The Graduation of a Lifetime

Marissa Lavigne

LIV VIE BOOKS

Published by Liv Vie Books in Denver, CO

ISBN: 979-8-9907716-5-9 (paperback)

ISBN: 979-8-9907716-6-6 (ebook)

Library of Congress Control Number: 2025905654

Cover design by Marissa Lavigne

Map illustrated by Esther Jamieson

1st Printing 2025

Dedicated to you

Nest *noun*

    1. a place or environment that favors the development of
something

DOME
RESIDEN
GRAND
HALL
IMPRESSIONS OFFICE

PODS
BUILDINGS
SIM BUILDINGS
CLASSES

The GRADUATION of a LIFETIME

Marissa Lavigne

CHAPTER ONE

"I feel like you've lived a thousand lives to my one," Nova grumbled longingly to Kirana as they entered the Grand Hall. Kirana smiled inwardly, thinking that it was probably way more than that. Placing a reassuring hand on Nova's arm, she whispered back, "You'll get there!" as they quickly took their seats along the edge of the room where Guardian Nika was starting to talk.

"Welcome to all of you just back in from self-assignments. We must start by warmly congratulating you on the successes you have all achieved. It's an honor to share the ongoing journey with you, and I hope everyone is feeling refreshed and ready to begin a new time of preparation and organization. We are populating your tablets with your new class schedules according to your last self-assignments, your preferences and your presumed arrangements as of now, though you can change these as needed. Drop by the Official Registry in the Impressions Office at any time to do this."

Nova was half listening, half trying to access her schedule, and half drowning under anticipation, excitement and desperation to get things moving. While digging in her bag, the whole thing fell off her lap, dumping items at her feet that started spilling down to the row of seats in front of them. She froze and stared straight ahead, holding her breath pretending nothing happened. Guardian Nika continued on as three different students in front of Nova quietly picked up writing tools, a refreshment carrier, and other items that had fallen to pass back to her. Kirana already had Nova's bag open and calmly put things back inside, elbowing Nova gently to take it.

"Don't sweat it!" she whispered with a small smile. "I've caused much bigger commotions." Nova looked incredulously back at Kirana and went to thank her, but Kirana was already focused intently on Guardian Nika as she was inviting Guardian Era onto the stage. In fact, everyone seemed to be glued in silence and awe.

Guardian Era smiled warmly at the group. He was a lot taller than Guardian Nika, older too. Nova had heard rumors about his self-assignments before becoming a Guardian. They were all experiences that warranted attention in many, many places. On his first self-assignment, the rumor was that he led an entire civilization at the point of extinction to a complete turnaround when he was less than middle age. She made a mental note to catch herself up on these details later. Her own first self-assignment felt like a disaster, and it made her a little embarrassed to think about it. She wanted to make sure this time was different.

"Esteemed colleagues," Guardian Era was saying, "I am thrilled to be here and ready to support each and every one of you in preparation for your next self-assignment. To our teams going on their first self-assignments, don't underestimate your potential, but don't overestimate the skills that you are able to exhibit here. Each self-assignment will test you in ways you have yet to experience, so preparation, as much and as best as you can, is key. You'll understand better what I mean by the time you get back."

Nova huffed at that remark, immediately glad that she had not taken a sip from the carrier still in her hand, imagining it would have ended up all over whoever was sitting in front of her. Kirana put her hand on Nova's knee, as if to reassure her, still with rapt attention on Guardian Era.

"To those of you entering your graduation iterations, this is just the beginning of an intense bout of radical shifts, and we are thrilled that you are up for the task! We will do our best to encourage you while on your self-assignments, and you can know for certain that you will not be alone. Prep the very best you can, and know that it will be enough." Guardian Era paused and sent a rippling sensation of joy, pride and encouragement through the crowd. Nova glanced at Kirana, whose hand was still on her knee. She could feel the low tones of... fear? No, not just that. It was like fear mixed with an absolute determination. Nova smiled and covered Kirana's hand with her own, glad it was her turn to offer some support. She felt Kirana relax as Guardian Era began to address the rest of the room.

"There is deep work being done by everyone here. We applaud you and your improvements. We all have the same goal. We are one. With every self-assignment, know that you are valued and worthy." He paused again, gazing around the room. "And with that, Guardian Nika, if you'll please rejoin me, along with Guardians Beck, Gaia, Cosmo and Alder, we'll get introductions started."

Everyone in the room radiated applause towards the stage as the group joined Guardian Era. He spoke again, gesturing down the line. "Welcome to all of our Guardians here, both those who have been with us for some time and those newly joining us. You've already heard from Guardian Nika a bit earlier, and many of you know her from supporting our second self-assignments and onward. She will be here again oversee-ing the same group, and we are thrilled." Everyone loved Guardian Nika. She had never intended to be a Guardian, but so many had asked for her to do it that she agreed and was appointed the following iteration. That was many iterations ago. She smiled and bowed her head at the crowd. Everyone sent a rush of light bubbles in approval. Guardian Era continued. "Guardian Cosmo has also been with us for some time now. We couldn't be more pleased that he is here. Would you like to share anything Guardian?" Guardian Era invited Guardian Cosmo forward.

Nova already knew Guardian Cosmo from her last self-assignment. He had a dramatic manner about him, both sudden and unmoving at the same time. He was bold, and despite Nova's experience, she really did think he was perfect for the position. He stepped forward and started to speak.

"I am really honored to be offering my council to those on their first self-assignments again. We had an incredible completion rate last time, and despite a hiccup or two, that we all learned from mind you, I am ready to get going again!" Guardian Cosmo emphatically punched the air upward, starting a vortex that Guardian Era quickly swept away as if it were completely intentional on Guardian Cosmo's part. Nova slid down in her seat.

"Thank you, Guardian Cosmo," Guardian Era began, stepping for-ward again. "Now, before we officially introduce our newest Guardians to the team, I have an announcement to make." Nova could feel as everyone's attention grew hard and strong.

"Many of you have known me to work with the graduating class as of late, however this time around, I will be joining Guardian Nika in assisting the group of you from your second self-assignment and on, up until the graduating class." A small flow of sparks of surprise seemed to touch down throughout the room. Nova tried to sneak a peek at Kirana without moving her head, but she didn't need to. She could feel the white buzz coming from Kirana's hand under hers. She closed her eyes and very softly moved her other hand on top of Kirana's as well, sending a cool blue through them. Kirana breathed a deep sigh as if to say *thank you* as the buzz dissipated. Nova knew how much she had been looking forward to working with Guardian Era and for how long she had waited. Now it seemed she wouldn't get the chance at all.

"I know it may come as a surprise," Guardian Era continued, "but all six of us came to the conclusion that this was the best course of action. We are confident that with Guardian Gaia being joined by Guardian Beck and Guardian Alder, we will be able to move faster and keep up with the massive shifts the graduating class is going to be experiencing. We know that you'll be in the best hands." Guardian Era stepped back and gestured Guardian Gaia forward. She was also quite tall, and her energy was almost swirling. She really was in constant movement, and it was hard to know where she started or ended. Her voice came from everywhere as she spoke.

"Thank you, Guardian Era. While I will miss working so closely with you, I am beyond grateful for our time together and thrilled to introduce everyone to our two new Guardians this year." Nova didn't hear any more because at that moment, she felt Kirana slump over onto her shoulder.

CHAPTER TWO

Kirana opened her eyes, wondering why she blinked for so long. She hoped she didn't miss too much of the introductions. However, she wasn't in the seat in the Grand Hall anymore. She took note of this quietly to herself as she felt the ground beneath her instead. She was propped up against a wall with a warm shoulder on one side. She must have moved her leg because Nova popped up around the shoulder she was leaning against.

"Welcome back," she grinned. Kirana let out a frustrated groan and closed her eyes again. She didn't have to ask what happened; she already knew.

"I told you I've caused bigger commotions," Kirana whined softly, realizing she didn't know who she was leaning against. Nova pulled her up slowly until they were sitting cross-legged on the ground, facing each other. "Do you know what we missed?" She turned her head to see who had assumedly helped her out of the Grand Hall.

"Nope!" Nova chirped happily, stirring Kirana's attention back towards her before she got a glimpse. Nova was actually happy for an excuse to leave after Kirana had the flash-out. It was harmless, she knew, and had happened before when Kirana got overwhelmed. She just needed some space and probably some refreshment. "Here," Nova said, holding her carrier out to Kirana, indicating that she should take it.

"Well," said the voice of the body behind Kirana. "I think I'm going to go find out, seeing as I'm new to two of my Guardians this iteration. Nova, if everything's okay here, I'll catch up with you later?"

"Sounds good!" Nova responded with a wave. "Thanks again for your help. Let me know what you find out!" she called after him as he walked away. Kirana turned and watched a figure walk back towards the Grand Hall. He was tall, dark and... she didn't know what else. She never saw his face, so she wouldn't even know if she ran into him again anyway. She turned back to Nova.

"Okay, first of all, how long was it this time?" she asked. Then lowering her voice a degree or two, she continued. "Second, who was that??" She tried not to deliberately point at the guy and instead pointed to where he had been sitting.

Nova turned to look back in the direction he had walked away. "Oh, Nox? Yeah, he's family! He was sitting behind us in there! You haven't met?" She made a humming sound, and her face turned contemplative. "Actually, I guess that makes sense. He has a way of staying in stealth mode." Her face turned back to a smile as she indicated to the refreshment carrier, implying she should have a little more. "You were only out briefly. We probably could've stayed in there." She shrugged. "Oh well! Are you feeling alright?" Kirana moved around a little bit and cautiously stood up.

"Yeah, actually, I feel fine. Just all that information and..." she trailed off for a moment. She sat back down again, as Nova hadn't moved yet. "We both have some really big things going on, don't we," she asked rhetorically, moving her hands to cover her face. Taking a big sigh, she smiled up at Nova. "Well, you're welcome," she teased. "I got you out of Orientation, but I actually do want to know more about the new Guardians I'll be working with. I think I might go back in and try to catch what I can." Nova was uncharacteristically quiet. "You okay?" Kirana asked her, reaching out to touch her knee. "Oh my gosh, I didn't even say thank you for real though! Thanks for getting me some space!"

"Oh, don't worry about it!" Nova responded airily. "I actually have something I need to go do, so if you're good, I'll see you later?"

"Yeah, for sure," Kirana nodded as they both stood up and picked up their things. "We got this," she breathed with another heavy sigh. The two waved at each other as they walked opposite directions, Kirana back to the Grand Hall, and Nova towards the Sim buildings.

Kirana cracked open the big door to the Grand Hall as quietly as she could and slipped inside. It was mostly dark with just the stage illuminated, but she could walk through this building with her eyes closed knowing as many times as she had been in here. It seemed like she had missed both Guardian Beck's and Guardian Alder's introductions.

"I'm probably the only one," she muttered quietly to herself, completing that thought out loud, eyes on the stage. Not a moment later, she walked straight into someone who she hadn't seen standing in her usual spot. It was her vantage point to the stage that she used when she was either late for a session or when she had to excuse herself briefly and return halfway through, like what had happened just now. It was above everything and everyone in the Hall. She'd never seen anyone else there before. With a small gasp, she clutched the arm in front of her to keep from falling as, "OhmygoshI'msosorry!" fell out of her mouth as one word. It was too dark to see who it was, but she could see that they had turned their head to look at her and turned back to the stage as if nothing had happened. She realized she was still clinging to the arm, so she stabilized herself and let go, taking a step and a half away from the other to give them some space back. Turning her attention to the stage again, she saw that Guardian Nika was there in the middle of explaining the campus map that was being displayed across, and slightly above, the stage. It was like a firm, holographic model that depicted various colors and vibrations, bringing the buildings to life and representing real-time information. She relaxed, knowing she was quite familiar with that, but then did a double take when it wasn't at all what she was used to. She opened her eyes as wide as she could, as if that would help her take in information faster.

"—wouldn't want to mix up those two buildings, so please remember that detail," Guarding Nika was saying. "And don't worry, the full map has already been updated in your tablets, so you can gain access to this again at any time. Your own energy will always show you where you are. Those of you who have already discovered this may have also seen that any notes or relevant directions you have added on your own maps can be shared with others, so please feel free to support each other as we all adjust to the additions." Guardian Nika zoomed the display out so the full map could be seen on the stage, and in that moment, Kirana realized that there were a *multitude* of buildings she didn't recognize. Her eyes stayed wide as she tried to take in as much as she could, but she knew she had missed quite a bit more of the session than she'd anticipated. This orientation was not what she had been expecting at all. Especially as she was going into the graduating class!

"Well, I literally already had a flash-out from information overload, so I guess bring it on now," Kirana muttered to herself under her breath, forgetting someone else was there too. "I'll have to make sure Nova knows." She whipped her head to the right realizing she had been talking out loud again. Whoever was there didn't seem to notice, so she faced forward again, silently admonishing herself and hoping it was quiet enough to not have been heard at all. Guardian Nika wasn't quite done talking.

"After everything we've gone over at this present moment, we expect some extra arrangements will probably need to be made, so keep your notifications from your Guardians on and know that you can stop by the Impressions Office at any time with questions. I am going to ask that our graduating class please stay behind for one more announcement, and to the rest of you, we're so excited for what's to come! Thank you for being here, and remember, we're always available." Guardian Nika held her hands together and bowed her head to the crowd. A dark pink static of gratitude flowed through the room, and most everyone stood, chatting quietly to each other while moving towards the exit. Kirana took the moment of extra light to look towards the one she had bumped into earlier, but they must have slipped away because she didn't see anyone there anymore. She considered going back to where she had been sitting earlier with Nova, but it seemed to make more sense to stay put instead of going against the traffic of those leaving the room. She couldn't imagine the last announcement would take too long anyway.

Once the room was pared down to just the graduating class, Guardian Gaia stood with Guardians Alder and Beck onstage. Kirana took in the two new Guardians that she missed introductions for earlier. Guardian Alder was by far the tallest and stood so still and solid that Kirana wasn't sure he ever blinked. Guardian Beck was sinuous and looked strong. She walked with a silent, elegant flow. Both of them looked like they were prepared for anything.

"We won't keep you too long now," Guardian Gaia began, "because we have plenty of time to figure things out, but there is one more change to be expected this iteration." The room glittered in anticipation for a moment. "We will be splitting into two groups, and as with everything else, it is your choice which group you join. If you're familiar with the activities of the graduating class from either your own experience or others' explanations, you may find things to be generally different this time, regardless of which group you decide to join. We are finalizing the details to share in group sessions later but wanted you to be aware of this change now. This is a very, very special time to be here, and we will support you every step of the way." Kirana shifted her weight from foot to foot. Maybe that was why the graduating class went from two guardians to three. Guardian Gaia continued. "We will start out classes with everyone together and split into the two groups as sessions progress. Thank you so much. We are honored by your dedication to all that exists."

Guardian Gaia, as well as the other two Guardians on stage, all gave the same small bow to the crowd that Guardian Nika had done, but this time with their arms outstretched and palms open. A pink and gold swirl of mist exploded throughout the room and felt like a breath of fresh air. The crowd sparkled rosewood gratitude in return and began to gather their things to leave. Kirana turned slowly to head towards the exit, without really watching where she was going and her head lost in thought. Her feet knew the way, and they took her outside to wait and see if she could find her friends to debrief on everything that they had found out, as well as what she'd missed. There were a few who she thought would also be in the graduating class this iteration, but she didn't see any of them as the building emptied.

"Hi, are you Kirana?" asked a voice behind her. She whirled around to see someone there she didn't know. He was her same height, with a brightness to him that couldn't be overlooked. She didn't think she responded, but she must have nodded because he continued. "I'm Ravi. I thought that was you. I think we'll be having some classes together this iteration." He held out his hand to her.

"Hi! Yes, that's me," Kirana smiled back, holding her hand out to him in response. "Nice to meet you, Ravi." As their hands touched, the soft, warm glow emanated much farther than the usual greeting. It surprised both of them.

"Wow, you really are radiant, aren't you!" Ravi laughed. "Kylo told me as much."

"Oh really? And what else did Kylo say?" Kirana joked back. Kylo was family. They had been through so many iterations together, taking turns in balancing each other in numerous ways. He was a constant for her. He was supposed to be joining the graduating class again, but she hadn't been able to catch up with him yet to confirm.

"He said we should meet. I'm one of his residence mates. Want to walk?" Ravi held an arm out, offering a direction. Kirana took one more look towards the last of those who were exiting the Grand Hall. Not seeing anyone she was looking for, she nodded and smiled at Ravi.

"Sure, let's stick to the part of the campus that's still somewhat familiar, if you don't mind. My head is swimming from everything we just learned, and I haven't had a chance to explore the new map yet."

"Cool, me neither. But I might know a little trick that could help us pick it up quickly..." Ravi hinted with a grin, his eyes glimmering. "Interested?"

CHAPTER THREE

Nova was already at the residence she would be sharing with Kirana and two other mates when Kirana arrived. The residences were geometric buildings, each one unique. Nova and Kirana were mates together in a residence last iteration as well, and that's how they had grown so close. Kirana preferred the residence building they shared now to the one they had before. It was unassuming from the outside. It was shaped like someone had been haphazardly stacking giant blocks that didn't entirely line up, but the inside was incredibly spacious and full of light. They could easily modulate the inside into nearly any configuration they wanted. The color pattern on their building changed depending on who was there and generally how things were flowing. Right now, the building had a midnight blue mist covering the outside, staying very close to the building walls. There was a faint green glow in one spot, near where Kirana knew Nova had said she was going to set up her nest. Nests were their private spaces, where each mate could have somewhere to go to study, to integrate new information and to process new developments from their sessions.

As Kirana walked up to her residence, she considered stopping by next door to see if Tali was in. Tali had shared the residence with Kirana and Nova last iteration. Nova had been so relieved that she was still nearby.

Kirana was happy too, though she hadn't shared as many classes as Nova and Tali had together. It was standard to mix some newer students with some more experienced students in the residences. She decided to let Tali settle in a bit before going to check on her. As she entered her residence, she saw the same light green glow that she noticed from the outside, as well as a bright orange curving flicker. There was low, warm chatter spreading along the walls. Nova sprung up when she saw Kirana.

"You're finally here!" she exclaimed. "You have to see my nest!"

"Sure, I'd love to! Hey, you're Anala, right?" Kirana responded, turning her attention to the other in the room. "We've had a number of classes together! Are you mates with us too?" She recognized Anala as possibly entering the graduating class this year as well. Anala smiled warmly. She spoke with a little crackle in her voice that made her sound almost sultry.

"Hi! Yes! I definitely remember you—shining just as brightly as always," Anala gleamed. "Excited that we're mates this time. Maybe the guardians put us together so you can teach me how to glow steady without flickering so much." She held her palm open to exhibit the bright dancing curve Kirana had noticed earlier.

"Deal," Kirana agreed, "if you'll help me to stay strong when things get in my way." Anala and Kirana laughed and gave each other a hug.

"Good to see you," Kirana whispered. Anala glowed back.

"Um, mates, I know I'm newer to all this, but I'm pretty sure Contracts class doesn't start for a while yet," interrupted Nova.

"You're so right," responded Anala with a smile. "I'm going to get back to setting up my nest and let you two catch up." She turned to head to the back of the building. "Oh," she paused, turning back to look at Nova. "Don't forget to ask Nox about that thing I told you." She gave a pointed look. Nova nodded quickly, grabbing Kirana's hand and starting to pull her towards the front room. Kirana let herself be moved forward, wondering what she had missed and why she was even curious about that comment at all.

Nova's nest was positively perfect. Everything had a shininess to it like a newly polished crystal. Kirana looked around with her eyes widening as she realized it actually *was* all crystal. There were 5 walls, all of them covered in sheets of glimmering moonstone. The light from the long, horizontal strips of window near the ceiling bounced around in rainbow shimmers everywhere she looked. The ceiling sloped upwards slightly into the center and was covered in emerald. The dark green created somewhat of an illusion that made the room look endless.

"Nova..." Kirana breathed. "It's stunning." Nova stepped up beside her.

"I'm focused on new beginnings," she murmured, "just like you told me to do when I got back from last iteration." Then she added with an excited hop, "I hope you'll take the space right above me at the front of the residence! Then you can get some of this energy too."

"Sounds like a great idea to me!" Kirana responded, suddenly re-membering everything that happened earlier. "By the way, did you get filled in on everything that we missed at Orientation?" Nova walked over to a pile of stuffed cloud-like cushions and jumped into them, landing somewhere in the middle, half hidden amongst them. She giggled.

"I will never stop loving these," she called from across the room. "C'mon!" Kirana made a show of running and jumping into a flip and landing in the pile of cushions. They both settled on their backs, as if they were floating on the surface of something, staring up into the endless emerald. "I'm pretty sure I'm caught up on the announcements at the Grand Hall," Nova finally responded. "The new Guardians sound pretty awesome actually. Want to trade spots? Then you can work with Guardian Era!" After a short moment, she rescinded the idea. "Actually, never mind. You're a much better candidate for graduating class," she admitted weakly.

"I guess we'll see," said Kirana. "Seems like a lot of things are changing this iteration. I feel a little lost honestly." She chuckled to herself as she remembered *actually* getting lost on the walk earlier with Ravi. His "trick" turned out to be less reliable than either of them expected, but he had made it fun. She had felt light with him, and he erased the feelings of overwhelm that she had prior to meeting him.

"Okay, spill it," Nova was saying, breaking through Kirana's memory. "What's so funny?"

"Would you have guessed that our campus would have light strings?" She didn't wait for an answer before explaining further. "They're super useful for getting around since the campus seems to be huge, but it turns out, you have to know what the colors mean first! I've only ever used the gold ones, but these ones change, and you have to time it right to try to jump on the right color." Nova sat up and stared at her for a moment, then burst out laughing.

"Kirana, that's not how they work at all!" Nova nearly had tears now, she was laughing so hard. "Sounds like you had a really good time though. Who were you hanging out with?" Kirana hesitated, wanting to laugh along with her but not sure what she had missed. "Oohh." Nova stopped laughing, and her eyes glowed large and round. "It was a guy! Who was it?!"

"His name is Ravi. He told me he's mates with Kylo this iteration. And he's going to be in the graduating class with me." She paused. "Well, maybe anyways. Apparently the graduating class is going to be split into two at some point." Nova looked confused for a moment.

"Two separate graduating classes? That's interesting." Nova seemed to contemplate this briefly, as Kirana realized Nova hadn't actually been caught up on quite everything. Although, that news was shared after the majority of the students had gone, so maybe that detail hadn't spread much yet. Nova seemed to pocket the information for later and turned back to Kirana with the shine back in her eyes. "So tell me about Ravi."

"Not much to tell really; he seems nice, and we had fun! Although speaking of, I haven't seen Kylo around yet. Have you?" Kirana turned to look at Nova who was now laying back and staring up into the ceiling again.

"I actually did. Briefly, but he's here. Don't worry." Nova swung her arm to lay between them, as if to offer comfort. "He... he actually stood up for me." Nova sighed. All of a sudden now it seemed to Kirana as if Nova's outstretched arm was asking for comfort instead of offering it. She laid her own arm across the space between them too, waiting for Nova to continue. Except she switched topics instead. "Remember how I said I had something I needed to go do earlier?" she prompted. Kirana nodded. "Well," she continued, "when Nox and I brought you outside during Orientation, I saw Guardian Cosmo do a split-energy and head towards the Sim buildings. I wanted to talk to him about what happened away from all the official meetings, you know? Seemed like I got my chance." Kirana nodded understandingly, though her interest was piqued hearing Nox's name and remembering what Anala had said to Nova. She lightly shook her head to return to Nova's story.

"It's a little odd that he would do a split-energy in the middle of a huge orientation like that, don't you think?" Kirana mused. Only Guardians could do split-energy on campus, mostly because it was actually just not worth the energy loss to both of the splits. "He did seem a little jumpy on stage though and had already done his introduction, so I guess just standing there wouldn't have been too noticeable." Nova sat up suddenly.

"You're right! I didn't even think about that!" she responded. "When I caught up with him, he was whispering to someone in front of the Gravity Sim building. He didn't see me right away, and when I said his name, he jumped! I apologized and said I didn't mean to startle him, but now I'm realizing that he expected everyone to be in the orientation. He thought no one else was around..." she trailed off for a moment. "Anyways, I didn't get to talk to him after all, because he muttered that he 'didn't have time for this' and hopped on a light string. I thought following him again might be too much. Plus I'm not familiar enough with the campus yet." She paused, flipping over onto her stomach to tease Kirana. "By the way, as long as you've chosen which color light string you want to take, you just hop on and you're good. You don't have to time anything right unless someone is purposefully changing it on you." She laughed, putting her head down on her arms for a moment. "Seems like your Ravi was playing games."

"He's not *my* Ravi!" Kirana huffed. "But good to know," she remarked, now able to join in on the laughter.

There was a light tap at the door turning their attention to the sound and color in the doorway.

"Open!" Nova called. The door opened soundlessly, and someone practically floated into the entryway. She was nearly clear in the way a quartz crystal was both very solid looking and yet flawlessly empty looking, but in the most elegant way. The purest of blue eyes blinked at them.

"Sorry to bother you! I'm Sora—I'm here for my first iteration, and we're mates! I just wanted to see if there was a specific nest space I should take?" Sora somehow sounded like a songbird. Kirana and Nova both jumped out of the cushions and greeted her with open arms.

"Welcome! This is so exciting!" Kirana took the lead. "I'm Kirana. I'm not sure if you've met Anala yet, but she and I are both in the graduating class. And this is Nova. She'll be a great resource for you on what to expect in your first iteration." Nova looked a little uncertain of that. "Here, let's go up a level and check out our nest spaces. I'll be up there with you." Kirana turned to Nova. "Conversation not over! See you later?"

"Of course!" Nova glittered, turning to Sora. "So happy you're here. Can't wait to see what you do with your nest!" And with a flourish, she waved the glitter around them in welcome as Kirana and Sora turned to go up to their nests.

CHAPTER FOUR

"Nova!" Kirana called down to her mate. "NOVA! You've got to see this! Get Anala, and come up here!" Everyone had gotten settled in now and were just about to head to their first classes. Kirana and Anala would have class together, Nova would rejoin Tali to head to their own class, and Sora would be starting in Guardian Cosmo's class with the others entering their first iteration. Sora and Kirana already stood at the window in Kirana's nest when Nova and Anala rushed in.

"What is it?" Nova asked breathlessly. She didn't need a response. Out the floor-to-ceiling windows from Kirana's nest was the most spectacular sight any of them had ever seen. Everything had gone dark, like accessing the depth of space itself. The first layer on that backdrop was a dark sapphire spray that subtly gleamed as they washed their eyes over the scene. Then, a dark cobalt marbled on top of that, elusively swirling its pattern. Lighter colors started to make splashes into it, disappearing and reemerging as smooth ribbons that fluttered across the surface until they exploded into millions of golden specks, twinkling in a flurry of brightness.

All of a sudden, the four of them were sucked into the scene itself, completely surrounded by millions of flowing colors, each of them becoming a part of the display in their own expression. Every one of them had a place in the scene and everything was connected to everything else. One blink or a decade later, the four of them were back in Kirana's nest, still glowing various colors and glimmering at various intervals.

"The Guardians have outdone themselves this time," Kirana breathed, reaching to link arms with Sora and Nova who were standing the closest to her. They all followed suit and stood in a circle together, arms linked.

"Everybody ready?" asked Anala, her voice shiny and crackling. They all nodded and beamed at each other.

"Let's do it. See you later!" Nova sent a cloud of courage through their little group and broke the chain to grab her stuff and meet up with Tali. Sora glided away just behind her, off to her very first class.

"Do you remember your first couple times?" Kirana asked Anala softly as they watched the other two leave.

"It always feels like the first time," Anala whispered. She disappeared out the door with a shimmer of orange. "Come on, we better get going!" she called back from the hall. "Meet you out front!"

As Kirana and Anala entered the room for their first session of their graduating class, Kirana heard someone call her name from somewhere in the center. As she scanned the group gathering to find seats on the cushioned flooring, she finally spotted who it was. Her face lit up.

"Kylo!" she squealed. "You're here!" She hurried towards him with a skip in her step, waving Anala to follow. Right as she almost reached him, her shoulder caught someone else's shoulder going the opposite way, and it spun her around with momentum. She stumbled, her legs not quite catching her all the way, landing her on her back where she ended up staring straight up into Ravi's smiling face.

"Falling for me already, are you?" Ravi teased as he helped her up. "Good to see you again!" Kirana's face always glowed, but this time it was one shade of pink more vibrant than usual. She looked over her shoulder to apologize to whoever she ran into, but everyone seemed busy with settling in and preparing for class. There was no sign of anyone getting bumped into. Kylo appeared next to Ravi just as Anala also caught up.

"Are you okay?" they both questioned her, looking her over as if the floors weren't super soft and nearly bouncy.

"Totally fine!" Kirana brushed them off, eager to move on from that. "Kylo, I'm so happy to see you!" she exclaimed, reaching her arms out for a hug. He grabbed her and spun her around a few times before setting her down again. Kylo was expansive in every way. He could hold on to a lot of information and organize it all in his head, he could empathize in a way no one else seemed to, and his shoulders were as broad as his legs were steady.

"I've missed you, Kir, wow it's great to see you!" Kylo responded, still with his arms around her. "Last iteration wasn't the same without you, that's for sure."

Kirana reached an arm towards Anala. "This is Anala, one of my new mates. Anala," she turned to look at her mate, "this is Kylo. He's family. A long-time teammate through many iterations with me!" The two of them greeted each other warmly. Then Kylo turned towards Ravi, who had gathered some cushions for them all.

"Hey Rav, come meet the one I've been telling you about! Well actually," he faltered with a grin, "I guess we'll come to you. We better go sit down."

"We've actually met!" Kirana mentioned as they took their seats. "But I'm not sure if Ravi and Anala have met before, have you?" she questioned as she looked back and forth between the two.

"Yeah, we've had a few iterations together," Anala sparkled. Ravi gleamed back.

"Good to see you again!" he added. "I hope your—" But he was cut off as Guardian Gaia walked to the center of the room to address the group.

"My dearest colleagues," she began. "We hope you enjoyed our collective display of joy and appreciation. I know I did!" The class was sitting in a circle around the center stage and passed a hazy glowing wave all the way around. "Good," she continued. "Let's keep up this momentum. If you'll notice, Guardians Alder and Beck are not joining us in this session as they are evaluating the potential for different plans regarding the announcement that was made at Orientation. So I don't have any further updates for you right now, but I can say that we will still be offering two paths to this class." Kirana felt like the only one that still didn't know anything about the two new Guardians. She'd have to ask someone later. She started wondering how Nova was doing with Guardian Era. Part of her wanted to backtrack out of the graduating class just to be able to work with him, but she knew she was ready for this leap. She had worked hard to prepare herself to take on a self-assignment that would (hopefully) have a bigger impact than she ever had before. Kylo leaned over, touching his shoulder to hers to bring her back to what Guardian Gaia was saying. She gave him a small smile. He knew her too well.

"Your sessions will be progressive, and remember that your self-assignments may all be starting at different times—as soon as you're ready for the position you've selected. Your coursework, as I'm sure you've already reviewed in your tablets, consist of four types of classes with focuses that will vary as you progress towards your self-selection. The class types will build from Practical History, which includes your Observation Studies and Location Choices, to Internal Development, Simulations, and then Communications, which will include Contracts and Teams. While these should all be generally familiar to you from previous iterations, you will quickly start to notice some rather large differences that define this group as the graduating class. Remember, you may repeat iterations in this graduating class as much as necessary, as long as you desire to do so. I suggest you take this moment to access your tablets, find an area around the outside edges of the room and watch your projections. They'll give you a debrief, complete with maps to get you started. Keep in mind that it might take some time to get accustomed to 3D. I'll be here in the center of the room if you need anything or have any questions." With that, Guardian Gaia drew a large sphere in the air in front of her and stepped inside it, letting it start to fill with blue and brownish-green swatches that shifted their edges continuously. White streaks circled around it, staying close to the surface, and it pulsed a very low frequency that surprised Kirana. Everyone else was already up and moving.

"Hey, are you coming?" Anala was asking her, while Kylo was making faces, and Ravi was offering a hand. She grabbed it, shaking off her stunned stare, and he pulled her up. As soon as they touched hands, that same bright light as before briefly shone from the two of them. Anala raised her eyebrows, and Kylo dug his elbow into Ravi's side.

"Well look at that, Kir. I didn't know your luminosity could be amplified like that!" Kylo grinned, winking at Ravi who was still turned towards Kirana, glowing at her. Kirana blushed back.

"Thanks," she practically whispered to Ravi. The four of them found a space at the edge of the room and pulled out their tablets. They laid the tablets on the floor facing up which joined their projected maps together to give them that much more space to study at once. It didn't have the same movement or vibration emanating from it as Guardian Gaia's did, and it felt rather flat in a way, even though she could walk around it and see it from all sides. Maybe this is what 3D was.

"What do you think the difference between the two groups is going to be?" Anala asked as they all studied the projection. They could really only zoom in and out with it and toggle layers on and off, but Simulation classes would allow them to explore in different ways entirely. Kirana always looked forward to Simulations. They always shocked her, but she felt like she achieved something once she understood how they worked.

"I don't know, but based on what Guardian Beck said at Orientation, I think it could possibly make this iteration more successful," responded Kylo. "Honestly, this graduating class was a struggle for me last iteration. I would take any support I could get."

"What did Guardian Beck say?" Kirana asked the question at the same time as Guardian Gaia rang the gong indicating class was over. Everyone turned to the center of the room and sent a dark pink static of gratitude towards Guardian Gaia and then began to pick up their things.

"What'd you say in there, Sunshine?" Kylo asked Kirana as they walked towards the door.

"It's okay, I just missed that part of Orientation when Guardian Beck and Guardian Alder were introduced, and I feel like I missed something important," she explained. Kylo stopped walking and grabbed her arm to stop her too.

"Kirana, did you have a flash-out again?" he asked with concern.

"Really, it's not a big deal!" she countered. "Anyways, Nova was with me, and she recruited family to help me too." She gave him a winning smile and a, "All's well that ends well." Kylo rolled his eyes.

"You two," he said, gesturing to Anala and Ravi, "keep an eye on her if I'm not around! This iteration is going to be a big one. I can feel it."

CHAPTER FIVE

Kylo invited everyone to the Sim buildings to play a round of X, but Anala and Kirana were anxious to get back to their residence to check on how Sora's and Nova's sessions had gone.

"Definitely later though," Anala reassured them.

"Yeah, it sounds fun!" agreed Kirana. "Hey, don't you guys have another mate in your residence too?"

"Yeah, we have one other mate. He's in the FI class. He's going to meet us at the Sim buildings," replied Ravi.

"FI class?" Kirana asked, tilting her head to the side.

"First Iteration," Ravi clarified with a fist bump to Kylo.

"X is especially fun with those in the FI class," added Kylo with a smirk. "But alright, we'll see you later!" he said while pulling Kirana into a hug.

"Yes, you will," she said muffled from his chest. After Anala and Ravi gave each other a hug, Kylo still hadn't released her. Ravi cleared his throat.

"Give everyone else a chance, hm?" he complained. Kylo removed one of his arms from Kirana and left the other around her shoulders. He pulled Ravi in with his newly freed arm, draping it around Ravi's shoulders on his other side.

"How did you two end up meeting anyway? I was actually planning to introduce you." Kylo looked back and forth between the two. Kirana and Ravi smiled big at each other, small sparkles in their eyes if you looked closely enough. Kylo was close enough. He quickly dropped his arms from both of them. "Right, sometimes no introduction is necessary," he chuckled softly. He turned to give Anala a hug. "See you later. So happy to meet another one of Kirana's mates." She sent an orange flicker in agreement and reciprocation. The two turned to see Ravi whispering something into Kirana's ear, making her giggle. That pretty pink was back in her face. Kirana looked over and saw them watching.

"C'mon Anala, we better go!" she said, quickly deflecting the attention. With last misty blue *see you laters*, the four of them split into two and two. While they were walking away, Anala and Kirana laughed quietly with hands over their mouths as they heard Kylo begging Ravi to know what he had said to Kirana.

"You don't have to tell me," Anala laughed when they were out of earshot.

As they approached their residence, there was a thickness to the air. It was clear, as in, devoid of color, but it was opaque in feeling. The mates exchanged a look that said *glad we came back*. They went inside to find Sora and Tali comforting Nova. Sora glided over to greet them.

"I was the first one back," she explained. "They just got here, and I'm not really sure what happened, but it sounded like someone doesn't want Nova here." Anala gave her a hug.

"Don't worry about it; I'm sure there was a misunderstanding," she encouraged.

"We'll help sort it out," Kirana agreed. "How was your first session? I can't wait to hear about your first impressions!"

"Oh," Sora breathed, starting to glow. "It was incredible. I'm actually going to go meet with some others from my class if you think Nova will be alright?"

"I'm fine," called Nova from across the room. "Really, don't worry about me. You should be out getting to know everyone." She flicked over as many specks of green dust as she could muster, but it didn't help prove her point of being fine. Sora kissed her fingers and blew white peace bubbles over to Nova, then waved at the rest of them while heading out the door.

"Nice to meet you, Tali!" she called as she disappeared. Kirana was already across the room enveloping Tali in a hug, happy to see her again. Anala sat next to Nova and put an arm around her shoulders. As Kirana and Tali sat down on Nova's other side, she began to tell them about the session.

"So I met up with Tali first thing, and we went straight to our session. We may have gone a little slower than normal because we were talking a lot, but it seemed like we might be the last to arrive. Then I thought I saw something outside the building and told Tali I'd meet up with her inside. I went around the building, and no one was there, so I turned back around to go to the front. Just then, I heard someone say something like, '—can't do it. You saw what happened last iteration.' Whoever he was talking to said something about watching for signs himself, but I kind of stopped listening and ran to the front. Once I got inside and found Tali, the session was starting."

"Wait a second," said Tali thoughtfully. "I think you arrived at the same time as Guardian Era. Guardian Nika was already there in the center of the room, so I didn't even think to expect anyone else, but he must have walked in like right when you did."

"Well, you definitely saw how things went the rest of the session. Guardian Era was practically staring at me the whole time!" Nova put her face in her hands. "I've messed up this iteration already, and it hasn't even started!"

"Okay, hold on," intercepted Anala. "You haven't messed up anything. You don't know who or what they were talking about behind the building, and you don't even know who was talking. Don't distract yourself with stories like this." She looked up at Tali who still looked rather deep in thought. She was giving off sparks, like she didn't know whether she was making a good connection or a bad connection.

"Actually, I thought I noticed Guardian Era eyeing us," Tali began, "but I wasn't going to say anything! I didn't know if he was just trying to get used to working with those of us who aren't in the graduating class or something, and Guardian Nika did tell us he was going to be doing a lot of observation in the first couple sessions. But he was definitely looking towards our group A LOT," emphasized Tali.

"Who all was in your group?" asked Kirana.

"It was just us and Tali's two mates," Nova said, her voice dimmed from speaking into her hands that were still half covering her face.

"I'm sure there's nothing to worry about. Did your session go okay otherwise? Why would Sora say it sounded like someone doesn't want you here?" prodded Anala. Tali and Nova exchanged glances.
"The session went well, great actually, but—" Nova faltered. Tali finished the sentence for her.

"She found a note in her bag right when we were getting ready to leave. It said, *How long do you think you'll last?*" she explained. "We've been trying to think of what other scenarios it could possibly be referring to, or if it was part of a project somehow and accidentally ended up there." Everyone was quiet for a moment. Nova pulled the note out of her pocket. It looked ripped off the corner of something.

"I'm sure it's not about you," Anala reassured her. "I'm glad you told us though. We're here for you, and we've got your back. No matter what." Nova nodded sullenly, clearly not believing that it wasn't about her. She did know that her mates would always support her though, and that cheered her up a bit.

"Where did Sora go—I need some more of those bubbles," Nova half whined, starting to smile.

"There we go," twinkled Kirana. "We've got a smile! What can I do to keep it going?"

"You know, I've seen your nest, but you haven't given me an official tour," Nova replied, silently asking for one. Kirana chuckled.

"Alright, let's go. There's no time like the present," she proclaimed. "After all, it's literally always the present." Kirana's eyes twinkled as Tali began gathering her things to leave. Everyone stood up in higher moods. Tali headed back to her residence next door, Anala went to her nest in the back to study her notes, and Kirana led Nova to her nest, up a level and in the front. Nova took her time to look around. Kirana's nest was mainly rectangular shaped, with one long wall and one short wall of entirely clear panels framed in black, giving her a fantastic view over the residences. The ceiling was both entirely non-existent but low and cozy at the same time. It shifted, changing the light ever so slowly, through a huge range of colors that appeared at different intervals but never exactly the same. There were soft, lush, sprawling mats on the ground and tons of green botanics of all kinds. Kirana sat on a swing and started to rock back and forth.

"I was inspired by my next self-assignment," she explained as Nova noticed something on the far end of the room and moved closer to inspect it. Kirana smiled, knowingly waiting for the next question.

"You put a light string in here?" Nova asked incredulously.

"I loved it so much when Ravi and I were playing with them the other day, and it turns out there are a few perks to being in the graduating class." Kirana paused dramatically. "One of which is that I can install light strings," she confirmed proudly. "Try it!"

"It looks like there are three colors, and only two of them are active. Which one should I try?" Nova asked.

"They can only be local for personal use, so don't worry, you won't go far. Try whichever one you want!" encouraged Kirana. Nova looked at the maroon and chestnut strings and chose the maroon one first. She hopped on and disappeared. Kirana waited where she was, resting her head back in the swing. In a moment, Nova returned to Kirana's nest, smiling.

"Well that's convenient, isn't it! Right down to the community space—I love it!" Nova ran over to try the chestnut string. Kirana got up and followed behind her, meeting her in a little nook that Nova hadn't noticed earlier, tucked in a corner near the changing ceiling. It felt like floating in a bubble, slow and smooth. There was a soft, warm glow that seemed to come from nowhere but shine everywhere. The feeling of contentment wrapped around them, and they laid down to enjoy the peace.

"This is really incredible," Nova whispered as she closed her eyes. "But wait," she said, as her eyes shot open again. "What about that evergreen string? Where does that go? Are you going to activate it?" Kirana hesitated.

"You know the strings go both ways. I was thinking it could be fun to connect our nests... only if you wanted to of course," she said with a hopeful smile.

"I absolutely love it," gushed Nova. She put her hands up in the air and showered both of them in soft, fizzy sparks. "This is going to be the best iteration ever!" But as soon as she said it, her concerns from earlier seemed to resurface. "Kirana," she began, "there's something I didn't mention with Tali and Anala there earlier." Kirana sat up.

"What is it? Are you okay?" she asked.

"Yes, I'm fine," Nova reassured her, "but I was sure it was Guardian Cosmo's voice I heard behind my session building. I asked Sora if he was late to her session, and she said no, that he was there before anyone arrived and even told them so. So if that's true, that means he did a split-energy again to talk to whoever else was there—and according to what Tali said, that could've been Guardian Era." She paused. "Something seems odd somehow, but I don't know what it is." She turned to look at Kirana, gauging her reaction.

"Whatever it is, we'll figure it out together. I'm sure it's nothing, but I believe you, so we'll just start with what we know," Kirana said as she reached for Nova's hand. Nova nodded, but her face wasn't as certain as her motion.

"I still have to tell you what Kylo did," she murmured quietly.

Chapter Six

"**M**ountains and valleys, rivers and alpine lakes, gorges, canyons, fissures and earthquakes. Oceans and isla—Oh!" Kirana had been reciting softly to herself while on her way to see Kylo, clearly not paying enough attention to where she was going. She smacked right into someone head-on and nearly bounced herself backward, automatically reaching out to grab anything she could to keep from falling. Before she found anything to grasp, two strong hands grabbed one arm each, keeping her upright.

"We've got to stop running into each other like this," said a voice that sounded slightly familiar. Kirana steadied herself and looked up at who was speaking, starting to apologize.

"I'm so sorry! I've been studying and—" she stopped as she connected eyes with this stranger who hinted that they had met before. He didn't look familiar to her at all. She would've remembered. His hair was matte black, but she was sure there were at least 3 different shades of black mixed in that she'd never seen before. His face was open and inviting, enticing her to mirror his small, amused smile back to him. The eyes though, she couldn't bring herself to look away. They were deep and dark and drew her in, like swimming through endless space among the stars.

"—and?" he prompted.

"I wasn't paying attention, sorry, I didn't mean to run into you!" she responded, not breaking eye contact.

"It takes two, so I'm sorry as well then," he responded with a shooting star in his eye. "I think you were at the part that goes, 'Oceans and islands, sand, beach and waves, gulfs, coves and cenote caves.'" Kirana looked both surprised and a little embarrassed.

"Oh, are you in the graduating class as well?" she asked with a touch of excitement in her voice. Something on the edge of her vision finally pulled her eyes away from his. It was like there was a faint, hazy green bubble surrounding them. She realized his hands were still on her arms. She was steady now so she gently took a step back. He dropped his hands away as he responded to her question, but she realized she didn't hear the answer because she was focusing on trying to perceive the bubble. She couldn't tell if she had made it up. It didn't seem to exist anymore so maybe she did.

"Kirana?" this someone was saying to her, pulling her eyes back to his.

"Yes, sorry, I got distracted for a moment—thought I saw something. Probably nothing!" she babbled, staring straight into those whirlpool eyes again. "So I guess I'll see you in class then." Kirana almost whispered this, just in case he had answered her question differently than what she was gambling on.

"Yes, I'm sure I'll run into you again there," he winked. The closing of his eye seemed to break the spell, and the two exchanged small silver sparks of acknowledgement as they turned back to the directions they had been going.

"Hey, is Nova still at your residence?" Kirana heard him call from several paces away. She turned back around and said, "Yes, she should be! She was there when I left." He nodded and tossed a spark of thanks to her. She smiled and watched him walk away for a moment. A lightbulb of memory came to her then. "Wait, was that Nox?" she asked herself. *Oh wow, I didn't even ask his name?!* she silently chided herself. She continued her walk to Kylo's residence, but her mind was no longer on her studies. Processing the conversation and replaying the interaction over again in her mind, she made note of the things she wanted to confirm later on.

As Kirana reached the building Kylo had described as his residence, she stopped for a moment to take it in from a distance. He had told her that it was quite different up close than it was from afar. It was a tall building with three round levels. Each level up was smaller than the previous. The sides of the building were covered in colored tiles that made a beautifully intricate image of what looked like a galaxy, though she wasn't sure which one. As she got closer, she could see what Kylo meant. The full picture wasn't as visible anymore, and she realized that each individual tile was its own picture—planets, stars, darker and lighter areas. They were all stunning. She wondered to herself if the pattern continued on the flat top of the roof.

"Hey, Kir!" Kylo called happily to her from the front. "Come in! I'll take you to the roof. Best place in the residence." Kirana grinned. As they made their way up to the top of the residence, Kylo told her about how they arranged the nests since there were only three of them.

"The main level is our community space and shared areas, and then Ravi and I both have our nests in the middle level. I'm in the front, he's in the back. We decided to leave the top level to our new mate since it's his first iteration," he explained.

"How's he liking everything so far? Is he doing okay in his sessions?" Kirana asked.

"Yeah, actually, I think he's loving it. That FI group seem to be super close already from what he's told me," Kylo commented. Kirana nodded.

"Makes sense from what I've seen from Sora too. What's your mate's name?" she asked.

"Name's Alev," answered Kylo. "If he's around while you're here, I'll introduce you." They reached the entrance to the rooftop. "After you," he said, holding his arm out to let her pass. Kirana stepped forward into a warm, bright space that had a soft sheen all over the golden surface of low, rolling mounds. Along the edges of the roof were curving ribbons of red and orange flickers in constant motion that were mesmerizing to observe. Around the circular interior was a path in a wavy surface of light blue, surrounding the center of white, fluffy cushions.

"All three of us had a bit of say in this," Kylo said, sounding proud of their creation. "Right this way please." He held his hand out to Kirana and stepped forward onto the wavy blue path. From underneath him, a soft, clear chair of sorts appeared. Kirana gasped and carefully took his hand as she stepped onto it. They sat down, and it began to lazily float along the path at the top of the residence. They had an incredible view of the campus that was similar to Kirana's view from her nest, just from a different perspective. She could see some of the new buildings from here.

"This is really amazing," she said, her eyes shining.

"Hey, turn down the brights a little bit, will ya?" Kylo teased her, putting an arm over his face as if to block his eyes. She lightly smacked his arm and exclaimed, "You know I can't!"

"Good," he said with a smile. They were quiet for a moment, floating around the rooftop and watching the view. When they came around to the new buildings again, Kirana tried to get a good look. She didn't have much information for that area other than the block title **Pods** on the campus map in her tablet. Apparently they weren't finished yet. There appeared to be two larger buildings in the center of the pods. These did not have labels in the map yet at all.

"Do you know anything about those buildings?" Kirana asked Kylo. He considered his answer, taking longer than Kirana expected. She leaned forward. "You know something, don't you."

"I don't exactly know anything for sure, not more than what they told us at Orientation anyways, but I think I might have heard something while I was in the Impressions Office," Kylo finally responded.

"Why were you in the Impressions Office?" Kirana asked, suddenly alarmed. Usually they only made appointments there when they were making changes to their self-assignments. Kirana was counting on entering her graduation iterations with Kylo so hearing that he had already had an appointment there made her nervous.

"Don't worry, Kir, I just wanted to see if I could get more information about the class split and what the choices are. I'm not going to leave you alone entering the graduating class." Kylo was quiet for a moment. He turned his glassy blue eyes to her. They were the same color as the wavy path they were floating on. "It was not easy," he said quietly. "I think you, and Ravi too for that matter, will do a lot better than I did last iteration."

"That's ridiculous. I'm sure you did great," encouraged Kirana. Kylo shrugged.

"Anyways, I'm not letting you head into this next iteration by yourself. That's for sure. I'll figure something out." He had a determined glint in his eyes. Kirana tucked this information away for later. When Kylo got like this, she knew he was concocting a plan. His plans were usually pretty good, she had to admit, but sometimes he took them too far.

"So what did you find out about those buildings?" she asked, returning them to the topic as they slid by that side of the residence rooftop again.

"Right," he said as he snapped back to attention. "So you know how the two big ones in the middle are like meeting spots for the graduating class and how it's important not to confuse them? Now that we know there is going to be a split in the class, it makes sense that each group will have their own. But what I think I heard in the Impressions Office is that they are looking at options to enforce that one of the groups will not be permitted to enter the other's building. It's just curious to me is all. Why can one group enter both buildings, and the other group can only enter one?" Kylo turned his head to Kirana. "Doesn't that sound sort of odd?" She didn't immediately answer. All of that was news to Kirana. She had missed most of the discussion about the campus map during Orientation. Ignoring his question, she asked another of her own.

"So this whole section is just for the graduating class? What are all those smaller buildings surrounding those two then?" She tried to piece together the information. Kylo looked sideways at her.

"Ah, that's right," he said with a sigh. "You missed part of Orientation. Every one of us will have our own pod," he explained. "After the last iteration, I understand why they did that. I think it's a really good idea."

"What about our nests?" she asked.

"I'm not sure. Maybe they'll move them to the pods, or maybe they'll just become more permanent for in-between iterations instead of moving us every time," he mused. Kirana considered this.

"I think I'd be okay with that," she said mostly to herself, referring to the residences becoming more permanent.

"By the way, I heard something else when I was waiting outside the Impressions Office." Kylo waited for Kirana to acknowledge this before continuing. "Someone was asking about a rumor he had heard about last iteration. It must have been someone from the FI class. He actually mentioned Nova's name. That's when I started listening more intently. He was saying he didn't feel comfortable knowing that she was still on campus. I kinda lost it when I heard that." Kirana stayed quiet, knowing the story wasn't over. "I went straight into the room and interrupted them. Set them straight. And I told them if they have a problem with her, they have a problem with me too. She's not leaving unless she wants to." He grinned. "I don't think they'll bother her anymore."

"I hope not," Kirana sighed, thinking about the note someone had left in Nova's bag. "But that's actually why I wanted to see you. I wanted to thank you for standing up for her." She glittered all over with mauvy pink gratitude.

"You know I've got your back, and I know how much you care about Nova, so that means I've got her back too," Kylo said seriously. "Alright?" Kirana smiled with a nod. Her family and her mates were truly incredible.

CHAPTER SEVEN

Kylo and Kirana were just about to leave the rooftop when a ruddy face poked around the door.

"Hey, there you are!" the face said. He came further into view. He looked stocky, but Kirana couldn't tell if that was true or if he was actually thin and had a thick layer of dense energy he carried around him. She suspected the latter when she saw how he communicated.

"I invited Ravi to join a bunch of us in the FI class to go play X and wanted to see if you would come too," he said. Then, shifting his attention to Kirana, he stuck his hand out towards her adding, "Hi! I'm Alev." Some talked with their hands, moving them around a lot to emphasize different things. Alev spoke with his energy. A sort of burnt orange color moved and jumped around him as he spoke. Kirana smiled in greeting, offering her hand as well. His thick energy was warm and soothing.

"Lovely to meet you," she responded. Kylo watched them silently for a moment, then came alive again, hooking his arm over Alev's shoulders.

"Perfect, glad you've gotten acquainted. So a game of X, huh? And Ravi's going? I'm definitely in then. Kir, you should come too," he said with a mischievous glint in his eye.

"Sure, why not." Kirana smiled, then hesitated to look in Alev's direction. "As long as that's okay?"

"Absolutely! The more the merrier!" Alev confirmed. He turned his attention to Kylo as he led the way down from the rooftop. "I've been telling everybody about X since you and Ravi took me. They're so excited. And now I get to see others try it for the first time too!" he said excitedly. "We're going to meet them in front of the Sim buildings." Alev kept chattering away as they met Ravi in the front of the residence. Kylo threw his arm back over Alev's shoulders and walked with him, just listening. That left Ravi and Kirana to walk together. Kirana didn't mind at all. Ravi was joyfully telling her stories to make her laugh. At one point, he touched her shoulder to emphasize the punchline of a joke in one of his stories. It created a bright flare of light that even caught the attention of Alev and Kylo, who were a fair distance ahead of them by now.

"Whoa, what was that?" Alev's energy bounced in surprise. Kylo responded for them saying, "Oh, don't mind the Sunshine Twins. They just amp each other up." He turned back with a quick grin directed at Ravi. Kirana blushed. As Alev and Kylo turned back around and continued on, Ravi suddenly darted behind a building. Kirana stopped in surprise. Ravi came back around the corner and grabbed her hand, risking another flare, but this time nobody looked.

"Quick, the coast is clear!" Ravi said in a theatrical whisper. He gently tugged her hand so she would follow. Kirana looked behind the building and saw what he was going for.

"Ohh, is that a light string?" she responded in the same hushed tone, delighted to try them again. The ones she had in her nest were amazing, but they were such short distances that she didn't get to enjoy the ride for very long. They stopped in front of the set of the strings. There was a clear field of white light over them like a box. She didn't notice it before she reached out to touch them, but Ravi quickly grabbed for her arm to keep her from doing so. He knocked her away just in time, but with the sudden movement and added force, the bright light that normally formed when they touched was stronger, creating a spark. The spark flew out in the direction of the light string box and hit it, which caused it to start emanating strong waves that pushed Ravi and Kirana to the ground. Ravi stayed on his knees, but moved in between the box and Kirana so that she was behind him, and he was taking the brunt of the force from the waves. After a moment, it slowed down and then stopped, like it had been a warning. Ravi and Kirana looked at each other, stunned. It had all happened so fast.

"What was that?" Kirana asked, still talking quietly. Ravi didn't answer right away as he got up to take a closer look at the box. He nodded to himself and looked up at Kirana in a way that was more serious than she'd seen him yet.

"I'm sorry, Kirana, I didn't see that they had added a white-out to this set until the last second. Kylo's not going to be happy with me." He said that last part mostly to himself. Kirana tried to give him an encouraging glint.

"Hey, it's alright. I'm the one who tried to touch it, and you stopped a worse situation from happening! What is a white-out anyway?" she finally mustered a glint and sent it to him. He gave her a small smile and breathed a sigh of relief to himself.

"Either this light string set is not fully set up yet and they don't want anyone to get lost while the destinations are still being activated, or..." He paused, turning to look back at it. "Or it's under some sort of restrictions." Kirana got up and joined Ravi at the box to take a closer look.

"I set up some local light strings in my nest," she began, "and I didn't activate one of them right away, but I can't see a need for something this intense. I could get on it, it just didn't really go anywhere." She looked up to see Ravi in a full glow, looking at her with glittering eyes.

"Color me impressed!" he exclaimed, no longer speaking so quietly, or seriously for that matter. "The same Kirana, the one who had only ever used the gold light strings and had never even seen the colored ones, set up her own?!" Gold light strings were common for celebratory events, still fun, but they were standard, with the only purpose of getting everyone from one place to the other. Kirana had discovered that a lot of other fun things could be done with them. "You are really something," Ravi added. His eyes were locked on her, and Kirana could feel herself matching his glow. He offered his hand to her in their overlapping gold. She offered hers back, and they both watched the light that emanated from their combined energy.

"I had so much fun that day," she said, her voice back to a whisper. "I wanted something to remember it by."

"I did too," agreed Ravi, taking a step closer to her. Just then, there was a small *ping* next to them. They both turned to see the white-out box disappear. "No way," he breathed. He looked back at Kirana. "I think we might want to get out of here. Someone might be coming to work on them." He turned to start walking away from the light strings, but Kirana turned towards them with a grin.

"Where are you going? Now's our chance!" Her eyes twinkled at him as she reached for the red string that would take them to the Sim buildings. Ravi looked shocked and then thrilled as he grabbed for Kirana's other outstretched hand, catching it just in time as she jumped on and pulled him behind her.

This light string ride acted like it wanted to prepare them for what they might encounter in the Sim buildings. It was fast, then slow, dropped them high and swung them low, twisted in corkscrews and then finally, deposited them at their destination. They were laughing and breathless when they arrived near the group that had gathered. Kylo spotted them and started to make his way over.

"There you are! I thought we lost you somehow." He looked back and forth between the two of them. "Everything good here?"

"Everything's great," Kirana assured him, smiling brightly at Ravi. "Have they picked teams yet?" she asked.

"Not yet. I think Alev is waiting for a few more," he responded. Ravi started to say something, but Kirana got distracted hearing her name from the small crowd. She turned towards the sound and saw Sora waving.

"Sora's here! I'm going to go say hi," she said excitedly, skipping away without waiting for a response. When Kylo joined them a few moments later, Kirana looked around him, confused.

"Where did Ravi go?" she questioned Kylo.

"He said he wanted to go look into something at the archives," he shrugged. "He said he'll try to make it back in time to play a round with us." He paused, looking closer at Kirana. "Did anything happen on your way over here?"

"If something did, this probably wouldn't be the best time to mention it," she responded, gesturing to the FI group standing nearby. Kylo made a clicking sound as if to represent *good point.*

"And speaking of," Kirana glittered, "this is Sora, one of my new mates!" In Sora's ever graceful way, she extended a hand in greeting saying, "I've heard so much about you from Kirana! I'm really pleased to meet you." Kylo smiled.

"The pleasure is all mine. Any mate of Kirana's is a mate of mine. Welcome to the campus," he said, extending his hand as well. They glowed an airy blue. It was always fun to see how energies combined. Kylo turned to Kirana.

"How many from this FI class have played X before, do you think?" They both scanned the group, noting that they were the only two from the graduating class there. Everyone else was in the FI class. It was a smallish group, probably only big enough for two or three teams. Kylo realized what that meant. "Oh no," he said, feigning horror. "They are going to split us up!" Kirana laughed.

"You're probably right," she moaned, feigning that same flavor of tragedy and clinging to his arm dramatically.

"Okay everyone," they heard Alev call out. "Time for the rules of the game!" Everyone quieted down and turned his direction. "How many do we have—one, two, three," he began, going through the group. "Okay, that's 11 total," Alev was saying. He seemed a little unsure about how to split the group. Kylo leaned over to whisper to Kirana.

"I think I'm going to give him a hand, seeing as he forgot to include himself in the total," Kylo chuckled, moving towards where Alev was standing. After some deliberation, they decided to go with two teams of six. And it would make things more even if Kylo and Kirana were on different teams, since they had played the most and would have the biggest advantage. Alev agreed to mates staying on the same team, probably just to make sure he could be on Kylo's team. But it also meant that Kirana and Sora got to be on the same team.

"This'll be fun," Kirana whispered to Sora, shining a bit in anticipation. "I haven't had a chance to beat Kylo in this game in a long time." Sora glowed light blue back to her with an excited bounce.

"Rules," declared Kylo, loudly and with authority. "One. No player may abandon his or her team. You must stay together. Two. Stay within the designated Sim buildings. In this case, we are using the Gravity, Sense, and Interaction buildings. Three. First team to make it to the X Spot wins. Ready? Get set, GO!" The two teams started racing towards the buildings, first clue in hand. As Kylo passed by Kirana, he squeezed her shoulder and gave her a grin.

"Let the games begin!"

CHAPTER EIGHT

The Sim buildings were widely used by everyone on campus. They were always open and available, both for studies as well as personal practice and exploration. Each building had a different focus, which influenced how individual buildings were designed. Sims, short for simulations, were available in small rooms inside each of the buildings so no one was ever disturbed by others during their studies. There were smaller solo rooms and slightly larger group rooms, with one extra large room available for entire classes as needed. These teams of six would easily be able to use the group rooms to enter simulations together.

X was a common game to play. It was played like a race. The final destination, after making it through several simulation challenges, would be marked with an X. There were infinite ways to play.

Kirana, Sora and their four teammates were running towards the Sense Sim building first, same as the other team. Kirana could tell they were all looking to her for direction, and she was happy to oblige.

"Have any of you tried any Sims yet?" she called out to her team while dodging a stray shower of sparks that Kylo had casually tossed their direction. No one responded. She looked over her shoulder at them. "Really?!" she exclaimed. "No one? Okay, well you're about to get a crash course on how they work!" They got up to the Sense building which had a somewhat aggressive entry; an assault on the senses. It was loud and disorienting with intermittent flashing lights that made it feel like they were moving both too quickly and too slowly at the same time. There were places where they had to squeeze through giant spinning brushes and walk through a sticky substance. Sora looked relieved as she made it into the building.

"I am SO happy that there were no tastes and smells to deal with," she chirped.

"I've heard that's because there's a slightly smaller percentage of the Sims that use senses like those," said one of their teammates.

"That's not it. I think it's because no one would practice in this building if they had to endure that every time!" said another. Someone else was sputtering and complaining about brush bristles in their mouth, muttering something like, "Speak for yourselves." Kirana smirked.

"Actually, it changes every so often. But let's go! Grab a room!" She began shuffling everyone into a group Sim room. After making a face at Kylo as he was also trying to get his group of bewildered teammates into a Sim room, Kirana shut the door and pulled up the screen. The room was dark and empty, aside from benches, the screen and the controls, along with a basket of bracelets. Kirana passed out the bracelets and started shuffling through the control options. "For this game, it looks like Alev has hidden one clue here, one in the next Sim building, and the X will be in the last building. That's the easy part. Right now, we need to figure out which galaxy to search, and then which planet in that galaxy. We'll determine where to go and then enter that Sim where we have to navigate to the clue. Obviously we'll have to figure out how to use whatever senses are available to us in this location to be able to do that. Can someone read the clue?"

The team figured out where they needed to go rather quickly and everyone was in agreement on where to start their search. This was a really impressive feat as new galaxies were constantly being added to the Sims. Luckily, Kirana was familiar with this one. She was excited.

"Oh, I've been here! Okay, one trick to remember—everyone hold on to whoever is next to them, and do not let go! We will be connected in a line. I'll stay on one end. Ready?" She hit the enter button and the team was pulled into the screen. They found themselves in an environment of endless white. It wasn't bright, just a flat, dull white. Not much to look at. With hooked arms or holding hands, the team very quickly discovered why Kirana had directed them to do that. There was very little friction here! Half the team had already fallen or slipped and would've been catapulted away from the others if they hadn't been holding on. They also couldn't hear much. Everything seemed to be soaked up and muffled by the surrounding whiteness. Kirana saw team members' mouths moving, but there was no sound to speak of. With her free hand in a fist, she swung her arm up above her head. There was a very low ceiling-like material above them and the force pushed a visual vibration of black across the otherwise white place, catching everyone's attention. She demonstrated how they could grasp the black rubbery pieces that hung down as long as they kept the ceiling vibrating. Kirana was pleased that everyone seemed to catch on quickly. They began their search for the next clue. They wouldn't run into the other team since they were in separate Sim rooms.

Kirana enjoyed watching the team as they interacted with the environment here. She enjoyed the tickles and suction and other odd internal sensations, but it looked like a few of them would rather be anywhere else. Sora seemed to become more opaque here, but still managed movement easily. She spotted the clue and made her way in that direction. When she reached out for it, she realized she couldn't reach it unless she let go of the black material. Kirana saw her looking around for options and started to head in her direction. Soon the whole team was nearby and reconnecting to each other so that Sora could let go of the black and get the clue. She held it up triumphantly, and the team looked happy. Everyone looked to Kirana as if to ask, *What now?* She smiled and held up her arm with the bracelet on it. She pushed the button on the side to exit the simulation. Everyone quickly followed suit. The team was hugging and cheering back in the Sim room congratulating Sora, who was looking much more clear again.

"Did you feel the fuzziness in your feet when you took a step like I did?" asked someone from the team, looking a little uncomfortable.

"I felt way too many sensations," said another. "I think I prefer my sensations on the outside rather than on the inside." Agreement rumbled through the group as they removed their bracelets to leave in the basket. Kirana reset the Sim and asked Sora to read the clue. It was obvious that their next stop would be the Interaction building.

"And good news," she added. "The exit to a Sim building is separate from the entrance. We don't have to go through anything but a regular door." Smiling and chattering amongst themselves, the group left the Sim room, went out the doors and began running towards the Interaction building. Kirana noticed that the other team's Sim room was already vacant. Hopefully they weren't too far behind.

The entry to the Interaction building was a series of small rooms, each blocked by someone different. There were huge words written on the wall behind each of those Someones. The words explained how to interact in greeting form. Greet the Someone, and they could pass into the next room. They successfully got through various greetings, some with certain words, some with gestures or body movements, and even one by humming in a certain key. They ran into a Sim room, now understanding better what to do. They put on their bracelets as Sora read the clue again. Kirana was glad it was another easy one. One of the team members even knew a little bit about the planet.

"Some of my family has been there!" he exclaimed. "They told me a bit about how they interact." His excitement dulled as he seemed to remember something. "Whatever you do," he warned, "do not lift your leg above your head." His eyes had gotten wide. Kirana nodded.

"Noted," she said. "Does everyone understand?" The team looked unworried. "Alright, let's head in!" She started the simulation, and they were sucked into the screen. Almost immediately, the team understood the warning when they saw the bodies they were in on this planet. Their heads were actually pretty low to the ground, and they each had five legs that sprawled out around them. It would be easy to lift one over their head. Luckily, it was just a simulation, so whatever that team member had heard would happen if they accidentally interacted poorly would not actually happen here. The worst that could happen is that they would get kicked out of the simulation. Then they would all have to exit and reenter so that they didn't break rule number one of the game: to stay together.

They moved around for a moment to get used to these bodies. They wanted to figure out how to interact with each other before they started to interact with all the beings around them. Some team members started observing common gestures and movements and started copying them. They discovered that if they faced each other and each put one leg forward, that appeared to be a greeting. It was similar to what they were used to, just with a leg since they had no arms. Then, if one of them put two legs out, they became the speaker. The one with the one leg out was the listener. Communication happened in their heads. The communication seemed to appear as an understanding, rather than words or sounds. The team started interacting with beings around them and asking where a clue might be. Almost immediately, the team member that had been somewhat familiar with this planet was rushing around to show that he had gotten the clue. Luckily, everyone kept their legs low until they got back into the Sim room where they were able to throw their arms up in triumph.

"Amazing job, team!" Kirana praised them. "Well, we already know the last building is the Gravity building, so that must be where the X is! We can read the clue when we get there." They dumped their bracelets in the basket and made a run for it. Kirana wasn't sure which room the other team was in, but she did see two other occupied group rooms. She hoped they were ahead now.

The Gravity building actually floated a bit off the ground. The door itself was in the middle of the face of the building, not at the bottom. It used to have a different type of entrance, Kirana remembered, but since the campus had added light strings this year, it seemed they made an update to this building. She thought it was a clever addition. Sora noticed the light strings first and called everyone over. There were two colors: one a navy blue and the other a gold.

"Which one do you think goes to the entrance?" she asked, looking up towards the door. The team discussed and came to the conclusion that it was probably the gold one because of the fact that those were standard issue. The blue one might leave them somewhere further away on campus or have some other use that they couldn't guess from the color. Sora was getting ready to jump on the gold one when Kirana noticed how pallid it looked next to her shiny transparency.

"Wait," she insisted, stepping closer to the light strings and holding Sora back. In her hand, there was no slight buzz of energy indicating a live light string, and there was no signal that it was just currently deactivated. In that moment, Kirana realized with horror that this light string had been cut.

CHAPTER NINE

K irana held the broken light string, mostly so no one would jump on it, and turned to her team from the FI class who were trying to see what was going on. When she had created her own light string setup, she had actually learned a decent amount about how they worked and what happens when they break. While it was quite rare for a light string to break, it was possible, so she didn't want to jump to conclusions that someone had intentionally cut it. They could be dangerous though. If you attempted to jump onto a broken light string, you could get stuck at the point of the break (or cut), and it would be nearly impossible to climb back out the way you came. Then, if it was closed off, you would really have no exit point.

All of a sudden, Kirana gasped, remembering that they didn't know where the other team was. *Could they have—no, no definitely not.* She shook the thought out of her head.

"What is it?" asked Sora gently. The blue in her eyes had intensified.

"I'm sorry, I don't think we'll be able to continue this game of X," Kirana responded, looking down at the gold light string. "Unless we want to take a chance at the navy blue one," she added weakly. The team started to talk in hushed whispers when they saw Kylo, Alev and the rest of the other team running their way. They were shouting excitedly, thinking they were catching up. Everyone slowed to a stop in confusion when they realized the other team was just standing there with serious faces.

"Hey," Kylo called as he caught up. He looked at Kirana holding the light string. "What happened? Is everything okay?"

"I'm not sure," she responded. "This light string is... broken," she added, not wanting to say what she suspected in front of everyone. Kylo looked her in the eyes, gathering the information he needed from there and turned back to the group.

"What do you say we finish this game later? We'll have the same teams and continue from this point," he announced.

"As long as we get a head start!" said someone from Kirana's team. "We were ahead after all." The rest of the team flickered in agreement. The other team was not concerned.

"Of course," nodded Alev. "Let's rejoin later!" Everyone casually drifted off, discussing their experiences with the game, how they figured out the clues and what happened to who in different Sims until only Kirana and Kylo remained at the Gravity Sim building. Kylo was inspecting both the gold and the blue light strings.

"I think you're right that the gold string goes to the entrance of the building," he stated, looking up at her. "I also think you're right that it's been cut. It's just too new to have broken like this." Just then, Ravi showed up from around the corner.

"Hey there!" he called with a shiny smile. "Perfect timing! Guess I caught up with you after all!" Looking around, a look of confusion came over his face. "Where is everyone?"

"Hey, Rav," said Kylo, a little less airy than usual. "We had to cut the game short. No pun intended, but Kirana discovered a cut light string, and this is the only way to enter the Gravity Sim building. Ravi looked down at the string that was still in Kirana's hand. He quickly grabbed it and dropped it so it was hanging on the wall again.

"Just in case," he reasoned, looked at her. She rolled her eyes playfully.

"I'm not going to fall onto the broken light string!" she responded, smiling at him.

"I don't know," he continued, "the second time we met, you were on the ground." He shrugged his shoulders and smiled back.

"But that—" Kirana started to respond when Kylo interrupted.

"Hey you two beams of light." Waving his arm between them, he wasn't smiling like usual. "Let's get some of that shine onto solving our situation here, hm?" Kirana and Ravi both snapped back to the seriousness of the situation.

"I'm so glad we caught this before anyone tried to use it," murmured Kirana.

"I'm so glad *you* caught it before anyone tried to use it," emphasized Kylo. "Especially our inexperienced FI teams."

"Maybe now is a good time to fill you in on what happened on our way over here earlier," Ravi began, speaking to Kylo but glancing at Kirana. They filled him in on their encounter with the white-out box on the set of strings near the residence buildings. "That's actually why I went to the archives," he said, looking at Kirana again as if to apologize for disappearing.

"What were you trying to find out?" Kirana asked him. "Did you learn anything?"

"Mostly just general information," he responded. "They're a sort of lock to keep anyone from using whatever light strings they're protecting, which we already knew. This would be an excellent time to use one actually," he said as he gestured to the ones in front of them. "What I didn't figure out is how it was there one moment, blocking us from using the strings and then how it disappeared the next, allowing us to jump on." His face showed the concern that Kirana felt when she realized that they could have unknowingly jumped on a broken string earlier. Luckily, it was fine, but she wasn't sure about the other strings in that set.

"I'm going to head back to the residence," Ravi said, finally pulling his eyes from Kirana to look at Kylo. "I want to check into a few things from there on my tablet. On the way, I'm going to stop at those light strings we used and see if it has a white-out on it again or not. I'll check out the strings and see if everything looks alright." Kylo nodded and sent him a dust of luck.

"Let us know what you find out. I'll catch up with you later," he said. Kirana sent a dust of luck as well. As Ravi left, Kirana turned back to the strings.

"Where do you think this blue one goes?" she wondered aloud.

"That's a good question," Kylo agreed. "Maybe one of us should take it and see where we end up while the other one guards the gold string to make sure nobody uses it. Whoever takes the blue string can just come right back, and we can figure out how to either install a white-out ourselves or find someone who can."

"Sounds like a plan," Kirana sighed, starting a bit of an internal battle with herself. She felt a responsibility to be the one to take the blue string and get more information as well as to be the one to guard the gold string to protect others. Kylo seemed to pick up on it.

"That's why there's two of us, Sunshine!" he reassured with a grin. "Here, let me hop on the blue string. I'll be back in a blink. Sound good?" Kirana gave him half a smile as he came close to give her a hug.

"Okay," she agreed, giving him the rest of the smile.

"Okay. Then I'll be right back," Kylo said as he gave her a small salute. He picked up the navy blue light string and hopped on, disappearing from view. Kirana sat down to wait. It shouldn't take him too long, but it depended on how far the destination was, how intense the ride might be and probably a few other factors that Kirana didn't know about light strings yet. As her mind drifted while she sat there, her thoughts meandered to Sora and how she managed in the simulations, Kylo and his laid back demeanor, Ravi and how much fun they had together and eventually landed on Nova, wondering how she was doing. She thought back to the note in her bag and how she had tried to talk to Guardian Cosmo the day of Orientation. Something buzzed in the back of Kirana's mind. Didn't Nova say that she had found Guardian Cosmo in front of the Gravity Sim building? And didn't he hop on a light string from there? Or, here, rather. She stood and turned to examine where the light strings hung on the wall. She scanned the area around and nearby, letting her thoughts continue to wander. Taking a step backward to widen her view, she bumped right into something. This something talked.

"Lost in thought again, are we?" said a low, but smooth voice that was definitely familiar this time. Kirana took in a breath, but didn't let it go right away. She covered her mouth as she slowly turned around.

"I. am. so. sorry," she said, as if each word were its own sentence. Nox's eyes were dancing. Dancing stars against the backdrop of the purest night. She stared into them.

"What are we looking for?" he asked, scanning the area like she had been doing a moment ago. Kirana worked to regain her clarity and nonchalance, but this time she couldn't help but acknowledge that there was an odd feeling deep inside her that seemed to get stronger every time she bumped into him. And then she remembered how many times she had bumped into him, and her cheeks flushed.

"Want to tell me about it?" Nox asked, sitting down near the wall that he was almost tall enough to lean against, even with the building raised off the ground. Kirana breathed out, not realizing that she had been holding it again. She sat down next to him. Somehow this was easier than looking at him directly—maybe because she couldn't get lost in his eyes from here. The green haze around them appeared again. Kirana could see it better this time, and she just watched it as she began to tell Nox what happened while they were playing X. She explained that she was guarding the gold string while waiting for Kylo to come back from testing the blue one. Everything just poured out. She felt... safe. She wondered if that was the green bubble around them or Nox himself. She finally turned to look at him. He seemed to be considering the information.

"I'll go after Kylo. It probably shouldn't take this long. Let's make sure everything is alright," Nox said, getting to his feet. Looking up at him from the ground while he was standing really made him look huge to Kirana. She quickly hopped up to her feet as well.

"Are you sure? What if he got stuck and you just get stuck too? Should we have some sort of plan to—" as Kirana was speaking, Kylo appeared, looking slightly out of breath.

"Kylo!" she shouted, running to give him a hug. "We were getting worried." She stopped hugging him when she realized that he really did need to catch his breath.

"I got back as soon as I could, Kir. I found something interesting. But I want to get back to my tablet and check in with Ravi on what he's discovered too," he breathed. "The blue string is fine. It just goes to the

Dome. I also ran into Guardian Era who will be on his way shortly to add a white-out to the strings here. Can you wait until he gets here if I take off?" Just then, Kylo seemed to notice someone else was there. He stood taller. "Nox! Wow, good to see you!" he said, offering evergreen sparkles. It was kind of like the color of the hazy bubble that formed when Kirana was with Nox, she noticed. But the bubble didn't seem to be there anymore. Nox smiled warmly.

"Kylo, you too, mate," he said, going in for a hug. Kylo accepted. Kirana looked at the two of them.

"You know each other?" she asked.

"We're old mates," Kylo responded with a faraway look in his eye. "Nox here got me through some rough times. I don't see you around nearly enough," he added, directing his attention to Nox. Kirana started to suspect that Nox's ability to lay low or stay somewhat hidden was intentional.

"You've done the same for me," Nox said quietly. Then they seemed to snap out of it, and Kylo went back into go mode.

"Alright, I'm going to head out. Can you two wait for Guardian Era?" Turning to Kirana, he added, "I trust Nox with everything I am. Maybe he can help us figure this out." Kirana felt a rush of relief, realizing she'd already told him everything.

"No problem, go ahead," she told him. "And you don't have to wait with me," she directed at Nox, silently hoping he would anyway. Nox looked back towards the spot where they had been sitting.

"My seat there was rather comfortable. I think I'll hang out a bit longer," he grinned. "As long as that's alright." Kirana glowed more golden than usual. Kylo's face gave away a small hint of surprise, like something just dawned on him. He tossed them a few more evergreen sparkles and ran off towards the residence buildings. As Nox and Kirana sat down to wait for Guardian Era, Nox absently scuffed his feet on the ground underneath the building.

"Hey, what's this?" he asked to no one in particular, picking up a small note that looked like it had been ripped off of something. He brushed it off and showed Kirana. It read, *I think I'm ready.*

CHAPTER TEN

"Can I see that?" Kirana asked, leaning towards Nox's outstretched hand holding the note. Somehow the closer she got to him, the stronger the feeling was to get that much closer still. She reached out her hand as he passed her the note. Their fingers touched briefly, and Kirana focused hard on pretending like she didn't notice. Completely comfortable with sharing information with Nox now, especially after what Kylo had said, she studied the note and mused aloud.

"I saw a note just like this earlier. Nova found one in her bag. I bet she still has it. Do you mind if I hold onto this? I want to compare the handwriting and the material it's written on with hers," she explained. Nox nodded, not looking like he needed any more explanation than that. Just then, Kirana remembered that they, Nova and Nox, were family. He probably already knew all about it.

"You saw her note, didn't you," Kirana stated, not really as a question. Nox's eyes connected to hers, and she was momentarily lost there in that moment.

"Keep me in the loop?" she heard him say. Kirana knew that Nova would keep him updated regardless, so this felt like an invitation to stay in contact with each other. To work on something together. This made something flutter in her stomach.

"Absolutely," she agreed, tearing her eyes from his. Someone was approaching them.

"Nox," Guardian Era glowed. "Delightful to see you again. And you," he said, turning to Kirana, "must be Kirana." He dipped his head into a small bow directed somewhere in between the two of them. Kirana had been wanting to meet, to talk to or to work with Guardian Era for as long as she could remember. Somehow, now that the moment had arrived, she said nothing and remained frozen in her spot. She had no idea how long she remained like this. Guardian Era did not seem to be in a hurry. He and Nox caught up for a moment, and Kirana realized they must have worked together through numerous iterations. Guardian Era asked him if he knew which of the two groups he intended to join, but it seemed like both of them already knew the answer. The groups hadn't been announced yet, but maybe Nox had special insight? Or maybe he'd just been around long enough to have seen the need for the split. All of this spun around in Kirana's head and only settled as Guardian Era addressed her directly again. She missed the question.

"Sorry, what was that?" she blushed, gathering her bearings. Guardian Era smiled.

"Not to worry," he said graciously. "You were the one who discovered the broken light string, yes? Would you like to tell me what happened?"

"Oh, yes, of course," she exclaimed softly. She walked over to the strings to show him and began to explain.

"A group of us were playing X—many of them for the first time. Kylo and I each ended up with a group from the FI class with us. My team reached the building first, and our last clue was here in the Gravity Sim building. We determined as a group that the gold string went to the entrance, and one of my team members was about to hop on—actually,"

Kirana stopped abruptly. "It was one of my mates. One of my mates, who was on my team, almost hopped on a broken light string." That reality finally seemed to hit her, how serious it could have been. She must have shown some distress on her face because Guardian Era sent her some white peace bubbles. Nox stepped closer to her, looking like he wanted to put his arms around her but holding back. Guardian Era spoke positively and gently.

"But you didn't let that happen. You trusted your instincts and protected those around you." He paused for a moment as Kirana nodded before he continued. "You know," he said, looking intently at Kirana, making sure she was hearing him. "Just because I moved stations this iteration to allow Guardians Beck and Alder to focus on the graduating class doesn't mean I'm not accessible. The first time you enter the graduating class is a big step. I'm still involved, and I'm still able to observe and guide wherever I see the need. Okay?" He gave her a big smile, hoping to coax one out of her as well. It worked. "There's that shine I've heard so much about," he grinned. "My personal office is open to you in the Impressions Office at any time." He waited for some confirmation from her that she heard him before turning towards the light strings. With his back turned as he inspected the strings, he added, "But with family like Kylo and Nox, you probably won't even need me." Kirana glanced at Nox sideways. He was still watching her silently, looking ready to jump in wherever or whenever he was needed. He didn't react to Guardian Era's words.

"Oh, we're not—" Kirana began. Guardian Era glanced back at her with raised eyebrows, turning back around without saying anything. Kirana didn't finish her sentence, but Nox chimed in saying, "We've run into each other a time or two," without taking his eyes off Kirana. She sparkled unintentionally. Everyone pretended not to notice. Guardian Era brushed his hands off.

"I'm going to go ahead and install a white-out box here and document the situation. Is there anything else I should know before I leave?" he asked. Kirana briefly thought about Nova seeing Guardian Cosmo there, but she had no real reason to mention that now. Then something else popped into her head.

"Actually, I saw another white-out box earlier near the residences. Was there another cut light string there?" she asked tentatively. "Or broken," she added quickly. Guardian Era did not react outwardly.

"We are aware and working on the issue," he responded indirectly. Kirana absently continued.

"Once it disappeared and we jumped on a string, it seemed alright, but it—" she stopped when this time, Guardian Era did react.

"What do you mean, 'it disappeared and then you jumped on a string,'" he repeated, somewhat alarmed. Nox's eyes intensified, which was hard for Kirana to believe was possible.

"We, Ravi and I," she clarified, decidedly not looking at Nox, "took the string from the residences to the entrance area of the Sim buildings."

White-outs had to cover all the strings in a set—they couldn't just block one string and not the others. However, the white-out automatically synced to the other end of the string with the issue and rendered it inactive from the other side. It would appear inactive without disturbing the other strings. That way, there was no ripple effect of having to take down an entire light string system for one broken string. When the white-out was installed here, it had to cover both the string to the Gravity Sim building and the one to the Dome. Someone at the Dome could still use the string to get to the Gravity Sim building safely though. Kirana noted to herself that apparently, it was not normal for white-out boxes to just disappear. She'd have to share notes with Ravi later. For some odd reason, it felt weird to talk about Ravi in front of Nox.

Guardian Era looked like part of him was deep in thought. Kirana briefly wondered if he was doing a split-energy, but he passed her another peace bubble and sent both her and Nox away, saying he had everything handled and would be done soon. Kirana found herself walking back to her residence with Nox beside her. Somehow she felt glad he was next to her. That warm glow of safety inside her grew ever stronger.

"Oh, you didn't have to come all this way with me!" she said, either betraying herself or her feelings, she wasn't sure. She sparkled some dark pink gratitude to make up for it. A lot of gratitude.

"Don't mention it. I wanted to!" he laughed, practically getting attacked by gratitude. They got to the front door, and he looked like he wanted to ask her something. She waited a moment, but he didn't say anything. She wracked her brain for what to say before she walked inside, leaving him, but nothing was coming easily. Then, she thought of something. She turned to him with her hand already on the door.

"Hey, what were you doing out by the Gravity Sim building earlier when I bumped into you?" She seemed to have finally accepted the fact that they just seemed drawn to each other. The closer they were, the stronger the impact. Nox stared into her eyes.

"I was actually looking for you. Nova told me you were with Kylo, and when nobody was at their residence, I figured you all might be playing X." His smile was so genuine, so warm and so open, Kirana almost completely melted on the spot.

"Oh—" she stammered, not sure how to continue. Just then, the door opened and Sora, Nova and Anala were all in the doorway scrambling to hug Kirana first.

"We could see your glow through the door, why didn't you come in?"

"Oh my gosh, I heard what happened! Are you okay?

"Kirana! I'm so glad you're back!"

Everyone was talking at once. Kirana looked back at Nox as she was getting swept inside. "We'll talk later?" she asked him. He smiled back at her, sent a handful of gold stardust and closed the door for them. Kirana addressed Sora first.

"Are you okay?" she asked intently, releasing her from a hug. Sora flickered opaque for a moment before returning to clear, as if remembering the events earlier.

"Yes, are you?" she responded. "Everyone came over after, and we were all talking about it. We were so distracted by the events of the game that we didn't realize..." she trailed off for a moment. Then in her sing-songy voice, she proclaimed, "You saved me. You saved all of us. How many of us could have been still trapped in there right now?" She hugged Kirana tightly again. Kirana looked over at Anala, and then at Nova from over Sora's shoulder. They were giving Sora a moment of space. When she finally let go of Kirana, she looked like she had soaked up some rays and was glowing. "I'm so glad I get to be your mate this iteration. And that goes to all of you."

"And we are so happy you're ours!" Anala spoke for the rest of them. Kirana noticed then that she was extra shiny, her flicker extra steady. Sora noticed Kirana noticing and smirked.

"Anala told us more about light strings," she began. "Alev was especially interested." Anala's face glowed a touch more red.

"Anyways," she said as if nobody had been talking about her, "I have to study a bit before class. I'm glad you're all here and that everybody is okay!" She blew them kisses as she walked to the back where her nest was. The other three giggled quietly to themselves, Kirana a little disappointed she hadn't gotten to see Anala and Alev meet.

"Same here," sang Sora. "Are you headed up too?" she directed at Kirana.

"Yeah, I think I need to process all of this," she responded, putting her arm around Sora and starting to walk with her. "Lots to catch up on," she said pointedly to Nova as they passed by, silently slipping her the note that Nox had found. Nova nodded knowingly, sent them some glitter, and headed in the direction of her own nest as well.

Chapter Eleven

A little while later, because Nova actually did want to make sure Kirana had some time to process the recent events, she took the light string they had connected from Kirana's nest to hers, carrying both notes with her. Kirana wasn't immediately visible in her nest.

"Knock knock," Nova called quietly.

"Chestnut light string!" Kirana called down from her hidden nook. Nova hopped on and after flipping through an apparently new loop, she met Kirana up there.

"Still playing with your light strings I see," Nova giggled. "That was a surprise, but I didn't hate it." She grinned. "Hi." Kirana grinned back.

"Hi," she began. "I feel like we have so much to catch up on."

"Tell me about it!" agreed Nova, flopping down next to her. "Can we start with these notes though? Because they look way too similar to be unrelated." She set both of the notes down in between them. *How long do you think you'll last?* with two ripped edges and two smooth, indicating a corner piece, and *I think I'm ready* with three ripped edges and one straight. Using one finger, Kirana moved one of the notes so that its edge fit on top of the other one. They seemed to share a ripped edge. She glanced up at Nova, silently confirming that the handwriting was also the same.

"Do you—" Kirana paused, wanting to ask this question carefully. "When and where exactly did you find the first note?" Nova looked like she understood what Kirana was halfway implying.

"You know, I've been wondering if maybe the note wasn't about me after all," she responded. "I'm not ruling it out just yet, but it's possible that it ended up in my bag by mistake." Kirana was silent, waiting for her to continue. "We were in class, working in groups. I was with Tali and her two mates." Kirana nodded, remembering those details. Nova continued, "I left my bag in the center while we moved to the edges of the room to work with our tablets. There was plenty of movement around there throughout class. When we went to gather our things, I saw the note. I'd say it was more *on* my bag than *in* it, if I'm being honest. It could have dropped out of another bag or fallen from anyone's pocket as they walked by. I was just already sensitive to what I heard outside of the building before class and obviously thinking about last iteration because of it. The message kind of fits my situation, but next to this other note, I almost read it as more of a legitimate question than I do as a threat. Does that even make sense?" She paused. "Like, if someone was threatening me, wouldn't it be something more like, *You shouldn't be here* or *You're making things worse for everyone,* or something like that." Her voice turned weak towards the end of her thought.

"I hope those aren't your thoughts about yourself," Kirana said gently, reaching to put her hand on Nova's knee. Nova didn't respond. She suspected they were both thinking about the student in the Impressions Office that Kylo had overheard and confronted. Kylo had said that student was from the FI class though, so he wouldn't have been in Nova's class to drop a note like that. "I see what you mean about the tone of the note though," Kirana continued, her face shaped into a look of concentration. "Even if I fit it to your situation, it is kind of an odd way to try to threaten or scare someone."

"Right?" Nova responded. "So tell me about this second one. Where did it come from? When did you find it?" Kirana's thoughts went to Nox and she felt warm. Nova looked at her curiously.

"Actually, Nox found it," she began. "We were waiting outside the Gravity Sim building guarding the light strings, and he found it on the ground under the building. He let me take it when I told him I wanted to compare it to yours. He didn't seem surprised by my request so I assume you already told him about it..?" Kirana turned her statement into a question at the very last word.

"Yeah," Nova said, looking thoughtful. "He had an interesting take on it." She seemed to say that last part to herself. Kirana was going to ask about it, but another memory popped in, distracting her.

"Hey, did you actually see who Guardian Cosmo was talking to that day you followed him? On the day of Orientation," she clarified. "Oh! And do you remember which light string he took?" She asked this last bit with anticipation. Nova appeared to be trying to connect the dots as to why Kirana was asking about this. Unable to do so, she went ahead and searched her memory for the answers anyway.

"I think I was so focused on talking to Guardian Cosmo that I have no idea who he was talking to. I remember a hazy red for some reason, but that's it. As for the light string, I'm pretty sure it was gold." She stopped when Kirana's eyes grew wider.

"You're sure?" she asked Nova. "There's only a gold and a navy blue one there in that set."

"Oh, then yeah. It was for sure the gold one. I remember I noticed how shiny it was when it was reflecting off of Guardian Cosmo's pendant," she confirmed. "Why?" The look in Kirana's eye answered her question. Kirana took a big breath and sighed it out.

"That was the broken light string. The gold one goes to the entrance to the Gravity Sim building."

"Interesting," remarked Nova. "Why would someone cut entry to that building?" She began to count on her fingers. "So Guardian Cosmo went to the Gravity Sim building during Orientation," she said, holding one finger up. She held up a second finger saying, "Nox found a note at the same building that matches another mystery note we have, and now the light string to that building has been cut," she finished on the third finger. "Popular building."

"What do you know about white-outs?" Kirana asked, not missing a beat.

"You mean like what they install when a light string is broken? I know you can't touch them, or they will push you away with a strong vibrational wave. Basically, they just keep anyone from falling into a broken string and getting trapped. When the light string gets fixed, they remove it," Nova said matter-of-factly.

"Have you ever seen one disappear?" she asked, wondering if it was there or not when Ravi went back to check.

"What do you mean, *disappear*?" Nova was saying as Kirana returned from her wondering.

"Ravi and I saw a set of light strings with a white-out box on them before our X game earlier," she said carefully, not wanting to upset Nova with more dangerous situations. But she had the opposite reaction than what Kirana was expecting. She brightened up.

"Oh, you were hanging out with Ravi again?" she teased. "Tell me more," she prodded with a grin. Kirana wasn't sure all of a sudden how she felt about talking about Ravi. Maybe a little conflicted somehow? But why, she wasn't sure. She took the bait anyway.

"I think we had a moment actually," she said, remembering how they had connected. "We were playing around, and then when we saw the white-out box and accidentally provoked it, he put himself between it and me, blocking me from the majority of the force of the waves. It was gallant," she reflected. "Then I told him about how I had set up light strings in my nest, and he was so impressed and all glowy, and we were just vibing." Kirana found herself smiling and remembering how much fun they'd been having. Nova was listening with great interest, but her face changed as Kirana continued. "Then, when the white-out disappeared, we were able to hop on and make it to the Sim buildings. We weren't even the last to arrive!" Kirana was still smiling, but Nova was not anymore. Kirana was quick on the pick-up. "Ahh, okay, so that really isn't normal then." Nova shook her head.

"I've never heard of a white-out box just disappearing and letting anyone use the strings. I'm so glad you're both okay," Nova said, looking a little pale.

Kirana felt like she needed to comfort Nova, even though she had been the one in all the dangerous situations. She was surprised at Nova's next question.

"Does Nox know?" Kirana tilted her head, wondering what she was really asking.

"Does Nox know about the white-out box?" Kirana repeated Nova's question back to her. Remembering that she had spilled everything to him, she responded without waiting for Nova to confirm. "Yes." Nova looked satisfied. Something else occurred to Kirana as she glanced at the notes again.

"You know what's weird? Why we now have two notes written by the same Someone, found in different places. Why wouldn't the intended recipient of the notes have them? Or have gotten rid of them? But both of these were found in pretty public places. I wonder if they were both intended for the same Someone," she mused. Nova's head was still focused on the puzzle surrounding the Gravity Sim building.

"Yeah, and what is it about that particular building that things seem to happen around?" she asked, knowing they didn't have the answer.

"I know both Kylo and Ravi have been looking into some stuff. I'll catch up with them in class and let you know what they've discovered," Kirana assured her. She looked sideways at Nova then, changing the subject.

"I talked to Guardian Era," she almost whispered. Nova knew how much she respected him and how she was still disappointed that he was appointed to Nova's group now, instead of the graduating class.

"And?" she prompted.

"He said I could go to his office anytime. He said just because he's not officially working with the graduating class this iteration doesn't mean he can't advise me," Kirana confided, her voice back to a happier tone.

"That's great," Nova responded, giving her a small smile. "He still hasn't been involved much in our class. He mostly observes."

"Do you feel like he's still observing you a lot?" Kirana questioned. Nova considered this.

"Either I've gotten used to it so it doesn't feel so obvious anymore, or he's toned it down," she said, not seeming confident in her answer.

"Well," Kirana offered, "I'm sure it's not anything bad. Let's just keep our eyes open for the next little while here and see if we can get some answers. We seem to be collecting more questions than answers right now!" She looked at Nova who had a faraway look. "Everything okay?" she prompted.

"What? Oh, yes, hey Kirana?" Nova said, without waiting for a response. "Just promise me you'll stay away from light strings for a while, yeah? Just until we know they're all working properly." Her eyes pleaded more than her words did.

"Okay, sure," Kirana said, again feeling like Nova was the one who needed comfort. "Don't worry about me. Besides, Kylo would never let anything happen to me," she said laughing, making an effort to relax Nova.

"And Nox won't either," Nova uttered like a previously discussed fact. Kirana was a little confused, but she had just learned that Kylo and Nox knew each other, apparently very well, so she assumed it was because of that and let it go.

CHAPTER TWELVE

Kirana needed to refocus. She was getting too distracted, and there was too much at stake this iteration for her to be playing on light strings and endangering her mates. She considered telling Anala to go ahead to class without her so she could... what? Arrive slightly later and be alone? It wasn't a solution to isolate herself either. She decided to dedicate herself to her studies as much as she could so she didn't fall behind. She'd work out a study routine and try to stay out of trouble. Nova was right.

Anala was waiting for her outside of their residence. "Ready?" she asked Kirana with a deep red, swirling glow about her. She looked closer at Kirana's face. "Hey, are you alright?" she asked. Kirana looked up at the concern in Anala's voice.

"Yes," she began, "I'm alright. I was just thinking about everything that's happened and realized I'm getting distracted. This iteration is really important to me, and I need to do well. I need to do the best I can. It's the graduating class!" Anala was nodding next to her as they made their way to their class building.

"I know what you mean. Hopefully things will calm down a little bit now that we've all settled into campus, met everyone and gotten past our first couple of classes," Anala commented. "I think I should probably try to focus a little harder as well." Kirana looked over at Anala to catch her looking down as if her head were somewhere else, even in that very moment. Anala saw her looking and blushed. "See? Even now when I'm talking about focusing more, I'm not focusing!" Somehow it made Kirana feel better that she wasn't the only one with distractions. Without any prompting, Anala shared more. "When everyone from the FI group showed up with Sora talking about the game of X they had been playing, at first I was annoyed, because I honestly was trying to study. But then I actually started listening. Nova heard too, and we both joined them and started asking questions."

Anala suddenly stopped talking, prompting Kirana to glance her way again, but there didn't seem to be a reason for her silence. She didn't say anything more, and they continued quietly until Anala stopped short a few moments later. Surprised, Kirana stopped and backtracked a few steps to where Anala had stopped. Anala looked her in the eyes and explained. "Kirana, I've just never felt that before. When Alev and I saw each other for the first time, our eyes locked. It felt like suddenly everything fell into place, and my entire life force was alive..." she trailed off, realizing she was making dramatic movements with her arms. Kirana was looking at her with big eyes. "Ugh, sorry," she said. "This is the opposite of focusing," she moaned, putting her palm to her face. Kirana seemed a bit stunned, so Anala continued to fill the silence. "Anyways, I had to try to act normal and talk about light strings with the group of them," she chuckled to herself. They began to move forward again. "He's mates with Kylo, right?" Kirana hadn't responded. "Kirana?" She looked up quickly.

"Oh! Yes, Alev and Kylo are mates," she smiled. Anala knew Kirana enough now to know she was in her head. She looked pointedly at her, waiting for some other reaction or explanation.

"I think that sounds really amazing, Anala. I hope you get to spend more time with Alev and explore those initial sparks. Maybe it will go somewhere! With him being Kylo's mate and in Sora's class, I'm sure he'll be around more." Kirana was trying to sound reassuring and involved for Anala's sake, but she couldn't help feeling her thoughts swirl about her own encounters lately. Anala was satisfied with Kirana's answer, so she didn't say more.

When they arrived to class and walked in, they immediately noticed that it was Guardian Beck in the center of the room instead of Guardian Gaia. They had progressed in their Practical History course quarter, almost complete with their Observational Studies and looking forward to their Location Choices. For several of them, it was easy because they already had family in certain areas, and they planned to join them there. For others, it was a brand new opportunity to make a decision. Once they recorded their decisions, that would mark their halfway point through the first semester. Guardian Beck had not been in any class yet, so this put a static in the air as the class anticipated an announcement. Anala and Kirana found Kylo and Ravi, as had become their norm, and the four of them sat abnormally quiet along with the rest of the class. Guardian Beck smiled pleasantly at the group, sweeping her eyes around the room in a wave all her own. Kirana's eyes were glued to her, as she still had no idea what to expect.

"Hello everyone," Guardian Beck began, her voice just as smooth as one would expect, but with a crash of power at the edges. "I'm thrilled to finally join you all in this session. I was given the honor to be able to share the news that we have determined the split for the two groups." She paused and let this information sink in for a moment. The static in the room only grew. Guardian Beck put up her hand to quell it. "There's nothing to be worried about. In fact, we anticipate this change to be a much needed support that will benefit all of us. This announcement arrives at the perfect time, because we do anticipate a need for this to be decided as you move into your next quarter. Internal Development may look slightly different depending on which group you decide to join."

Kirana's eyes widened as she realized what that meant. They would be choosing not only their location at these midterms but the group they would join as well. She thought they'd have more time. And selfishly, she wasn't sure what would happen if some of her and the little group she'd formed made different choices. Someone put an arm around her, but she didn't know who. Guardian Beck continued speaking.

"As we briefly discussed at Orientation, Guardian Alder and I have been brought on so that we can provide guidance in smaller groups. This will give us an opportunity to spend more dedicated time with each of you before the iteration officially begins. Guardian Gaia will still be just as available to everyone, in a more general sense, at a higher level. Now, let's get into the details about the groups."

Kirana blinked. Too long. She blinked again, thankful she was still seated in the same place as she remembered, and Guardian Beck was still in the center of the room speaking. She took in a deep breath and felt the arm around her.

"I've got you," Kylo whispered. "You didn't miss much. I'll fill you in after." Kirana mentally kicked herself, feeling ridiculous that she let anticipation get the better of her. She touched Kylo's knee in a flurry of mauvy gratitude. Too much. She saw Guardian Beck's attention move their way, and she froze. Guardian Beck didn't blink an eye and continued speaking, just looking directly at Kirana and Kylo. Kylo whispered, "breathe," under his breath. She took a breath and tried to act casual.

"The second group," Guardian Beck continued, finally looking away, "will be called Guides. This group is just as crucial and will have just as difficult of a job. In a practical sense for your sessions, Guides will be cutting their Simulation training in half to start early on Communications. Also, some of them will likely leave for their locations early, which means team discussions will be moved up as well. When we are building your teams, there must be a mix of Seeds and Guides. We can help match those of you in your first iteration of the graduating class especially, though remember that this plan is new for everyone." Kirana looked over her shoulder at Anala and Ravi, who were on the other side of her. Their eyes were locked on Guardian Beck. She turned to Kylo, who had his arm around her less intensely now. He looked back at her so she mouthed, "Seeds?" to him as a silent question. He gave her a half nod and raised his eyebrows back to Guardian Beck as if telling her to pay attention. She obliged. Guardian Beck shared a few more logistical things, including an update on the new buildings.

"We will begin using the new buildings as soon as groups have been officially chosen. We will remind you again later, but Seeds will be restricted to their own building. Only Guides are able to go freely back and forth between the two buildings, though most sessions will occur in their own location. Pods will be opened shortly after that, and we will discuss more about their use at that time." She paused, scanning the room, and Kirana didn't miss that she caught her gaze for a sliver longer than anyone else. Or maybe it was in her head. "Thank you for your dedication and attention. We really do appreciate everything you're doing." Guardian Beck offered some glowing gratitude to the group. "Please take this time to digest the new information and make your final decisions on your location choices. If you need support on this upcoming decision, Guardians Gaia, Alder and I are available any time." She gave a small bow and glided away from the center of the room. Kirana's eyes followed her as she met with Guardians Gaia and Alder in the back. She hadn't realized Guardian Alder was there as well.

The room started buzzing as students began moving around to gather and start discussing. Kirana and the three in her group all turned to each other to do the same. Kirana was quiet. For the second time, she felt bombarded when everyone else started to talk at once.

"You didn't miss much. The first group w—"

"I have to tell you what we learned about light st—"

"What group do you think you'll join?"

They realized at the same moment that they all had separate topics on their minds. Anala was the quickest.

"Wait, who missed something? We were all here," she said, looking around. Kirana shook her head, silently begging Kylo to not make it a big deal. At first, Kirana thought he would listen. But no, apparently he changed his mind.

"Remember Kirana mentioning that she had a flash-out at Orientation?" he began.

"I did not men—" Kirana interjected, because she definitely had not intentionally brought it up that day in class. But Anala looked at her with a spark of warning as if to say *you literally just told me that you needed to focus.* Kirana sighed and stopped the attempt at modifying Kylo's story, and he continued.

"Well, it seemed brief anyways. You're feeling alright now, right?" he checked. She nodded. "Okay." Satisfied, he started again. "The first group Guardian Beck talked about was called Seeds. Essentially, this is the same thing as what we usually anticipate for an iteration, where you have a task to complete while you're at your location and all that. The reason they are splitting it this year is to try to make it a little easier on, well, the Seeds. Teams will be a mix of Seeds and Guides for that reason. I think it's a great idea. After one iteration in this class, I can see how much this could help." He stopped talking, but for some reason, Kirana got the feeling that this announcement was not the first time he had heard about the details of the split.

CHAPTER THIRTEEN

I t didn't go unnoticed to Kirana that Ravi had been quieter than usual. He seemed disinterested in talking about the announcement of how the groups would be split, fairly indifferent about which one he would join and even unconcerned about Kirana's flash-out. The only thing he wanted to talk about were the light strings, and Kirana had just recently decided that was a topic she didn't want to talk about.

"I've decided that I'm going to take a break from light strings and X and any distractions from my studies right now," she said to Kylo and Ravi. Anala nodded, as if she was doing the right thing. Ravi seemed shocked.

"Does that mean I can't share anything we found out? Don't you want to know?" he asked her. Kirana hesitated, but then Kylo stepped in.

"Honestly, that's probably for the best right now, Kir. For several reasons. Whenever you want to talk about that stuff again, just say the word." Kylo gave Ravi a look to let it go. He obliged, but he seemed frustrated about it. Class was over and almost everyone had gone by now. Anala offered to wait for Kirana so they could go back to the residence together, but Kirana declined.

"You go ahead. I'm going to go over a few more things from here. I want to use Guardian Gaia's globe," she explained, pointing to the center of the room. It was so much better than their 3D ones, though she knew it could be taking a step backwards in preparing her. Maybe, maybe not. Anala nodded and waved a red flicker to say, *see you later*. Kylo and Ravi both seemed like they were hanging around to be the last one in the room with Kirana, like they each wanted to say something to her without the other one hearing. Kirana didn't feel like monitoring that for either of them. She gathered what she needed from her bag and headed towards the center of the room, tossing some golden flecks behind her. Kylo got the hint. Ravi didn't seem to though, and he turned to jog up behind her.

"Kirana," he called after her. She turned around with a tired smile. She didn't think she had actually heard him say her name before. It had sort of a shiny bounce to it when he said it. He reached her and gave her that glowing smile, and she felt some energy return to her own smile for a moment. She could see the gold in his eyes. They were directly eye to eye after all. He reached over to touch her arm, and she watched him do it without moving.

"I wanted to see that shine again," he gleamed, as their amplified glow gave them a show. It really was spectacular, but Kirana was just not really in the mood for this right now. She politely smiled back, but her own personal glow didn't come through it. Ravi didn't seem to notice. "Nah, I'm kidding, but what I actually wanted to tell you was that there's someone in my family who has the same thing as you. The flash-outs I mean." Kirana's face turned surprised. So he *had* noticed. Somehow that made her feel better. "I know she always keeps some sort of refreshment with her, and it seems to help," he said with a shrug. He reached in his pocket and offered her something small and wrapped. "Maybe that'll help." She was touched.

"That's so kind of you, Ravi, thanks!" Kirana's smile turned more genuine. But then it turned hard when Ravi kept talking.

"You're welcome! Hopefully it's a flavor you like. And before I go, I just have to tell you, light strings keep a record of everyone who has used them. Including when they were used." He stopped, glancing back towards where Kylo was waiting for him impatiently at the door. Kirana followed his gaze. She couldn't tell if he was waiting because he wanted to talk to Ravi himself, or if he didn't want Ravi talking to her. The latter seemed odd, because up until this point, she had gotten the opposite impression. "I'll tell you more later," he called, already on the move to meet Kylo.

After they left, Kirana felt even more drained than when class had finished. That temporary bump of energy had dropped immediately when Ravi started talking about light strings again after she had told him she didn't want to be involved for a while. Of course it was an interesting piece of information, but she needed her energy focused elsewhere. She knew she'd be tempted to continue to go after more answers if she knew what they had discovered so far. Maybe that's what Ravi wanted. For them to go on this mystery adventure together. While the idea was charming, this was the biggest upcoming iteration yet, and she wanted to take it seriously.

Kirana turned her attention to where Guardian Gaia had shown them how to use her sphere projection. She drew it in the space in front of her and worked with it until she saw the same blue and brownish-green shapes and felt the low vibration coming off of it. She wanted to memorize every bit of it and every bit of what it felt like until it felt normal. She knew she would have plenty of opportunities to work in the Sim buildings later on, but she wouldn't get this part of it. She basked in it. It didn't feel particularly good, if she was being honest with herself, but it didn't feel bad either. It just, was. It existed in such a heavy way that she felt the potential.

She was down to two choices for her location. She wanted to solidify her plan as soon as possible—some already had. As far as she knew, Kylo hadn't chosen yet. She definitely wanted to touch base with him before giving her final response. She knew they had some more family in various locations, and being that it was her first iteration in this class, she wanted as much support as possible. After Kylo was talking about how difficult it was for him in the last iteration, she was assuming he'd agree, and they would choose the same location. She leaned more heavily on one of her choices than the other, so she'd confirm with him first.

As for the group choice, she still wasn't completely clear on what the difference was or why it was such a big deal, but if she went the normal way that she had been expecting anyway, it just sounded like she'd be a Seed with that much more support being offered through having Guides. Satisfied with her progress, Kirana swiped away the projection and gathered her things to head back to her residence. As she moved towards the door, she thought she heard something. She turned back around briefly and scanned the room. She wasn't convinced it was empty, though she didn't see or hear anyone. She didn't have any more bandwidth for playing sleuth, so she walked to the door and pushed it open in defiance.

"Oh!" said a surprised voice.

"Oh no, I'm sorry, did I hit you with the door?" Kirana fretted.

"Actually, no," said the voice as Nox came into view, holding back his laughter. "That would be the first time we ran into each other without actually running into each other." His grin was lopsided. "I rather liked getting hit with a sunbeam now and then. Or at least I was getting used to it." He winked. Kirana relaxed but wasn't sure what to say. She thought she fell into his eyes again, and the wink brought her back out. She smiled, feeling like she needed to explain why she was there even though nobody asked.

"I was just working with Guardian Gaia's projection. Something about it is so... potent, in a way. I don't know if that makes any sense," she said, rushing out the last sentence. Nox just nodded calmly, as if he completely understood.

"Are you headed to your residence? Want some company?" he asked. "I was thinking to stop by and see Nova anyway."

"Sure," she smiled again. After a few moments, she realized it was actually really nice to have his company. She wasn't sure if it would be weird to say that now. She glanced at him sideways while her mind filled with so many questions. She decided her first thought was probably the least weird of all of them, considering they didn't know each other that well, so she went for it. "This is actually really nice. I'm glad I ran into you so we could walk together." Saying the words made her smile somehow, and then giggle. She had no idea where that came from.

"How did the class go? They made the announcement, didn't they?" he asked her.

"Yeah, they did. Well, Guardian Beck did," she answered. It popped into her head that he was in the graduating class too. So wasn't he there? Wouldn't he have known that? He asked another question before she could ask him though.

"And do you have an idea of which group you think you might choose?" he asked. "Or not yet?" She didn't really see it as an option for herself. That was probably one of the easier answers she'd been able to give in a while.

"Based on what I understand, I'm going to be a Seed," she said confidently. "You?" she asked, turning to look at him and tilting her head slightly. She thought she saw a hint of a smile but couldn't read what was behind it.

"I'm leaning the same way," he said, purposefully not looking in her direction. Somehow she wanted him to. And she wanted that safe green field around them. She thought about telling him about how she and Nova had discussed the notes and what they had determined, but she just didn't want to get her head back into all those distractions right now. She kept the conversation on their studies.

"Were you not in class?" she asked, hinting back to earlier. He spoke clearly, and low.

"I do a bit of my own coursework, and this iteration I've taken to more independent studies. You'll understand better once you've done a few iterations in the graduating class. He glanced her way, as if trying to gauge her response. She took it lightly. Then something seemed to click in her mind.

"Ohh, so is that why you showed up after class was already over? Did you have a meeting with one of the Guardians or something?" Somehow she felt obtrusive asking that, but it already left her mouth, and he was already answering.

"Sometimes I meet with one of them after the class is over, yes. This time, I was just going to use the projection for a while," he responded. "Looks like we're here!" He stopped in front of her residence that she hadn't even realized they had walked up to. It appeared calm inside based on the slow moving colors sticking closely to the building walls.

"Thanks for walking with me!" Kirana exclaimed sincerely, sending him some dark pink gratitude more gently this time, remembering last time's attack.

"Anytime," Nox replied with a puff of evergreen smoke. He was gone before Kirana even entered her residence and realized that:

A. She had occupied the time that Nox had just revealed he was supposed to be doing classwork with the projection, and

B. He didn't talk to Nova.

CHAPTER FOURTEEN

The door to Nova's nest was open a crack when Kirana went inside their residence, so she knocked softly and poked her head in.

"Hey!" Nova said brightly when she saw her. "How was class?"

"Kind of eventful actually," Kirana responded, letting the positivity coming off of Nova soak into her. "How was yours?"

"Ours too. There was an announcement. Guardian Era finally seems to be getting more involved. He told us that based on how you all broke into your groups, they may be making some changes with ours as well," she explained.

"Oh?" Kirana raised her eyebrows. "That's interesting. I wonder why that makes a difference," she wondered aloud.

"Does that mean you also got an announcement about those groups?" Nova asked her. Kirana nodded, now fully in Nova's nest and preparing to make a dive into the cloud cushions. She landed without a sound, sinking in deep.

"Honestly, it all seems a bit dramatic with this built up anticipation. I guess it makes more sense for the Guardians and those who have already been through iterations in the graduating class, but for me, it's all going to be new anyway, you know?" Kirana turned to look at Nova. Nova stared back, giving her a face. She knew what anxious anticipation did to her. Kirana rolled her eyes and smiled at Nova. "I'm fine. Kylo was there. Why can't they just make things less dramatic though?"

"Have you ever thought that maybe you're the problem?" Nova asked her, feigning seriousness and throwing a cloud cushion at her. It practically dissipated before reaching her, and Kirana laughed. Nova continued, "So what are the two groups? I haven't actually heard any details."

"The first one they are calling Seeds, and the second one is Guides. Seeds are basically on the normal path that I was expecting anyways, so that's my plan. Did you know that all those new buildings are for us? The graduating class I mean. The two big ones in the middle are for the two groups." She seemed to consider the rule about those two buildings for the first time. "Apparently Seeds can only use their own building, but Guides will be using both. And then all those pods are for individuals. I hope that I'll get to keep my nest here with all of you though," she said optimistically.

"You think they'd move you and Anala out?" Nova asked, showing on her face how much she disliked that idea.

"I don't know," Kirana admitted. "It doesn't seem like it would be a good idea. We need these debriefs and to be able to support each other in different areas, you know? Like Sora being in her first iteration, and you entering the next one. And it's Anala's and my first iteration in the graduating class. It's actually really nice for me to have a connection with all of you for different reasons!" It was almost like she was just coming to these conclusions by speaking them out with Nova. It only confirmed her thoughts about the situation. "Have you gotten to spend much time with either of them?" she asked Nova.

"A little bit, yeah," Nova responded. "And I think you're right. I love being able to help Sora with any of her first time questions, especially having been in her shoes such a short while ago. And Anala gives me great advice too." She stopped for a moment as if she had just gotten an idea. Kirana waited expectantly, but Nova didn't reveal anything right away. She seemed to finish her previous thought first. "And you're alright as a mate too," she said, making a face at Kirana. This time Kirana tried throwing a cloud cushion at Nova. "Actually," Nova continued, getting more serious, "You're the best mate of all. I know I can lean on you, and I feel that you trust me enough to know that I'm here for you to lean on too. I'll start a petition if they try to move you and Anala to the pods for good!" The two laughed, and Nova's eyes got bright. "I have an idea," she said. "How about after this semester, the four of us go on a trip together during the break." It was more of a statement than a question. Kirana twinkled.

"I love it! That's a great idea! And it'll be fun to plan together too. Should we tell them now?" she asked, already climbing out of the clouds.

"Sure. Just let me finish up a few things in my journal. I'll send a message to everyone through the tablets," she responded.

"Oops," Kirana whispered loudly as if Nova was working right now. "Didn't mean to interrupt!"

"No, no, I was hoping you'd stop by," Nova insisted, waving her hand dismissively.

"Okay, well I'll see you soon." Kirana went over to the light string that would take her to her own nest. Before she jumped on, she turned back to Nova for one last question. "Hey, were you expecting Nox to stop by just now when I came in?" Nova looked a little puzzled and shook her head.

"No, why?" she asked.

"No reason," said Kirana with a smile as she hopped on the light string and disappeared from view.

Back in her own space, Kirana went to her tablet and saw the group message from Nova. They would meet in the community area. Sora and Anala both responded to the notification, so everyone must be at the residence already. She was actually super excited about Nova's idea. And it was also really good to see Nova enjoying her classes more. Distancing herself from Guardian Cosmo and the idea of feeling scrutinized for her last iteration seemed to be doing her a lot of good. She was glad they decided to give the notes a break too. Maybe it was all nothing. Distraction, just like the light strings. This trip would be really fun! Kirana started formulating a plan in her head.

1. Touch base with Kylo to confirm location choice with him.

2. Turn in location choice.

3. Turn in decision to be in the Seeds group.

4. Start classes on Internal Development while planning a trip with her mates.

5. Take the trip!

Kirana was in the community area of their residence first, thanks to her light string connection to get there. Anala showed up next.

"Hey! Did you get your observation studies finished up?" she asked Kirana.

"Yeah, I did! I'm feeling pretty good about it now," she responded. "What about you? And have you thought about the groups at all?"

"Oh good! Yeah, I think I'm ready to submit my choices too!" Anala's eyes flickered a little. "I think I'm going to go with the Seeds group," she said, almost anxiously. "It seems like that's the one that I was expecting anyways so I might as well give it a shot with my first iteration." She shrugged.

"Me too!" declared Kirana. "And that's literally my same thought process." Anala seemed to relax a little bit hearing that.

"They kind of seem to make it a big deal, don't you think?" she asked. Kirana chuckled.

"Same thoughts exactly," she agreed.

"Was everything okay with you and Ravi in class?" Anala asked suddenly. "The space around you two seemed a little dimmer than usual or something." Kirana looked startled. Anala had left before it had even gotten tense.

"Really?" she asked. "I guess I was just trying to be clear that I don't want to talk about light strings for a while."

"Oh I think you did the right thing for sure," Anala confirmed, "but when I was leaving is when I noticed it."

"Yeah, he got a little—" Kirana started to answer, but Sora and Nova walked in. This wasn't a conversation she wanted to have as a group. She gave Anala a look that said *let's continue this later*, and Anala gave her a small nod before she turned to greet their other two mates.

Sora was crystal clear with a glowing face, and Nova was laughing at something she said as they entered. Once they were all sitting in a circle around the central fireplace that Anala had added, Nova addressed the notification she had sent asking them to meet.

"Kirana and I were talking about how much we enjoy our mates, and we thought it would be super fun to celebrate it! What do you think about going on a trip together, just the four of us, during the break at the end of the semester?" she offered, graciously including Kirana in her idea. Sora gasped with her hands together, and Anala sparked.

"I love it!" said Sora. "What a great idea!" She looked at both Kirana and Nova to offer her thanks.

"Really it was all Nova's idea!" Kirana indicated. Except Nova shook her head.

"The thought wouldn't have come to me without you and the conversation we were having, so I definitely cannot take all the credit." Nova corrected.

"I'm on board too," joined Anala.

"Perfect!" said Nova. "This is so exciting! So let's all think about what we want to do, and we can start making plans." They shared some initial ideas, and then Sora and Nova went back to their nests leaving Anala and Kirana alone again.

"Do you want to talk about it?" Anala gently nudged, starting up their conversation again. Kirana sighed.

"I do, but I don't. After you left, Ravi told me something he found out about light strings anyways, ignoring my request." She shook her head slightly as if to shake it off. "It's probably not a big deal, plus he gave me a refreshment because he said it helps someone in his family who has flash-outs too, which was really kind of him." Kirana looked up at Anala. "So it's fine. I think I was just kind of depleted." Anala looked unconvinced. Kirana continued, "Then when I was leaving, I ran into Nox, and he walked me home. But I felt kind of bad because he was supposed to be studying. He told me he was going to talk to Nova anyways, but Nova said they didn't have any plan to talk."

"Why would you feel bad about that?!" Anala asked, surprised. "That was so kind of him! Aww. You realize he wouldn't have walked you back if he couldn't or didn't want to. So feeling bad about it is definitely not the correct response." Her eyes bore into Kirana as if to make sure she got the point.

"Yeah, you're right," Kirana said, really trying to believe it for real.

"You should feel special," Anala insisted. Kirana let herself realize that she kind of did.

CHAPTER FIFTEEN

Kirana had just gotten back to her nest when she thought she heard a commotion outside of the residence. Being in the front of the building, she looked out, trying to see down to the front door. There was definitely someone there, or a few someones, but she couldn't tell who. There was a knock on the front door. Kirana walked to the hallway where Sora was already poking her head out of her nest across the way.

"Did you hear something?" she asked breezily.

"Yes! I think someone is here," Kirana said as she started to head down a level. There was something curious enough about the scuffling and loud whispers they were hearing for Sora to follow. Anala and Nova had also been rustled enough to lose their attention on what they were doing. All four of them ended up in the entry. Nova reached to open the door. As she pulled it open, three Someones dressed in crazy costumes burst into the room, using percussion and playing other musical instruments, shooting sparks around and overall just making noise. They began to do some sort of poorly choreographed dance, though Kirana wasn't sure it could even be described that way. The four mates had not moved, stunned in place, still standing in the entry. Once the noise and dancing stopped and the three intruders took off their masks with a "Ta da!," they burst out laughing. Anala was barely breathing, Kirana had tears in her eyes she was laughing so hard, and Sora and Nova fell to the floor in a fit of laughter. Kylo, Ravi and Alev were congratulating each other, looking proud of themselves.

"What—," Nova tried to speak through her laughter. "—is wrong with you."

"Well you're the one on the floor!" said Kylo, pulling her and Sora to their feet. They still buckled over in laughter.

"That, my friends, is called disturbing the peace," Anala teased them, finally able to breathe again. She was looking like she could breathe for all of them now, so full of fresh energy. Kylo had moved on to Kirana.

"C'mon now, nothing to cry about. We weren't *that* bad," he said, grabbing her and spinning her around, literally making her tears of laughter fly off her face. Ravi seemed to catch one on his arm with a glow. They all wore silly grins.

"Oh, but you were," Kirana squeaked, wiping off her face as he set her down. Kylo turned to Ravi and Alev.

"Guys, all I see are happy faces here, so I consider our mission a success. Good work!" he said. They all cheered and sprayed more multicolored sparks around the room. Everyone except Sora rolled their eyes, with grins still ear to ear. Sora was thrilled for the excitement and offered everyone some refreshment. They all gathered in the community space.

"So what did you think of our performance?" Alev asked, only half joking. "We were practicing forever!" His energy was solidly glowing a deep burning red, and he looked like there was nowhere else he'd rather be. The room noticed he seemed to just be asking Anala, who was failing at trying to look nonchalant.

"Yeah, I guess we can count that one time we almost made it through the routine before deciding we were ready as practicing forever," Kylo said, slapping Alev on the back and looking like he might be the one to burst into laughter this time. "Ehh, I think we've lost those two," he said, turning away from Anala and Alev. He sat down next to Nova as Ravi helped Sora and Kirana gather refreshments and set them out for everyone.

"How are you doing? How have things been going around here?" he asked her. Nova knew he was not looking for a surface answer.

"Better," she responded. "We've decided to plan a mate's trip actually! Something exciting to look forward to." She glanced in Kirana's direction. She was busy laughing with Ravi. "Have you told her yet?" Kylo shook his head.

"She seemed to have a lot going on with worrying about you, the whole light string situation and not knowing about the groups and everything. I couldn't really say anything until the Guardians shared more information to the whole class, but that's when she wasn't really in a place for my news," he explained. He waved his arm out across the room saying, "This whole thing was to try to cheer you all up." He grinned, "Seems to be working." Nova looked around the room. Alev and Anala were engrossed in discussion, oblivious to the rest of the room, and Sora, Nova and Ravi were chatting happily. "I'll tell her soon," he promised Nova. She nodded.

Kirana was feeling much better. That laughter really seemed to knock the last of the gloom and doom out of her, and Ravi wasn't saying anything about the light strings, which allowed her to just relax and hang out with everyone. Having a trip to look forward to with her mates was super nice too. They hung out for a while before she started picking things up a bit as they were finishing their refreshments. She found herself alone with Ravi when he got up and started to help.

"Are we good?" he asked, stopping her in the other room for a moment. Kirana suspected he had gotten a Kylo talking-to. She smiled politely, but genuinely.

"Yeah, we're good," she responded, connecting eyes with him. "I still don't want to get into the light strings stuff right now, but this has been really fun."

"Yeah, I totally get it," he said, not looking like he did at all. "And this is fun for me too. I was wondering, would you want to do something together soon?" He scratched the back of his head. "Like, just us, maybe after class or something?" Kirana paused for a moment, having an entire thought-processed conversation with herself in her head in just a fraction of a moment.

"Sure, that sounds nice," she smiled. She'd like to get back to how she felt around him before, and maybe this would do it. He did always make her laugh, after all. She wasn't sure what the difference was or what had really happened, but for some reason, things felt different between them lately.

"Great!" Ravi resounded, making Kirana glad that their conversation was semi-private. "Maybe we can go dancing." After seeing Kirana's eyebrows go up in skepticism, he added, "Don't worry, that little show was just for fun. I'm actually decent at it." They returned into the main room together, both laughing, though Kirana did notice Kylo watching them enter. She saw him lean over and say something quietly to Nova and then stand up and smile at the room.

"Alright mates, I think we've caused enough mayhem, or disturbing of the peace according to Anala," he said, turning to wink at her. "Shall we?" Ravi turned towards Kirana while touching her hand lightly (still setting off that bright glow between them) and said, "I'm glad you're feeling better about things. I'm looking forward to our date." She didn't have a chance to respond before he was offering his farewells to everyone else and heading for the door. Her attention shifted to Kylo, who still had that look like he wanted to talk to her. As he sparkled a little gold mist her way, imitating her shine, she decided to ask him.

"I feel like you want to tell me something," she said, narrowing her eyes just a little. He made a sound like a sigh mixed with a groan.

"Later," he smiled. "Nothing to worry about right now."

"Promise?" she pushed.

"Promise." He glanced towards Ravi in a quick reflex that Kirana didn't even think he realized. He almost went to say something and stopped himself, giving her a quick hug and following Ravi and Alev out the door. "See you later!" he called as he disappeared. Nova was immediately at her side.

"Did I hear the word date?" she asked, feigning shock. Kirana's cheeks went pink.

"I mean, he asked me to hang out, but I don't know if I would call it a date. We've hung out before," she shrugged.

"Well, looks like he wants to 'hang out' officially." She gave a knowing face and used air quotes with her fingers. "Do you not want it to be a date?" Anala and Sora were listening now too. Kirana squirmed.

"Yeah, I mean, it's fine. We have fun—" she paused. "You know what, I do want it to be a date. I'll just go and be able to see if there's something more there, you know?" She looked up at Nova, expecting her to gush and tease, but she didn't. She came across a bit serious, even though she was smiling.

"Good! Well, I'm excited for you," she stated. "You're definitely bright together." Nova looked to Sora and Anala for confirmation, and they nodded in agreement. Kirana smiled back at them, genuinely looking forward to exploring what was between her and Ravi and thinking about how similar they were to each other. She let that thought slip into her statement to Anala.

"You and Alev seem to have a connection," she thought aloud. "You're pretty similar to each other too."

"Anala," Sora corrected, "is over the moon." Anala spun in a circle, holding her hands together at her heart.

"Wait, have you already been out with him?" Kirana asked, feeling behind.

"Just a couple of times," Anala gleamed. "He's the best," she practically sang. Nova was watching Kirana. "And he brought me this." Anala opened her palm where she was holding a smooth red stone in the shape of a flame. It seemed to flicker as the light hit it. The mates all oohed and ahhed over it.

"That's stunning!" praised Sora.

"It really is," glowed Anala. She looked up at Kirana. "Maybe we can go on a double date together sometime!"

"Yeah, that'd be fun!" agreed Kirana, but she couldn't help wondering why she wasn't over the moon like Anala was.

CHAPTER SIXTEEN

"It's time," Kirana said to herself as she looked out over the campus from her nest. It felt like things were about to get more real as soon as she turned in her choices at her upcoming class. Midterms were upon them. She felt pretty clear though, and it seemed like Anala and Sora did too. Nova, however, had seemed noncommittal on her location choice so far, at least when speaking with her specifically.

Kirana had asked Kylo to meet her before class just to confirm everything with him before she made it official. They planned to head to class together, so she went to the front of her residence to wait for him. Looking back at the building, there was a lot going on. There was a spikiness near where Nova's nest was, an orange flickering glow near Anala's, and a sort of white softness near Sora's nest. This all combined to make textured patterns moving around the building. She checked her own energy and felt rather calm and a little excited. After class, she would be hanging out with Ravi. She didn't really know what to expect, so she decided to think of it more like how they always hung out and not make a big deal of it.

"Lookin' bright and shiny and ready to go!" boomed Kylo from behind her. She grinned.

"Hey! Thanks for meeting me here. I wanted to touch base with you before turning in our midterms," said Kirana.

"Let's go then, shall we?" he replied, holding one arm out to her and one open towards the direction of the class building. As they began walking, Kylo actually spoke first. "So there's something I have to tell you. Actually two somethings, but—" He stopped and turned to look at her.

"Can we just stick to talking about Location?" she pleaded, thinking he wanted to talk about light strings. Kylo considered this, slowly nodding.

"Okay," he said haltingly. "Well, where did you land with your choices?" She told him where she wanted to go, as well as her second choice just in case. She was willing to change her decision at the last moment if he preferred the other. She just wanted him to go with her like they had done so many times before. "Fine," he said nodding, "No, that's fine." Kirana could tell he wanted to say more.

"What is it?" she asked, looking at him closely. He didn't react, and she couldn't read anything in his face.

"I'm assuming you're going to join the Seeds group, correct?" he asked. Kirana nodded, waiting for him to continue. "It seems that most of you in your first iteration of the graduating class are. Can I tell you something that Guardian Gaia shared with some of us?" He was hesitant, wanting to make sure he respected Kirana's wishes to stay drama and distraction free.

"What is it?" she asked again, this time with a different tone.

"They are kind of experimenting with all these changes, and they think in the next iteration after this one, they might make another split. They might officially split the graduating class to offer extra support to those in their first iteration of *this* class. Crazy, huh? But it makes sense. It's kind of like how the FI class is separated from the rest of the group. After that first round is when you'd be able to make the choice between Seeds and Guides. Guardian Gaia said that they expect the split to happen almost naturally, and that seems to be the case from what I've noticed too." He took a breath. "I guess we'll see." He turned his head slightly to peek at Kirana's reaction next to him. She didn't seem to have one.

"Hm," she said pleasantly. "Yeah, I guess it will be interesting to see." She didn't have quite as much context as Kylo, so she didn't seem to mind either way. Kylo was a little relieved but decided to keep the other piece of news he had to himself for now. They were getting close to the class building, and Kylo excused himself rather suddenly.

"Hey, I'm going to catch up with Nox real quick. See you in there?" He was already on the move when Kirana responded.

"Oh! Okay, sure, see y—" she stopped talking when she realized there was no point as he was already out of earshot anyway. "Curious," she whispered to herself, thinking about Kylo and Nox knowing each other. She wasn't sure how this was the first iteration she had encountered Nox when two of the closest ones to her both had history with him.

"What's curious?" said Anala's voice behind her. She walked up next to Kirana. "Hey! Perfect timing to catch up with you I guess." She had a gleam to her, looking ready for anything. Even though she had complained with Kirana about being distracted, something about her connection to Alev had really seemed to make her more steady, not less.

"Hi, Anala," Kirana laughed. "Yeah, perfect timing 'cause Kylo just ditched me! I mean, not really, but still." She said it all in good spirits.

"Did you make a plan to choose the same location for this iteration?" Anala asked.

"Yep!" Kirana confirmed. "And he told me that it looks like most of us starting our first iteration in the graduating class are choosing to join the Seeds group. It should be interesting to find out."

"Cool!" Anala answered. "And is Kylo too?" Kirana and Anala had entered the building now and were making their way to the spot at the center where they usually sat. Kirana frowned slightly.

"Oh, he actually didn't say." She looked around, watching the door to see if he had entered yet. By the time he walked in to join them, Guardian Gaia was making her way to the center of the room. She was about to start speaking so Kirana couldn't get Kylo's attention.

"Thanks to everyone gathering here now," Guardian Gaia began, beaming at the group. Her energy was moving faster than usual. "It's a privilege to be here with you all as you make your first big decisions of this iteration. One at a time, we will ask you to come up to the center and enter your choices." She drew up her globe hologram and set pings of light to the side for them to grab and place on their locations. "We will be further zeroing in on the specifics as we continue this semester, although hopefully most of you have already gotten somewhat precise. And while you are up here, please choose which group you will be joining for the rest of this iteration." Guardian Gaia pulled up a board with two sides on it. One was labeled *Seeds* and the other *Guides*. "Press the button of your choosing, and your name will be recorded on the board. Let's get started with those of you in your first iteration of this class!"

Anala and Kirana gave each other excited looks. One by one, everyone was placing their golden dot on the globe and pressing the button for the group they decided to join. Anala went up and made her selections, and pretty soon, it was Kirana's turn. She confidently went up to the globe and placed her dot. Then she pressed the button for Seeds and returned to her spot. It felt like the first accomplishment of many to come. She watched Ravi go up and place his dot in the same vicinity as hers. He also pressed the Seeds button. He gave her a glowing look as he sat back down. When it was finally Kylo's turn, after all the newer ones in the group had finished their selections, he went up and put his dot almost on top of Kirana's on the globe. She smiled. This was going to be great. She watched as he walked over to the buttons. He stood in front of them for a moment before pressing the button for Guides and going back to his seat next to Ravi. Kirana blinked. She thought maybe she had seen wrong, but sure enough, there was his name on the board. She wasn't entirely certain what this meant, except for the fact that she knew they wouldn't be in class together anymore. They would be in different buildings. Anala leaned over to whisper in her ear.

"Guess we got the answer," she said. "But at least you know you'll be there together," she shrugged, referring to his location dot. Kirana tried to give her a small smile. She realized she didn't actually know what all this meant and started to doubt her choice. She spent the rest of the class trying to remember everything she had learned about the two groups and almost missed it when Nox went to the center of the room to record his choices. He placed his dot nearly on the opposite side of the globe to where Kirana, Kylo and Ravi had. But then, with no hesitation, he pressed the button for Seeds. He returned to his seat, which Kirana saw was almost exactly opposite her in the room. She hadn't noticed because he never actually seemed to be in class, so she never thought to look for him. Now that she knew he was there, she could barely keep her eyes from pulling towards him. Just then, Ravi leaned over and whispered to her, tearing her attention from Nox.

"Ready for some dancing after this?" he asked. "We can celebrate midterms being over!" She smiled back, nodding quietly, not trusting any words that might come out of her mouth right now. He seemed happy enough with her small response.

After everyone had been to the center of the room to make their choices, Guardian Gaia returned to the platform. "We are so proud of all of you and pleased with your dedication to the process. Congratulations on your choices! Please note, we will be moving to our new buildings immediately, starting our next sessions accordingly. Seeds, you will report to the Green building with Guardian Beck, and Guides, you will report to the White building with Guardian Alder. I will still be available, though working more one on one as needed, here in this room. Please feel free to stop by. That's all for now, and we will see you soon in the new buildings!" Guardian Gaia sent them a burst of silver streaks, bowed her head slightly and left the center of the room.

There was a buzz all around them as everyone stirred to pick up their things and check in with their friends. Kylo was on the other side of Ravi so Kirana didn't have direct reach to him to ask anything about the Guides. She tried to get his attention, but she was blocked by Ravi who was talking to him emphatically about something. She glanced back at Anala, who had already gotten up and gathered her things.

"Have a good time!" she waved. She gave her a little flourish and was gone. Nox had also disappeared from where he had been seated across from her on the other side of the room. She started to get up, and Ravi turned to her with a huge smile.

"Ready?" he asked. "I have a plan!" She nodded, then glanced behind him to Kylo who was talking with someone else now. She'd just have to catch up with him later. "Kirana?" Ravi was waving a hand in front of her face. She ignored it.

"Let's go," she said with a strained smile. They walked out of the building, and Kirana took one last look behind her. "It's kind of crazy that we won't even be in this building anymore." Ravi didn't seem to share her nostalgia, looking away towards the Sim buildings. She wasn't sure if he even heard her.

"This way!" he said excitedly. He started off without her, paused and seemed to think better of it, then turned back her direction. He stood still and held his hand out to her, beckoning her towards him while glowing a shimmering gold. Kirana stepped forward, taking his hand, and they stood for a moment absorbing the bright shine that emerged. Ravi's eyes were already on Kirana's when she looked at his face. "I'm so glad we're doing this," he said quietly. Kirana relaxed and decided to allow her mind to let go of everything for now and just focus on enjoying herself.

"Me too," she responded, getting a much needed burst of energy. It lasted just about as long as it took for Ravi to lead her directly back to the light strings at the Gravity Sim building.

CHAPTER SEVENTEEN

"Ravi, what—" Kirana began. "What are we doing here? Why did you bring me here?" She stopped, even taking a step backwards as if preparing to turn around altogether.

"We're going to the Dome! This is the quickest way." Ravi's smile started to dim at her reaction. "I thought you liked light strings, no? What's wrong?" Kirana could see that he really didn't mean anything by bringing her here, and he was right that it *was* the quickest way to the Dome. It just felt insensitive to her. Ravi had taken a step closer to her, reaching for her hand again. "Are you worried about it being broken? The white-out box is gone, and I even went there earlier to make sure all was in working order. Nothing at all to be concerned about." Kirana tried to smile back. She hadn't been on any light strings (besides her own personal ones) since Nova had asked her not to.

"Yeah, no, I mean I'm sure it's fine. You've checked it so I guess it's alright to go this way," she thought aloud. She looked down at her hand that Ravi was holding. He was smiling at her, and she decided she was probably just making a big deal out of nothing. She smiled back. "Let's go," she confirmed. Ravi was thrilled.

"After you," he said, as if he was afraid she wouldn't follow if he went first. Kirana took a breath, closed her eyes and jumped onto the navy blue light string headed to the Dome. It was far, making this a really relaxing and fun experience. The ride was smooth with a few ups and downs but no loud movements or loops. She was feeling a lot more relaxed when they arrived, and she decided to herself that she'd focus on the positive and just try to enjoy her time with Ravi.

The Dome was generally multipurpose, used for any event with a large audience, including both multidimensional and multigalactic meetings, occasions or gatherings. Kirana didn't go to the Dome often, but she knew some that attended events here regularly. She had no idea what the schedule was or what Ravi had in mind.

"So are you okay with light strings again then?" Ravi cautiously asked when he arrived. Remembering her promise to herself a moment earlier, she replied pleasantly.

"Yeah, I guess I am! It was a really nice ride actually. Thanks for pushing me," she said. Ravi absolutely beamed. As they turned to start making their way into the Dome, Ravi took her hand again, that flare of light catching the attention of several others around them. Kirana wanted to hide. Instead, she turned to Ravi and started asking him about what they were getting into.

"What kind of event is this? We're dancing, right? Is there going to be live vibration?" she looked around, trying to gather clues. There was a decent sized crowd, but the huge dome was by no means packed. Everyone was down on the main floor with barely anyone in the stands.

"You'll see," Ravi replied as they made their way towards the group that had gathered. "We're right on time!" He seemed shiny and pleased. Kirana tried to match his energy but found it odd that she had to try. On average, Kirana was the most radiant in the room, everywhere she went. She pushed the feeling aside as someone in the front began speaking.

"Hi everyone," said the Someone at the front with a flourish. "Who's ready for some salsa?" The crowd cheered. Lively vibrational sounds began and someone else joined the front so there was a pair of dancers, preparing to start teaching them the steps. Ravi was practically overflowing with excitement.

"I chose a dance that we'll probably encounter during our self-assignments! Maybe we can get some muscle memory going," he gleamed. Kirana did think that was sweet.

"Oh! What a great idea!" she responded, still struggling to match his energy. He didn't seem to notice, so she decided it wasn't that big of a deal. They definitely stood out with their combined energy though, as his hands moved to her hand and waist and they practiced the steps. The glances started to diminish as everyone was practicing their own moves.

After the lesson, the vibes and dancing continued. Kirana and Ravi were both breathless in the best way when they finally stepped away from the group to take a break.

"Isn't this great?" Ravi asked. "I told you I'm pretty good." He beamed proudly.

"Yeah, this is really fun!" Kirana agreed. She hadn't stopped smiling which felt really good. Everyone must have needed a bit of a break at that point because the vibrations changed to more drawn out notes. From where they were sitting now, off to the side, they noticed the other dancers start to sway to the slower sounds. Ravi stood up and held a hand out.

"May I have this dance?" he asked softly.

"Right here?" Kirana practically squeaked.

"Well, we wouldn't want to blind the others, would we?" he replied with feigned seriousness. Kirana smiled and took his hand, and he pulled her up and right into a twirl.

"Oh!" she gasped.

"You're right," Ravi laughed. "Wrong dance. Here..." He placed her arms around his shoulders and settled his around her waist. "There. Now this matches the vibes." They began to sway like the rest of the crowd, with Kirana purposely trying to keep a small cushion of space between them so they were not pressed together, though it did keep happening. She was focusing more on keeping space than dancing, and Ravi finally said something. "You feel tense. Just relax!" He shook his arms gently to emphasize being relaxed, but his arms were on her waist which meant she shook a little too. All of a sudden, she didn't feel like dancing anymore.

"I think I'm going to get some refreshment," she said, pulling away. "Do you want anything?"

"Sure!" he said unphased. "I'll go with you." He reached for her hand. Kirana looked down at their hands, not really holding his hand back and stopped.

"You know what," she began, "I've had a really good time, but I think I need things to go a little slower than this. I might just head back to my residence now if you don't mind." Ravi looked confused.

"Are you okay? Is holding hands too much? I'm sorry, we don't have to do that," he rushed, letting go of her hand.

"Sometimes is okay," Kirana responded, "but maybe not all the time. It's just a little fast, don't you think?" Kirana wasn't sure that she even believed herself. Not in a general sense anyway. But in this moment, that's how she felt. Luckily, Ravi took it well.

"Of course. Let's just take things slowly." He smiled. "I really like hanging out with you." Kirana relaxed.

"I had a great time! Thanks for planning this," she said, looking back at the dancers, almost wanting to continue now that she wasn't so tense.

"So are you still going to leave?" Ravi asked her.

"Are you going to stay?" Kirana asked, surprised. Ravi looked at the dancers and back at Kirana.

"I'm walking you back. It was a date after all. Unless you want to just have one more dance? I saw you looking over there," he teased. Kirana considered it for a moment, but she knew one more dance would turn into two and then three, and she was happy with the amount of time they had already spent together.

"I'm ready to go," she confirmed. Ravi went to reach for her hand and stopped himself, reaching an arm out ahead of them instead, as if to show her the way.

"After you," he said. As she stepped forward towards the Dome exit, he put his hand on her shoulder, then lifted it back off and walked next to her. "Light strings?" he asked, turning to look at her. It kind of felt like their thing now. She smiled.

"Light strings," she agreed.

When they made it back to Kirana's residence, Alev and Anala were also walking up, giggling to each other. They didn't notice anyone was there. Ravi cleared his throat as they approached. They looked up simultaneously, both grinning widely, glowing shades of orange.

"Hey, you two," greeted Anala. "Did you have a good time? You went dancing, right?" She was mostly looking to Kirana for an answer.

"Yes! We went dancing at the Dome. It was a lot of fun! What were you guys up to?" Kirana reciprocated.

"We walked through this beautiful display of art and gardens and colors," Anala said, with vibrant expression in her voice. "And Alev made us refreshments so we sat on a big blanket nearby and enjoyed that. It was wonderful." She turned to look at him.

"*You're* wonderful," Alev said to her quietly. Anala giggled. Kirana turned to Ravi to give the illusion that the other couple had some privacy.

"Thanks again for walking me back. I'm glad we did this," she told him.

"You're welcome. I'm glad we did too," he responded, looking unsure of what he wanted to do next. "Maybe we should all hang out together next time!" he said to the group of them there, not joining Kirana in her illusion of privacy as Alev and Anala whispered to each other. It didn't seem like they heard him.

"Well, I'm going to go in," said Kirana. "See you later? Oh, we'll have class in the new building!" She wished she hadn't said that last part. It almost felt like rambling. Luckily, Anala joined her at the door.

"Wait for me!" she was saying. Then she called, "See you later, Alev!" blowing flickering kisses behind her. They disappeared inside the residence as they heard the two mates start to chat and head back to their own residence. Anala practically melted to the floor with a sigh as soon as the door was closed. Kirana chuckled and sat next to her.

"You're really into him," she said as a statement. She didn't need to ask that—it was plain to see how much Anala and Alev were into each other. Anala turned her head to Kirana, still foggy-eyed. She was quiet for a moment, looking like she was thinking.

"He feels like home," she said finally. It sparked something in Kirana. She wasn't sure what it was though.

"That's beautiful," she told Anala.

"But what about you? Tell me about your first date with Ravi!" Anala turned the attention towards Kirana. Kirana tried to speak passionately like Anala did, but it just wasn't there.

"We had a great time. I mean, I always have fun with Ravi! That didn't change. The only thing different was that he kept holding my hand and wanting to dance really close and stuff. I told him I wanted to move a little slower," she explained. Anala nodded reassuringly.

"Sometimes it takes more time for things to develop! Definitely don't put any pressure on yourselves. I'm glad you told him how you were feeling. How did he respond?" she asked.

"I think he understood," Kirana reflected. "He didn't try to hug me at the door, which is kind of the space I asked for, but we've hugged a lot as friends, so it's a little confusing." Kirana shook her head slightly as Anala was nodding in understanding, creating a small friction in the space between them. Anala gently brushed it away.

"You'll figure it out. The energy has shifted so you'll have to discover what works now, even if it's not the same as how things were before," she told Kirana. It made sense, but Kirana wasn't sure that she wanted the energy to shift after all.

CHAPTER EIGHTEEN

Anala got up and went to her nest to do some preparation for their next sessions, which would be focused on Internal Development now that they had most of their Observation Studies completed. Each set of classes built on the information from the last set, so she was really just getting ahead. Kirana was still sitting on the ground near the entrance, thinking about their conversation. Before Anala had gone, Kirana had asked her if she was worried about Alev being in his first iteration and her being in the graduating class and therefore, not being able to experience the iteration together. She shrugged, not seeing it as any sort of issue. She figured that soon enough they would get to do that, and it was probably better for Alev to learn on his own first anyway.

Kirana was about to get up and head towards her nest, where she'd probably continue to do more of the same contemplation, when Nova poked her head out into the entry from her nest.

"I thought I heard you guys get back!" She looked around for Anala, looking confused when she realized Kirana was just sitting there by herself. Noticing her face, Kirana explained.

"Yes, we arrived back at the same time! Anala already went to her nest to do some preparation for class. I'm just..." Kirana didn't know what she was doing. "—thinking I guess."

"I see," said Nova. "Can I join you?" Kirana smiled and patted the ground next to her. "How did the date go? Only if you want to share of course," Nova added.

"I'm finding myself comparing things to Anala all of a sudden," Kirana reflected, responding more to her current thought process than the actual question. Nova nodded as a silent acknowledgement to continue. "She and Alev have one of the dreamiest, family-at-first-sight types of relationships going on," she said, "which I love to see!" Then she was quiet.

"And you're comparing that to you and Ravi?" asked Nova gently.

"Look, I know it doesn't make any sense. I already know I don't have that same connection with Ravi that Anala has with Alev. And actually, I'm totally fine with that. My concern is that I don't know whether I should continue pursuing this connection with Ravi at all. Like, if I want to or not. I know every relationship looks different and goes with its own rhythm. Ravi and I have so much fun together, and we're similar in a lot of ways. I definitely like spending time with him. But there's something that I can't quite put my finger on that makes me question if we are right for *that* kind of relationship. Plus, it feels like I'm risking my friendship with him to try dating." She finally stopped her stream of thought and realized that the last sentence might've hit the root of her concerns.

"Ahh," Nova replied, realizing the same thing. "Well that makes sense. It's a tough decision." She thought a bit more about what Kirana had told her so far. "So then if it's not the relationship stuff that you're comparing with Anala, what is it?" Kirana looked up at her.

"I think it might be that she makes everything look so easy, but it doesn't feel easy to me. She falls into an easy relationship that gels so perfectly. She's not concerned about going into this iteration on her own.

It seems like she doesn't have any other stressors, and then here I am with a friendship turned into a date that I'm unsure about, wanting to make sure that I have Kylo in this next iteration with me and all these other thoughts that keep nagging me. The light strings, those notes and other conversations we've had about Guardian Cosmo and—" Again, she found the root. "I can't do it all. I can't concentrate on all of it." Nova took Kirana's hand.

"You don't have to do all of it," reassured Nova. "No one expects you to." Kirana looked guilty then for a split moment, but Nova caught it. "Did something happen on your date with Ravi?"

"We took light strings to the Dome. And also back to the residences. All the white-out boxes seem to be gone, and everything worked fine," she confessed.

"And how did you feel about that?" Nova asked her. Kirana considered this.

"Not good at first. I almost left to be honest. But Ravi convinced me it was all good now, and he was actually right," she explained, as if she was convincing herself all over again. "I do feel like I want more details though, now that I'm taking light strings again. I want to know what happened and why it happened." Kirana didn't know she felt like this until Nova had asked. She was almost surprising herself with what she was saying. Nova didn't respond, just listened. Kirana started counting on her fingers. "Kylo is going to be in a different building than me for classes now,"—Nova raised her eyebrows but didn't interrupt—"Ravi and I went on a date, I don't know any updates on the notes or light strings or Guardian Cosmo. (This part counted as three fingers). That's a lot of things on top of being in the graduating class for the first time, which is likely to be the hardest iteration I've experienced yet." Nova gave Kirana's hand a squeeze.

"So what are you saying?" Nova asked her with narrowed, yet hopeful looking eyes.

"I don't want to date right now," Kirana confirmed for herself. "What I do want is to get some answers. There's something different about this iteration, and I think somehow all these pieces go together." She waited for a reaction from Nova, who's face slowly turned from serious to happy, almost excited.

"Okay, first of all," Nova began, counting on Kirana's still outstretched fingers. "I don't like that Ravi convinced you to go on the light strings. I know it all worked out and all, but pushing and convincing, it's not really ideal. Second, Nox found something out potentially related to the notes. I've been wanting to tell you, but it didn't seem like the right time. He told me what he saw after we had already decided to take a break from it. Third," she said, smiling now because Kirana's eyes had lit up with a glint of curiosity about that last bit, "just like you think everything looks so easy for Anala, I often think that of you! You always know what to say in every situation, everyone always wants your advice or to know what you think. You can draw every eye to you, not just for your looks, but for your kindness and authenticity. You really are like a bright light for all of us to follow." Kirana's eyes were wide and slightly glinting as she felt seen all of a sudden.

"I probably only know what to say because I've talked it all out with you first!" Kirana laughed, also brushing a small tear from her eye. "This is why we're mates." Kirana and Nova hugged. "Okay, I have some things to take care of now! I'm going to have to talk to Ravi, and then once things are settled in my new class, will you fill me in on what I missed?"

"Absolutely!" Nova confirmed. "I'm excited to puzzle out some clues with you! Since we know we're such a great team and all," she added teasingly.

"Hey, how are your classes going by the way?" asked Kirana. "Has everything calmed down?" Nova looked thoughtful for a moment.

"Yes," she said slowly, "but I think I'll hold off on more information until you're ready." There was a hint of something in her eye that Kirana couldn't wait to find out more about. "And wait, why is Kylo going to be in a different building than you now?" she asked.

"Oh, so we made the group split official. I'm going with the Seeds group along with Ravi and Anala, and Kylo is going with the Guides group. I haven't gotten a chance to talk to him about that yet." Nova didn't ask any more questions, and it actually looked like something clicked in her mind. "Oh, and Nox is going to be in the Seeds group. I never see him in class, but he was there and joined the Seeds," Kirana told her, still not quite understanding all these details. This bit of news lit a fire in Nova's eyes. "What?" prompted Kirana.

"Nothing," Nova responded quickly, as if Kirana couldn't see that something had changed. "I better get back to finishing up my—" she looked at Kirana briefly—"classwork. By the way, you might want to talk to Anala about how you were feeling too. Just since she seemed to catalyze some answers for you."

"Yeah, you're right," Kirana agreed. "I will, thanks." She sent a wave of sparkling mauve gratitude to Nova as she was skipping back towards her nest, leaving Kirana to herself again in the entry.

The conversation had stirred the energy in Kirana, and she felt almost exhilarated. She had been feeling so different just moments ago, and talking with Nova had breathed a new life into her. Being able to talk everything out helped her organize her thoughts and feelings. She got up and went into the community area to take her light string up to her nest when something shiny caught her eye from the fireplace. She reached in and picked up a piece of stone, similar to the flame that Alev had given Anala—at least in color. It just seemed like a broken piece of an unknown shape, but it was still pretty. Kirana rubbed it off in her hands and took it with her as she jumped on her light string. This one was boring. No real ride effects or visual displays. She decided to tinker with it and remembered what Ravi had told her about how light strings track who had used them. "I bet I can figure out how it works," she murmured to herself.

After spending a bit of time working on her light strings, she figured out how to see the records. They hung in the air if she kinked the string in a specific way on the color she wanted to check. She was looking at the maroon one only because that was the light string she had just used from the community room. She saw a list containing mostly her name, but then she blinked in surprise when she saw another name there. "Alev," she whispered to herself. "That's odd." She quickly checked the chestnut and evergreen strings, but those lists only contained hers and Nova's names. She looked back at the maroon string's list. His name was definitely there. She thought Ravi had told her it should identify when the string was used, but she didn't see that information. She also thought it was curious that his name was only listed there once. If he stumbled across the light string and hopped on, once he realized he was in someone's nest it would probably make sense to hop back on it and leave. So his name should have been there twice, but it wasn't. That would mean he would've had to have gone into her nest and then out the door, or into her nest through the door and then used the light string to leave, which seemed way more unlikely.

As she puzzled over this, she realized she was thrown right back into mysterious things happening. This time she decided to take a different approach. She was going to jump in, both to solve all these puzzles and finish out this semester knowing exactly what internal development she wanted to focus on this iteration, and then she'd celebrate everything on the mate's trip. When they got back, she'd be ready to seriously prepare for her self-assignment. "Easy," she thought to herself. "Let's go."

CHAPTER NINETEEN

Kirana's first order of business was to talk to Ravi to find out what he knew about the light strings. She also had to tell him about just staying friends for a while, but that seemed pushed to the side in order of importance. She could wait until class and talk to him there, but with the new split and new building, there might be too much else going on. If she went over to his residence, she might even have the opportunity to ask Alev about using her light string or talk to Kylo about his decision to be a Guide. This idea sounded like it gave her better odds of gathering at least some answers from somebody.

As she left her nest with her things for the next class, in case she didn't have time to come back, Sora was also on her way out.

"Hi!" she glowed. Sora had such a lightness to her that seemed to wrap around everyone who was nearby. It was that similar expansive feeling Kirana got when she was around Kylo. It made her smile.

"Hi!" Kirana echoed back. "How have you been? Headed out?"

"Yep, going to meet some friends before class. Everyone has been so friendly and amazing, and we're having a great time," she said in her songbird voice.

"And that's exactly how it should be," Kirana validated. It made her happy that the FI class had bonded so well. They would hopefully make a great support system for the iterations to come. "Have fun! See you later!" she called after Sora, who scampered down to the entry and out the door. Sora threw some white sparkles behind her.

Kirana made her way through the residence buildings, letting her thoughts drift per usual. The idea popped in her head that she should take Guardian Era up on his offer to advise her. She added stopping by his office to her mental checklist. As she approached the residence where Ravi, Kylo and Alev stayed, something about the building seemed slightly different, but she wasn't sure what it was. She settled on the idea that it was a different color palette. Somehow the colors seemed heavier? More dense? She wasn't sure. She didn't notice that someone had opened the front door. A bouncing voice called out to her.

"What a great surprise to find when I open the door! To what do I owe the pleasure?" Kylo called, smiling.

"Hey!" Kirana laughed as she reached him and gave him a hug. "I came by to talk to Ravi. Is he here?"

"I see," Kylo responded, looking interested in what she wanted to talk about. It still seemed to Kirana that he didn't quite have the same attitude about her and Ravi together as he did originally. Maybe she was just making it up. "He's not here, so I guess you'll have to settle for little ol' me," he answered, feigning a meekness that was not at all his personality. "Just kidding. But maybe I can help with whatever you needed...?" He looked at her cautiously.

"Actually you probably can for the most part," Kirana remarked. "But first, what has changed about your building? Something seems different, but I don't know what it is, and it's bugging me!" Kylo stepped out of the residence and walked further back from the building to take it in. Kirana followed.

"Oh! Yeah, I know it shifts galaxies. Not sure what it's showing now." He studied it a bit more. "Actually I think it shifts less now. Since we have all chosen our locations, it's only showing the galaxies that my mates and I will be visiting this iteration. Alev to one, and Ravi and I both to another. This is home for a little while!" he confirmed.

"Wait, so is this where I'm going too?" Kirana asked, looking at it with new eyes. She definitely had noticed that Observation Studies had been a lot more zeroed in for this iteration than what she was used to in prior ones. She used to have the pick of the galaxy. Numerous options. This iteration had been focused entirely differently, and she was only putting the pieces together now. "Wow, they did a good job of still making it seem like a variety of options for our self-assignments, but now I'm realizing just how limited it actually was," she murmured with her eyes open just about as wide as they could go.

"There's a reason for that," explained Kylo, as if he didn't want to say more. "This is the toughest one of them all." Then his tone changed. "But you've got this! Nothing to worry about, especially with a whole team to support you!" Kirana didn't really have the context to under-stand what Kylo was saying, but she felt like she understood well enough. She knew that the purpose of all her previous iterations culminated with the graduation iterations. Nobody else had access to these particular self-assignments. Kirana decided to take advantage of the moment.

"Why did you choose to be in the Guides group instead of the Seeds group with the rest of us? We won't get to have class together anymore," she complained. Kylo didn't answer right away, and when he did, he was careful with his words.

"It was the best option for me," he explained, knowing Kirana would never want him to do something other than what was right for him. He expanded, "You know last iteration was really tough for me, and this gives me the opportunity to take a step back while still continuing to have a big impact on progressing the overall mission."

"What do you mean, 'take a step back?'" Kirana asked, though she wasn't super worried since Kylo had still put his light pin on the same location as her.

"That's one of the details that is..." Kylo struggled for the right way to say it. "Some information will be shared with Seeds and Guides at different times." It appeared to be enough information for Kirana for now, and he breathed a small sigh of relief.

"Was that the other thing you wanted to tell me when we were talking before we turned in our midterm locations?" she asked him. "That you were going to choose the Guides group?" Kylo nodded. "Oh," she said quietly. "Sorry, I shouldn't have cut you off. I thought you were going to talk about light strings, and I wasn't ready yet. Which, by the way, that's what I came to talk to Ravi about." Kylo didn't say anything, waiting to see if she would continue. She didn't though, so he prompted her.

"Are you wanting to know what happened to the light string at the entry of the Gravity Sim building?" he asked.

"Yes," Kirana responded with an absoluteness to her voice. "That, and why that white-out box disappeared and let us use the light strings when it shouldn't have." Kylo bobbed his head in an understanding way.

"Well, he and I have talked about it, and he knows everything I know, so I'll let him tell you what we found out. We don't know everything, but I have a hunch at minimum," said Kylo. It didn't escape Kirana's memory that Ravi had played with her lack of understanding about light strings the first time they had met, so it was good to know that she could confirm any additional questions she had with Kylo later.

"Okay," she responded, "that's good to know. Well, I'll have to catch up with him in class I guess. I'm glad you were here though!" She playfully smacked his arm.

"Always here for you, Kir!" Kylo glittered. "See you later." Kirana waved a colorful mist in his direction and turned to head back to her residence. It looked like she'd have more time before class after all. She considered stopping by the Impressions Office to see if Guardian Era was there, but she suspected he would be preparing for class in Nova's class building. She already had her stuff so she didn't need to go back to her residence, she reasoned, so maybe she could stop by Guardian Gaia's building. Her old classroom, she reminded herself.

When she arrived, the area around the building was quiet, which made sense as class wasn't going to be there anymore. She opened the door and walked inside and the room appeared empty. She thought she might play with Guardian Gaia's projection and see if it could zoom out so she could see the galaxy. As she made her way towards the center of the room, she heard voices that seemed to be coming from the back.

"Your students need you. You've already committed to that role in this iteration," someone said.

"Correct, and I will stand by that commitment. I've already proven I can do a split-energy efficiently enough to take on two roles," a different voice said.

"Maybe, but not *this* role. You can choose something else for this iteration as a trial. I cannot permit you to enter the location of the graduating class right now," said a third. "Besides, we have our eye on a few potential prospects already and are evaluating the feasibility with how we can best build out their teams." Kirana had made it to the center platform of the room now where it was brighter than the edges. The voices hushed and Guardian Gaia appeared in Kirana's view from the back of the room.

"Kirana?" she said pleasantly. "Can I help you with something?"

"Sorry," Kirana stated, "I was just a bit early for class so I was going to review your projection. Is that alright?"

"Certainly. Do let me know if you need anything. I'll be in the back," smiled Guardian Gaia, already disappearing into the shadows of the room again.

"Oh, can I zoom out in this projection?" Kirana called after her, but she got no response. She suspected Guardian Gaia had gone through the back doors to continue the conversation with the other voices. "Oh well, let's see if I can figure it out," she murmured to herself. She drew the projection as she normally did and then started fiddling with it. These things were more like light strings—no specific buttons or controls like the Sim buildings used. You had to use other means of discovery, like how she kinked the light strings to find the records of use. She tried different motions and gestures with her hands and arms, but they didn't have any effect on the projection. She would have to try something else.

She concentrated on the projection in front of her and imagined it shrinking and allowing her to see what was around it. She allowed her energy to focus in on this idea, and it actually started to work. She pulled harder with her energy and saw that she could now see the center of this little corner of the galaxy. It looked like one of the tiles on Kylo's residence. She kept pulling it and pulling it further out until the galaxy itself was visible. Kylo was right. It looked like the one on his building. She also realized that even though they had been limited to locations within this one galaxy, there should have been billions of location choices available for the graduating class. Even though she was now alone in the room, she loudly acknowledged, "There's been a mistake."

CHAPTER TWENTY

"Guardian Gaia?" Kirana called in the direction towards the back of the room. No response. She left the projection zoomed out as it was and walked to the back. Nobody was there. She thought she might just poke her head out the back door real quick, and then she would need to leave for her new building. As she pushed open the door, something whooshed and seemed to push against her. When she managed to get it open, she didn't see anything or anybody. "Guardian Gaia?" she called again. Still nothing. She'd have to ask someone later—maybe in class she could talk to Guardian Beck.

She walked back inside to pick up her things and looked closely at the projection one last time before shutting it off. On her way to the new building, she saw several others looking excited and realized that she had completely forgotten that this was a big deal! These buildings were a brand new addition to the campus. She'd also get a closer look at the pods that they'd start using next semester. She tucked her thoughts about her discovery from the projection in the back of her mind in order to enjoy this new experience.

The two buildings were identical and right next to each other. They were completely devoid of color, and Kirana wondered if she had heard the directions wrong. She remembered them on the map as a sort of creamy white, but she was sure Guardian Gaia had said Seeds were in the Green building. But in this moment, they were just a smooth, opaqueness in no particular color at all. Maybe it was just a title and not a descriptor?

The entrances to the two buildings did not face each other. They both faced the same direction with twin entrances. Kirana realized she was not 100% certain which was for Seeds and which was for Guides. As she hesitated in the front, she heard someone call her name. Anala and Ravi were walking up together, and Ravi waved to her.

"Hey! I stopped by your residence thinking we could walk together, but you weren't there!" said Ravi. "But I found your mate."

"That's funny, because I just went to your residence too," she laughed.

"Oh, that's sweet!" Anala joined in, making a face at Kirana. "And you didn't run into each other half way?"

"I guess not," Kirana admitted, deciding to change the topic. "So do either of you know which building is ours?" Both of them pointed to the one on the left.

"If you look closely above the door, they've added a light green symbol. Honestly, I don't think these buildings are finished," said Anala, letting her face contort to a thinking position with a touch of distaste. Kirana turned towards the other building to see if Kylo happened to be in sight, but she didn't see him.

"Alright, well, let's check out the inside I guess," Kirana mused. "Maybe they did more on the inside than the outside?" She led the way towards the two sets of double doors. The second set did not open until the first set was closed. They thought it was locked at first. Then there was a light blue shine that moved up from the ground. Their names appeared on the door.

"Does this mean we can go in now?" Ravi asked, pulling on the doors again. They opened and Anala and Kirana gasped. On the inside, it didn't look like any kind of building Kirana had ever seen. It was so solid, so stunning, so heavy and dense. They stood with their mouths agape until Ravi grabbed a hand from each of them and pulled them through the doors. "Let's let the next group stand in the doorway now," he jokingly chided them.

Guardian Beck greeted them with a roaring, quick moving energy. "Come in!" she exclaimed. "We are gathering just over there. I will meet you shortly." She indicated over to where a group was sitting next to a Being that Kirana was not familiar with. She walked over with wide eyes.

"Our building is basically a Sim, but we can't just hit a button and pop out of it," whispered Anala, looking around somewhat cautiously. Ravi rubbed his hands together.

"This is going to be great," he concluded. "Too bad Kylo's not here though."

"Ohh yeah," breathed Kirana. "I wonder what his building is like!" Just then, Guardian Beck walked to the center of the group, then thought better of it and moved to the side, standing up on a ledge. This way, she had everybody facing one direction towards her.

"Welcome to the new building! I hope you're all as excited as we are to introduce it. I want to clarify that we will still be using the Sim buildings next semester, but we want to do everything in our power to make your transitions to your self-assignments less jarring. This is all part of the trial with splitting the graduating class. The Sim buildings will be used for drills and exercises to keep your minds as open as possible, and we're hoping that spending more time in the environments your self-assignments will take you to will help ease your work when you arrive. We are not sure how many of you this will work for so we will be assessing the results when you return, which may result in more changes for further iterations."

Guardian Beck stopped talking and looked around at their faces. Since they were not in a circular room like before, she was the only one who could really see any reactions. It appeared that maybe it was a lot to take in for some of them because Guardian Beck smiled and floated several white bubbles of peace out over the group. "This class is open for you to explore the building. Do remember that this will be similar to your projections, where everything is 3D for the most part. Feel free to interact with the environment, though it is not as potent as the Sims will be." She released them to wander after that. Her comment about the projections reminded Kirana about what she had discovered before class. As they got up to explore, Kirana quietly addressed it with Anala and Ravi.

"I have to tell you something," she divulged. She was battling for their attention with the room though. "I was studying Guardian Gaia's projection and I zoomed out, and it turns out there are numerous other locations that we should have had available. I guess I didn't realize how zoomed in we were—they made it seem different somehow."

"Hmm?" asked Anala passively.

"The galaxy," insisted Kirana. "We didn't even get to choose from the billions of options in one galaxy. Location choices in the past started with the galaxy, then we narrowed down from there. Remember?" she prompted. Ravi gave her a funny look.

"The graduation iterations are different. You know that. Pretty much everything else has been practice because these will be the toughest self-assignments and the hardest jobs," he said louder than Kirana would have liked. She decided to let it go. Maybe it wasn't as big of a deal as she thought. It just seemed so odd that the focus was so intense. "You volunteered for this, remember?" Ravi started to tease her.

"No, I know!" she tried to explain, "but—" She stopped, deciding they weren't going to understand what she was trying to say. She decided to take her sentence in a different direction. "There's just so many changes this iteration. Not even just for us. All the other classes are here on the same campus, you know?" Anala put her arm around Kirana.

"Well, we'll be on self-assignments nearby," she assured her. "Ravi and Kylo will be even closer to you. We'll figure it out together." She gave her a big smile, flickering just a little. Ravi nodded in agreement.

"I can't wait to ask Kylo about his building," gleamed Ravi. They continued walking through various types of landscapes with all kinds of Beings that looked so odd to Kirana. Some things she found to be familiar from other self-assignments she had done, like the liquid sounds of rushing, though she was generally more comfortable with the substance in solid form. She was also quite used to standing somewhere and looking out over either huge, gaping holes or towering mounds. Most of the Beings that persisted throughout the building were new though. They were all unmoving, which must be one of the main reasons they still needed the Sim buildings. They couldn't fully interact with things too much here. There were also other types of Beings that appeared to be actually rooted in place entirely. They were beautiful things that were saturated with color. It was all still very gripping. Guardian Beck appeared next to Kirana as she stared at some of them.

"We've represented things in their true form here. Everything gets a little dulled when you arrive. Not because they are duller, but because you won't be able to see in quite the same way. I hope you can remember how they really exist," she said quietly. Kirana looked at her, unsure at what her face might be doing. "How are you feeling about everything so far? I understand it's your first graduation iteration," she said kindly.

"Pretty good," Kirana responded. "Though there's a lot of changes this year." She wavered. Guardian Beck nodded knowingly.

"We are going to be there every step of the way. You will never be alone," she told her. Kirana knew that it was supposed to be reassuring, but it kind of felt ominous. Why was everyone so obsessed with how hard these self-assignments were at this location? She really thought she knew what she had signed up for, but she was starting to doubt herself now. She tried to smile at Guardian Beck so that she wouldn't have to say anything more. It worked. Guardian Beck moved on to speak with others.

Anala walked over, looking as if she was on clouds and didn't have a care in the world. "I'm going to head out. Want to walk together?" she asked Kirana. Kirana looked back at where Ravi was talking with someone else. Anala grinned. "Or do you want to walk with your boyfriend?" she asked lightly. Kirana did want to talk to Ravi, but not for reasons that Anala thought. She'd catch up with him later.

"It's okay, I'd rather not wait for him now anyways," she responded. "Also, he's not actually my boyfriend!" she emphasized.

"What was that about a boyfriend?" said a voice behind Kirana. She glared at Anala, who turned with a flourish, waving soft orange behind her. Kirana took a breath and turned around to face Ravi. She wasn't entirely certain she was ready to have that conversation with him, but it looked like she was going to have to.

"Nothing," she replied. "Anala was just—" She didn't know how to finish that sentence. "Anyways, are you heading out? Want to go together?" she asked, not helping the impression it gave that she wanted to be more than friends. "I mean, like talk about some things," she added, making it even worse. She was cringing inside. Ravi, however, was positively glowing.

"I would love to, but I'm going to hang back with some old mates over there," he said, gesturing towards the small group he was just talking with. "Let's meet up later? I'll swing by your residence?" Kirana nodded, not wanting to continue digging herself in a hole with more words. She mustered a flutter of gold specks, which he made a show of collecting. "See you later then," he said, turning away. Kirana made her way out the exit as quickly as she could to see if she could catch Anala, but she was nowhere in sight.

CHAPTER TWENTY ONE

"**I**'ll catch up with her if I go fast enough," Kirana whispered to herself, picking up her pace as she went around the edge of the building. The entrances of these buildings faced away from where the other classes and residences were, and the pods were surrounding the two buildings, except for on that one side where the rest of campus was. She slowed her walking, trying to get a better look at the pods as she passed and noticed someone standing among them. He was alone and appeared to be working on something outside one of the pods. Kirana glanced in the direction of the residences and decided Anala would be there when she got back. She'd have plenty of opportunities to talk to her. She may even already be hanging out with Alev, she reasoned.

She pivoted direction and started walking cautiously towards the pods. Nobody had mentioned them in class yet so she assumed maybe they weren't finished. It appeared to be a good guess as the Someone who was working on this one wasn't a Guardian or anyone she had seen around campus before. He saw her approaching and stopped what he was doing for a moment.

"Can I help you with something?" he asked in a very friendly way.

"Oh, no," explained Kirana. "I was just passing by and curious about these. We haven't used them yet. Are they done?" The Someone seemed eager to talk about what he was doing.

"I'd say they are just about ready!" he said proudly. "I'm just finishing up some testing. I expect these pods will be ready to go shortly!" There was a panel off the wall of the mini dome structure, and he showed her various pieces inside while talking about conductors and electrical energy. All of a sudden, Kirana felt a presence behind her. She stood up quickly, turning around as she did so. She would've knocked right into whoever was there had they not taken a step to the side in anticipation of her surprise.

"See, now I'm getting it. Did you feel that?" Nox said with an open expression and sparkles in his eyes.

"Nox! Hi!" Kirana stumbled over her words. "I—yes, I felt something and just reacted I guess. Sorry," she continued a little sheepishly. "I don't know why that keeps happening." She muttered the last part to the ground, which happened to be towards the Someone who was still working on the pod. He watched their interaction with interest.

"Looks like standard magnetism to me," he shrugged with a grin, standing not quite as tall as Nox. Addressing Nox directly, he continued. "I tweaked the grounding cord, which should allow you to settle in more fully now. Let's run one more test to confirm, and then we should be all set here!" Nox nodded and sent him a ball of evergreen mist. Turning to Kirana, he raised an eyebrow and held out his hand.

"Care to join me, Little Miss Curious?" His eyes danced. Kirana was already lost to them. Luckily, her arm responded and reached her hand out to Nox's. He led her around the pod to what must be the front. "The identifiers are not turned on yet, so you can come in with me. Eventually you will only be able to enter your own," he explained. He placed his hand on the side of the small dome and a piece of the wall pulled inward a little bit before sliding open. The inside was similar to a room in the Sim building, except there was no screen or bracelets, and there was an area with cushions on the floor instead of a bench.

"Is this one yours?" asked Kirana.

"Probably not," Nox responded. "This one will likely remain as the test pod and be used for other experimentation and demonstration purposes." He turned to face her as the door of the pod closed. Though the dome was all black, the energy glowed in the room creating plenty of light. Even so, Nox disappeared into the black as he walked to the edge of one side. Kirana realized two things in that moment. One, she realized the majority of the glowing source was her own self. Two, she realized that same feeling she felt earlier of a *presence* allowed her to know exactly where Nox was, and she kept her face directed towards him as he moved. When he came closer and reappeared, he had a knowing smile.

"You feel that too, don't you," he said, half rhetorically. "I started noticing it after maybe the third time we ran into each other. That's how I've been able to sidestep the last couple crashes," he chuckled. Kirana wasn't sure what to say. She had twelve different thoughts going on at once. Things like, *Have I really run into him that much? That's so sweet that he says 'we' and doesn't blame it entirely on me! What is magnetism? Is that what we have?* along with many more. She finally settled on responding directly.

"I do feel it! I just felt it for the first time in front of the pod, but now it's like I'm somehow drawn to where your energy is." Then she started rambling. "How did I not notice before? Is that why I kept running into you? But how would I even have known because—" She stopped abruptly, her eyes going to his with alarm as she realized her inner thoughts were starting to get out. He looked calm and collected. Interested even.

"... because..." he prompted. He remained in the perfect energetic space between distance and pushing her. Surprised at his response and the way it felt like he created a space where she could exist and release these thoughts, she finished her sentence.

"Because if I didn't recognize the feeling, I wouldn't know how to respond to it," she said quietly. She blinked and added, "Kinda silly, I know."

"No, that's exactly how it works. And you have responded perfectly to the whole process of discovering that. Often we need to feel something multiple times until we can identify what it is and why it's happening. Then," he added carefully, "then we decide how to respond to it." Kirana disappeared this time, straight into the shooting stars in his eyes until a knocking sound caused them both to turn towards the entry.

"If it's working alright, I'll just be on my way," said the Someone who had been working on the pod. Nox went to the door and opened it, speaking quietly to him. When he returned, he brought a small control panel over to Kirana from the front of the pod.

"Do you want to see what it'll be like? As an example of course," Nox asked her. Kirana looked at him wide-eyed.

"Absolutely," she confirmed. *Just wait 'til I tell Nova about this*, she thought to herself.

"Alright," said Nox. "A few things to remember. It is similar to a Sim, so you shouldn't be too shocked, but it may be surprising at first. Prepare yourself mentally. Also, I will still be there with you, and we will be both connected and individual, so don't panic. Just think about several

Sim building experiences combined. Are you ready?" He looked at her closely.

"Yes, I'm ready," she confirmed. Nox gave her a nod, looking convinced of her answer.

"OH, one more thing. The most important," he stressed. "I have no doubt this will not be an issue, but we will be sharing space. We must remain mindful of those already there. The respect you show now will follow you for many iterations. We will still be in this room, but taking space there, unlike a Sim. Do you understand?" The way that Nox spoke made his eyes go deep black, covering the stars. He glowed the deep green of respect, and Kirana realized how much he must trust her to take her in this pod and show her how they worked.

"I understand," she said, in her most serious voice. Her seriousness broke his, and his eyes twinkled again. Without another word, he did something on the control panel and everything around them started to change. Instead of getting sucked into a screen like the Sims did, it was like they were the screen and the environment got sucked to them. Kirana was still herself, but her knowledge-set changed. She somehow just knew things about where she was that she didn't know before, and she knew what to do and how to do it. The feelings were foreign at first, but a moment later, she felt like it had always been that way. She felt heavy and thick, but also light and airy. There was every kind of contrast happening at the same time, and she felt it all. She discovered she could identify her separate self but also feel for her connection to Nox. They could communicate, but it was in an entirely different way. Somehow, she just knew how to do it. In the Sim rooms, one of their practices was to figure out those things that she intuitively was just picking up on here.

She felt exhilarated and overwhelmed and completely normal, all at the same time.

In what could have been decades or seconds, Nox returned them to the pod. Kirana was speechless.

"It's a lot the first time, I know," Nox said softly, watching her carefully. Whatever he saw in her caused him to step forward and wrap his arms around her, somewhat tentatively at first. When Kirana melted into him, he held her more firmly. When Kirana regained her senses, she bursted with energy.

"That was beautiful! Magnificent even. Whatever that was, that's what I want to be when I start my self-assignment!" she said, exuberantly moving around the pod. Nox chuckled.

"You certainly could," he said smiling, "though I have a feeling that you'll end up going with another type of self-assignment." Kirana didn't have any other context to respond to that, so she changed the subject.

"How did I just know things? And I felt everything. It was like you said actually," she realized, "like multiple Sims all at once." She shook her head in disbelief. "But I also felt so grounded to myself. Why is everyone so concerned about these assignments?" She finally got to the question that caused a look of concern on Nox's face.

"Well," he began, "this is not exactly what the self-assignments will be like." He seemed to be treading carefully. "Think of it as an advanced Sim maybe. It will get you one step closer and help you transition fully into your self-assignment."

"Okay," said Kirana, nodding while trying to understand what he meant. As they left the pod, her mind was still working. All of a sudden she had a realization. She stopped on a dime and looked at Nox who did not look surprised at her sudden action. He waited for her to talk. With her voice full of awe, she asked, "Did we just do a split-energy?"

CHAPTER
TWENTY TWO

Kirana made her way back to her residence, replaying it all in her head. She couldn't help but think that something was missing. That some piece of information that she didn't have yet would bring it all together.

Nox had offered to go with her to her residence, but she had declined when he said he'd have to go quickly, as he was needed by the Guardians to discuss the results of the pod testing. He insisted he would be happy to go with her, but she wanted the time to mull over these ideas in her head anyway. Repetitive movements helped things to process. She thought mostly about her upcoming self-assignment, then a little about past self-assignments (of which there were many), and finally, she thought again about her first experience doing a split-energy. She was kind of shocked that all of them, all of them in the graduating class anyway, would be doing it. It used to be unheard of—even rare for Guardians. A memory pinged in her head.

Who had been talking when she had gone to work with Guardian Gaia's projection? She knew Guardian Gaia's voice well enough now, but she wasn't as familiar with the other two. Her mind had been on other things, and she didn't pay close attention to what was being said, but now she recalled that someone was definitely talking about split-energy. The only Guardian she knew of that had been seen doing that lately was Guardian Cosmo. Nova had told her of two different instances—although one of them was just a suspicion. She reviewed them in her head. The first time, Nova had seen him in front of the Gravity Sim building during Orientation when he was on stage. The second time, she had heard his voice behind her building where she had class with Guardians Nika and Era, yet Sora had confirmed him in another location in her own session building. It seemed feasible that the second voice she had heard was Guardian Cosmo, trying to convince Guardian Gaia and someone else that he was practiced enough with split-energy to continue working with the FI class as well as taking on a self-assignment.

"Why would he even want to do that though?" she wondered in a whisper to herself. *And why would he not be permitted to do it?* she asked in her head. Kirana was close to her residence now. The building was light yellow with soft white streaks floating casually. She only saw a faint light blue inside. She guessed that Nova and Anala were not there. As she entered, this was confirmed. She seemed to be striking out on having any and all of the conversations she had wanted to have lately! First with Ravi, then with Anala and now with Nova. Although, to have that sneak peek of the pods with Nox was worth it, she decided.

As she went up a level to her nest, she decided to check out her light strings again. Nothing had changed though. They had no more use, and no other names showed. She stared at Alev's name, thinking about when he might have used it, and why. He and his mates had all come over dressed up that one time doing their ridiculous dance, but no, he had been glued to Anala that whole time, deep in conversation. Was he here other times? Actually, yes, she remembered. The time they had all played X. Everyone had gone with Sora back to their residence. That was when Anala and Alev had met. Kirana had already installed the light strings at that point. She looked harder at the record that she still had up, showing the comings and goings on her light string. Ravi had told her it showed when they were used. How could she get that to show?

After a lot of playing around and getting nowhere, she decided to give it a break. It would be easier to just ask someone who already knew how to do it at this point. With that thought, she hopped on her chestnut light string and snuggled into her nook to start reviewing her plan for Internal Development. Her first list had been things like trusting herself, getting comfortable with being uncomfortable and finding balance in, well, so many things. How to fight for things but also know when to let go. How to be stable and yet open to change. How to stand up for herself and still be able to admit when she was wrong. The list went on. Many of these had been on previous lists, and she hadn't quite moved the needle enough to be satisfied that she had really developed in these areas enough yet. She would probably end up taking most of this with her into this self-assignment.

Just then, she heard someone enter her nest through a light string. Alarmed having just been thinking about Alev not too long ago, she peeked down. Nova was there, looking wild and with her energy whirling around her.

"Chestnut?" Nova called out, not seeing her.

"Chestnut!" Kirana confirmed, making space for her arrival. "Hey!" she added cheerfully as Nova appeared. She waited for Nova to address what all this high energy was about. She doubted she'd need to ask.

"Hey!" Nova began. Kirana was right; Nova jumped into it right away. "Remember how I told you that Guardian Era said that based on how the graduating class split into groups that it might make changes in ours as well?" She didn't wait for Kirana to respond. "Well now that you have made the split official, Guardian Era confirmed that we will potentially have a new opportunity this iteration! Even me! And I'm only in my second iteration!"

"Okay, hold on," laughed Kirana. "So now that there are Seeds and Guides in the graduating class, how does that make a difference for everyone else?"

"Apparently they had a theory that most of you who are in your first graduation iteration would choose to be Seeds, and that happened. The remaining members of the graduating class were about half and half," Nova explained. Kirana realized that she had not really paid much attention to how many of them were in each group, as she had been focused on who was and wasn't in hers. Nova continued, "They don't have as many Guides as they want for the number of Seeds, and there's a good chance they will open up the option to everyone else to add to the group of Guides! Well, besides the FI class. They don't have this opportunity."

"Why do I feel like they don't tell us anything?" asked Kirana rhetorically, still feeling like everyone else had information that she didn't. Nova pointed to herself.

"Remember your mate? Here? Telling you all the things?" she said. Both of them laughed. "Anyways, Guardian Era said it wouldn't be exactly the same as what the actual Guides will be doing, but it would still be a self-assignment in support of a Seed. And you're a Seed!!" she said, getting louder at the end. Kirana considered the opportunity to be able to have a self-assignment with Nova. Her eyes got big to match Nova's.

"Wow, do you really think we could potentially have an iteration together?!" she asked with a hopeful excitement beginning.

"I don't know, but when Guardian Era said it, it seemed like a possibility!" Nova squealed. Kirana remembered that she wanted to visit Guardian Era's office soon. She added this information to her mental note to bring up with him.

"Well, I have some crazy news too," Kirana twinkled. She told Nova about running into Nox when he was helping to run tests on the pods that they would be using. "Can you believe that I actually did a split-energy?! Honestly, I'm not sure if anyone is supposed to know that until they actually assign our pods to us, so maybe don't mention it." She made a pleading face at Nova, but she seemed to be thinking about something else.

"No, of course not! I would never," Nova confirmed, then carefully shifted the topic. "Do you and Nox run into each other often?" she said pleasantly. Kirana thought about this for a moment.

"For as much as I rarely see him in class, I guess we kind of do! Why?" Kirana looked curious but also remembered what the Someone who had been working on the pod said to them.

"No reason," Nova smiled. She changed the subject again. "Speaking of Nox, can I finally tell you about what he found? We think it's connected to the notes!" Kirana smiled, excited to get back to this adventure.

"Yes, for sure. What is it?" she asked.

"Okay, so he was in the Gravity Sim building, Nox was I mean, and he saw that a corner of the wall material had been ripped up in one of the back corners by a single Sim room. He never would have thought anything of it, but then he realized the material was familiar. I think we should bring the notes with us to the Gravity Sim building and see if they fit in that torn up spot!" Nova's energy was swirling again.

"No way!" Kirana's eyes were wide. "I mean, it must've really been a secret for someone to do that instead of just communicating by tablet, you know?

"Yeah, but anything written on a tablet can be traced. It's not really a secret. You'd either have to tell somebody something in person, OR," Nova emphasized, "you could use some wall material to write on and leave the note somewhere for someone to find."

"Well, I'm in!" confirmed Kirana. "And I'm not even concerned about the light strings anymore!" And then a little quieter she added, "Though it doesn't hurt to let someone else go in first before us. Test it out." She made a face at Nova that made her laugh. "When should we go?"

"Looks like you're working on something, but I could totally go right now..." Nova said with anticipation.

"Oh, this can wait! I made some good progress anyways," said Kirana, already hopping on the light string. When Nova joined her coming down from the nook, Kirana paused, remembering another predicament she was dealing with. "Wait a sec though. I want to show you something," she told Nova. She kinked the light string on the maroon one that went to the community area, bringing up the record of who had been on it.

"Whoaaa," Nova reacted as she saw the names pop up. She immediately went to touch them, enticingly hanging in the space above the string as they were. She slid her finger to the left on one of Kirana's names, and a small hologram appeared that showed Kirana taking the light string from her nest to the community area right before they met to chat about the mate's trip. Then it disappeared. "This is so cool! How did you find out about this?" Nova looked like she was just having fun with it. Kirana's eyes got big.

"How did you do that! How did you know how to do that, Nova?" Kirana stared at her, unsure if she should be annoyed that again, she didn't know what everyone else did, or if she should be impressed. Nova shrugged.

"I didn't. I had no idea light strings kept this information. I just swiped—" Then she realized something. "The Gravity Sim building. I'd be curious..." She looked Kirana in the eyes. They didn't speak for a moment.

"I didn't even think about that," Kirana practically whispered.

"Do you think anyone can look at the records for any light strings?" asked Nova.

"We're about to find out," Kirana replied.

Chapter Twenty Three

In the renewed excitement to get to the Gravity Sim building, Kirana didn't remember to swipe on Alev's name in her records until they had already grabbed the notes and left their residence.

"Oh my gosh, I forgot to show you the thing I was going to show you in the records!" she complained.

"There was more?" Nova responded.

"Yes, but I can show you later. And now that I know how to see the rest of the information, thanks to you," she smiled at Nova, "I'll be able to figure out when it happened."

"Wait, when *what* happened?" Nova started putting the pieces together. "Was someone else in your nest?" Her face turned serious, then lightened up again. "Besides me, of course."

"Let's just deal with that later. We have another puzzle in front of us," Kirana requested. Nova agreed, though a bit begrudgingly. Kirana pulled the notes out of her bag.

How long do you think you'll last?

I think I'm ready.

"Do you think they were written in this order?" Kirana wondered aloud. "Like if they tore the corner first and went back for another piece later?" She turned her head to look at Nova, who had become alert to something she saw ahead of them. In an instant, Nova grabbed her arm and pulled her behind a building. She held a finger to her lips, notifying Kirana to be quiet.

"If we get caught, pretend you had a flash-out and that I'm helping you," she said in a whisper Kirana could barely hear. She nodded in response, and they waited silently. Finally, two figures talking to each other appeared, and they would have directly passed them on their way to the Sim buildings. It was not immediately clear to Kirana why Nova had them hiding, but she was ready to fake a flash-out if needed. She recognized a voice as they got closer. She was pretty sure it was the same voice that she heard speaking with Guardian Gaia earlier that she suspected was Guardian Cosmo. Sure enough, it was him. She didn't recognize who was walking with him, but whoever it was had a faint red haze around them. Kirana and Nova exchanged glances. They seemed to be thinking of the same thing. *The red haze that Nova saw when Guardian Cosmo was doing the split-energy at the Gravity Sim building.*

"—can't let it get to this point." Guardian Cosmo was saying. "Burn-outs have terrible side ef—Nova?" They were spotted. Kirana immediately slumped herself down further against the building and half closed her eyes to appear as if she had just awakened. Nova hovered over her, blocking Guardian Cosmo from fully seeing her. She turned her head to him.

"Guardian Cosmo! Kirana just had a flash-out, and I was just about to call for help when she woke up," she said quickly and loudly, as if it were true. She pulled Kirana up straighter, and Kirana rubbed her eyes.

Guardian Cosmo whispered something to whoever was with him, and they scampered off in the direction of the residences.

"I've heard about this issue," said Guardian Cosmo. "Let's take her to the Impressions Building. I think it's worth a chat with Guardian Era about this." The mates exchanged looks.

"Oh, no, I'm okay Guardian Cosmo. Nothing to worry about," Kirana said. "Thanks though! Nova knows what to do."

"Nonsense," Guardian Cosmo said, gesturing for them to get up. "This is serious and must be addressed before the next steps in this iteration. Do you need help to walk?" It didn't seem like they would get a choice. Kirana leaned into Nova as she stood, whispering to her to go check the notes without her. Nova shook her head.

"I'm not leaving you alone with him! Lean on me like you need support," she insisted quietly.

"Nova's got it," Kirana said louder to Guardian Cosmo. He looked at them suspiciously, then turned and led the way to the Impressions Offices. By the time they arrived, Kirana was walking normally on her own, as would have been typical by now if she had actually had a flash-out. Guardian Cosmo went inside, telling them to stay put for a moment.

"Nova, you should go check out the Gravity Sim building. Seriously! I'll catch up with you there after. It can't take that long I'm sure," Kirana insisted, watching the doors of the Office. "I wanted to meet with Guardian Era, but not like this," she said mostly to herself. Nova looked a little guilty.

"Sorry about that," she said. "But did you hear what they were saying? Also, no, I'm still not leaving you," Nova solidified.

"Well, take the notes then, just in case," said Kirana, looking around for them before realizing she didn't know where they were. "Oh no!" she expressed in a whisper yell. "I must have dropped them." She covered her mouth with her hands, and just then, Guardian Cosmo appeared at the door.

"Kirana only, please," he said, looking at Nova. Kirana shot her a look silently begging her to keep going on the mission they had started. Nova looked like a mixture of protective and determined but didn't say anything. Guardian Cosmo ushered Kirana into the office and straight to Guardian Era's office. He entered with her but quickly got a taste of his own medicine.

"Kirana only, please," Guardian Era said, smiling politely at Guardian Cosmo, who looked like he wanted to argue but decidedly did not. He stepped out of the office and left the door slightly ajar. Guardian Era's office was everything and nothing. It seemed to be no color, but all colors. It was expansive, yet contained. Kirana felt the vibrations of connectedness and trust, and she knew that whatever she told Guardian Era would be handled with care.

Guardian Era casually moved to the door and closed it all the way, gesturing for Kirana to take a seat.

"I've been wanting to check in with you," he said pleasantly. Kirana looked up in surprise from the hammock-like seat she had chosen. She drifted softly back and forth.

"I actually had planned to stop by soon," she admitted.

"Oh?" replied Guardian Era, sounding equally surprised. "And what did you want to talk to me about?" he asked.

"A couple things," Kirana responded. Guardian Era waited. "Like, I wanted to know what happened with the light strings when I saw you before and also just talk about how you said you could still advise me, even though I'm with Guardian Beck now." Guardian Era was nodding.

"Guardian Beck," he said. "So you've chosen to be a Seed?"

"Yes," Kirana nodded. Guardian Era didn't say anything, so Kirana kept talking. "It's my first iteration in the graduating class, and this role seems more aligned with what I expected to be self-assigning anyways." She blinked at him. He must have known what she had chosen already, but he wasn't showing it.

"Tell me, how are you feeling about your classes, your mates and your general experience in preparing for this iteration so far?" he asked her. "I understand you came here just now with a mate," he added, right as Kirana opened her mouth.

"Yes! My mates are incredible. We're actually going on a trip together after the semester—" She stopped, realizing that was irrelevant to him. Guardian Era smiled. "Anyways, yes, classes are good too. I feel like I'm on top of everything and confident with my choices so far."

"That's excellent," replied Guardian Era, looking genuinely pleased. "Anything else you think I should know?" he asked, looking at her closely. A few things ran through Kirana's head, such as her experience with the pod, wondering about Nova being able to join her this iteration, and that she didn't actually have a flash-out just now, but she decided to take the opportunity to ask about the white-out box she had encountered with Ravi.

"I don't think so, at least not right now," she said looking up at Guardian Era who was watching her with interest. "But I was hoping you could share with me what happened to that white-out box that disappeared and let me use the light strings it was blocking." Then adding quickly, "Just so I know what to do if it happens again." Guardian Era did not respond right away. He leaned back in his chair and spoke quietly.

"That shouldn't have happened," he said carefully, as if trying not to scare her. "You may come to me personally at any time if you see any other white-out boxes in use. If I am unavailable, find Nox." He appeared to be watching for a reaction, but Kirana just nodded, because somehow that made sense to her. "Okay," said Guardian Era, seeming satisfied with the interaction. "I have things to get back to, but Kirana, please feel free to come by anytime you wish. It was delightful to chat." He pressed his hands together and sent a puff of gold sparkles. Kirana repeated the gesture and got up. As she left the Impressions Office, she realized two things.

1. He hadn't actually answered her question, and
2. He said absolutely nothing about her flash-outs.

Kirana wondered if Nova would still be at the Gravity Sim building if she went there now. She decided to go by there anyway, and if she wasn't, then she'd just catch up with her back at the residence. She went back to where they had been hiding to see if she had dropped the notes there, but she didn't see anything. She guessed that Nova would have done the same thing, so maybe she had found them. When she finally reached the Gravity Sim building, she inspected the light strings. Everything looked okay so she took a deep breath and hopped on the gold one. Being a gold light string, it was a standard ride, but the entry of the building was a whole different story. She was pulled down with an intense pressure and then bounced outward, getting flung out so she spun without knowing up from down. Finally, she was floating slowly down to where the Sim rooms were.

"Oh, I forgot to check the records on the light strings!" she said to herself, putting a hand to her forehead. Then she quickly looked around, realizing she had said it out loud. She didn't see anyone and breathed out a sigh of relief. She went to the back corner of the singular Sim rooms as Nova had instructed, looking for a tear in the walls. It actually was not that easy to spot, but once she did, it was unmistakably the same material that those notes were written on. She was sure of it. She tried to imagine the sizes of the two notes and the edges they had and how they might fit in the ripped area, but it was a bit difficult to imagine. It looked like a bigger hole than the two notes put together. *Are there more notes?* she wondered to herself.

Nothing else really looked out of the ordinary in the building, and she didn't see Nova, so she decided to go back to the front and check out the light strings real quick before heading back to her residence. She made her way out the back and around to the front again, but before she could take a look at the light strings, a group from the FI class appeared, excitedly waiting to enter.

"Kirana!" one of them said, recognizing her. "We're finally finishing the game of X! Your team just went in 'cause they had a head start, but you can probably still catch them!" She smiled brightly.

"Oh, that's amazing! I can't right now, but you all have fun. Let me know who finds the X Spot!" she said, running a brief scan over the group. Kylo wasn't there, but Alev was. Her eyes snagged on his for a moment, but he looked completely normal and pleasant and happy to be playing. "See you later!" she called to them as she turned away.

CHAPTER TWENTY FOUR

Kirana made a beeline back to her residence. She was sure she wasn't too far behind Nova, except when she got back, Nova wasn't there. Nobody was. She decided to wait and knew exactly what she'd do in the meantime. She went through the community area to where her light string hid in the corner next to a shelving unit. It wasn't super obvious, but could definitely be stumbled upon. As she took it in her hand, a glint of something on the shelf caught her eye. She reached across the shelf and picked up another piece of stone.

"Again?" asked Kirana to no one. It looked like the same stone that Anala had, as well as the piece she had found in the fireplace. She pocketed it and did a quick sweep of the room with her eyes. Nothing else stood out, so she hopped on her light string. She had made it a bit more fun, though it did take a little longer than the direct path it took before. It climbed rather steeply upwards and then dropped her down into her nest. She took the piece of stone over to the piece she had found before and held them up next to each other. Surprisingly, or not, they literally fit together. They were pieces broken from the same original stone.

"Why are pieces of this stone littered around the community area," she mused, "and WHY do I keep finding pieces to multiple puzzles without being able to solve one?" Then she laughed to herself. Shaking her head, she put the pieces down and returned to her light string set. Just as she was pulling up the records on the maroon string, Nova popped in, jumping off the evergreen one.

"Perfect timing!" said Kirana. Nova looked like she was bursting to say something too, but held it in as she watched Kirana pull up the records and scroll up.

"Alev?!" Nova said, shocked and now completely distracted from her own news. She swiped left on his name, and they both leaned in to watch the hologram. It showed Alev in the community room, looking strangely at the light string while the group from the X game were distracted behind him. He had a hand on the shelves, which is what it looked like he was actually perusing, and seeing that no one was paying attention to him, he hopped on the string. When he landed in Kirana's nest, he didn't know where he was at first. The hologram showed him look around and walk towards Kirana's bag. He dug through it, and then the hologram cut out. Kirana's eyes were wide with curiosity. She got up and went to get her bag. Nova was angry.

"How dare he!" she voiced with indignation. She began scrolling the list looking for more instances of his name. Not seeing any, she looked back to Kirana who was pulling everything out of her bag.

"I don't see anything odd here, nothing removed and nothing extra. Plus, I've had a lot of classes since then, and I never noticed anything off," she confirmed. "He might've just been trying to figure out who's nest it was." Nova went back to scrolling. She started swiping left on random entries and watching Kirana use her light string in the holograms.

"Kirana, oh my..." Nova suddenly gasped.

"What?" she responded, rushing over. They watched a hologram of Alev that showed him use the light string with purpose this time. Like he knew exactly what he was doing and where he was going. This time, he went to her bookcase and desk, then seemed to scan everything, looking for something in particular. It seemed like he didn't find what he was looking for though, at least by the time the hologram cut out. Kirana's eyes remained widened.

"I didn't see his name on any other records," she said as she looked to Nova for answers. Nova was shaking her head.

"It wasn't his name. It was yours," she said as she scrolled to show Kirana the one she had just swiped on.

"Records can be changed," they said practically in unison, overlapping each other's words.

"Looks like the holograms can't be changed though," Nova added.

"What was he looking for?" Kirana inquired, her mind buzzing.

"We have to check all the records," Nova said in a determined voice. She kept going through the maroon string. Finally, the second to last one showed him again. The mates looked at each other in alarm. It was just about the time when they were out on their mission to the Gravity Sim building. "How could this be?" hissed Nova angrily. They watched as Alev hopped on the light string straight into Kirana's nest and then studied the two remaining colors. Chestnut and Evergreen. He hopped on the Evergreen one that led into Nova's nest.

"He's testing them all to see if he can find... whatever it is he's looking for!" said Nova, at the same time as Kirana said, "I'm sorry."

"Why are you sorry?" Nova asked her, putting her hand on Kirana's shoulder. "You didn't do this."

"I know, but because of me and my light strings, someone is snooping in both of our nests!" she lamented. They watched the look of surprise on Alev's face as he discovered he was in another mate's nest. He didn't seem interested and immediately left.

"That must've been right before you got back here," Nova said with wide eyes. "Did you see him near the residence?"

"Oh my gosh, I saw him in front of the Gravity Sim building! They had just gathered to finish the game we had started before the broken light string debacle. He didn't look suspicious or anything. Wow," Kirana divulged.

"Oh, so you did end up going there? Me too! Did you see what I saw?" Nova asked.

"Wait, what was that," Kirana asked flatly. The hologram they had just watched popped up again and started to replay. Kirana thought she saw something on Alev's wrist. It looked like a bracelet with red stones. "Do you see that?" Kirana asked, pointing it out. It was a little hard to tell. She got up and grabbed the two pieces of red stone she had found and handed them to Nova.

"Do you think they're a match? Where did you get these?" Nova paused. "You didn't find them in here, did you?"

"No, not in here, but I found both of them in the community area at different times. One was in the fireplace and the other on the shelf near my light string. Don't you think they look really similar to the stone Alev gave to Anala?" Kirana questioned. Nova gasped.

"You're right!" she agreed. "They really do." Then she muttered, "Geez, this guy really leaves a lot of breadcrumbs." Kirana laughed, breaking some of the tension.

"Let's just see if we can see the bracelet more clearly in the first hologram," suggested Kirana. Nova nodded. They reviewed the first situation, the one where Alev had clearly forgotten to cover his tracks in the records. While he was first examining the light string, his hand was up on the shelf.

"There!" Kirana pointed. When Alev turned back to look at the room to see if anyone was paying attention to him, his arm twisted, and they could see a small piece of something left behind. "It looks like he lost a piece from his bracelet! This one." Kirana pointed to one of the stones in Nova's hands. Nova nodded seriously.

"I can't wait to see him again so I can ask him about his bracelet and why it has missing stones," Nova said wryly. Kirana chuckled.

"Actually, that's a good idea. But let's just start with seeing it ourselves and looking for those missing spots," she conceded. "Oh! Did you find the notes?" Kirana had just remembered that they didn't have them anymore. Nova looked even more annoyed than she had a moment ago.

"No," she snorted. "And I have a theory." Kirana blinked, waiting for her to continue. She started by reviewing the main points. "You were holding the notes in your hand when Guardian Cosmo arrived. From that point to the point where we were in front of the Impressions Office, somehow they disappeared. It seems to me the most likely place it happened was immediately, right behind that building. You don't remember putting them in your bag or your pocket or anything, right?" Kirana tried to remember, but she couldn't recall doing anything with them after she pulled them out of her bag.

"You might be right," she said. "I went limp with them in my hand, so it's very possible that I just let them fall." She hung her head down a little bit.

"Hey, it's alright," Nova assured her. "My point is that the notes were visible and likely in that spot." Kirana nodded in agreement. "So from there, I have two suspicions," she continued. "Either someone happened to find them after we left and picked them up, or what I think is more likely, Guardian Cosmo simply did a split-energy after we already turned around and were walking away from the area, and *he* picked them up." Kirana gasped. Nova explained further. "They would've been really noticeable, and we were concentrating on making things look like you had a flash-out. He's apparently well rehearsed with doing split-energies, so we wouldn't have noticed a thing." Kirana thought about this.

"But why would he want those? What's the significance to him to make it a secret or take them from us?" Kirana questioned.

"I don't know, but he could've just said, 'Hey, you dropped something,' but he didn't. You know?" Nova responded.

"I guess," Kirana said tentatively, before shifting the subject. "So you saw the wall in the Gravity building, right? What did you think?"

"That is definitely the same material," Nova confirmed immediately. "Also, I think the space was bigger than the two we had combined. So I suspect there's another note." She looked at Kirana.

"I had the exact same thoughts," said Kirana. "Now I guess we'll have to try to remember the shapes and what the handwriting looked like without them. Oh, I better write down what they said so we don't have to rely on our memory for that too." She hopped on the chestnut light string to go up to her nook and get her journal. As she wrote the sayings down, she realized that there was potentially a lot of sensitive information in her journal. Things that someone might be potentially interested in knowing that she had been looking into or working on. Or even details of her plans for her next self-assignment, which was information generally kept private, except for in contracts. She tucked the journal under a cushion and took the light string back down to where Nova had been looking through the records on the remaining two light strings.

"I didn't see anything else in the holograms from the chestnut or the evergreen light strings," Nova confirmed, satisfied. "Besides the one we already knew about on the evergreen one to my nest."

"So he hasn't found what he's looking for because he hasn't taken the chestnut light string and found my journal..." Kirana suspected. Nova turned sharply to look at her.

"How do you want to handle this? Break the maroon light string and let him get trapped?" Nova suggested. Kirana laughed at the harshness.

"I was thinking more like disabling them when I leave," she said smiling. "Even if he came in through my door, he wouldn't know the nook existed. And if he did, he wouldn't be able to reach it with a deactivated light string."

"But you'll have to remember to do it every single time you leave," Nova warned.

"Maybe there's a way to set it up so that it's restricted only to me," Kirana mused. "I wouldn't be surprised. That actually sounds fairly feasible! How about this. I'll figure out how to do that, and in the meantime, I'll just keep them deactivated when I'm not here." Nova seemed to be agreeable to this idea. She picked up the stones again and looked at them intensely in her hand.

"We're going to get to the bottom of this," Nova remarked heavily. Kirana had no doubt that they would.

CHAPTER
TWENTY FIVE

"How did I beat you back here to the residence?" Kirana asked Nova, just remembering that she had expected Nova to be there when she arrived, and yet she wasn't. Nova came to life, and her eyes sparkled with excitement.

"Ohh that's right! I actually came with news for you, and you distracted me!" she complained, feigning annoyance. "I ran into Tali on my way back, and she told me that one of her mates got approached by Guardian Era about potentially being a Guide!" She was buzzing with excitement and almost hopping, leaving Kirana to believe that Nova thought it might be possible for her too. She easily matched Nova's energy.

"Really?! Okay, that's a good sign!" she said, spraying some silver sparks above them. "Do you still attend your classes as a group with Tali and her mates?"

"Yep!" Nova responded. "We've been able to stay together for the most part so far, although just like you all, we'll probably have to work a bit more individually soon." Nova continued to ramble. "I really like Makani. I can see why Guardian Era would make her an offer like that. I think she's really close to joining the graduating class—like an iteration or two away—so definitely a good option for her to get more insight sooner. Hmm," she said, all of a sudden producing a change of tone.

"What is it?" asked Kirana.

"Well, I just realized, it makes sense *because* she's so close to joining the graduating class anyways. I'm like, the farthest from the far." She slapped her palm to her forehead.

"Maybe that was only part of the decision. You never know!" Kirana encouraged. "Do you know if she accepted the offer? Or was it more of a preliminary idea that Guardian Era presented her with?"

"She didn't have to answer yet. He told her she could think about it and potentially do some observation of the graduating class before she decided. He said she'd still have a little time to think about it," Nova explained.

"So there's plenty of time for you as well," Kirana concluded, smiling. Nova smiled back and glittered a little. Kirana was glad to see her looking forward to this iteration versus how she was feeling before.

"Hey," Nova said, as if something just popped into her head. "Did you check the records on the light strings at the Gravity Sim building?" Kirana shook her head.

"I forgot when I arrived, and then when I was leaving, I was going to check, but that's when I saw Alev and them. They were all waiting to enter, and I didn't want to do that with all of them watching. Did you?" Kirana's eyes widened with hope. Nova furrowed her brow just a little.

"I fiddled with them, but maybe I just don't know how to do it properly. I didn't get anything to show up," she said, turning to look at Kirana's light strings.

"Can you bring up the records on mine? Someone obviously can if they've meddled with changing Alev's name," Kirana said with a wince.

"I guess I had them up already the times that you've seen them." Nova didn't respond and walked over to the light strings. She kinked them precisely right, and the records appeared.

"That's what I did at the Sim building, and it didn't work. There must be restrictions of some kind on the campus ones," she decided.

"It wouldn't surprise me," Kirana mumbled. "Guess there's a lot to learn about these things!"

Just then, the mates heard hearty laughter and more than several pairs of feet near the entrance. They rushed over to Kirana's vantage point at the front of their residence to see if they could see who was coming. What looked to be like most of the FI group that had been playing X was approaching, including Sora and Alev.

"They must have just finished their game," Kirana guessed. By the looks of them, she could not tell which team reached the X Spot first.

"The bracelet! I'm going to go down to meet them and see if I can get a glimpse!" Nova exclaimed, hardening her gaze. "You should disable your light strings." Kirana realized that's where her head should be too.

"On it!" she called, already heading back to her strings. "I'll meet you down there when I'm done. I want to know who won," she grinned.

Before Kirana went down to the community area, she stashed the red stones up in her nook and deactivated all three light strings. As far as she knew, they couldn't be reactivated by anyone who didn't know where they led. Only she and Nova would be able to do that for the nook, even if someone tried with the other two. Everything should be fine. She still thought it was odd that Alev might be trying to see her iteration and self-assignment plans. Very odd.

She went down a level to greet everyone and found Sora was playing host again, happily floating around and providing refreshments. When she saw Kirana, she lit up.

"Kirana, guess what!" Sora sang as she fluttered over to hug her. "We won! Our team won!" Kirana smiled broadly and produced a congratulatory rainbow of glitter. The group all started talking at once, telling her what happened and the challenges they faced. Having had more classes and exposure to more things now, they said it was easier than their previous experiences when they really needed Kirana's and Kylo's help. She was glad to hear they were all progressing.

The door in the entry opened again, and Anala came in with Ravi right behind her. The group swarmed Anala like they had Kirana, but Ravi stayed in the entry, gesturing to Kirana.

"Hey!" she greeted him.

"Hey! I saw Anala on her way here and came back with her to see if you were here and still wanted to talk?" he said, speaking as if he already knew the answer. "Although, I didn't know you were having a party and didn't invite me!" Kirana turned back to look at the group in her community area. She couldn't tell if he was being serious or not, so she decided to ignore that last bit.

"Maybe we should walk?" she suggested, not wanting an audience. Ravi looked unsure for a moment, like he wanted to stay and hang out with everyone instead. "Er, I guess let's just sit outside at least. It's loud. Then you're welcome to stay for a while if you want." Kirana felt like she was bribing him. Ravi agreed with a nod and half a smile.

"Sure," he said, opening the door again. As Kirana went to follow, she saw Nova's door to her nest slightly ajar. Nova peeked out and wrapped one thumb and forefinger around her other wrist like a bracelet and shook her head. Kirana gave her a disappointed face, and Nova disappeared. As she walked out the door, she realized she wasn't sure if Nova was saying that Alev's bracelet wasn't missing any stones or that he just wasn't wearing it. Maybe he'd still be around when she was done talking to Ravi.

"That was nice of you to come by," Kirana said as they settled in the front of the residence. Ravi sat a bit too close and reached for her hand. Apparently they had different agendas for what they wanted to talk about. She started to wonder why he seemed to be walking everywhere with Anala all of a sudden and then remembered that she didn't even want to date him anyway. She shook that thought away all too easily.

"Of course! You wanted to talk to me earlier, so I came as soon as I could," he said, giving her hand a little squeeze. It actually felt nice, and they glowed so much. They were a bright bubble of golden light together. Kirana decided that for now, holding hands was okay. She *had* told him it was okay after all. Just not all the time. "So what did you want to talk to me about?" He leaned in a little closer.

"Light strings!" said Kirana quickly. "We never actually got to talk about it. I wanted to know what you found out." Ravi's face went a little blank. "Remember you and Kylo did some research on them a while back?" she prompted.

"Oh yeah," Ravi said, leaning back again and making a face as if he was thinking. "I thought you were all good with light strings since we took them on our date," he said, looking confused. Kirana tried not to show what she was thinking and slowly repeated what had happened.

"When we played X, we took a light string that previously had a white-out box on it. Remember when it disappeared? You went to the archives and then went to see if it was still there or not on your way to do some research on your tablet." Kirana looked for any signs of recognition.

"Yeah, yeah of course," Ravi said. "But I already told you what I found out, remember?" This time, he was the one looking like he was trying to hide what he was thinking. "… about how light strings hold records of who has used them and when?" he said, as if intending to jog her memory.

"But," Kirana sputtered, "is that all? I thought there was more. Have you pulled up any records on the light strings we used? Was the white-out box still there when you went back? Do you know if records can be changed?"

"Changed?" Ravi asked, the look of confusion back. "I don't know about that. I haven't actually looked at any records. Only the Guardians have the ability to do that."

"You're sure?" pressed Kirana.

"Yeah, that's what the text said." Ravi shrugged. "Are you alright?" He leaned in a bit closer again—though not as close this time—which Kirana appreciated. She nodded.

"Yes, I guess I just thought there was more information," she sighed. "So, the white-out box was still gone when you got back to it?"

"I don't really remember. That was a while back, and everything is fixed now, so it's all okay anyways! No need to stress," he said, moving his thumb on the back of her hand rhythmically and smiling at her. Something about it rubbed Kirana the wrong way. She wasn't stressed, and she couldn't understand why he was so excited to talk about the light strings before, only to act uninterested now. She realized they weren't getting anywhere.

"Let's go back in," she rasped, trying not to show her disappointment and surprise at how this conversation she'd been waiting a long time for ended up unfolding.

"Are you sure?" asked Ravi. "It seems like there might be something else on your mind."

"I'm sure," Kirana said, taking a deep breath and giving him a genuine smile. Ravi caught eyes with her and held her gaze as he slowly kissed her hand.

"Okay," he whispered, "then let's go." They stood up and went inside. The room was joyful and buzzing. Anala and Alev were in their own blazing bubble, and Kirana tried to nonchalantly see Alev's wrists, looking for a bracelet. She didn't see one, but maybe it was tucked up under his sleeve. She couldn't tell. Ravi caught her staring at the couple and pulled her close to whisper something in her ear. "That could be us," he said. Kirana blushed, which Ravi took the wrong way. He grinned. "You're so cute," he said, thinking the blush was indicating that she wanted to be that close with him.

"No, I was just..." Kirana started to say, then trailed off realizing she'd have to explain more if she said what she was looking for. The miscommunications needed to stop. "Actually Ravi, I don't think we should go on any more dates for a while." She clamped her free hand over her mouth, realizing she had just said that in public and hoping that nobody had heard her. About twelve more things entered her mind that would've come out and made things so much worse if she wasn't clamping her mouth shut. Ravi gave her a funny look.

"What'd you say?" he asked, as if he definitely heard her wrong. Kirana realized that nobody else seemed to be paying them any attention.

"Sorry," she said, pulling him over to the side just in case. "I just really need to focus on everything that's going on this iteration. I still want to hang out and have fun with you, but let's not make it about dates and couples for now. Can we go back to being friends?" Kirana looked at him with pleading eyes.

"Of course!" he said, much to Kirana's relief. "It's all good! We're friends, and there's nothing to stress about." He was smiling at her, but didn't let go of her hand. She gently released his grip, and he looked down at their hands and back up at her, still smiling. "Oops! I didn't even realize that was still there. Your hand just feels like home for mine." His eyes twinkled at her, and then he settled himself in the middle of the chatter and fun in the community area of her residence, leaving Kirana to wonder if he actually understood her at all.

Chapter
Twenty Six

The semester was rapidly coming closer to its end. Finals were coming soon, and Kirana expected to hear that the pods would be fully completed almost imminently. Ravi had been distracted with another group in their Seeds classes lately, which Kirana did not mind because it took the pressure off. She and Anala had still been sitting with each other and exploring together, though the work was heavily individual for this quarter. It was only as private as each individual wanted, and sometimes it helped to talk each other through ideas.

"I'm kind of stumped," Anala said all of a sudden. "I've almost finished everything else, but this one is tougher."

"Go on," prompted Kirana. They were sitting together under a canopy of lush green, listening to a background of tweets and twitters of all kinds of creatures in the Seeds building. Anala sighed.

"Okay, so one of my Internal Development themes is Not Jumping to Conclusions," said Anala slowly, as if she could come up with a plan before she had to say it. "I'm quick, I get answers before others and I respond in conversations before others have even finished a sentence. But more often than not, I didn't actually understand what was being said.

I mean, I understood it from my lens, but not theirs. Once I slow down and loop back to see from their perspective, there could've been a completely different—and significantly better—response." She thought for a moment and Kirana stayed quiet, reading in Anala's face that she wasn't done considering her task. "But how would I do that? What situations can I build into my experience that would be significant enough for me to grasp the lesson and improve?" This time, she turned to look at Kirana, who took it as a sign that she wanted input now. Kirana considered the situation.

"Can I share an example from my list? Maybe that will help spur something in your mind for yours," she suggested. Anala nodded. "One of my themes is Creating Balance. I used to use Finding Balance, but as I thought about it situationally, I know I'm ready to push it a little further. To find something just meant I was looking for an option that already existed, or I was choosing to trust myself to know how to respond appropriately in different situations. Being that Trusting Myself is a theme I've taken with me for a while, I decided to combine those two to give me space for Creation. My Creating Balance theme is more like..." Kirana paused for a moment, and this time it was Anala's turn to quietly give her space to think. "It's being in situations where it looks like there are only black and white options and being able to make something out of the gray. Or when a situation presents as a 'this or that' decision, creating a third option to satisfy both. Or getting stuck between a rock and a hard place on either side and knowing to look up." Kirana glanced towards Anala. "Does that make sense? I don't know if that helps." Anala's eyes were wider than normal.

"Yeah, I think it did. For my theme, it shouldn't be about *not* doing something, but about looking at it almost in the inverse. I think my theme needs to be around Being Empathetic. Having situations where I won't understand others unless I look at things from their perspective from the beginning. I'll need to learn how to connect with all kinds of different backgrounds and viewpoints, keeping my own opinions as opinions instead of facts. Flexibility of Mind, might be a good add-on." Her face was one of concentration, and then it broke into a smile as she looked at Kirana again. "Thanks! This is definitely getting me on the right track."

"I'm glad it helped!" Kirana acknowledged. She preferred sharing examples from her own experiences than outright giving advice because it provided all the necessary context for why she may have chosen what she did. Sometimes explaining how she solved problems seemed to help others solve their own without them even needing outside advice.

"Well, I think that might be as far as I'm going to get for now," said Anala as she reached over Kirana to grab her bag. "Excuse my reach!" As she stretched her arm, the sleeve of her sweater came up a bit, revealing a bracelet of red stones. Kirana nearly choked on her gasp. "Are you okay?" Anala said urgently, looking at her closely.

"I just breathed in funny and choked on nothing," Kirana said in a strangled voice.

"Oh, I hate it when that happens!" Anala sympathized. "Sure you're good?" Kirana cleared her throat.

"Yes, wow, that was not fun. But hey, cute bracelet! It looks like your flame stone!" Kirana prodded. Anala touched the bracelet and smiled.

"Yes! Actually it was Alev's, but he said that he lost a couple of stones from it so he restrung it smaller, and then it didn't fit him anymore. But it fits me!" she laughed.

"It's really beautiful," Kirana said sincerely, debating momentarily in her mind if she should tell Anala about the stones. "Well, I have good news for you then! I actually found two pieces of stone in our community area! I didn't know what they were from, and they were so pretty, so I just brought them to my nest." Anala wasn't really reacting in any sort of way. "I'll bring them down to you when we get back," she added quickly. Anala shrugged.

"Keep them! The bracelet is the perfect size for me now, and I'm sure Alev won't mind since he thinks he lost them anyways," she insisted. "I think he said it was fire agate, containing the quintessence of fire. They should suit you well too." Anala smiled brightly. "Make earrings, and we'll match!"

"Thank you!" Kirana said, sending Anala a small mauve puff of mist. They both finished gathering their things and headed towards the exit together.

"Wait! One moment, please!" they heard someone calling after them. It was Guardian Beck. As they turned to walk towards her, she came rushing up to meet them before they barely took two steps. "Sorry to keep you; I've just been notified that there will be an announcement in the Grand Hall. Everyone needs to meet there shortly. You may have time to get back to your residence and leave your things if you wish, but please join everyone there as soon as you can." As soon as Guardian Beck was sure they understood, she jetted off to continue spreading the news. Anala and Kirana looked at each other with surprise.

"Everyone?" Anala questioned. Usually Orientation was the only time that everyone came together. After that, announcements were given by class.

"Interesting," Kirana murmured. They turned back to the exit and made their way out of the building where they saw Kylo exiting his Guides building next door at the same time. Kirana lit up. "Kylo!" she called. He saw them and came sauntering over.

"Hey, mates!" He pulled both of them into a rough hug at the same time, one in each arm. "Haven't seen you in a while now!" He paused, glancing around. "And where's Ravi?"

"Er, he's been hanging around with another crowd pretty much since we split groups," Kirana informed him. Kylo looked surprised.

"Oh?" He seemed puzzled but didn't say anything else about it.

"Are you headed to the Grand Hall?" Kirana asked, changing the subject.

"Yep," he confirmed. "Apparently it was a last second decision. Guardian Alder was trying to catch everyone by the door."

"Same in our building with Guardian Beck," Anala said, nodding. They continued on towards the Grand Hall quietly for a moment. Kirana broke the silence.

"How's your class going over there with Guardian Alder? Are you ready for finals?" she directed at Kylo. He appeared to be considering very hard how to respond. Finally, he gave them a little window into the Guide's sessions.

"We've actually been doing a lot in the Sim buildings and starting on Communications," he said, as if he didn't want anyone else to hear.

"What?" Kirana said in a much louder tone. She realized her outburst and lowered her voice to continue. "What do you mean? Are you skipping Internal Development altogether? You're really ahead." She was a little concerned about what that meant for her. He confirmed her fears.

"We'll be leaving before you," Kylo admitted. "We still have so much work to do and not a lot of time left. But not to worry!" His big grin came back, and he looped his arm around Kirana's shoulders. "We've still got the same location, remember?" He winked at her. It did help Kirana to know that that hadn't changed.

When the three of them reached the Grand Hall, many were already inside. They filed in and found seats while Kirana scanned the crowd for Nova. A few moments later, she spotted her and Tali along with two others who Kirana assumed were Tali's mates. She tossed a small gold spark in the air towards Nova and caught her attention. The four of them made their way quickly to get seats nearby. Guardian Nika was walking onto the stage by the time they sat down, so introductions would have to wait. They gave each other smiles and small waves. Kirana thought she saw a certain glow in Kylo's eye that she'd not seen on him before and followed his gaze to one of Tali's mates. She looked back at Kylo and poked him. He quickly snapped out of it.

"What, are we starting?" he said, looking to the stage. Kirana giggled.

"Have you met her yet?" she asked him. Lucky for him, there was no time to answer because Guardian Nika started speaking.

"Thank you all for joining us on such short notice. As you are all aware, we've had many changes happening across campus and across groups in preparation for this iteration, and we want to tell you again how much we appreciate your work and your dedication as you volunteer for these self-assignments." She gave the room a small bow and the room fizzed orange sparks in response. "We just have a short announcement that is worth it for everyone to be aware of, and then we will dismiss those of you in the FI classes." She took a breath. "Because there is so much work to be done and we are rapidly coming to the end of this first semester, we are going to ask that everyone remains on campus during the break in case we need to reach you."

There was a small ripple of surprise that went through the crowd, but no dramatics. Kirana, Anala and Nova all made eye contact. Looks like their mate's trip was off. Guardian Nika continued. "Those of you in the First Iteration group do have an exception, although we understand from Guardian Cosmo that many of you have asked to stay anyway. Any other concerns or issues with this should be brought to the Impressions Office as soon as possible."

"Does that mean Sora already knew about this?" Kirana whispered to Anala next to her. Anala shook her head and mouthed, "I don't know."

Guardian Era stood from his seat in the front row and began to move towards the stage as Guardian Nika finished her announcement.

"Thank you, FI group. We deeply appreciate you and your passion and excitement. You are now dismissed, and we ask everyone else to please remain in their seats as Guardian Era makes his way up for some additional announcements."

A small buzz erupted in the room as various groups got up to head towards the exit. Kirana tried to spot Sora in the crowd, but hadn't seen her by the time everything became quiet again and Guardian Era began speaking.

"Well, first things first, yes?" he said, trying to get the crowd a little more energetic. "The pods are ready!"

CHAPTER TWENTY SEVEN

Kirana was trying her very best to make sure she did not have another flash-out and miss any more big announcements. She was over it. It was annoying, and besides, she couldn't help but feel like there were eyes on her. The Grand Hall was full though, so that couldn't be avoided, she guessed. So far so good anyway, as Guardian Era talked through some details about how they would get assigned to their pods. She already had great insight into how they worked, thanks to Nox, so this part was definitely not overwhelming.

Kylo, next to her, seemed distracted though. He kept fidgeting, which really wasn't like him. She took a peek in his direction and caught his eye. Just knowing that someone else was noticing his movements immediately made him stop. Kylo liked to keep his reputation as someone who was steady and reliable. He never let anything phase him. Except now. Kirana had a suspicion as to why. She grinned and then realized she wasn't paying attention! Guardian Era seemed to be giving a small history on how they operated in previous iterations and how the pods would change things.

"—given us a great opportunity to be even more efficient, which is growing ever more important. However, this does come with new challenges that we have not had before, so please be sure to find a Guardian, or Nox, if you experience anything odd," Guardian Era was saying. Kirana shook her head as if to get herself out of a daze. How had she missed Nox being on stage? When did that happen? It made sense that he was the point person for the pods. Guardian Era thanked Nox, and he went to sit back down again in the front row. She was sure that he caught her eye for the briefest of moments. Now she was the one who was squirming.

"What this also means," continued Guardian Era, "is that residence mates will remain the same for the most part. Instead of the constant shuffle every iteration as some come and go into different classes and such, the pods allow us the opportunity to keep mates together." The crowd really liked this. Hands went up in the air and gave a silent cheer in multicolored sparks. Guardian Era looked pleased.

"What we've seen from the FI class recently has led us to consider opening residences just for them, starting next iteration with the newest group of course, to orient them and let them build bonds as a larger group." He nodded satisfactorily. "Now, one more thing." The room stilled. "Most of you have heard at least parts of this, but let me explain the details to everyone. The graduating class has been split into Guides and Seeds for some time now, and this is giving us the opportunity to provide larger teams for our Seeds as they take on their self-assignments. As Guardians, we are always available to help Seeds as much as we can, but in this critical time, having the opportunity to provide dedicated teams to each individual is very exciting. According to the self-assignments, Seeds will be provided a team of 2-3 Guides."

Kirana did not want to miss a word. She knew some of this, but not all! She worked to squint her widened eyes and took deeper breaths to calm herself. Then she felt eyes on her again. From across the room, it was unmistakably Guardian Cosmo's eyes. He didn't look away when they connected eyes; he didn't even blink. Something stirred in Kirana. She sat up straighter and made sure he could see the determination in her face. She felt far from having a flash-out now. He finally looked away.

"It's important to note that currently there are not enough Guides to partner as a 2:1 with Seeds, and we are working tirelessly to provide opportunities to those of you who are not yet in the graduating class but would like to take that step to help support a Seed this iteration. We know that it will disrupt the plans you have already been working hard on for your current iteration so we are trying to reach out as soon as we possibly can. That's why we ask that everyone stay here on campus during break." Guardian Era glanced around the room, gauging how the room was taking in what he had said so far. More so than not, there were positive murmurs and excited whispers fluttering around the room. He continued.

"Those not yet in the graduating class who decide to support a Seed will be referred to as Jr. Guides. Their role will be performed a bit differently than those who are. As such, pods are still only reserved for the graduating class, to be clear. Once we have the full group of Jr. Guides, training will begin immediately in the building that the graduating class has vacated. You may keep your current plans and set them aside to be used for the following iteration, if you so choose." He paused. "How is everyone doing? I know there's a lot of change and a lot of information, but can we keep going?" The room sparkled. Everyone was more than ready to keep going. "Excellent. I think we'll let Guardian Gaia take over from here for a bit, shall we?" Guardian Gaia was already moving on stage, practically spinning as her voice surrounded them.

"I am so excited to be a part of this iteration," she gleamed. "You are all so valued, and I'm delighted to support your next steps." She gathered herself a little bit and the swirling calmed down. "You may have heard that Guides will be leaving quite a bit earlier than Seeds to begin their self-assignments. This is necessary to provide a sort of on-the-ground support, we'll call it. To account for Guides leaving earlier, the classes in the next two quarters will be swapped. As soon as finals are turned in, each Seed's information will need to be made available to their Guide team as it is built. Then after the break, we will be moving straight into Communications, which as you know, includes Contracts and Teams. Simulations will be completed at the very end before the iteration officially kicks off. This applies to everyone here. Those in the First Iteration will follow their original course, so no need to confuse them." She gestured to Guardian Nika, and this signaled to Kirana that the information overload was coming to an end.

"Thank you, Guardian Gaia, and thank you, Guardian Era, for all of your dedication to everyone here," Guardian Nika said, issuing a wave of dark pink gratitude to each of them. The audience followed suit with their own. "I think that will just about do it for now. If you have any questions, always feel free to visit us in the Impressions Office or speak to a Guardian in class. We appreciate your time as this was so sudden and also because we are asking you all to stay here during break. Now, I have one last, very small announcement." She stopped with a grin and the anticipation was palpable. "As soon as finals are over, we are going to throw you a big party in the Dome. We will announce the theme soon, so stay tuned! Thanks everyone!" She had to close down the speech quickly because the room had erupted and nobody could hear her anymore anyway. Groups at a time began spilling out of the Grand Hall. Anala, Kirana and Kylo filed out of their row while Nova, Tali and her mates filed out of theirs a couple rows back. They all made their way to the exit.

"Okay, so no mate's trip, but we get a theme party!" Anala celebrated as they reconvened outside the building.

"Aaand," Nova said, drawing out the sound, "we get to remain mates!" Everyone looked overall happy and unstressed, even though they had just had their semester flipped over, and some would be completely starting over to be Jr. Guides. "It's cool," said Nova, "that I have two groups who are really special to me." She looked from Kirana, Anala and Kylo, to Tali and her two mates. "Oh! Introductions! Obviously you all know Tali, and these are her two mates, Celeste and Makani. And these are my mates, Anala and Kirana, and Kirana's family, Kylo." They were all exchanging greetings and Kylo was uncharacteristically quiet instead of being his usual boisterous self. Kirana was watching him, which she was sure he could feel, and it seemed to help kick him into gear.

"The pleasure's all mine; pleased to meet you," he said to Celeste and Makani, reaching a hand out with beautifully arranged colorful bubbles and making them 'ooh' and 'ahh.'

"Makani has been—" Nova stopped suddenly and looked to Makani for permission. She nodded brightly, and Nova continued. "Makani has been approached about being a Jr. Guide, and she accepted!" Everyone congratulated her warmly, making Makani blush a little. She had light eyes, and Kirana could almost see movement in them. She moved gracefully, like Sora, but in a fierce way that she seemed to be able to control. She seemed very gentle, but Kirana suspected that she could be quite forceful if the situation called for it. She'd be a great Jr. Guide.

"Whoever gets to have you on their team will be very lucky," Kirana praised her.

"Thank you so much," expressed Makani. "It really feels like the right thing for me to do right now. I'm almost ready to join the graduating class, and I think being of support in this way will be a really special step for me."

Out of the corner of her eye, Kirana was distracted by a dark figure approaching.

"Nox!" Nova called, running to give him a hug. She did quick introductions for him before he excused himself, taking Kylo with him for an "urgent matter," so Kirana really didn't get to talk to him. What she did get, though, was to feel that pull that seemed to get stronger every time he was in her presence. It was a pull towards safety. A pull towards a contented state of calm.

"Kirana? Hellooo," Anala was saying. Kirana came back to attention and laughed a little at herself. Anala continued. "Want to head back together? It sounds like these four are going to stop by their building to get a little more done since they were called out of class early." Kirana nodded, and they all whisked various "see you laters" and mists of blue to each other as they departed.

Kirana thought about asking Anala how things were going with Alev, but Anala beat her to it.

"How are things going with you and Ravi?" she asked. Kirana responded with her own question.

"Why do you think he doesn't sit with us or study with us that much anymore?" she asked. Anala looked like she might know something but didn't want to say it. She looked down before she continued speaking.

"He's talked to me a bit before and after classes when we've walked together. He thinks maybe he's stressing you out," she explained.

"So, he's avoiding me?" Kirana asked with surprise. Anala shook her head in thought.

"No, I don't think so. I actually don't know why he's hanging out with that other group in class now. But I don't necessarily think the two are related," she said. That didn't make sense to Kirana, so she waited to see if Anala would say more. "This might sound weird," said Anala slowly, "but I think there's something strange going on, and I think Ravi and Alev are both involved."

Chapter Twenty Eight

Anala and Kirana both looked around to see who was nearby and then at each other.

"Back at the residence?" Kirana said quietly. Anala nodded. They picked up their speed a little bit and started talking about other things. "What do you think the theme of the party is going to be?" Kirana asked, louder now.

"I hope it's something like the Gold Party I went to a few iterations ago," Anala responded, her demeanor completely changing from suspicious sleuth to dreamy partygoer. "I had some family who invited me, and it was spectacular! Or maybe a Once Upon A Dream bubble party!" Those both sounded amazing to Kirana, who started to glow.

"Wow, yeah! Or maybe even a Flicker Fest!" added Kirana.

"Ohhh," Anala cooed. Both of their eyes were lighting up thinking about costumes and how much fun it was going to be. "You know what, we can definitely use this party as a replacement for our trip. Honestly it might be even better!" she remarked. "We can plan outfits together and get ready together and everything!"

The mates were practically skipping by the time they reached their residence. The building was sort of an unmoving, dark blue. As they went inside, Sora was there waiting for them. She was rather opaque and not as light on her feet.

"Hey," she said hesitantly. "I'm so sorry I didn't say anything."

"What do you mean? Are you talking about how we won't be able to take the mate's trip?" Anala asked, as both she and Kirana moved closer to Sora to hug her. She nodded.

"I didn't know for very long, but I didn't want to be the one to have to tell everyone, so I kind of avoided you all. I'm really sorry," Sora said in a quiet voice, with less bounce.

"No no no, you have nothing to be sorry about!" Kirana assured her. "We were disappointed at first too, but I guess they forgot to tell you about the party?"

"Party?" Sora perked up.

"Yes! That is, if you decided to stay on campus. They told us at the very end of the announcements that they would be throwing a party at the Dome to make up for asking us all to stay!" Anala reported. Sora was turning transparent again.

"So, you're not upset with me for not telling you?" she asked carefully.

"Of course not!" Kirana promised her. "We were surprised, but I definitely understand that it's not fun to be the bearer of bad news. Besides, Anala and I were just talking about how much fun it will be to get ready together and plan our theme outfits and everything. And Nova is excited too! Wait—" Kirana paused. "Do you think you're still going to leave for break? We would definitely understand if you did and—" Sora stopped her.

"No way! I'm staying out of solidarity for you, because maybe you'll need me? And also because I want to take this as seriously as everyone else! Actually most of us in the FI class are planning to stay on campus," she told them.

"We definitely need you," confirmed Anala, giving her a gentle squeeze. By this point, Anala and Kirana had infused their party excitement into Sora, and she was back to her poised, floating self. Pleased that everything was back in order, Anala asked Kirana if she wanted to study in her nest with her for a bit. Kirana knew it was just to avoid making Sora feel excluded as they talked about the topic from earlier. She agreed, and Sora happily made her way back up to her own nest, feeling relieved.

Kirana hadn't spent any time in Anala's nest, so she was looking forward to experiencing her design. As they entered, there was a warped curtain of warmth that they walked through. It was pleasant, like a hug. The floor was a stunning marbled look of oranges and yellows that flickered up the sides of the room, which was rather circular. It was sectioned off with more curtains, which gave a hazy, curving, distorted appearance, allowing the spaces to be mostly separate but without doors or specific entry points of any kind. Anala walked Kirana through another curtain into an area with lounges that looked like moving lava.

Anala sat in one and gestured Kirana to another. As she sat and stretched out on the lounger, she discovered the movement to be warm and massaging. She was instantly calm and relaxed.

"They're nice, right?" said a grinning Anala.

"Wow," was all Kirana could say in that moment. Anala laughed. They reclined in silence for a few moments, and then Kirana turned to look at Anala.

"What did you mean when you said you think Ravi and Alev are involved in something strange?" she asked. Anala swallowed.

"Well, it could just be my perspective, so take it with a grain of salt, but there seem to be some small oddities going on. I didn't really think anything of most of them, but when I put them all together, something seems off." Kirana waited for her to explain further. "For example," Anala began, "Alev started wanting to hang out with me here. Like, here in our residence specifically. We used to go out a lot, but more and more, it seemed like he wanted to be here. It was fine, but looking back—" she shook her head and didn't finish her sentence. "And then with Ravi, all of a sudden he always wanted to walk with me. Like, he always acted like he came by to look for you and then just walked with me instead, but then he'd ask me so many questions about you." She eyed Kirana and confirmed, "Don't worry, I never really told him anything he wanted to know, but it was just a little weird. I feel like the two of them are up to something," she concluded. Kirana was silent, wondering if she should tell Anala about the light strings. She knew she had to.

"Did you know that I had light strings in my nest?" she asked, aware that this would seem like a complete change of topic to Anala. Understandably, she looked confused.

"No..." Anala responded. Kirana continued then.

"I wasn't going to tell you this because I didn't want you to think that I didn't like Alev or something, but I have a light string in my nest that connects to the community area." She was watching Anala for any signs of recognition or insight, and she didn't find any. Yet. "I have recently learned that light strings hold records of who has used them and what the circumstances were. I pulled up the records on that particular light string and—" Anala's face was showing now that she was terrified about what Kirana was about to say. Kirana lowered her voice and spoke more gently. "I saw Alev's name on the records. He's been in my nest."

Kirana had never seen Anala get upset. She seemed to burn at her core, with waves of red flowing from it.

"You could have told me!" she quickly said to Kirana, confirming that she was not upset at her. "I can't believe he thought he had the right to use me to get to my mate... for, do we know what he was doing in there?" she asked. Kirana shook her head slightly, then stopped.

"Not entirely, but I have a theory. It looked like he was looking for something," she explained.

"What's your theory?" Anala prompted.

"I think that maybe he was looking for my journal. The one that describes my iteration plans in detail," she said. "Though I'm not sure why someone in their first iteration would care at all about that information," she mused. Anala thought about this for a moment.

"Well, that actually sounds like some of the things Ravi was asking me about too," she acknowledged. "I thought it was weird but since I didn't tell him anything, I didn't really think to tell you. I just thought maybe it was because he liked you and was trying to find ways to be closer to you? That sounds silly when I say it now. Plus, he's kind of ignored us in class lately. It doesn't make sense," she finished.

"No, it doesn't," agreed Kirana. "Are you going to confront Alev? I'm sorry, I know you are so good together, and I don't want it to affect anything."

"You're not the one affecting things. He is. And yes, one hundred percent I will be talking with him. This is a matter of trust, and he's broken mine." Anala went from upset to sad. Her fire turned soggy and her flicker, weak. Kirana reached for her hand.

"And I'm going to talk to Kylo. When I talk to Ravi, it doesn't go anywhere. I think Kylo will have better insight into what's going on. Especially because he is mates with them," Kirana encouraged. Anala nodded.

"I'm sorry about Ravi," she said. Kirana shrugged.

"I like him better as a friend anyway, if I'm being honest," she admitted.

"I thought it would be so fun that we would be dating mates," Anala said. "I didn't really think that maybe you and Ravi weren't connecting the same way as Alev and I were. Sorry, I guess I've been in a bubble."

"No need to apologize for that!" Kirana assured her.

"Well anyways, I think the bubble has burst," Anala said, looking like some anger had resurfaced.

"Let me know if you need anything," Kirana said pointedly to her. "And I will let you know what I learn from Kylo." Anala nodded.

"Thanks," she said weakly. Kirana got up to give Anala some space and as she was walking out of her nest, Anala called after her.

"Have you added restrictions to your light string?" she asked.

"No, but I've disabled them. Do you know how to add restrictions?" asked Kirana.

"Yes!" Anala declared, getting up as well. "Twist the light string at the source, and hold it until it blinks. That should do it." Kirana had tried twisting it before but didn't hold it very long at all, so she hadn't discovered it. "That will restrict it to allow only you to use it. Since the light strings are your personal ones, installed by you, you don't need to do anything else. If you want someone else to also be able to use them, both yours and their hands need to be on it at the same time, and you can do the same motion. Twist and hold it together until it blinks."

"That's great, thank you!" Kirana exclaimed. She passed a frosted peace bubble to Anala as she saw Anala pick up a note that was sitting on a small table and drop it to the floor. "Are you ok? Want me to stay a bit longer?" she asked Anala.

"I'm just not sure I can trust him at all anymore," Anala responded. "Like, was any of this even true?" She picked up the note she had just dropped and showed it to Kirana. It was a little poem. *You're my fire, ever true, burns so bright, it's only you.* There was a little flame drawing next to it.

"Did Alev write this?" Kirana asked. Anala nodded. Kirana gave her a hug. "I'm sure it was true. Just talk to him." Anala nodded again.

"I will," she said quietly. "But yeah, I'm okay. I just need to think about how I'm going to bring this up. I'm sure he'll be happy to come back over here to talk," she said, rolling her eyes.

"Let me know if you need anything," Kirana said again. They smiled softly at each other, and Kirana left to add restrictions on her light strings immediately. As she worked, she brought up the mental image of the note she had seen in Alev's handwriting. At least they could eliminate him from their investigation of the notes that she, Nova and Nox had found. The handwriting was not a match.

CHAPTER
TWENTY NINE

When it came time for finals, Kirana was ready. Just as with midterms, she was confident and ready to turn in her plan for her self-assignment. It took a lot of work, and she was happy with the results.

Anala had been slightly more sullen lately, but oddly enough, Alev had been so busy that they hadn't had a chance to get together and talk yet.

Sora was glowing and excited to finish her first semester, and Nova was still hoping she would get approached about being a Jr. Guide.

"Mates," Kirana addressed them—all gathered at the entry before leaving for their respective finals—"good work so far, good luck, and when we get back, we're celebrating!" They all threw glittering energies of various colors up in the air to rain down over them, and Sora scampered off first. Anala and Kirana left Nova at Tali's and then continued on to their class building.

The Green building never actually became green on the outside, although it did turn a little more cloudy white in color like the map originally showed. The White building didn't change either, though the name actually made a little more sense for it. When they arrived, it was relatively quiet, and Guardian Beck was smooth and calm. She handed each of them a tablet, and they arranged themselves around the building to work on filling in their official plan. All of their notes and everything they had been working on would be combined in their file on the tablet. Typically, only the Guardian of their class would be able to access their file in order to best support them during their self-assignments. But this time, there were multiple Guardians, plus Guides and Jr. Guides that would all have access. Kirana suspected that she may have up to seven different witnesses to her plan, not including herself. It made her just a touch more self conscious to make sure that she was clear and that her ambitions and plans were thorough enough.

Kirana went over everything three times before she took a deep breath and hit the submit button. A green screen came up that said, *Thank you for your submission. A Guardian will be in touch shortly.* She got up and stretched as she looked at the screen. It was a little different than she was used to. Typically, the screen color didn't change and there wasn't a note about a Guardian getting in touch. She assumed it must be due to her being in the graduating class. She gathered her things and walked towards the exit with the tablet. Guardian Beck was waiting there to receive it.

"Thank you, Kirana," she said with a big, kind smile. "Go enjoy yourself for now. Being that you'll be here over break, someone will reach out to you soon for a meeting."

"A meeting?" Kirana asked. That was new. Guardian Beck nodded.

"Your screen turned green, correct? You may qualify for a special assignment opportunity. Of course, it is always your choice whether you take it or not, and it will be discussed with you in detail first."

"Oh," Kirana said, a little surprised. "Okay! Thank you, Guardian Beck. See you later then." She put her hands together with a dark pink glow, dipped her head and made her way to the exit. *How curious*, she thought to herself as she went back to her residence, making a mental note to ask Anala if anything happened to her screen too. She decided to make a quick stop on her way back to pick up a little something special for her mates to celebrate their progress. She was the last one of her mates back at their residence. The building was gold and actively glittering. She smiled as she entered.

"Kirana's here!" Nova called towards the community area, which was looking pretty full. Sora and several others from the FI class were there, as well as Tali, Makani and Celeste, along with Anala and Nova. She glanced around, curious if Alev and Ravi would be there. Anala seemed to pick up on who she was looking for.

"Apparently Alev, Ravi and Kylo are all coming by soon," she said with a knowing look in her eye. "This might get interesting." Then Kirana remembered the last time they all showed up together.

"Oh no, are we going to be subject to another weird dance show?" she groaned, laughing.

"We better not!" agreed Nova. "I'll keep them locked out if I see those costumes again!" she teased. Kirana joined everyone in the community area where they were playing the most joyful waves of sound, making everything vibrate in the most satisfying way. Kirana went to the center of the room to the fireplace and covered it to make a table of sorts. She set something down on the top. As interest started to grow around her, she made an announcement to the room.

"I got this for my mates to celebrate getting to this point, but sharing it with even more of you makes it that much more special." She smiled brightly. She knew she must be glowing solidly from within as everyone around her seemed to reflect it right back. She pushed a button on the disc she had placed on the makeshift table. A hologram appeared with two Beings who began to dance and twirl together. It was a perfect match to the melodic notes her mates already had playing, and everyone watched the hologram, entranced with the ebbing and flowing of the movements. When the dancers stopped moving, they both put an arm upwards and created a sparkling banner that read *Congratulations!*, and then everything dissolved into gold glitter. The room loved it. Sora brought out more refreshments, and everyone just enjoyed themselves.

Between the two semesters was often when the celebrations occurred. It was common for self-assignments to start up at different times during the second semester, so this was the moment when everyone was still aligned, the planning phase mainly over, and the training, fieldwork and actual self-assignments yet to come.

Their residence became more and more full, and then there was a knock at the door. Mostly everyone had just come in, so this knock stood out a little bit. Sora skipped over to open the door. As she did, the room turned dark. So dark, in fact, that everyone quieted down and looked towards the entryway. Lasers of light entered the room in fantastic colors and sequences that evoked sounds from the crowd in appreciation of the display. Kylo, Ravi and Alev entered the residence and the lights sparked, glittered and jumped around the room, sending dazzling colors in every direction. Their light show ended with a flourishing vortex of lights, swirling and spiraling before dropping away under their feet. As the room regained its normal light, everyone cheered.

"We've upgraded our surprises," Kylo said, smirking at Kirana, who was cheering along with everyone else.

"That was incredible!" she squealed in response, along with several others. Kirana didn't know when it happened, but somehow their residence had become the official party place, and she loved it. Some were dancing, some enjoying refreshments and some engaged in lively chatter. She finally sat down on some cushions in the corner, and Kylo joined her soon after.

"I need to talk to you soon," he said.

"And I need to talk to you!" Kirana returned. They smiled and nodded at each other, both knowing it wasn't the right time and place. "Well, we have a break from classes now, so it's a good time to catch up," she added. Kirana saw Anala across the room, looking slightly strained as Alev appeared to be joking with her. Alev still didn't know that Anala was upset, and he was just thinking everything was normal. Anala spotted Kirana and made a beeline over to the corner to them, with Alev following close behind.

"Just need a bit of a buffer for now, until we can talk in private," Anala whispered to Kirana before Alev could catch up. Kylo's face changed like he heard her as well. The four of them sat and discussed their finals briefly before Kirana turned to Anala.

"Hey, what did the screen say after you submitted your plans?" she asked her. Anala thought for a moment.

"I didn't really pay attention. Something like, *Thank you for your submission*. Why?" Anala, as well as Kylo and Alev all seemed to lean in for the answer. Kirana suddenly felt a little uncomfortable.

"Your screen didn't change color?" Kirana asked Anala, trying to just look directly at her and ignore the other two. Anala shook her head.

"Change color? No. Nothing happened to the screen," Anala confirmed. Kirana didn't say anything else, hoping she could get away with it, but Kylo and Alev appeared highly interested.

"You got the green screen," Kylo guessed, not phrasing it as a question. Kirana looked at him, eyes darting quickly to Alev as she noticed his intensity on her, and then back to Kylo.

"Yeah, do you know what that means exactly?" she asked him. Kirana noticed how light Kylo's eyes were in that moment. He looked at her in a certain way, *like, with admiration*, she thought.

"You'll find out soon," Kylo said, beaming at her. Alev, on the other hand, jumped up and announced he had to go do something and practically ran out the door. Anala looked shocked. "Not one for subtleties, that one," muttered Kylo. "Sorry Kir, I'm going to have to go too. We'll catch up soon. Lots to talk about." He smiled at her again and gave both her and Anala hugs.

"What just happened?" Anala asked Kirana after he had gone. They both laughed.

"I'm not exactly sure," responded Kirana quietly.

CHAPTER THIRTY

After everyone had gone, the four mates sat together in the community area, glowing and happy.

"Nova, how did your finals go?" Kirana asked her. Nova was reclining back on a lounger, looking upward. She didn't answer right away. "Nova…" Kirana said in a lower tone. "Did you—" She didn't finish her sentence. She knew the answer. Kirana sat up, and Nova finally looked at her.

"What did she do?" Sora asked. Kirana wasn't going to say anything. That was Nova's story to tell. Anala was quietly listening, looking interested but not surprised.

"Okay, don't worry. I've been working with Nox a lot!" Nova finally said. Kirana looked like she was about to jump up or scream or something, but she remained still, waiting for more. Nova lowered her tone quite a bit and said, "I don't think I'm ready for another iteration right now." That's when Kirana accepted what she had done. She had foregone her finals. She didn't turn in any plan for the iteration, and now Kirana was worried that she would be leaving campus.

While it was common to be on different schedules, with some taking a break after tough iterations and then returning later, they may not return at all. Or schedules may overlap, as some self-assignments took longer than others. Like with Kylo. He had a shorter iteration, came back and prepared for his first iteration in the graduating class and completed that self-assignment all before the current moment that aligned Kirana's and Kylo's schedules again. That's how Kylo had entered the graduating class an iteration prior to her.

He said his iteration was tough too, Kirana was thinking. *And now he was going to be a Guide.* She still didn't really know what that meant, but the system seemed to be expanding to allow for a sort of break after a tough iteration while still allowing those that wanted to volunteer in some way to do so. This helped put it in perspective for Kirana.

"Does Nox know of other assignments you can take? So you can stay?" Kirana asked her with pleading eyes.

"I'm not going anywhere," Nova responded fiercely. This made Kirana smile.

"Okay," she breathed. She hoped Nova would find a way to stay. Only Nova was stubborn enough to do it, and it helped to have Nox on her side.

Sora seemed unperturbed, and Anala a little relieved herself. Kirana wondered if Anala already knew about Nova's decision. She didn't ask the question, but Anala answered it anyway.

"I knew she'd been working with Nox, but I didn't know the details," she said to Kirana.

Just then, the sound of tinkling chimes could be heard from the entryway. The mates all turned towards the entry to see swirling ribbons of shimmering silver and shiny black twisting and falling on themselves in circular patterns. As they fell to the floor, a large, silver envelope appeared on top of the pile of ribbons.

"The party!" Nova said, catching on first. She jumped up and went to pick up the envelope, bringing it back to the community area. All four mates crowded together over it. "Who wants to open it?" Nova asked excitedly. Everyone looked at Kirana; she didn't know why.

"How about Sora?" she suggested. "This will be her first party! They don't do this every iteration you know." There were grins and nods of approval, so Nova passed the envelope to Sora who took it with shining, crystal blue eyes. All four of their names were written in silver looping letters on the front. She carefully pulled the tab to release the note from the envelope.

"To our dearest colleagues, shining volunteers and all those who work tirelessly for the betterment of us all," the note spoke in Guardian Nika's voice, "we hereby invite you to this iteration's Shimmering Horizons Ball to celebrate your growth and personal evolution. Prepare to stun in shades of silver and black, and let yourself be dazzled by mirrored decor and reflective art installations where you will both lose yourself and find every missing piece, all at once. We look forward to seeing you there." The note sizzled then, and it popped in Sora's hands, leaving behind a flourish of silver specks that reflected their faces for the slightest of a moment. Sora squealed with delight, and they all jumped up and down in anticipation.

"What should I wear?" Nova asked to everyone and no one, already twirling about as if she was at the party.

"We have to find silver and black!" said Sora, already concocting something elegant in her mind. Kirana noticed Anala was not quite showing as much excitement as the rest of them, though she knew she was excited and assumed maybe she was thinking about Alev.

"Since this is kind of a replacement for our mate's trip, do we want this to be *our* event?" Kirana hinted to the group. Nova caught on quickly.

"Like, nobody brings dates, and we go together as just the four of us? I'm in!" she confirmed.

"Love it!" agreed Sora. Everyone looked to Anala, who actually seemed a bit relieved at the prospect.

"That sounds perfect," she said. They all cheered and sprayed silver flecks around the room.

"Where do we even start?!" Nova asked. "Should I go sleek? Or really get into the ball gown look. It is a Ball after all. What are you going to wear?" Nova turned to ask Kirana directly, who laughed and shrugged. Obviously she didn't know yet, and Nova had moved on to Sora now anyway. "Sora, you would look amazing in all silver!" She gasped. "Or wait, all black! No, Anala in all black." She framed her hands around Anala and squinted an eye.

"Okay, Nova is going to be my stylist. I'm leaving that decision up to you," Anala told the room, laughing.

Another small chime came from the entry. All four heads turned quickly to look. A gold light string appeared with a note attached. Nova was quick. She bounced over and read Kirana's name. When she flipped the card over, it was a summons from Guardian Era and Guardian Gaia. Nova looked like a mix between excited, nervous and confused.

"Why are you being summoned?" she asked Kirana.

"Oh, that's probably related to my finals. When I turned it in, there was a message at the end that said a Guardian was going to be in touch," Kirana explained. "This is kind of a lot though."

"Was that the green screen that Kylo mentioned?" Anala asked. "That made Alev jump up and leave?" she added under her breath.

"What?" pushed Nova, looking at Kirana.

"Yeah," Kirana nodded. Then she paused, feeling like this was turning into a big deal, but she didn't even know what *this* was. "When I finished my finals, the screen turned green and said a Guardian would reach out soon. When I asked Anala if she got that too, it was in front of Kylo and Alev. Alev jumped up and left in the middle of the party, and then Kylo ended up leaving too. Although I'm not sure if it was related."

"For Alev, it seemed related," Anala reflected. Sora, who had been quiet, had a look of concentration on her face. Then she spoke.

"Alev hasn't been hanging out with us as much anymore. I thought maybe it was just because he was with you," she said, indicating to Anala. Now Anala looked surprised.

"I haven't seen him much lately either," she said quietly.

"That's odd," said Nova, "but Kirana, I think you might need to get going. They even sent you a direct ride." She gestured to the light string. Kirana hesitated for just a moment. Nova got the hint and did a quick check on it. "It's a gold one anyways. Standard issues are harder to mess with because they have less capability," she reminded her reassuringly. Having a random light string pop up in one's residence was not a common occurrence. Kirana nodded and took the light string in her hand.

"Alright, wish me luck," she said to her mates. Everyone responded at once.

"You've got this!"

"Let us know how it goes!"

"We'll be here waiting for you!"

Kirana took a deep breath and jumped on the light string. It was smooth and quick, and she landed directly in Guardian Era's office.

Both he and Guardian Gaia were already seated, conversing quietly. They smiled as Kirana arrived.

"Welcome, Kirana," Guardian Era began. "You may have a seat wherever you'd like." Kirana moved towards the hammock seat she had sat in last time she was here, and then changed her mind and chose a circular seat with several cushions. It was even more comfortable than she was expecting. It added to the peace she felt in this office. Once she was settled, Guardian Era spoke again.

"I had a feeling that we might be having this discussion. You've been on our radar," he told her. "I've reviewed your files, and you do indeed qualify for a special self-assignment." Seeing her blank face, Guardian Gaia jumped in.

"Are you aware of what your green screen indicated?" she asked Kirana gently. Kirana shook her head no. Guardian Era and Guardian Gaia exchanged glances.

"I had forgotten this was your first experience in the graduation iterations and that you might not have known," admitted Guardian Era. "It's not common for someone to qualify so soon. But you certainly have a fantastic profile for this. Kirana," he said, changing tactics, "why did you decide to join the graduating class, and why did you join the Seeds group?" Kirana thought for a moment, wanting to answer correctly.

"I wanted to join the graduating class because I—because I think it might be important. I mean, I think I can be important to the cause. I think I can help," she finally got out. Guardian Era nodded.

"And the Seeds group?" pressed Guardian Gaia.

"Well, I knew what I was signing up for, for the most part anyways, and so it just seemed obvious that I would continue on that path," Kirana said, looking back and forth between them to try and pick up more clues as to why she was here.

"According to your file, you're brave and stubborn and don't believe in good intentions," Guardian Gaia said with half a grin. Kirana assumed she was asking her to explain.

"To intend to do something is not the same as doing it. You can intend all you want, but if it's not followed through on, what worth does it have? I measure trust by actions. Not intentions," she explained. Guardian Gaia considered this.

"I understand, and I agree for the most part," she said, "though I might offer that you learn to extend a bit of grace in this area as you go into your new self-assignment, or you may experience some unnecessary difficulty." Kirana considered this, not entirely certain how she felt about it. Guardian Gaia seemed to notice this. "Try thinking of intention like a direction. If someone intends to do something, that is their compass. That is the way they are trying to go. Sometimes they don't always get there. Maybe there were stormy conditions or the path was fraught with holes and challenges." Kirana was listening intently, and it was starting to make sense.

"I think I understand," she told Guardian Gaia. "I'll try," she promised. Guardian Era nodded in approval and took the conversation straight to the point.

"Kirana," he said, "we'd like to offer you an opportunity." It was quiet in the office for a moment. "This would be on top of your plans that you've already organized, but we would provide you with extra guidance as well. You would have three Guardians available to you should you need them, potentially four with me involved as much as I can, though I do have my hands full with this iteration's other group. We would also build a team of Guides specifically for you and your assignment." Kirana was still not entirely certain why there was so much fuss over this.

"Okay," she said simply. The Guardians looked at each other.

"You do not have to take it," Guardian Gaia reminded her. "But we do think you can complete this assignment, and it will definitely have an impact that will provide a huge boost to our overall mission." Kirana nodded confidently.

"I understand. I can do it. I'll do it," she said.

CHAPTER THIRTY ONE

"Well then," Guardian Era said, leaning back in his chair and closing Kirana's file. "Thank you, Kirana, we look forward to helping you along your journey to achieving what you set out to do. It's almost like your intentions are all spelled out right here." He winked at her. Kirana blinked back.

"Fair enough," she admitted with a smile.

"Alright then," Guardian Gaia said in a caring tone. "We appreciate you, Kirana." She was looking her straight in the eye. "And you won't be alone in this." Kirana nodded and sent a small blast of mauve sparkles.

"Thanks to you as well—for your support and for helping all of us do these things," Kirana said earnestly. "Does Guardian Beck know?" she asked, suddenly realizing her most recently assigned Guardian wasn't even there. Guardian Era nodded once.

"Yes, don't worry. She will be updated on your plans for your self-assignment as well as your team, as necessary," he responded. "Now, you are going to return to your residence by the same light string you took here, please, and bring this note back with you for your mate, Nova." He handed her a summons card, just like the one she had received. She took it and looked at Guardian Era with questions in her eyes, but without asking anything out loud. Guardian Era said nothing in return, and gestured to the light string. "Thank you, Kirana," he said, indicating that it was time to leave the office. Kirana took the hint and hopped on the light string.

When she got back to her residence, her mates were still in the community area discussing dresses and designs and possibilities for the Shimmering Horizons Ball. There was animated talking as she arrived. She expected to get bombarded with questions as usual, but this time, there were none. They all waited for her to enter the room, their attention glued to her.

"Did you plan a dress for me yet?" Kirana asked, trying to break the odd tension.

"Word travels fast," said Nova. Kirana stared at her, confused, until Nova pointed to a pile of notes stacked on a small table.

"What's all this?" asked Kirana, still holding the summons for Nova from Guardian Era. She picked one of them up from the pile with her other hand. It was handwritten with her name on it. Nobody hand wrote anything except for on very specific occasions.

"Your green screen," said Nova. "I suppose they all assumed that you accepted the assignment." She paused and leaned forward. "Have you?"

Kirana flipped the note over. It read, *I always knew you were special. I'm here to support you in any way you need. Don't hesitate to reach out!* Kirana looked up at her mates, then back down to the pile of notes. She was not intentionally ignoring Nova's question, she was just a little baffled. She picked up a second one and flipped it over. *You've got this! Way to be a leader!* She picked up a third. *Congratulations! I know you'll pull it off.*

"Did you all see these?" she asked her mates. They stared at her. Obviously they did. "I mean, of course you did," she chuckled at herself.

"Yeah, I—so I *did* accept it." As soon as she said that, all three of her mates jumped up and hugged her.

"You're going to be great!"

"I can't think of anyone else that could be a better option."

"I'm so proud of you."

Kirana laughed. That had been the original response she had expected. "Thank you, really, thanks for being the best and most supportive mates I could've possibly ever been given!" She hugged them all back.

"Hey, why is the light string still here?" Sora asked all of a sudden. "Is it just going to disappear at some point or something?"

"Oh! Nova," Kirana said, turning to face her. Nova's face turned a little pale. "I have something for you." She held the summons out to her. Nova took it with shaking hands and flipped it over. "Nova, what's wrong?" Kirana asked. "You don't think it's something..." she trailed off, not wanting to say it out loud.

"Well, I did fail my finals after all," Nova said in a very quiet voice.

"It's going to be okay," Anala assured her, rubbing her arm. "I'm sure of it." Nova nodded tentatively and started taking very small steps towards the light string.

"We'll wait for you, Nova!" Sora called behind her, sending white peace bubbles to her. Nova took them gladly and gave them a wavering smile.

"You're the best mates," she said, and she hopped on the light string.

"Okay, you two need to fill me in on what I missed with the party planning talk!" Kirana was hoping to both lighten the mood in the room and distract herself at the same time. Sora immediately took the bait.

"Ahh, I can't wait!" she said. "We have a whole dress scheme idea for all four of us. I'll be in a smooth, shiny, silky, silver gown with black feathers in my hair," she gushed. "Nova is going to be in mostly silver too, in a shorter gown with reflective pieces all over it, each framed in black. She'll have dazzling strings of gems that hang down from her waist to the floor and accent one of her shoulders. She thinks you and Anala should both be mostly in black."

"Especially you," said Anala. "She says you're made for gold, so we've been trying to find a way to sneak some gold into your look. Kind of hard to do at a silver and black party!" she laughed.

"What are you thinking about wearing?" Kirana asked Anala.

"I've always wanted to wear a big dress. Something with a lot of volume in the skirt. So I'm thinking about a silver strapless bodice, covered in silver crystals, and then a smooth, black skirt with a lot of fabric that twirls when I do!" Anala demonstrated with her arms out at her sides, imagining the skirt was flowing out under them as she spun. When she stopped, she looked at Sora. "Should we tell her our plan for her dress? Or wait until Nova's back?" Sora looked ready to burst.

"Let's tell her!" she squealed. Anala laughed.

"Ok, you go ahead," she said. Kirana was excited to hear what they had come up with, and there was no way Sora was going to be able to wait.

"We think your dress should be shorter, like Nova's, and soft." Sora's voice made it sound dreamy. "A stretchy fabric that is luxurious to the touch. It will be super black, but with dimension and covered in silver flecks like stars. Imagine the shimmer when you move!"

"It sounds lovely," praised Kirana.

"What we're trying to figure out is how to incorporate some gold. Maybe you could have some gold jewelry or add some gold dust to the silver flecks in some areas, but I don't think we've quite figured it out yet," Anala added. "Nova says it's a must," she giggled.

"I trust her," said Kirana, laughing as well. "We'll figure it out." Kirana began randomly shuffling through the notes from the pile on the table. "When did these arrive?" she asked absently.

"Oh, they keep coming," Sora said nonchalantly, like it was the most normal thing to happen. Almost as she said it, another note seemed to flutter down out of nowhere, landing haphazardly near the pile. Kirana looked up, surprised.

"I actually wrote one of these notes before for someone I knew a while back that got a green screen," Anala remembered. "I had no idea how it got to her, so this is interesting to see.

"Did she also accept the assignment?" Kirana asked.

"Yes, she did. And from what I remember, she accomplished it in her iteration," Anala confirmed. Somehow that made Kirana feel better, which was weird, because she hadn't realized she was feeling anything but fine.

"Well, is she still in the graduating class? Maybe I can talk to her," Kirana suggested.

"She had been in the graduating class for many iterations at that point, I'm pretty sure," said Anala. "I think she's been off campus for quite some time now."

"Ahh," Kirana sighed, then carefully, she shifted topics. "Anala, when do you think you'll be able to talk to Alev?" Sora turned to look at Anala too. Anala looked guilty.

"Admittedly, I haven't tried very hard to reach out to him," she began. "But it's also true that he hasn't really messaged me much either. Always saying he wants to stop by but he can't or that we'll see each other soon and stuff. He made it sound like the FI class had a lot of work, or he had a big project or something. Does that make any sense to you?" she asked, directing the question to Sora.

"No," Sora said slowly, trying to think of what he might be working on. "He hasn't even been to all our classes to be honest. Sometimes he's just not there lately. And sometimes he comes in late and stays in the back, kind of away from everyone." Something popped into Kirana's head.

"Is Guardian Cosmo always there?" she asked.

"Yes, he's always there. Why?" asked Sora, confused at the connection.

"Do you know what it means to do a split-energy?" asked Kirana back. Sora thought about this briefly.

"Like when someone is in two places at once, sort of," she concluded. Kirana nodded.

"Yes, they literally split their energy and can exist twofold," she confirmed, "though with half of their energy in each direction. It takes a lot of practice, but it's possible to get really good. Do you think Guardian Cosmo is doing that?"

"Hard to say," said Sora. "He seems like he's always the same." Kirana had a strong hunch that he had probably been doing split-energies the entire semester. "Although," Sora said haltingly. She looked at Anala. "That kind of makes sense for why Alev looks so weird on the days he comes in late."

"What do you mean?" asked Anala curiously.

"He has so much excess energy around him… that's part of what makes him Alev. But on the days he comes in late, he's not really like that. He's thinner. He's like, half of his energy? It's weird to say that, but it really does seem that way now that I think about it. He stays in the back, further away from us, so it's hard to tell sometimes." Sora stopped talking when she saw Anala's and Kirana's somewhat horrified faces. "What?" she asked in growing alarm.

There was a knock on the door, and they all jumped. Anala got up and opened the door. She came back with Kylo.

"Hey!" Kirana greeted him.

"Hey, Sunshine," he said with a smile, but without his usual exuberance. "I think we've got a lot to talk about," he said, surveying the room with the new gold light string and the pile of notes. Kirana nodded. Everyone in the room seemed to have momentarily forgotten the conversation about Alev.

"Nova's not back yet, so I don't want to go far," Kirana said. Anala and Sora took that as a clue and got up. "No, you don't have to leave!" she insisted. They both smiled and continued heading towards their respective nests.

"Let us know when Nova gets back?" requested Anala.

"I definitely will," Kirana told them. Kylo sat down next to her, and they took a moment to settle and regroup.

"So," Kylo said, "where do you want to start?"

CHAPTER THIRTY TWO

As Kirana and Kylo were sitting in the community area of Kirana's residence, notes continued to appear, congratulating her on her self-assignment opportunity. She was ready to get answers for so many different things, but she wasn't sure where she wanted to start.

"I think," Kirana proclaimed, "that this conversation should be as light as possible. We need refreshments." She got up and brought back some leftover items from their party. She and Kylo got comfortable again, turning on the fireplace and the low hanging globe lanterns around the room. It felt like a cozy holiday. Kirana smiled. "That's better," she declared. "Can we go back to the light strings first? I know it's weird, everything was so long ago, but I didn't get answers." Kylo furrowed his brow a little.

"I thought you talked to Ravi, no?" he asked her.

"I did, and he didn't tell me anything I didn't already know. He acted like it was old news and was wondering why I was talking about it at all," she said, remembering how that conversation had gotten a little uncomfortable.

"Well, you can ask me anything you want," confirmed Kylo. Kirana looked down to think. Now that she had the chance, she wanted to clear these things up in her mind once and for all.

"The day that we played X and discovered the broken light string to the Gravity Sim Building," she stated, setting the scene, "you took the navy string and discovered it went to the Dome. That's when you ran into Guardian Era and told him about the broken string, which he came to fix it later." Kylo was nodding, waiting for a question. Kirana continued by asking, "What else happened when you went there? You were gone for a while, and then when you came back, you left to do some research on your tablet." She finally stopped, and Kylo actually started by answering an unasked question.

"The light string wasn't cut, Kirana," he explained, jumping right to the point. "It was burned." Kirana stared at him, trying to understand what that meant. "I suppose Ravi didn't share this bit of information, did he," Kylo said, stating it as fact. Kirana remained silent, so he continued. "Sometimes when someone is doing a split-energy, they can burn themselves out. Kind of like your flash-outs actually! It's sort of the opposite though. In your case, you reach a max capacity of energy and flash, bringing yourself back to stabilized energy. If someone pushes themselves too far while doing a split-energy, they can deplete it so much in the opposite direction that they have a burn-out. It appears that someone was taking that light string and had a burn-out while on it." He paused for a moment to gauge Kirana's thoughts and level of understanding.

"So, the string broke, but what happened to—" she didn't seem to want to complete the sentence.

"What happened to whoever was doing the split-energy?" Kylo asked for her. Kirana nodded, so he answered. "I think it was all kept quiet, but as far as I'm aware, whoever it was is alright. Being that only half of their energy was affected, they just needed a fair amount of recovery time and were likely sent off campus to do so. I don't know who it was," he said, before she could ask.

"How do you know they're alright though?" Kirana pressed.

"When I took the light string to the Dome, I saw them," he said.

"Them?" asked Kirana, realizing he was referring to more than one.

"Guardian Cosmo was there with two others from the FI group. I've had a suspicion for a while now that he is intentionally trying to teach some of them to do split-energies." Kylo didn't want to purposefully hide any information from Kirana, but he also didn't want to create suspicions or distrust if he was mistaken. "I don't really know what his motive is, but maybe it's none of my business. Guardian Era was nearby, also dealing with the situation. That's how I was able to notify him that you were guarding the light string." Kirana's mind started to fill the holes she had in the story to make it complete.

"When someone is about to have a burn-out, might they have a red mistiness around them?" she asked Kylo.

"I'm not sure," he responded. "But that sounds feasible. Actually, that sounds likely," he amended. "Why? Have you seen someone like that?"

"Yes, when Nova and I were on our way to check the source of these notes we found, we were walking opposite Guardian Cosmo and someone from the FI class. We hid behind the building, and when they got closer, Guardian Cosmo saw us. I pretended to have a flash-out, but we saw that whoever it was with him had a red mist around them. Guardian Cosmo sent him away and then made us go to Guardian Era's office." She stopped, realizing she didn't think Kylo knew about the notes. He surprised her.

"Nox told me about the notes. But Kirana, you didn't actually have a flash-out that day?" Kylo asked, looking happy for some reason.

"No," she said, a little confused as to why he would know about it. "Nova and I faked it because something seemed suspicious. We were hoping they wouldn't see us at all."

"You should tell Guardian Era," Kylo said matter-of-factly. He didn't explain further on that topic. "Any other questions about light strings before we go to the next thing?" he asked her.

"Just the white out box that disappeared. I want to know what happened," she said.

"I think it was a fluke. A mistake. A dangerous one at that," he confirmed. They both silently breathed in gratefulness that nothing had happened. Kirana shook it off.

"Oh! Yes, more light string questions." She cut straight in. "Any idea why Alev has been using my light strings to go into my nest and look through my things?" Kylo's eyes went dark and stormy.

"I better have heard that wrong," he growled. Kirana told him about how she had discovered how to read the records of use on the light strings and watch the holograms. She also told him which light strings Alev had used and how he even tried to cover his tracks in the records. When she noticed a cloudiness that had cropped up in Kylo as she had been talking, she quickly added how she had already put restrictions on the light strings so that it would not happen again and sent him some white peace bubbles. They only seemed to mix in at first. He glowered for a moment and then finally regained some clarity. She saw it pass over his face like a realization.

"What did you just think of?" she asked curiously. Not wanting to hold back anything while they had the time to clear everything up, he told her what he was thinking.

"It's just a hunch, but I think Alev has been working on doing split-energies with Guardian Cosmo. I don't think it necessarily would have been his choice to do that. I think he's being used somehow. But for what, I don't know," Kylo mused. Kirana nodded.

"We were just talking when you got here about that exact thing," she said. Kylo's eyebrows shot up, so she continued. "Sora has seen him looking oddly smaller when he comes into class late and sits in the back. He's been avoiding them a lot. Avoiding Anala too for that matter." They both caught eyes with each other and had the same thought.

"It's almost like Guardian Cosmo has been burning out his students, and Alev is the next potential victim. He has so much energy that he's perfect for it. But why is he doing this? What does he want?" Kylo asked rhetorically. Then turning to Kirana he asked her, "What was he looking for in your nest?"

"I'm not certain, but I think he was looking for my journal with all my iteration plans," she explained.

"You did just get a green screen," Kylo mentioned. "What if he was looking for those, but for somebody else?" Kirana thought they were starting to get an idea of what might be going on. "Kir," Kylo said, "any other big questions before I take off? I think you gave me just as much information as I gave you, and I need to talk to Nox." Now all Kirana wanted to ask about was what Nox's involvement was in all of this, but she shook her head.

"I don't think so," she said, "although I'm probably forgetting something at the moment."

"No problem. I'm going to touch base with you more often, okay? Sorry we've been so busy. Er, sorry *I've* been so busy. I'll take the responsibility on that one," Kylo said, standing up to give Kirana a hug. She stood up, and he grabbed her and spun her around, making her laugh. "Good to see you!" he proclaimed.

As Kirana walked Kylo to the door, Nova appeared next to them coming off of the light string from Guardian Era's office.

"Nova!" she said, "You're back! Let me tell Anala and Sora." While she called to them that Nova was back, she saw Nova whispering something to Kylo. She assessed that Nova looked fine, not upset or anything, so she hoped everything went okay. Anala and Sora showed up quickly.

"What happened?" asked Anala for all of them. "Is everything okay?" Nova hesitated.

"Yes, I mean, I think so. I hope so? I have to talk to Nox before I can say anything," she said, the slightest uncertainty showing through. *Why did everyone need to talk to Nox?* Kirana was wondering. She saw Nova watching her face as if she could read the question that Kirana was thinking. "I'm going to go with Kylo now," she said. "Since he's going to meet up with Nox too," she added quickly.

"Okay," said Anala, looking just as confused as Kirana felt. "Well, let us know if you need anything."

"I definitely will! Thanks all!" Nova blew them kisses and Sora returned the favor. Kylo didn't say anything else, just gave a wave of blue fizz, and the two of them walked out the door.

Anala, Sora and Kirana stood in the entryway for a moment.

"What do you think her meeting was about?" asked Sora. Kirana shook her head, not coming up with an answer. A new note floating down caught her eye, and the notes that she and Nova had found popped into her head. *The handwriting*, she thought.

"Hey," she said to Anala and Sora. "If you're not busy, do you want to help me with something?"

"Of course!" Sora responded.

"What do you need?" asked Anala. Kirana explained to them then about the notes. She didn't have them anymore, but she had copied them into her journal. Her copies might still help them identify who wrote them.

They all sat down, split the stack of notes and began looking through them. Every once in a while, it looked like they might have a match, but it was more of a match to Kirana's forgery of the notes than the real things. She didn't think they had matched the handwriting in any of the notes they currently had.

"Well, thanks anyways," she sighed, feeling defeated.

"Let's keep this stack over here," said Sora, placing them on the book-case near where Kirana's light string was, "and then when more come, we can keep going through them."

"Good idea!" agreed Anala. Kirana smiled in agreement as well, but couldn't help but feel unsatisfied somehow. She felt so close to putting together the whole puzzle, yet just as far as before at the same time. And how did Ravi play into all this? Maybe he didn't at all. But he hadn't even talked to her at the party.

"You look like you just decided something," Anala called her out.

"Yeah," Kirana said. "I guess I did. I'm going to confront Ravi. I need some answers."

CHAPTER THIRTY THREE

As Kirana made her way to Ravi's residence, she tried to focus on her body rather than her mind. What the ground felt like as she took a step, how her foot rolled from heel to toe, the way her arms hung at her sides and moved with her. Sometimes, being in her body took the pressure off, and her mind could process without her involvement. She didn't know if Ravi was going to be there, but she had to try. This wasn't a conversation she wanted to have at the upcoming party, and then when they were back in class, it was going to be very busy with her Communications schedule, especially with her new assignment addition. It just needed to happen now.

As she approached the residence, she noticed the galaxy on the building was still set to the graduation iterations' destination. She took it in with appreciation from afar and stopped to look at a few close-ups once she was near the tiles. It was amazing how just one universe held hundreds of billions of galaxies, and each of those galaxies held hundreds of billions of solar systems with multiple planets in each one. And somehow, it was narrowed down to one particular location where she would visit. She wanted things resolved here before she left.

She knew Kylo wouldn't be there, because he and Nova had gone to see Nox, but Ravi and/or Alev could be. She took a deep breath and knocked on the door. When Ravi finally cracked the door open, Kirana was sitting on the step facing away from it, thinking nobody was there. She turned as he spoke.

"Kirana! Hi!" he said, sounding like being chipper was straining him. "How're you doing?" He hesitated in the doorway, as if he was unsure if he wanted to come out or invite her in.

"Hey, Ravi, I think it's time we talked, don't you?" Kirana said, friendly and polite, but serious.

"What do you want to talk about?" he asked, still not moving either out or in. Kirana stood up and faced him.

"Us," she said. "Why we don't hang out anymore, why you avoid Anala and me in class, why you didn't tell me about the light strings—" she stopped herself, realizing she was attacking him in a way. "Look, I miss you, and I miss how we used to be. We're getting so much closer to starting our iteration, and I have a lot on my plate. I really want to have your friendship back." She dissolved, just a little bit. That got Ravi's attention. He took a step towards her.

"I thought you didn't want to," he responded.

"Didn't want to be friends?" Kirana clarified. "Ravi, what's really going on?" He sighed like he was weighing his options.

"Fine," he said finally. "Let's talk. Do you want to go up to the roof?" He opened the door wider for her, inviting her in. They walked in silence up the three levels to the roof. They went over to the ledge overlooking the campus where they could see their class buildings and all the pods. Kirana hadn't been up here since Kylo had shown it to her before she knew what those buildings were. As they gazed out over the view, Ravi softly placed his hand nearer to hers on the ledge, but not touching. She could feel him looking at her. She turned to him, giving him a small smile and put her hand out like he had done when they met. He grinned and when he put his hand up to hers, they enjoyed the shine that illuminated the roof.

"That doesn't get old, does it," he said, sounding more like his normal self again.

"How have you been?" Kirana asked.

"Good! Yeah, good," he responded. "You?"

"Good! I've been busy with finals. Now that they're over, I'm looking forward to the party before we have to get back to planning the iteration. It's kinda cool that we'll have teams, don't you think?" She was trying to get him to say more. If he kept acting like a brick wall, this conversation wasn't going to go any further than the last one did. Obviously, giving him space didn't work, but all he did in response to her question was nod. She looked down, deciding whether or not to give up.

"I thought we might set up a contract or two together," she admitted, "for this iteration. Like, I thought we'd be connected somehow since you're not going to be all that far away." He was quiet for a moment, then stayed on the same path of playing like nothing was wrong.

"Won't we?" he said, not following it up with anything else. Somehow the sadness turned to anger in Kirana.

"You know what, forget it," she said. "This isn't working." She turned and started walking towards the door, ready to leave and make Ravi a stranger.

"Kirana, wait!" Ravi snapped back into action. "Hey," he said, catching up to her and lightly touching her hand again. "Okay, I'm sorry. I'll talk. I just—," he paused. "I think you're going to hate me." He looked down and then said in a quieter voice, "But I guess you hate me now already so it doesn't matter anymore." He gave her a pleading look.

"I don't hate you," Kirana declared, but she didn't smile or offer anything else.

"Let's sit?" he offered, holding an arm out towards the clear chair that she had ridden with Kylo. She didn't say anything, but she did move over to the chair and sit down expectantly. He got on as well, and it began to float along the path of their rooftop. They were quiet for a moment until Kirana raised her eyebrows at Ravi.

"Right," Ravi said, scratching the back of his head. "So, you know about the light strings?" he said, sounding guilty.

"I know a lot about the light strings, no thanks to you," she said. "But what exactly are you referring to?"

"Alev asked me to do it, and first I told him no, but then Guardian Cosmo got involved, and I just thought it would be easier to avoid you, both of you, and maybe we could still, I don't know, maybe once all this was over, we could still date." He finished his rambling rather tentatively, bordering on awkward. Kirana stared at him, trying to figure out what to address first.

"Alev asked you to do what, exactly?" she demanded. Ravi thought maybe she just wanted him to admit it out loud, so he huffed a little as he spoke.

"To change the record on your light string. I'm sorry," he said. When her eyes grew big, he realized he had it wrong.

"You knew he was sneaking into my nest? And you covered for him?" She stood up, making the chair rock. She went from surprised to angry and then to betrayed. "And you didn't tell me, you just avoided me entirely. You did something to me and made me feel like I did something wrong," she squeaked out. Ravi went from golden to ashen. He crumbled in front of her.

"Kirana, I—" he started and then stopped. Now he realized how much he screwed up. "This was never supposed to go like this." He put his face in his hands. "I didn't want to do it, Kirana, I promise you. I told Alev no, I did. Then Guardian Cosmo summoned me, and I didn't think anything of it until he asked me to change the record. I couldn't tell anyone. He was going to find an excuse to kick both of us out of the program." He waved his hand back and forth between the two of them.

"He was going to get *us* kicked out of the program?" Kirana reacted. "How?"

"He didn't say. I'm sure it was just an empty threat. He said Alev was too important to this iteration and couldn't get in trouble for accidentally taking a light string into someone's nest," Ravi explained.

"Accidentally?" Kirana blurted out. "Ravi, he went in three times. That wasn't an accident. He was digging through my stuff." This time Ravi looked surprised.

"He must have watched me clear his name and then did it on his own after that," Ravi mused. "So wait, I thought you knew. I thought Alev told Anala who then told you. I know Alev and Anala aren't talking right now, and I thought if I stayed away for a while, maybe it would all blow over. I also thought he only did it once, by accident." They both sat quietly, contemplating this new information. Ravi spoke first.

"If his name was cleared from the records, and Anala didn't tell you, how did you know?" he asked.

"There was an earlier record. Maybe the very first time he entered my nest was actually a mistake, but that record didn't get cleared. And when you told me that day after class about how those records existed, that's when I found it. And even if the name is changed, the hologram shows the entry. I checked all of them and found him entering. Actually, Nova found them for me," she explained. Ravi was shaking his head.

"I didn't know, Kirana." He looked her directly in the eyes. "I thought it was a lot less than this, and even then I thought you'd be upset. I never wanted to—" That's when something flipped in Ravi. "What was he doing? And why does Guardian Cosmo care about what's in your nest?" he asked, putting two and two together. His reaction made Kirana feel just a tiny bit better, like they were on the same team again.

"I don't know," she whispered, suddenly feeling tired. Ravi was looking hard at her.

"May I?" he asked, and she looked up. He wanted to sit next to her instead of across from her. She nodded. He moved and carefully put his arm around her. He felt warm, and the brightness between the two of them felt like it would rebuild their energy. Slowly but surely, it seemed to work.

"I'm really sorry," Ravi said again, "about all of this." Kirana could tell that he meant it.

"I accept your apology," she said. Ravi brightened. His voice turned mischievous, and Kirana began to feel like things might be able to turn back to normal.

"Did you know that this little path has another setting?" he hinted with a gleam in his eye. She shook her head.

"What do you mean," she stated flatly, rather than asking.

"Do you trust me?" he asked, then winced, hoping it wasn't too soon to be asking that. Something passed between the two of them, and she understood his sincerity.

"Yes," she said quietly. He smiled big and touched something on the other side of the chair where he had been sitting before.

"Hold on," he said, and the chair began to move faster. It was like riding on a light string. It moved up and down and tilted them to the side at one point, doing a spin in another. They went around a few times, and then it slowed down to a stop where they had originally got on. They were laughing, smiling so big it hurt. It had been the final healing touch they needed. Kirana and Ravi were happy, bright and joyful together. It felt good to be back.

"So, you mentioned you're going to the party?" Ravi asked her once they had gone back to the ledge of the rooftop.

"Yes," Kirana responded. "Since my mates and I couldn't go on our trip together because we had to stay on campus, we decided to go to the party together as a group." She stated this clearly, just in case he thought of asking her to go together. "Are you going to go?" she asked him.

"I wasn't sure if I was, but it could be fun," he said nonchalantly. "Especially if I can run into you all there. You're a really great group." Kirana smiled.

"Yeah, I got very, very lucky," she agreed.

"I'm going to make up for everything," Ravi said suddenly, surprising Kirana a little with his determination. "I'm going to fix this." Kirana wasn't sure how to respond and decided maybe a response wasn't necessary. Ravi walked her out, and she was glad she had come by. As she started to head back to her residence, she tossed some golden flecks to Ravi.

"See you at the party?" she called back to him. He sent her golden orange sparks in return.

"See you at the party," he confirmed with a twinkle in his eye.

CHAPTER
THIRTY FOUR

Nova's news about her summons was going to have to wait. All of them were back at their residence, and it was time to get ready for the party. If anyone had walked by their building at that moment, they would've seen swirling silver dust creating patterns across a matte black background. Everyone was getting dressed, doing their hair, accessorizing and doing spins around the room. They had all found nearly exactly what they had been looking for.

"Sora," gasped Kirana, "you're stunning! I've never seen someone so elegant!" She was as graceful as ever, floating in a long, silver silk dress. She had a headpiece with black feathers that stood out dramatically, and the black that was lining her ice blue eyes was striking. Sora herself was glowing crystal clear and gave them a twirl. Nova was doing Kirana's hair, and neither of them were dressed yet.

"Here," smiled Nova. "Let me add a little bit of this." She reached over and sprayed something in Sora's hair to smooth what was already smooth. "It'll add shine!" she said. Sora looked pleased.

"Anala!" Nova called towards her nest. "Almost ready for you!" She kept working on Kirana's hair, and soon Anala joined them, already dressed. She had exactly what she wanted. She wore a gorgeous gown with a silver jeweled top that glittered with every movement. It was like a play on her natural flicker, taking advantage of that energy. The skirt was full and very twirlable. She added large glittering earrings that went perfectly with the ensemble.

"Oh, wow!" they all complimented her.

"And we'll do something a little fiery with your hair!" said Nova. "Alright," she said, turning to Kirana, "I have one last surprise for your hair, but go get dressed, and I'll come up and add the finishing touch after I finish Anala's." Nova had done very little with her own hair, except for parting it in the middle and adding silver head jewelry that was decorated with strings of crystals and one slightly larger piece that fell on her forehead. It matched the strings of crystals that were hanging on her dress and decorating her shoulder.

"Okay," responded Kirana, "but put your dress on first! I can't wait to see it!" Kirana got up and headed up to her nest. Her dress was luckily so comfortable. Stretchy, black, soft material. One might describe it as matte, but someone else would see it as shiny. It had so much depth and dimension somehow. The silver sparkles that covered it looked like they were popping out, with more coming along behind in the distance. Someone could float right off into space staring at her dress too hard. She easily slipped into it and went to add some golden flecks to her eyes as Nova had insisted. "Nobody else is doing gold, Nova," she had complained. "It's a silver and black event."

"Nobody else is you," Nova had responded, as if that was some kind of reason that made any sense. She settled to wait, but it didn't take long. Nova showed up quickly, taking the light string from her nest.

"Nova!" Kirana breathed. Nova's fully silver dress was covered in the hanging crystal strings that made delicate, tinkling sounds when they bumped into each other as she moved. One could almost catch their reflection in the many reflective pieces that covered her dress in patterns. Both Kirana's and Nova's dresses were shorter in length and closer fitting.

"It's fun, right?" Nova sang, holding her arms out and turning slowly so Kirana could see the whole thing.

"Incredible," Kirana agreed.

"Okay, I just need to add some finishing touches to you," Nova said, quickly getting to work. She brushed something through Kirana's somewhat slicked back hair that was curled up at the ends. She added a little more of the large gold flecks to her eyes and brushed something along her shoulders and collarbone as well. She stood back and studied Kirana before giving one firm nod and saying, "Perfect."

"Are we ready?" Kirana asked excitedly.

"Let's go down!" Nova expressed, with just as much excitement. They headed back to the community area where Sora and Anala were waiting for them. When they walked in, both mates just stared at first, so Kirana spoke.

"Oh, Anala, your hair! It's fantastic!" She turned to Nova. "You did such a great job!"

"You really did," Anala agreed, but not speaking about herself. "Kirana, have you seen yourself?"

"You are luminescent against that backdrop of a dress!" Sora sang. Nova was grinning from ear to ear. Kirana caught some of her reflection in Nova's dress. There was twinkling gold intertwined into her hair, bronzed golden specks across her shoulders and the additional large golden flecks on her eyes.

"I tried to tell her it wasn't a gold party," Kirana laughed pleasantly, but the looks on Anala's and Sora's faces said nobody really heard her. Kirana hooked one arm to Nova's arm and the other to Sora's, and those two both hooked onto Anala's arms so that they stood just like they had on their first day of class. This time, much wiser, much more dressed up and much more ready to party.

"Shimmering Horizons, here we come!" Nova called.

The mates took a different path to the Dome than Kirana had taken with Ravi when they went there for dancing. There were silver light strings set up all over campus to make it easy for everyone to arrive. It was a simple ride, although quite a visual masterpiece. Parts of it looked like Kirana's dress, like one was getting catapulted through space and time, and others were reflective in ways that confused the mind. Inverse, upside down, and at times, even backwards. It was an individual journey, as all light strings are.

When they had all reached the Dome, they stopped to observe the building and other partygoers entering. Just like the mates, there were combinations of silver and black, all silver, all black, and black and silver. For a moment, Kirana was self-conscious. Why had she let Nova use all this gold on her? It was probably her imagination, but as they moved towards the building, she thought everyone was starting to stare. They made it to the entrance where there were enormous doors, decorated with immense amounts of silver and black crystals that shifted and moved to greet groups as they approached. They watched as the patterns shifted to write each of their names in looping letters, allowing them into the party. Kirana's name came last, along with some extra words. It read, *Golden One*. Kirana stared wide-eyed for a moment, and it disappeared as quickly as it had appeared. She thought maybe she made it up.

"Kirana!" Nova called from ahead of her, gesturing for her to catch up. She quickly walked through the doors without looking back. Any words she might have said were stolen right out of her mouth as she entered the massive room. She wanted to exclaim something. It seemed like everybody was, but she was so stunned that she stood and spun in a circle to try, impossibly, to take it all in. It was like the light string ride, but in the form of one room. Everywhere she looked, there was something to take in. The room was so dark from the black, but so bright from the shine on the silver. The room looked endless in all directions. Sora, who had never been to the Dome at all, was breathless.

"You went on a date *here*?" she asked Kirana.

"It looked a bit different then," she chuckled. Now there were costumes everywhere. Elaborate masks, completely disguised walls, beautiful gowns and to Kirana's dismay, no gold. She felt like she was catching just as much attention as the room. When whispering started, Kirana turned to her mates, sure that she must be making it up.

"Where should we go first?" she asked them, a little anxious to move away from the entry. They did a quick sweep and saw a place for refreshments, another for dancing where the lights were playing all kinds of tricks, an area for group posing where artistic keepsakes could be created, a station where they could interact with—wait. What was that exactly? "Do you see those?" Kirana asked her mates, angling them towards what looked like a variety of reflective surfaces of all different shapes and sizes.

Some warped, some stretched, some hung diagonal and all kinds of other fantastical oddities.

"Let's go!" said Sora, leading the way. As they made their way to the Hall of Reflection, as they saw it was called, Kirana noticed a shimmering line across the room. It was so perfectly straight, and yet it wavered somehow. It seemed like an important fixture, but she couldn't really tell anything about it from there. She fixed her attention back to the Hall of Reflection. Sora was giggling up ahead at one of them, Nova covering her mouth in laughter at another and Anala was twirling her skirt back and forth in front of a third. As Kirana stepped up to a very thick reflector, she saw it was called Peacekeeper. She saw herself far away at a distance, sitting in a glamorous chair made of opaque and swirling white pearls. They looked just like the peace bubbles that Sora was often using. Her reflected self showed the splendor of the gold she was dusted with. She blinked in surprise at herself and quickly moved on to another. This one was round, and at first it looked like just a frame with no reflective piece. Then she saw the label. *Step in, to step out.* She cautiously put a finger through the frame, then a hand, an arm, and finally just ducked her head in. It was quieter on the other side. She stepped through and turned back around to see where she had just come from, and she gasped. The party was gold. Everything was golden—all the elaborate decorations, the costumes, even the reflective surfaces somehow were glowing gold light. The brilliance and grandeur was two steps beyond the silver and black party, and she didn't know how that could be possible. She turned around to see where she was. It was like a reflection of the silver party, and for a moment, she wasn't sure if she had stepped through that round reflective piece at all, because she seemed to be on the correct side.

"I'm sure I just stepped through though," she murmured. But as she looked around, it was definitely the silver party, and through the reflection, was a gold party.

"Hey, Kir!" she heard Kylo's voice call behind her. She turned, still confused. He was with Makani, and they made their way over to her. Before she could speak, he continued. "Nox is looking for you," he said smiling. She stared at him. There was something subtly different. She glanced to Makani and back to Kylo. He appeared to be waiting for a response of some kind.

"Okay," she stammered. "Thank you?" She ended up making it sound like a question. Kylo took a step closer to her. "Ahh," he said. "You should be getting back." He winked and turned her back towards the reflection where the gold party was going on. She carefully followed the same pattern as before, starting with a finger to test it, a hand, an arm, and before she stepped through completely, she turned to see Kylo walking away, holding Makani's hand. She blinked in surprise. She decided to quickly go through the reflector again, and she could just confirm from the other side if it was gold or not. She dashed through, nearly falling to the other side. She looked around and breathed a sigh of relief when everything was silver and black. The reflector just looked like a frame.

"There you are!" said Nova. "We're going to go into the maze! Want to go?" She pulled Kirana through the Hall of Reflection, pointing out different ones she had tried. "Oh, that one was so funny. You'll have to see it later for sure!" Kirana shook off the daze and hurried to keep up with Nova.

"Where is there a maze?" she asked. Nova stopped suddenly, and Kirana almost ran into her. There were tall columns of silver reflectors, some clear and some opaque, creating an angled path that they could see twisted away somewhere beyond their line of sight. Sora and Anala were at the entrance.

"There!" said Nova. "C'mon!"

CHAPTER THIRTY FIVE

K irana's mates had already slipped inside the maze. She could hear laughter and the tinkling of Nova's dress. She caught glimpses of them sometimes as she tried to keep up, but she wasn't sure if they were reflections or if she was seeing them through clear sections. Kirana made her way carefully with her arms out in front of her to keep from walking into walls. She was getting used to the crooked path, until it split into two. She looked down one way and down the other, and they essentially looked the same. Someone else came by and briefly paused at the split next to her.

"Which way should I go?" Kirana asked pleasantly.

"Where are you trying to get to?" the other asked her in response. She realized she didn't know. Maybe there were multiple exits?

"I'm not sure," she told them.

"Then it doesn't matter!" the other called back to her, already disappearing down one of the paths. Kirana shrugged. *Good point,* she thought to herself. Several others streamed by her, all down that same path. Kirana took a step in that direction too, but her curiosity got the best of her and she ultimately took the path the others had not taken. It appeared to have a good amount of clear panels at first, and she tried to get an idea of where she might be going or get a glimpse of any of her mates. She saw movements of silver and black all over, but it was disorienting. Even through the clear panels, she might be seeing a reflection from a completely different side through it. Gradually, there were more and more reflective panels. She encountered a room in the shape of a dodecagon. It was circular, but used twelve panels of reflectors contributing to that shape. She didn't immediately see another exit, but turned around slowly in the center of the small room and saw every angle of her reflection.

"Wow," she said aloud, as she allowed herself to appreciate the full effect of the gold in her hair and the depth of her dress.

"Wow, indeed," someone agreed, stepping into the room.

"Ravi? Where did you come from?!" she exclaimed. She didn't immediately go for a hug, and neither did he. He had chosen to wear mainly black as well, being another bright one that would do better at a gold party too. He wore a simple black mask covering half of his face. "You look great!" she told him.

"But you," he responded, "you look magical." He reached a hand out to her, and she responded, anticipating the glow that they were used to creating together. What they didn't anticipate was the magnitude of the twelve reflections of the glow. As soon as they connected, the shine that ensued blinded her, making her jump back and cover her eyes. As the glow dissipated, she opened her eyes again.

"We don't even know our own strength," she laughed to Ravi. She looked around, finding herself in the pathway again. She must have stepped back enough to leave that circular room. "Ravi?" she called quietly, stepping forward into the reflective room again. All she saw was herself, twelve times over. Even behind her.

"Wait a second," she said to no one. Where she had just stepped in from had closed into another panel. She gently touched it, and it moved silently, revealing a path. She quickly touched every panel around the room, and every single one opened to a path behind it. "Okay, well, guess it's just me again," she spoke to one of her reflections. She was so turned around, she had no clue which way she had come from. She decided to randomly walk straight, because how else was she to choose? As she moved closer to the reflection in front of her, a pearly word appeared on the reflection. *There's*. She paused, turning to the right, where one more word was written. *power*. She continued to turn, reading the rest of the sentence, one word on each surface. *in knowing your own strength and following your own path.*

Kirana was thrilled because it gave her something to go off of, rather than a random direction. She went to the reflection that had the word *knowing* and went through it. This path was a random mixture of reflective and clear panels. It looked like it went straight, but after walking into clear panels twice, she put her arms up in front of her again.

"I think I'm ready to be out of here now," she mumbled, talking to herself again. She thought she heard a tinkling sound. "Nova?" she called. No response. She saw some distorted silvery movements to her right through a clear panel showing her a reflection from somewhere else. She moved a little faster and began to see more shapes of movement, indicating a busier area, which to her, meant she might find a way out. When she came to another split in the path, she stood in front of them and peered down as far as she could. One looked like a dead end, with two reflective panels coming together at a point. The other looked like mainly clear panels, and she could see Nova from a distance through them! She was smiling and chatting with someone standing just out of Kirana's sight. She smiled, feeling relieved, and took a step down the clear path. Something felt off though. She felt drawn towards the other path, as odd as that seemed to her. She looked back that way and decided she would go down it a little ways and just confirm the dead end and turn around and come right back. She started walking down the path, and it felt good somehow. It felt right. As she got close to the end of the path, she was smiling and nearly turned around too soon. She happened to catch that the reflection wasn't perfectly aligned. She looked a little closer, moving cautiously so she didn't run into the walls again. She realized that the path continued behind one panel, so that from afar, it would look like a dead end. The path doubled back on itself and shortly after that, she exited the maze with relief.

"Kirana!" Nova called to her, making her way towards her. "Wasn't that fun? Did you get lost? I found a room like a cube and every single part was a reflection! Looking up, looking down, everything! That was so cool. We should go in again!" She grabbed Kirana's hand like she was going to pull her back in, and Kirana stopped her, laughing.

"Whoa, hey, I think I need a break! By the way, I ran into Ravi in there," Kirana told Nova. They hadn't fully caught up on how her latest conversation had gone yet. Nova cocked her head.

"In a good way?" she asked.

"I think so," Kirana said, shrugging. "We didn't talk much because the reflection of the shine we made when we greeted each other practically blinded me. I stepped back through a reflection unknowingly and lost him." Nova was staring at her, then turned to stare at the maze.

"Wow, what maze were you just in," she said in a dazzled kind of way, not actually asking the question. "Well," she sighed happily, "I also ran into someone! I left him over there to come get you. C'mon!" Nova took off again, and Kirana started to be very concerned that this party was creating a pattern of her getting lost trying to follow Nova's exuberance. But she grinned, and followed suit. As they went around the edge of the maze, she saw Anala and Sora standing with Nox. She took in a breath at his appearance. He was in glowing silver that seemed to be reflecting itself upon itself, making it hard to look directly at him, but hard to look away. He wore crisp black underneath the silver, which could be seen at the collar and wrists. He also had on black gloves and black, opaque glasses. *Probably to shield his eyes from himself*, Kirana joked to herself. As she approached, she moved faster, the feeling of *rightness* she had felt in the maze growing ever stronger. She was beaming, and she didn't even know it. She was also holding her breath. She remembered to breathe out then. She couldn't see his eyes, but his gaze was in her direction, and he was completely still and unmoving. She forgot Anala and Sora were there.

"Nox," she said, forgetting any normalcy for how to communicate. He finally moved then, holding his arms open as if to invite her for a hug.

"Kirana, you take my breath away," he said as she moved towards him. She felt lost in a moment of time and wasn't sure how long he held her until she heard Anala, Sora and Nova talking about different things they had discovered in the maze. Nox released her, and she stepped back.

"Did you go into the maze?" she asked him. He shook his head that he had not. Just then, they heard an announcement from the stage, near where there was dancing and beautiful waves of sound.

"Ooh, they're going to do the costume contest I bet!" Sora squealed. She gave a little hop and a skip that gave way into her floating stride towards the stage, and the rest of them followed.

"Welcome to the Shimmering Horizons," the voice was saying across the room. "You've all been working so hard, and we are delighted to share this event with you. We hope you are enjoying the fantastical world we've created here, with all its wonders and delights. The dance floor will be open again right after the performance." By the time they reached the stage, Kirana could see the shimmering line much better. The stage seemed to be just above that line that stretched off along both directions. Performers started to appear as if out of nowhere as they moved up from that line. It was an incredible show with amazing acts and wild costumes. Everyone had sparkling stars in their eyes.

When the show finished, the announcer returned. "How did everyone enjoy that performance?" The crowd went wild. There were silver and black blasts of glitter and sparks of every size. "Excellent!" he boomed. "Don't go far, we will be running our contest for those of you who have dressed the best for the occasion shortly, so take a break, and come right back!" There was a flurry of movement after that as everyone went off for refreshments and to find mates and family. Nova and Nox were talking quietly to each other, and Anala came to stand next to Kirana.

"Have you ever been to a party like this?" she asked, looking more relaxed than she had since her troubles with Alev had come up.

"Not exactly," said Kirana. "This is probably two steps above any party I've attended!"

"And it's not even over yet!" Sora added as she joined them. From behind Sora and Anala, Kirana spotted Kylo and Ravi walking together.

"Kylo!" Kirana called to him, waving an arm in the air. He heard her and turned, and as he laid eyes on her, he stopped in his tracks. He quickly regained himself and with a huge smile, he walked up to the group.

"Kirana!" Kylo breathed as he held one of her hands and twirled her around. Kirana paused with a weird memory for a moment. Kylo never called her by her full name. She had ended up on the right side of that reflective frame, hadn't she? "You've outdone yourself!" he was saying. "I hope you entered the contest!" Kirana shook her head.

"No," she laughed, looking for signs that everything was normal. Nova and Nox had rejoined them then.

"I nominated you." Nova said, as if it were nothing more than a friendly hello.

"So did I!" joined Sora. They laughed. Ravi moved towards Kirana, distracting her from being horrified that she was nominated for a costume contest without knowing. Maybe nothing would come of it.

"That was crazy what happened in the maze, right?" Ravi said to her. Nox seemed to perk up. Kirana could almost feel him listening from her other side. For some reason, she wanted to clarify what had happened.

"Yeah, after we greeted each other, I was practically blinded and stepped backwards through what ended up being a secret door, and you were gone!" she laughed. She wondered if Ravi and Nox knew each other.

"What are you talking about?" chuckled Ravi, acting like she was kidding around. "You showed me how to get out of the maze! But then I lost you." He shrugged. Kirana just stared at him, confused. They heard the emcee back on stage, so she didn't say anything else.

"Welcome back!" he was announcing. "Who's ready for our costume contest? Nominees, please make your way to the Horizon Stage as soon as you can. We are starting shortly."

CHAPTER THIRTY SIX

Nova gently nudged Kirana.

"Nominee," she whispered. "You're one of those. You have to go backstage!"

"Nah," Kirana whispered back. "I wouldn't have known I was nominated, so others probably don't know either." Just then, a list of names came up on an invisible screen above the stage. Her name was there, floating alongside several others in beautiful, silver glowing letters.

"Give it up for our nominees!" rang out the emcee. "If your name is here, please meet me backstage." Nova smirked at Kirana, who glared back. Sora joined them and helped Nova push her towards the stage.

"Fine!" Kirana relented, finally walking on her own. She went backstage where a few others had gathered. All of them had exceptional costumes or were decorative in some extra way to warrant a nomination for this contest. She didn't quite feel like she measured up because she was still relatively simply dressed in comparison. But fine, she'd walk on stage, smile for her mates and get back to the party.

The emcee began to call their names. One by one, they walked up the steps that placed them directly in the center of the stage. They walked straight towards the crowd to various displays of sparks and mists in response to their looks, turned around and descended the same stairs again. Kirana was trying to get it over with quickly and was entirely focused on staying upright, so she didn't pay much attention to what the crowd was doing. As she descended the stairs, she meant to keep right on walking back to her mates, but someone grabbed her arm and insisted she wait.

"One last round of sparkle for our nominees! Absolutely amazing!" the emcee was calling out. The crowd glitzed and sparkled in silver, black and gold. *Gold?* thought Kirana. "And our winner, please meet us back on stage to receive a special gift..." The emcee paused, looking out over the crowd before dramatically announcing, "Kirana!"

All sound fell away from Kirana, and she wasn't sure if it was the audience or her ears that were the problem. Someone pushed her up the stairs until she finally got her legs to work properly. She walked up and stood on the stage with the emcee. "I can certainly see why you have been voted our winner!" the emcee was saying. "Congratulations!" He placed something on her head, and then all the activity of the audience suddenly and loudly came into Kirana's awareness. She smiled politely and sent some golden flecks towards where she knew her mates had been standing.

"Thank you," she said graciously to the emcee. He beamed back at her. She didn't know if there was anything else she was supposed to do, so she bowed her head to the crowd, putting her hands together in front of her as a gesture of gratitude, and turned around to walk back down the stairs to backstage. The emcee had continued to talk, but she didn't hear him. Backstage, the other nominees congratulated her warmly.

"You all look incredible, really!" she told them in reply. As she made her way back to her group, she thought even more attention was on her now than before. She'd just have to act like she didn't notice. When she made it back to her mates, Ravi actually rushed forward to greet her first.

"Incredible!" he said. "You actually impress me more and more every time I see you!" He had a favorable look in his eyes, and she wanted to tell him she was not trying to impress anyone, but she didn't say anything.

"Congratulations," Nova said quietly with a big hug and a huge smile. Sora joined in their hug and then Anala. When they let go, Kylo spun her around as he often did.

"I knew it would be you, Sunshine!" he said warmly. Kirana's face hurt from smiling so much, but she was just about done with all the attention.

"Should we get some refreshments?" she posed to the group.

"Let's go back in the maze!" said Nova. Sora and Ravi seemed to be in agreement there, so the three of them left to explore the maze further. That left Kylo, Nox, Anala and Kirana. Kylo asked Kirana to dance, so the four of them found a spot on the dance floor.

"Where's Alev?" Kirana whispered to Kylo so that Anala wouldn't hear. He shook his head.

"I don't think he's coming," he said.

"Why not?" she asked.

"He said he wanted to and would try, but he had to finish something for Guardian Cosmo." Kylo gave her a knowing look. Something was up. Kirana decided not to ask any more questions for now and just enjoy the party.

"I think I need a refreshment now!" Anala breathed, after they had been dancing for a while. "Anyone else?" Kylo jumped at the idea, and the two of them went off to the other side of the enormous room. Nox put a hand out to Kirana and led her off the dance floor as well.

"How has the party been treating you?" he asked her. She indicated towards the prize on her head and laughed.

"Better than I deserve!" she responded. "And you? Are you having a good time? I'm glad you're here!" Nox didn't respond to her questions, only her first statement.

"Oh, I think it's exactly what you deserve. Did you even see what he gave you?" Nox asked. "Here," he said, walking them towards the Hall of Reflection again. He walked her through half the hall like he was looking for a specific reflector. He found what he was looking for and moved it aside slightly, gesturing for her to step between two frames. As she did, she noticed another reflector with no frame tucked in the shadows, making it dark and nearly invisible.

"How did you know this was here?" she asked incredulously. He just smiled and gestured for her to look into it. As she stepped closer to the reflector, it began to show a scene. It was that line again. That perfect shimmering line that stretched on from side to side. She now knew it was the Horizon Stage. It was mostly dark, though she could still see the line, and everything above that line began to lighten up. There were colors starting to be thrown around—reds, oranges and yellows. Kirana was mesmerized. She took a step closer and continued watching as it intensified. Then, she noticed bright, shining gold crest the top of the line. It lightened everything and continued up, casting the light in a more even way across both the parts above and below the line. Below the line, she realized, there was a crowd. She looked back up above the line—the stage—and watched herself walk out fully onstage. She was positively glowing. She stumbled back from the reflector as she realized she was watching the replay of the contest from Nox's perspective. He didn't step out of the way of her sudden movement this time, but anticipated it and caught her, keeping her from falling back. He turned her around, smiling.

"It looked something similar when you walked back down off the stage," he said quietly. Kirana felt a little confused still.

"But those other nominees, their costumes were more elaborate and spectacular than mine. They must've been incredible to see as well," she said. Nox considered this for a moment before responding.

"Yes, there were some really great costumes," he agreed. "But nobody else did that. I think you won not for your outfit"—he placed his hand over his heart—"but for *you*." He took one of her hands and turned her around ever so slowly, and she could see herself normally now in the reflector. All she could think of as she looked at her dress full of depth and stars, were Nox's eyes. Then, as her eyes went up to the headpiece that the emcee had placed on her head, she saw it was intricate and delicate, and interestingly, golden.

"Hey, why do you think they had a golden prize for a silver and black party?" she asked him.

"Maybe they anticipated something extra special," he said softly, guiding her back through the space between two reflectors.

"Oh, now it's *my* turn to show *you* a reflector!" she exclaimed, remembering the frame she had stepped through earlier. They walked through the hall back to where she had seen it last. "Hmm," she said, "maybe someone moved it?" She couldn't find it anymore. They walked up and down the hall, but the frame did not show up.

"That's okay," said Nox, when he saw she was disappointed. "Should we go find the others? I think the party may be starting to come to a close." They walked back to the main dance floor and looked around from there, spotting the group gathering near the art displays. They were waving over to Nox and Kirana, telling them to hurry up.

"It's almost our turn!" called Nova.

"Perfect timing!" said Anala. All of them squeezed onto a platform, and they could see themselves in a reflector of sorts. Everyone looked amazing. They smiled and posed and had a few art pieces taken that showed their exuberance in that moment. Everyone agreed it had been an incredible party.

"About ready to go?" Anala asked the group. Everyone nodded, smiling and in good spirits. Several of them hooked arms around each other and began heading towards the exit. As they made their way out of the Dome, chatting and recounting their experiences, someone appeared to be coming towards them, glowing faintly red.

"Alev?" Anala said, stopping in her tracks and halting the rest of them that were linked.

"Hi—," he croaked. He could barely make a word out, using what seemed like the last of his energy, and collapsed just a short distance in front of them. Kylo and Nox immediately ran to his side and leaned over him, checking his condition. Kirana glanced at Ravi who was staring, seeming frozen in place. She rushed up to Kylo.

"How can I help?" she asked.

"Nox and I will help Alev. Can you go to Guardian Era as quickly as you can and let him know what's going on?" Kylo responded.

"I'll go with you," said Nova. Kirana gave her a brief nod, and the two of them took off.

CHAPTER
THIRTY SEVEN

Anala had wanted to stay with Alev, even though they had been distant for a while. Sora stayed with Anala for support while Kirana and Nova dashed off to the Impressions Office, hoping that's where they would find Guardian Era. As they rushed up the stairs to the offices, Guardian Gaia was on her way out.

"Kirana?" Guardian Gaia uttered, appearing a bit stunned, maybe at Kirana's appearance or maybe at her panicked energy.

"Guardian Gaia, we have an emergency. Is Guardian Era in his office?" Kirana was direct and at high alert.

"I'm afraid he's occupied at the moment," Guardian Gaia told them, looking back in the direction where Guardian Era's office was. "Can I help you with something?"

"It's Alev, a FI student. He had a red mist around him, and he collapsed near the Dome," Kirana explained. "We think he may be close to having a burn-out. Please, we need Guardian Era's help." Before Kirana could even finish her sentence, Guardian Gaia was back inside and rushing into Guardian Era's office without knocking, paying no attention to the fact that the door was closed. Kirana and Nova followed, with only slightly more caution. Guardian Era was sitting with Guardian Cosmo, and they both looked up in surprise at the three intruders barging in. Guardian Gaia noticed that the mates had followed her and nudged them back into the hall, though not fully closing the door behind her. Kirana and Nova listened at the door.

"Case in point, I'm afraid," sighed Guardian Gaia, her tone turning more urgent. "Outside the Dome, one of *your* students, Guardian Cosmo, near burn-out right now." They heard shuffling around and a few murmurs, and then it was quiet. Kirana and Nova looked at each other. Kirana cautiously and slowly pushed on the door that was not latched, poking her head into the room. Seeing nothing, she pushed the door open fully and walked in.

"Guardian Era?" she called. The room was empty. Nova followed her in.

"Where did they go?" Nova gaped, looking around. At the same moment, they seemed to have the same realization. "They must've just created a light string and hopped on." After all, both of them had just experienced how Guardian Era could place light strings anywhere he wanted in the blink of an eye.

"I guess they all went," Kirana remarked as she sat in the hammock chair and leaned back. "I hope he's going to be okay." She felt exhausted all of a sudden, like she had completed her mission and sent help, and now she needed to rest. Nova sat down next to her and put her hand on Kirana's arm.

"With three Guardians there, plus Nox and Kylo, I'm sure he's going to be okay," she assured her. Kirana nodded but didn't move otherwise.

"I hope Anala is okay too. She's been having a hard time with their relationship lately, and I'm sure this doesn't help. Maybe it will bring them back together?" Kirana asked hopefully and somewhat rhetorically. She gave a big sigh as she let her body further relax into the hammock. "Do you think Guardian Era would mind if we waited in his office? If we tried to make it back to the Dome now, I doubt they would still be there."

"That's probably true," agreed Nova. Then she changed the subject. "Is that where you sat when you were summoned?" Kirana looked at her in surprise. Maybe she was trying to distract her. She welcomed it.

"Actually, no," Kirana responded. "I sat here when Guardian Cosmo made us come here when we told him I had a flash-out, but I sat there," she gestured to a round seat full of cushions, "when I was summoned. Why?" Nova looked interested.

"When I was summoned, I sat where you're sitting now," Nova said. "And Guardian Era made a comment to me at one point about how he can get a sense of how someone is feeling and how to engage with them based on where they choose to sit." Kirana looked at the room with new eyes. Nova continued. "He said the hammock chair is often chosen when there is some nervousness or tension of some kind. We naturally choose an opportunity for some movement or swaying to soothe ourselves."

"Wow!" Kirana expressed. She took in some of the other seating in the room. There was a long lounger in one area and some low to the ground seating in another. Nova was currently perched on a chair next to her with wheels and no back, and there were several more styles as well. "What do you think that round one represents?" she asked Nova. Nova flopped into it to test it out.

"Definitely comfort," she confirmed with a smile. "You must've been feeling confident and were comfortable with Guardian Era when you came to his office for a second time. It makes sense. You really didn't seem nervous when you left." Kirana considered this.

"Wow, I think you're right. When I got summoned, I literally was about to sit in this hammock like I had the first time, but then I made a different choice." She laughed. "How interesting. Good strategy actually!" Then she remembered what Nova had said. "You sat here when you were summoned. You were nervous."

"Yes," said Nova quietly. "They had every reason to ask me to leave campus." Kirana stared at her.

"Are you—" Kirana started to ask, letting the words hang in the air.

"I have a choice," Nova stated. "Well, kind of. Obviously after only one iteration that didn't even go well and then failing my finals in preparation for a second one, it's not likely that I can continue this iteration. At least for my own work. And I'm fine with that. You know I am, right?" Nova asked Kirana. Kirana knew that Nova was struggling, but wished she had kept a closer eye on how things were going. She had always played it like everything was fine and that she was progressing. Plus, Tali and her mates were by her side in class.

"I'm sorry, Nova," Kirana apologized. "I should have been there for you more."

"No! Don't say that, Kirana," Nova insisted. "I know you're always here for me! Besides, Nox had an idea. That's what Guardian Era wanted to talk to me about." Kirana listened intently, remembering how Nova had wanted to go speak with Nox after being summoned. "I'm not sure if I should tell you now just in case I can't handle it. I don't want to disappoint you." Nova hung her head down, and Kirana reached over to put a hand on her shoulder.

"Whatever it is," Kirana reassured her, "you would never disappoint me. Is it something I can help you with?" Nova shook her head.

"No, because it's something I'd be helping *you* with." Nova seemed to be hinting at something but not wanting to say it outright. Kirana thought back to how excited she was when she found out that Makani was asked to be a Jr. Guide. She thought maybe it was possible for her too, until she found out that Makani was super close to being in the graduating class anyway. It was hard to believe they'd let Nova do that with how little experience she had. *Unless*, Kirana thought to herself. Something about the way she looked at Nova changed, and Nova gave her the tiniest smile. Kirana gasped.

"Are they going to let you be a Jr. Guide?!" she shrieked. Nova covered her face with her hands for a moment.

"Maybe?" she squeaked out. "Guardian Era said I would have to work really, really hard and do extra time with Nox if I want to be able to do it. But he's considering it because of our connection and your particular self-assignment. He said I could be an asset and a huge help to you in completing your tasks. And since you have such an important assignment, it could be of benefit to you to have guides that know you really well." Kirana jumped up and was hopping around in excitement. "But don't get so excited!" Nova whined, covering her face again. "What if I can't do it? It's a lot of work to catch up on, and I don't want to let you down!" Kirana stopped hopping and crouched in front of Nova.

"Nova, you will not let me down. I know you can pull this off. Actually, you're the only one I know who can pull this off!" she laughed. "And if you decide it's too much to take on for this iteration, I completely understand. I will support your decision, whatever it ends up being!" she promised. "Okay?" she said encouragingly, looking Nova directly in the eyes.

"Okay," Nova agreed with a small nod. Then she smiled brightly. "I could actually be part of your team this iteration!" And she let herself get a little excited, and she hopped around too.

Kirana and Nova had been in Guardian Era's office for a while now, and nobody had returned.

"Maybe we should head back to our residence and see if Anala and Sora are back," Kirana suggested. "It doesn't seem like anyone is coming back here."

"Yeah, I'd like to check up on them," agreed Nova. "Let's leave a note for Guardian Era letting him know that we're waiting for an update." She went to his desk and found something to write on, scribbling a quick note. As they left the Impressions Office, it seemed deserted. They didn't run into anyone all the way back to their residence. They were still dressed in their party attire too.

"Part of me is tired of making noise when I walk, and part of me wants to wear this dress forever," Nova grinned.

"Now we have some inspiration for our own parties that we have at our residence!" said Kirana. "Although ours always seem to be impromptu," she chuckled. "Hey, did I tell you about the reflector I stepped into?"

"Stepped into?" asked Nova, confused.

"Yeah," said Kirana. "There was a round one that looked like a frame with words that said, *Step in to step out*. So I stepped in and everything was backwards... or, something," Kirana stammered. Nova gave her half a frown. "The reflector showed a gold party, so then I was confused if I actually stepped in or not, because the side I was on was silver and black. And I saw Kylo, and he was holding hands with Makani. He told me Nox was looking for me, and then I stepped back through the reflector." Nova was silent. Kirana considered what she had just said. "Wow, hearing myself say it out loud makes it sound kinda crazy," she admitted. She wondered if she had made it all up.

As they approached their residence, the building looked dark and the energy was moving downward as if it was continuously falling. Kirana and Nova looked at each other with trepidation.

"C'mon," Kirana said, giving them both a boost of positivity. "It's going to be okay." They stepped in the door and found Anala and Sora in the community area. "Are you alright?" Kirana asked as they rushed over to hug them.

"We waited at Guardian Era's office for a while, but it didn't seem like anyone was coming back," explained Nova.

"So you don't have any news?" sniffled Anala.

"No, I'm sorry," Kirana said quietly. "What happened at the Dome after we left?" Sora responded this time.

"Nox and Kylo got him out of the way of passersby, but we had to stay close because we knew you would tell Guardian Era where we had been. Anala and I stayed in that spot to direct the Guardians where to go when they arrived. You were fast. They got there so soon. Once they arrived, they made us leave. Even Nox and Kylo had to leave. They walked us back here and just left not too long ago," she explained. "Nox thinks he's going to be alright." She glanced at Anala.

"He also said he might not be able to finish this iteration, depending on how bad he is," Anala said quietly. The mates all sat down together, putting their arms around Anala.

"Well, we don't know anything yet," said Nova. "Do we know when we might be able to get an update?" Anala and Nova shook their heads.

"We were hoping you'd hear something from the Guardians," Sora told them.

"We left a note for Guardian Era telling him that we're waiting for an update. Hopefully he'll tell us something," Nova informed them. Anala nodded weakly.

"Here," said Kirana, "Let's all focus our energy to send positive and healing thoughts, okay?" The mates arranged themselves in a circle on the floor. They closed their eyes and meditated on healing thoughts, sending them to Alev, wherever he was.

Chapter
Thirty Eight

As Anala, Kirana and Sora got ready to start classes again, Nova prepared for some intensive lessons with Nox and Guardian Alder, who was working with the Guides. She would have until midterms to get up to speed, or she would need to leave campus until the next iteration. She had more than one thing to motivate her.

"I really think this is where I can excel!" Nova told Kirana. "I'm going to be the best Jr. Guide on the most important team!" she declared.

"All the teams are crucially important," Kirana reminded her, though she couldn't help but smile. "Good luck in class! Keep me updated, okay?"

"I will," said Nova. Kirana gave her a hard look, because she clearly didn't keep her updated before. "I *will*!" Nova insisted.

Sora was upbeat and looking forward to getting back to her classes. She floated out the door with a swirl of light blue twinkles. Kirana looked at Anala, as they were the last two left at the residence. Anala had been doing alright, and the mates had been trying to keep her distracted.

"Ready to go?" she asked her. Anala gave her a small smile, and they left, heading towards the Green Seeds Building. Anala was quiet, seemingly deep in thought. "If you want," Kirana said to her, "I'll go with you to Guardian Era's office again after class, and we can see if we can get some information." They hadn't heard anything about Alev's condition yet, or any details about what had transpired.

"It's the not knowing that feels the hardest," said Anala. "But at the same time, I feel like I do know. He's alright," she said, turning to look at Kirana. Kirana nodded. It made sense to her. The two of them seemed to be of the same flame from the moment they met. Anala looked down at her bracelet with the fiery stones that had been Alev's and touched it fondly. "I miss him," she said. "And I just—" She didn't finish her sentence. Kirana gave her a moment, but she still didn't continue.

"What is it?" asked Kirana. "I'm here for you, and you can tell me anything." Anala looked at her.

"I know," she said. "I've just been feeling kind of"—she paused—"off lately. Like, everything seems to be going so perfectly for you, and I wonder why I can't keep up." Kirana looked at her in surprise.

"What?" she said to Anala, trying not to let the surprise show in her voice too much.

"Well, you got the green screen on your finals, you got a summons from the Guardians and you won the contest at the Shimmering Horizons party. Everyone is just enamored with you right now, and I'm… I'm just here." Anala looked down, and Kirana couldn't help but let out a little chuckle. She stopped and grabbed Anala's arm to stop her as well.

"Anala," she said gently, "I know I never got a chance to tell you this, but I had a talk with Nova a while back where I was telling her that I felt exactly the same way. Except it was about you." Anala looked up and met her eyes.

"Really?" she asked.

"Yes," Kirana said definitively. "You had such a great thing going with Alev that wasn't working out the same with Ravi and me, you were having such an easy time in class and you didn't have any fears! I mean, you *don't* have any fears! You're ready to dive into this big mission on your own without a second thought, and here I am clinging to my family."

"But that's different," said Anala, shaking her head.

"And that's the point," said Kirana. "It's different. We all have different struggles, and it doesn't make sense to compare ourselves to each other. We'll be average in some areas and fantastic in others. That's why it's so awesome that we're here to support each other and balance each other out." That finally got a smile out of Anala.

"You're right," she sighed. "Thanks." She gave Kirana a hug. "Now let's go, before we miss class!" They took off laughing and made it to the building just as Ravi was entering.

"Hey!" He greeted them. "You two look happy." It seemed infectious as his grin also widened.

"Ravi! Are you going to join us?" Anala asked him. Ravi glanced at Kirana, and his eyes sparkled a little.

"I sure am," he said. The three of them entered and joined the group that was gathered waiting for Guardian Beck. She appeared nearly soundlessly just a moment later.

"Welcome back!" she said with a liquid smile. "Seeds," she addressed them, "it's time to start putting your plans into action. We are moving straight into Communications, and all of you will be getting teams. Since we have a bit of a delay as the Guardians are still gathering Jr. Guides and making sure you will all have enough support, we'll start by focusing on contracts. Since you will likely be setting up contracts with others who are not in this particular class, many arrangements will need to be made. You can still start your drafts now based on your self-assignment plans. Luckily, this part of the semester is quite similar to what you've prepared in previous iterations, and everyone else will be on the same subject. Always feel free to loop me in if you get stuck!" She finished by spraying them with a deep blue mist of encouragement, and the group started pulling out notebooks and supplies to begin drafting their contracts.

"Sometimes these are so hard," Kirana sighed. "Well, I guess sometimes they are obvious and easy too." She was thinking of Kylo and the sheer number of contracts they had completed for each other over their many iterations together. "Wait," she said, turning to look at Anala and Ravi. "Can we make contracts with anyone from the Guides group?" She suddenly got very concerned.

"Good question," Ravi responded. "Might want to ask." Kirana got up and went to Guardian Beck.

"Hi, Kirana. How is everything going?" Guardian Beck greeted her.

"Good, thank you. I just had a quick question," Kirana said hesitantly.

"Go on," Guardian Beck encouraged.

"Are we able to make contracts with the Guides? I'm not really sure about the nature of their self-assignments," she asked. Guardian Beck looked thoughtful.

"Short answer, yes," she began, "but it may look different than it otherwise would. It also depends, because you will likely not be able to have contracts with Jr. Guides. So if there is someone who is a Guide that you'd like to set something up with, go ahead and create a draft. They will let you know during your appointment if it's feasible or not and how to modify it. Good question!" Guardian Beck smiled at Kirana. "Anything else?"

"No, that's all. Thank you," Kirana said, sending lilac gratitude. She went back to where Ravi and Anala were laughing with each other. She was happy to see them also getting along again. They looked at her as she rejoined them.

"So, what did she say?" asked Ravi.

"She said we can still draft a contract with a Guide, but when we meet with them, they may modify it. I'm not entirely certain what that means, but I guess it depends on the Guide. Oh, and also, we can't have contracts with Jr. Guides," she answered quickly.

"Okay, I guess I'll write up all my drafts and then figure out who to set them up with after the fact," Anala thought aloud.

"Good idea," Ravi said as he shuffled some things around. He dropped something, and Anala reached down to pick it up for him and handed it back. "Hey, thanks!" he responded to Anala. "It's nice to be back with you guys. We should set up contracts with each other." He said this last part looking intently at Kirana.

"Yes! That would be great," agreed Anala. Kirana nodded passively. She knew she likely would, but she wasn't sure how she wanted to arrange her contracts just yet and didn't want to commit too soon. Her nod seemed to be enough for Ravi though, who went back to working in his journal.

After class, they all walked out together. Anala shuffled a little, slowing them down. Kirana noticed, but Ravi kept on walking until he was further ahead before he realized he was walking alone. He turned around and gave them a wave while continuing to move.

"I've gotta get back to the residence," he said, walking backwards. He sent them a handful of silver sparks and turned back around.

"See you later!" Anala called. Kirana looked at her curiously and then remembered to respond to Ravi as well.

"See you!" she called to him, not certain if he even heard her at this point. "What's up?" she asked Anala.

"Oh my gosh, I've been wanting to talk to you since Ravi dropped those papers in class, and I couldn't wait for him to leave!" Anala blustered. "Remember how you told us about those notes, and we were looking through the congratulatory notes you got to see if we could match the handwriting?" Kirana froze. Anala noticed and quickly fixed the impression she had given. "Oh, no, sorry. His handwriting didn't match the notes. *But*," she emphasized, "it matched something else!" She fished around in her bag for a moment and pulled out a small note that Kirana hadn't seen before. "I forgot to tell you about this!" she exclaimed. "When Alev collapsed and Nox and Kylo moved him to a quieter location, Sora and I stayed in that spot to direct the Guardians when they arrived. I found this on the ground right about where Alev was." She paused for a breath. "And *this* is Ravi's handwriting based on his notes that I just saw." She handed Kirana the note which read, *Dome, come now*. She looked at Anala as if she might have more answers, yet knowing that she didn't. She was right that it didn't match the handwriting of the other two notes they had come across, but the material it was written on was the same.

"Want to check something out with me real quick?" Kirana asked. Anala didn't ask any questions. She just agreed and let Kirana lead her to the Sims buildings. They entered the Gravity Sim building, and Kirana took her to the corner behind the last singular Sim room. Sure enough, the tear in the material on the wall was much larger now. It seemed like a lot of notes must be floating around.

"I suspect he's using these notes as a means of communication," Kirana explained, "and it just so happens that Alev keeps losing the ones written to him." That almost made Anala laugh.

"He does have a tendency to break things and lose things," she smiled, touching her bracelet again. Kirana remembered Kylo making a similar comment about him not being very subtle. It seemed to be a likely scenario.

"But wait, that can't be," Kirana realized. "Because the first note that Nova found was in her class. And Alev is in the FI class, not hers. There has to be someone else involved."

"Or someones," Anala said, making it plural.

Chapter
Thirty Nine

Nova finally came back to the residence after what Kirana felt like was a long time away. But she came with news. When she arrived, Sora wasn't there, so just Anala and Kirana joined her in the community area.

"I don't have a lot of information, but I do know a little," she began. "I was working with Nox when Guardian Era stopped by. They went into the other room, but Nox didn't close the door all the way, and I could hear parts of what they were saying. Alev is okay," she made sure to say very clearly, looking at Anala, "but he won't be finishing this iteration. They've already moved him off campus to recover." She waited to say more to be sure Anala was handling the news alright.

"It's okay," Anala said. "I kind of expected as much. I'm relieved he will recover, and we weren't going to be able to share this iteration together anyways, so I was prepared for a delay." Kirana and Nova silently confirmed to each other that she seemed to be accepting the news and handling it well. Anala surprised them with what she said next. "I've been messaging him. He hasn't responded yet, but I just want him to know I'm thinking of him. Now I can tell him things with more certainty, like

I'm glad he's going to be okay." She gave them a small smile. "Thanks Nova." She sprinkled a bit of dark pink towards her.

"There's more," said Nova. "I found out he's not the first one that this has happened to. Even from what I've seen myself, he's the third one that had a burn-out, and all of them have been connected to Guardian Cosmo. That student we saw," she said, turning to Kirana, "when you pretended to have a flash-out, had that red mist around him, remember?" Kirana nodded, remembering well. It didn't feel like a good thing at all at the time. "He's not on campus anymore. And I don't know for sure about the one that I saw on the day of Orientation because I wasn't paying attention at the time, but I'll bet it's the same story there. He could've been the one that burned the light string."

"So this, whatever it is, has been going on since Orientation?" Anala asked, somewhat shocked. "With brand new students?!" This made her angry. She flickered fiercely and turned white.

"Nox wouldn't tell me much when I started asking questions after Guardian Era left, but he did say that it hadn't ever really been an issue before. Most of us have never been taught how to do a split-energy," she added, "so it never happened. But it seems like Guardian Cosmo has been teaching it," Nova attested.

"But, why now?" Kirana wondered aloud. "You didn't see anything like this last iteration when you were in his class, did you?" she asked Nova.

"I've been asking myself the same thing and can't think of anything unusual," she responded. "We know there have been a lot of changes this iteration. Maybe something that's still to come has triggered him to start doing it now."

"But it can't be class-wide," added Anala, "or Sora would've learned as well." They all considered this for a moment.

"Do we know if she knows about split-energy?" Kirana asked carefully. They all looked at each other and realized they weren't sure. Sora could've been practicing doing split-energy right there in their residence for all they knew!

"Okay," sighed Kirana, "so let's ask her about that." She tried to smile, but it came out as a worried wobble on her face. Then she looked at Anala, remembering the note. "Oh! Nova, Anala found something out too." Anala, who had finally cooled off a little, got up and went to her bag and pulled out the note. She handed it to Nova, who read it aloud.

"Dome, come now?" she read it as a question, though it wasn't written that way. Anala blinked.

"And I know—*we* know—whose handwriting that is," she added. Nova didn't say anything but looked nervous. Then something steeled behind her eyes, as if at that very moment, she decided she was going to be strong and became so.

"Whose?" Nova asked. Anala took a breath.

"It's Ravi's handwriting, and I found this on the ground where Alev collapsed. My theory is that Ravi somehow got this note to him, and he followed the instructions, making it to the Dome right as we were leaving," she went on. "The delivery would've been right around the time that he was in the maze at the party. He went with you and Sora, right? Did you all stay together in there, or did you split up?" Nova's eyes were widening as Anala spoke. Then her eyes unfocused on them as she tried to remember that part of the party.

"We mostly stayed together, actually," she finally relayed. "I remember he wanted to find a specific area of the maze. He said it was a room of reflectors in the shape of a dodecagon, but we couldn't find it. I told him I could find where the cube room was, but he wasn't interested." Nova darted a look between Kirana and Anala. "Sora and I lost him shortly after that, but only briefly. He caught up with us again, and we kept exploring. Do you think he found a way to deliver a note to Alev right then? To have Alev come meet us? Why? And how?" Nova started pacing. Kirana was trying her hardest to believe that it must've been for a good reason. They had only just repaired their relationship. Was he keeping things from her again already?

"We just had class with Ravi. He actually sat with us again for the first time in a long time, but this is not looking good," said Anala, trying to gauge Kirana's reaction.

"What is this all about?" Kirana whispered, as if she was just asking herself. There was something she was missing. "We don't have a motive," she said, looking up at her mates.

"A motive?" asked Nova.

"Yeah, like, all these things seem to be connected—the notes, the burn-outs, the broken light strings, Alev sneaking around, Ravi avoiding us, Guardian Cosmo—but we're missing the thing that connects them," she explained. "We've connected pieces, but the big picture isn't clear." Just then, a memory popped in her head. The look on her face must have changed because Anala and Sora watched her curiously.

"What is it?" asked Anala.

"I overheard part of a conversation a while back, and I didn't really pay much attention to it in the moment, but—" she appeared to be trying to remember what had been said. "I think that Guardian Cosmo was trying to convince Guardian Gaia that he could do a split-energy this iteration to keep working with the FI class *and* take on a self-assignment. They weren't going to permit it though."

"They?" pressed Nova.

"Well, Guardian Gaia and someone else. I can't remember who else's voice I heard. I just remember Guardian Gaia because she came out and talked to me," Kirana commented. "And—" she looked up at them now, thinking hard. "They were going to consider it if he was going to take on a self-assignment in general, but it just couldn't be with the graduating class. I think." She wasn't entirely sure she remembered correctly.

"Why would Guardian Cosmo be so obsessed with proving that he could take on a self-assignment and work with the FI class at the same time?" Nova puzzled, crinkling her nose.

"Do you think that this is the connecting piece somehow?" Anala asked Kirana.

"It might be," she reasoned. "But we need to know why so we can stop it. We can't let this keep happening. What if Sora is next?"

"You're right," agreed Anala. "We need answers. I'll talk to Ravi about the note. If that's alright with you," she said, checking with Kirana.

"Absolutely," she confirmed, somewhat relieved it wasn't going to be her.

"And I'll talk to Sora," Nova joined in. "I'll find out more about what she knows about doing split-energy and see if she's seen any more of her classmates in trouble." The mates nodded. Kirana wasn't sure at first where she could contribute, but then she decided on something.

"I'm going to talk to Guardian Era," she committed. "I have a weird feeling about Guardian Cosmo. Besides, Guardian Cosmo is the one who made me go to his office that first time, and then Guardian Era never even mentioned the flash-out to me at all." They all agreed to let the others know as soon as they had any more information.

Kirana went up to her nest to process their discussion before going to talk to Guardian Era right away. She wished Kylo was there. She missed him. She knew he was busy doing important Guide things, whatever those were. She hoped maybe they'd get some more time together once the iteration began, even though he would be leaving before her. She had heard that the Guides were going to start training in the pods soon. Maybe they already had, she wasn't sure.

She took her light string to her nook and journaled for a bit. She wanted to be clear with how she would approach Guardian Era. It was important to her to be seen as capable of handling tough situations—especially with the self-assignment coming up that she had taken on. When she felt ready, she left her residence and headed over to the Impressions Office. As she approached the building, she recognized someone who was leaving.

"Makani?" Kirana smiled, capturing her attention. "Good to see you again!" She saw Makani's eyes brighten and swirl ever so slightly.

"Kirana! Hi! How lovely to see you!" she replied. "I was just changing my status and schedule, so I'm officially a Jr. Guide now!" She glowed with excitement. Kirana's smile widened.

"That's amazing! Congratulations!" She gave her a hug, which Makani happily returned. "Any idea how teams are being set up yet?" she asked, knowing that Makani could probably not tell her anything, even if she knew.

"No, but there is a proposal out right now," she said with a twinkle in her eye. "I better go before I say anything else!"

"Fair enough," Kirana laughed. "Tell Tali I said hi! And Celeste too." She waved a ball of sparkles towards her as she skipped away.

"Will do!" Makani called behind her. As Kirana entered the building, she noticed Guardian Era's office door was partially open. She stepped up to it and knocked, seeing Guardian Era sitting inside at his desk. He looked up and gestured for her to come in.

"Hi, Kirana. I can't say that I haven't been expecting you," he said mysteriously. He gestured for her to take a seat, but Kirana remembered what Nova told her about how he used the seating as a gauge, and she remained standing.

"I need to talk to you," she said simply. Guardian Era nodded.

"Close the door behind you, please," he said.

CHAPTER FORTY

"Would you like a refreshment?" Guardian Era asked Kirana.

"I won't say no to that. Thank you!" she responded. Something inside her knew that this was going to be an interesting conversation, so she might as well relax. Guardian Era walked her over to the far corner of the room where two large, puffy armchairs were sitting tilted towards a table in front of them. It made it feel more like a community area in a residence than sitting to face each other directly like what typically happens in an office. Somehow Kirana picked up a vibe of respect between the two of them. Guardian Era cleared his throat as they placed their refreshments on the table and settled themselves in the chairs of fluff.

"Before we get started, Kirana, I need you to know that I will answer everything that I can, but I may not be able to provide insights into things that are not my own to share," he explained. "Where would you like to start?" Kirana thought for a moment. It wouldn't hurt to confirm certain details while she had his attention.

"Can you confirm my understanding of a situation if I list it out?" Seeing a nod, Kirana continued by recapping what happened with Alev. She decided to keep it basic, but threw in one extra piece of information to see if he reacted. "Alev had been practicing doing split-energies, received a note to go to the Dome when the Shimmering Horizons party was nearing its end, began to have a burn-out by the time he arrived and collapsed, but is now okay and recovering off campus, where he will not complete this iteration." She stopped and waited for the reply.

"Mostly correct, with caveats," stated Guardian Era. "I'm not aware of a note, but I'd be happy to discuss what you know. And as far as Alev's recovery, he has been insisting that he wants to come back and finish this iteration. I'm not sure we have the time or resources to support the full situation that would allow him to return at this moment, but you can tell your mate that he is insistent that he needs to make it right with her." He paused, watching Kirana's expression. Kirana abandoned her line of questioning for a new one.

"What exactly does he want to make right?" she asked.

"That," replied Guardian Era, "is an example of something that I cannot speak to, as it belongs to him. But we can still discuss the topic in general. Being in his first iteration, everything was new for Alev. What he spent his time working on and practicing was all valuable classwork from his understanding. I have another piece of that story which I am open to sharing with you, but perhaps you can fill in a blank for me first. Can you tell me about the note you mentioned?"

"Yes," Kirana agreed. "When Alev collapsed, he dropped a note that Anala found. It said, *Dome, come now*. It's written in Ravi's handwriting."

"Ravi is Alev's mate, correct? In the graduating class?" asked Guardian Era with interest.

"Yes," Kirana confirmed. "And there were other notes that we found, and likely more that we didn't. Actually..." Kirana tilted her head to the side, thinking this might be a good time to bring up something else.

"Guardian Era," she began again, "do you remember the first time that I came to your office? When Guardian Cosmo brought me."

"Yes, of course," Guardian Era said softly, accepting the shift in conversation.

"Nova and I were on our way to the Gravity Sim building to check the source of the notes, and we came across Guardian Cosmo with a student who had the red mist around him. We didn't recognize him. He ran off, and I pretended to have a flash-out so that Guardian Cosmo didn't suspect anything of our hiding." Guardian Era was listening patiently, but he got up to pace as she continued sharing the story. "I had the notes in my hand and dropped them when I faked the flash-out, and they disappeared shortly thereafter. We suspected Guardian Cosmo took them. Anyways, that's when he brought me here," she finished. She assumed he would ask her what was written on those notes or something about the Gravity Sim building, but he didn't.

"You didn't have a flash-out that day?" he asked instead, grinning just a little. Kirana shook her head.

"No! I completely faked it! I've been quite calm and handling things well for a long time now," she insisted. To her surprise, he laughed.

"Thank you for filling in the rest of the pieces of the puzzle I've been missing Kirana. Now," he said, sitting back down. "I think it's fair that I fill in the rest of yours." He took a breath. "Guardian Cosmo has been a great addition to our team over the last couple iterations. He also understands the complexity behind some of the changes that we've put into place this iteration and is on board with them. He is so on board, in fact, that he has taken it upon himself to find other ways to discover how we might accelerate some students towards, different paths, we'll say." He was eyeing Kirana as he spoke. "You may be familiar with one such example." Kirana nodded, thinking about Nova. "In his defense, he did very quickly guide her towards a different type of role, right off the bat."

"Guardian Cosmo—" Kirana began, feeling a bit hot. Guardian Era put his hand up to pause her.

"—let her do everything she asked," he said, finishing her sentence. "Let me clarify that Nova, just as with everyone on every assignment, is in one hundred percent control of their own *self*-assignment. The difference is that when working with the First Iteration group, sometimes they need some encouragement to not try to take on everything at once before they really understand what an iteration may be like. This is especially true for the graduating class." He watched Kirana blink, but she remained fierce. There really were no signs of a flash-out. He smiled at her. "Guardian Cosmo believes that there should be no outside influence on someone's decisions. He also pushes those who seem to have extra potential. While it's not my philosophy, it has uncovered some interesting prospects across the groups that have gone through him."

"But why was he pushing Alev and the others to do split-energies?" Kirana asked, still deciding how she felt about this method.

"Our understanding is that he wasn't pushing them any more than they were asking to do. He did teach them, and the ones who caught on quickly continued to get coached," Guardian Era explained. "Like I said, it is not my method, and it's been quite disappointing to see some of our students have burn-outs already before being able to complete an iteration. From what you've shared with me, it seems like most of their communication happened by handwritten notes, which would've been a test of sorts to see if they could deliver something physically beyond themselves while practicing the split-energy. What's written on them likely wasn't the point."

Interesting, Kirana thought to herself. *That's why he didn't seem to care what the notes said.* There was one other thing she wanted to bring up with Guardian Era but wasn't sure how to take the conversation there. She didn't fully understand the conversation she overheard in Guardian Gaia's class building when she went to study the projection, but part of her didn't want to admit to overhearing it. Guardian Era began speaking again before she could bring it up anyway.

"Kirana, there's something that we weren't going to share with you because we were concerned about a perceived additional pressure that you might take on in your self-assignment. However, finding out that your incidences of flash-outs are not quite as persistent anymore, I am willing to share it with you now if you want to know. It might fill in the final blank for you," he offered. Kirana considered this briefly, feeling comfortable that she did want to know. What she hesitated on were somewhat unrelated thoughts about how Ravi had gotten involved in all this, clearing Alev's light strings on Guardian Cosmo's request and his handwriting being on that last note. It seemed like something she'd need to take up with him though, she decided, not Guardian Era.

"I really do feel confident about this iteration," she told Guardian Era. "I know it will be harder—it is the graduating class after all—but I feel ready. I'm prepared, I know I'll have a great team supporting me and I actually think knowing whatever it is will help clear my field of vision and let me put all this to rest before I leave."

"Alright," Guardian Era conceded, jumping straight into it. "Guardian Cosmo had requested the assignment that we offered to you after you received the green screen." He stopped there to let her digest that piece of information. All of a sudden, things started falling into place, centering around Guardian Cosmo. Alev looking for her iteration plans for him, him trying to make her flash-outs a problem with Guardian Era and then even the fact that he was doing split-energies since Orientation. And she no longer needed to ask about the conversation she overheard that she hadn't been sure how to bring up with Guardian Era just now. It made sense, and she was relieved they had told him no to taking on a self-assignment even then.

"For the record," Guardian Era continued, seeing the light of understanding dawn on her, "he had already committed to being a Guardian this iteration and we are not permitting him to do anything with the graduating class at all. The graduating class takes full attention, no exceptions. AND," he emphasized, "as we already mentioned, though it's worth saying again, we are very confident that you are an excellent candidate for this assignment. We look forward to supporting you to achieve this very important mission."

Kirana let this information simmer for a moment longer. It didn't make her feel more pressure, like she had to get it right because someone else wanted the job. Of course others wanted the job. They were all here on this campus to take on these tough assignments and make things better. She felt honored. Honored that they believed in her and honored that she was qualified.

"Thank you, Guardian Era," she said reverently. "Thank you for supporting all this work that we're doing. He leaned forward and looked her in the eyes.

"And thank you for doing the work," he echoed. "Now," he leaned back again. "Is there anything else that we need to discuss?"

"I think that's quite enough for now," Kirana smiled.

"Good," Guardian Era proclaimed. "I agree." He walked Kirana out of his office and into the hall. As she walked towards the exit of the Impressions Office building, Guardian Era called after her.

"I look forward to talking again very soon!" His eyes were sparkling, and Kirana remembered how she had been dreaming about working with him for so many iterations and thought she had lost her opportunity when he switched groups. She felt so unbelievably lucky now, and she was not going to let him down.

CHAPTER FORTY ONE

K irana returned to her residence to see the most beautiful display of colors arranged all over the building. There were long marks of green near the bottom, and overflowing out over the top of the green lines were swirls of hundreds of colors in all different shades. They layered over and under each other, casting shadows in some places and catching light in others as they moved and gently swayed together. There was a feeling of softness, almost delicate, and the aroma evoked freshness. It felt like hope, in a way. She took it all in as she approached. This was an aesthetic she could get used to! When she reached the door, there was a smaller version of the same energetic display sitting on the doorstep that she could hold. She didn't even realize how wide her smile was when she bent down to pick it up. There was a note attached.

To: Kirana, the one who brings out the blossoms. She turned it over, but no one had signed it. Who was it from? It was stunning, and she didn't know who to thank! She stepped inside to see if anyone was there. Anala came from her nest as she heard Kirana enter.

"Beautiful, right?" Anala was grinning from ear to ear. "I have some too!" She showed Kirana a similar display of dazzling colors, hers leaning more towards shades of red and orange. She handed Kirana her note which read, *To: Anala, a touch of light and warmth to the one who provides it for me. Love, Alev.* Kirana got excited for her.

"You spoke with him?! Have you cleared things up? Anala, this is beautiful!" she exclaimed.

"Sorry that you have to share this beautiful gift with me," Anala said, casually extending her hand towards the display on the building.

"Um," Kirana corrected, "it looks like I'm the tagalong here." She laughed. "This note doesn't even say who it's from."

"It doesn't?" Anala said, looking at her note. "Well, it's from Ravi. They decided on a little joint surprise for us."

"Ohh," Kirana breathed. "You spoke with both of them?"

"Yes!" she responded. "Should we wait for Nova before we talk about it? I was hoping we could chat before class, so I guess I can fill her in later."

"Okay," agreed Kirana. It seemed important, and they didn't know how long it might be if they waited for Nova. Kirana followed Anala back into her nest, entering the waves of warmth. Anala seemed to be gliding, and she was humming to herself. Kirana hadn't seen her like this in quite some time, and it was energizing to witness.

"I had a heart-to-heart with Ravi," Anala began. "Well, both Ravi and Alev," she smiled. "When I went over to their residence, they were both there."

"Alev is back on campus?!" Kirana gasped, in a good way. Anala nodded.

"He's looking dim still, and his energy is quite weak, but he said he needs to be here. He's begging the Guardians to let him stay. I'm not sure if they will, but apparently Ravi is supporting him staying and finishing the iteration. He is super intent on getting past his first iteration because he thinks he has 'enormous potential' and wants to get into bigger self-assignments, faster." Anala shrugged.

"Sounds like someone told him that," Kirana ventured, uncertain of what Anala thought about it yet. Anala looked down.

"Yeah, we talked about that. How he'd literally worked so hard that he practically had a burn-out. I mean, realistically, he did," she recounted. "We talked about everything, Kirana." Anala looked back up at her. "He told me about Guardian Cosmo encouraging them to try doing split-energies, about how he had gone to get extra coaching from him, how a small group of them used the notes to practice with each other—" Anala paused for a moment. "And he told me everything about using your light strings." Kirana had been nodding along because none of this was news to her at this point, but she was glad that Alev had confessed everything to Anala.

"And Ravi was there the whole time while you were talking?" Kirana wanted to clarify. Anala nodded.

"Ravi has been supporting him all semester. He thought what Alev was doing was harmless, until it wasn't. When he realized Alev was taking it too far, he knew he had to get him some help. He knew if he could get Alev back to us, that maybe we could talk some sense into him. I'm a little concerned that even now, he's not willing to rest and just wait an iteration," she admitted. "He started writing to me," Anala said quietly, changing the subject. "After I was messaging him when he was off campus, he started writing me notes and sending them here." She gestured towards a small stack of handwritten notes on the table. Kirana glanced at them, seeing them glow faintly and emit a soft humming flicker. When she looked back at Anala, she saw that same loving flicker across Anala's face.

"Is everything back to normal with you two? As much as it can be, I guess?" Kirana asked her.

"Well, it feels wonderful to have cleared things up with him. He apologized so many times for so many different things. He said he wished he did things differently and wants to start over with me." She glanced at the colorful arrangement, then seemed to snap to attention. "Ravi and Alev both recorded a message for you, together," she grinned. "They knew I'd be filling you in on everything and wanted you to hear it from them." She pulled up her tablet and set it flat on the table as a projection popped up of Alev and Ravi. Anala was right. Alev did not look like he was ready to continue this iteration. The projection of the two of them flickered, and they shoved each other playfully until Anala's voice told them it was recording. Alev spoke first.

"Kirana, I have to confess, even though I know that you're already aware, but I did go into your nest, and Sora's. The first time was by accident, but I entered twice more, and I have no excuse for that." He was looking incredibly pale and ashamed. Kirana wanted him to stop, and she wanted to tell him she would accept his confession, but it was just a recording. It continued. "I wanted Guardian Cosmo to help me advance, and it was my idea to get your journal because I knew he wanted the assignment they were going to offer to you. It wasn't that I didn't want, or don't want, to support you, I just felt like I was in the inner circle. I had insight into Guardian-level information, and I wanted to make him proud. I'm so, so sorry." He hung his head, and Kirana took it seriously.

"I forgive you," she whispered, even though he wouldn't have heard her. Anala reached a hand over and squeezed Kirana's arm.

"I know, kinda hard to watch," she said quietly. In the projection, Ravi put a supportive hand on Alev's arm too. Then his projection spoke.

"And for my part, dear Kirana," Ravi began, "I am also terribly sorry. I thought I was doing the right thing by giving you more space. I kind of got wrapped up in Alev's pursuit and started hanging out with the group in the graduating class that were also working on doing split-energies." He looked very guilty then. "And when we talked recently about the light strings, I already thought you were going to hate me, and then you didn't. And I was so relieved about that, but I've been so scared to actually say the wrong thing since, thinking you'd never speak to me again." He was speaking in a rush. "But then I talked to Alev and found out everything, that I'm sure you know by now too, and we had to have our own moment to clear things up." He was looking at Alev, who was just looking awful by this point. When he turned back to the recording device, Kirana felt like he was looking directly at her. "I never meant to hurt you. That's the opposite thing I've ever wanted since the very first time I met you after Orientation." The memory seemed to make him smile. "I want to make it right, and I want to support you in this iteration." He had a pleading look in his eye. "Please accept my apology. Again," he added sheepishly.

"And mine," Alev included. They began to blow all kinds of sparkles and shimmers at the recording device that was held by Anala at the time, and she was getting bombarded before the projection cut out.

"By the time I got back from their residence, these gifts were here, and our residence was decorated," Anala cooed.

"It's certainly a nice gesture," Kirana noted. Picking up on Kirana's quiet behavior, Anala looked at her closely.

"How do you feel about all this?" she asked. Kirana sighed. She honestly wasn't sure.

"I guess I just need to let it all settle for now," she replied. Anala seemed to understand, but it could've just been that she was back to the dreamy, happy self that she was when she was with Alev.

So much had gotten revealed. She was a bit concerned about Guardian Cosmo wanting to take on her self-assignment and hoped it wouldn't continue to be an issue. But the part that troubled her the most was that she had *just* spoken with Ravi. How were they in a situation not that much later where he was apologizing again? And it had been so hard to get him to talk the first time! He was definitely avoidant. She would need to be cautious with any contracts she made with him for this iteration.

While Anala stayed in her nest to prepare for their upcoming class, Kirana went to hers to do the same, and they agreed to meet out front shortly. Kirana sat and looked at how gorgeous and bright the bouquet was, and her mind played through the conversations she'd recently had. Why didn't she feel satisfied? Was it because everyone just played it off as if the entire previous semester of secrets and sneaking around was normal? Or maybe it was because she still didn't know everything she needed to know, and her departure date was quickly approaching? She had mixed emotions on it and would just have to let things play out a bit more. She decided to refocus herself. Contracts needed to be finished soon, she needed to know more about her team of Guides, and she needed to start doing drills. Maybe she could skip the Sim buildings practice altogether since they had pods now. As she gathered her things for class, she let her mind work through it all. When she left her nest to go meet Anala, Sora was also heading down.

"Hi, Kirana!" she sang brightly. "I love the gift you and Anala got delivered on the front of the residence!"

"Isn't it lovely?" Kirana smiled.

"It really is!" Sora said as she stopped in the entryway. "Real quick, if you have a moment, I want to tell you what Nova and I talked about. She had to leave already, so I told her I would."

"Of course! What is it?" Kirana replied.

"Well, she asked if all of us in the FI class had been taught about doing split-energies." Kirana waited patiently while Sora shifted on her feet. "Guardian Cosmo had us try it, and he said that we'd need to do it eventually so it was okay to assess us and see who may have a knack for it right off the bat."

"Could you do it?" asked Kirana. Sora tilted her head and shuffled again, which wasn't like her.

"Not exactly. I'm pretty clear to begin with so I have to be in a state of high emotion to go opaque and have enough extra energy to do it. But—" Sora paused. Kirana looked at her curiously. "I—I kind of discovered something on my own."

"Okay," said Kirana expectantly. "Well, we're all here for you if you have any concerns."

"I know," continued Sora. Then she took a deep breath. "I realized when I *can* do it, my split is... my split is invisible."

CHAPTER FORTY TWO

Kirana and Sora stood in the entryway of their residence in silence. Sora was in her first iteration. Everything was new to her. Kirana had never been taught about doing a split-energy since it was kept to the Guardians until this iteration. Neither of them knew if what Sora did was normal.

"Does Guardian Cosmo know?" asked Kirana.

"I don't think so," replied Sora. "At least I didn't tell him. I've only told a few classmates and now, you and Nova."

"Okay," Kirana uttered. "Maybe you can ask your classmates to keep it to themselves? It might be a good idea to keep this from Guardian Cosmo for now. I have to get to class, but let's talk more about it later?" Sora nodded, looking like she wanted to say something more.

"What is it?" Kirana asked.

"I don't want him to find out! I don't want to end up like Alev or the others," Sora admitted nervously. Kirana realized she had potentially scared her. She put her hand on Sora's shoulder and went to say something, but Anala poked her head inside.

"You coming?" she asked Kirana.

"Yep! Right behind you!" she responded. Anala felt the serious tone in the air and nodded, quietly closing the door behind her. Kirana turned back to Sora and looked her in the eyes.

"You're not going to have a burn-out because you're not going to take it too far. You are in complete control of whether you do split-energies or not. Even if Guardian Cosmo knows, *you* get to decide. Remember that, okay?" Kirana passed her a hazy, white peace bubble and smiled. "You get to decide." Sora took a deep breath and let it go. Then she smiled and nodded at Kirana.

"Thanks," she said, adding, "I can show you later." Kirana tried not to assign any meaning to that last statement for now. The two mates walked out of the residence to where Anala was waiting, admired the building display again and headed off to class.

When Anala and Kirana entered their building, there was a huge campus map displayed in the air, zoomed in on the Green and White buildings and all the surrounding pods. Anala gasped.

"Do you think we're getting our pod assignments?" she asked excitedly. Kirana grinned at the memory of her experience with Nox when he was testing the pods.

"I hope so!" she responded.

"Welcome all!" Guardian Beck called out to get everyone to gather together. "Exciting news!" Anala and Kirana exchanged excited looks. "We are prepared to assign pods—" She wasn't finished speaking, but she had to pause as the class almost burst with excitement for a moment. They had been waiting for this! Bubbles and fizz were everywhere. "However," she had to cut in, "we will not be using them just yet." The excitement simmered down a little bit and Guardian Beck was able to lower her voice. "The Guides need to start using them, so we are going to make sure everyone has appropriate arrangements, which means you will at least get to know which one will be yours. As the Seeds, your pods will be evenly dispersed, so you may find yourself near our class building, all the way over on the other side of the Guides building or anywhere in between. This will allow space for the Guides on your teams to have a pod near you. Just a reminder that Jr. Guides will not exactly have the same role as the Guides, and therefore will not need pods. Now, when I display your names on the map, you may go find your pod. Make it a comfortable space for yourself and decorate however you please. Remember your nests in your residences will still be waiting for you after the iteration, and pods will likely shift each iteration." With that, Guardian Beck waved a hand towards the map, and all their names appeared throughout the sea of pods. Kirana was hoping to see Guides names too, but those pods on the map were left blank.

"Wow, your spot is like front and center," laughed Anala. Kirana hadn't spotted it yet and looked to where Anala indicated. It really was. There were no pods right in between the Green and White buildings, but a little ways in front of the entrances was where they began. Kirana's was the first one someone would reach from the entrance of either one of them.

"Where's yours?" she asked Anala, eyes roaming the map. "Oh, there!" She found it not too far away, just behind Kirana's by a couple pods and to the right, closer in the direction of the Green Seeds building. Kirana kept searching the map until she found Ravi's and Nox's names as well. Nox's pod was near Kirana's too, but closer to the White Guides building, and Ravi's was the opposite direction, practically on the edge of the map. Kirana looked around for him.

"Have you seen Ravi yet?" she asked Anala. Anala looked at her with uncertainty.

"To be honest, when I was talking with him and Alev earlier, I didn't get the impression that he was going to be joining," she said carefully. Kirana glanced at her, feeling like there was more to the story. Anala confirmed. "I think he was going with Alev to talk to Guardian Era."

"Hmm," was all the noise Kirana made. Other students were starting to make their way to the exit to go examine their pods, and Kirana and Anala joined the rush. As they reached Kirana's pod, Anala gave her a wave of gold sparkles and continued on towards her own. Kirana sent orange sparks in return. As she stood in front of the entrance of her pod, she placed her hand on the side like she remembered Nox doing. Sure enough, the entire doorway pushed inward slightly and then slid to the side, creating an opening. Her name hung in the air just inside.

It was dark and empty inside the pod. She closed the door behind her and walked around slowly, taking in a lot of nothing, contemplating what she wanted to do with it. She started talking to herself.

"I'll be back and forth a bit at the beginning, so I want it to be comfortable, and I want an easy transition back after the iteration. So, I think darkness will be good." She looked up at the domed ceiling. *Dimension*, she thought. *It needs dimension.*

She wasn't sure how long she had been working on her pod, but she was very happy with the results. The dome remained dark, but not as a flat blackness. She took inspiration from the reflectors at the Shimmering Horizons party and added lines in strategic places to cast light and shadows in certain ways, allowing a multidimensional darkness that also dispersed a glow throughout. She added flecks of gold across the ceiling, though these were more for fun than utility. She toyed with the idea of adding a softness to the ground, something cushy, but decided a solid ground might feel better upon her return. She did add a small section to the floor that provided a little bounce, though. Jumping on it would spring her into a cozy, floating bubble, but that was about the only extra she really added. She stood back and took a look at her work with a satisfied feeling. Wanting a fresh perspective on it, she decided to leave the pod and check on Anala. She would see what she thought of it when she returned.

As she walked up to Anala's pod, it appeared like she had just about finished too. She could tell because Anala's door was open. Kirana reached the door and noticed a silvery film over the opening. She reached out a finger to touch it just as Anala came from behind her pod.

"Wait, don't touch it!" she said urgently. Luckily, it was in time. "Phew!" Anala breathed. "We are the only ones allowed to enter our own pods. This thing would've zapped you or something! I heard it's kind of like what happens if you touch a white-out box on light strings." Kirana's eyes went wide.

"Oh! Thanks for saving me!" she laughed nervously. "Well, that's a good thing, I suppose." Anala walked up and through her door just fine.

"Yeah, that's weird," she noted, looking at the air between them. "I don't see anything there, but you do, don't you?" Kirana nodded, then shrugged.

"Well, I just came to check on you! I think I finished mine but wanted to see it with new eyes, so I decided to take a break," Kirana said.

"Me too!" Anala chimed. "I went basic except for a few features. Can you see inside? Or no?" she asked Kirana.

"Kind of," she responded, trying to see in. It was all wavy and warped from the film at the entrance.

"Well, I made it really warm," Anala began. "Obvious for me, I guess," she said, chuckling. "And I did the bright light so I can use it as a signal to myself when I enter and leave the iteration." Kirana had heard that many in the graduating class used the bright light and seemed to like it. It helped them to identify those transitions. She decided she could always try it next time but didn't really understand the need for it yet.

"I think I'm done for now. I'm going to head over to Alev's residence to see if a decision has been made," Anala announced. "Want to come with me?"

"Maybe I can catch up with you later. I want to take one final look at my pod," Kirana responded. "If I don't catch you, let me know what you find out!"

"I will!" assured Anala, seeming more in a rush now that she felt closer to knowing if Alev was going to be able to stay. She closed her pod and walked with Kirana back to hers. Kirana opened her door and showed Anala where she supposed the film was that covered the entrance. Kirana couldn't see one on her own door. "Oh yeah! I see it!" Anala squinted. "Weird," she said, shaking her head. "Okay, I'm off!" They exchanged a soft blue mist.

Kirana looked around her pod again, and it felt right. She was pleased with it. Now that it was set up, she wished they could start using them. She sighed, but in an excited and contented way. As she closed the door to her pod, she heard a familiar voice and walked around behind it to investigate. Sure enough, she saw the owner of that voice chatting happily with someone else, walking in her direction.

"Kirana!" Nova exclaimed. She and Nox came closer and met Kirana next to her pod. "Is this your pod?" she asked.

"Yep! I just finished the inside!" Kirana responded.

"You're so close to Nox!" Nova said excitedly. "He just showed me his."

"Can you go inside?" Kirana asked, surprised. She looked back and forth from Nox to Nova. Nova looked at Nox as if she wasn't sure how she should respond. Nox grinned.

"Nova may have some special privileges," he said, grinning at the two of them. Kirana tilted her head, and Nova seemed to pick up on what she was thinking.

"I can't go in all of them, only Nox's, and only until the iteration starts," she explained, playfully shoving Nox as hard as she could which barely nudged him at all.

"What are you up to now?" asked Kirana. She just wanted to extend her time near Nox somehow, if she could. She unconsciously had shifted her body to face his, where he was squared to her as well.

"Welllll," said Nova mischievously, "I've been trying to convince Nox to actually let me test the pod with him." She blinked rapidly at him with big eyes. "I almost convinced him." Kirana looked at Nox, whose eyes were already locked on hers. She felt herself fall right into them. She thought maybe she had moved closer to him but couldn't be sure. Something clicked in her mind, and she realized the inside of her pod looked just like staring into his eyes. Then she remembered the feeling she had when Nox had given *her* a trial of the pod before too.

"I—I think it's probably important that she knows what it's like," Kirana stammered, trying to think of any reason she could to get Nox to take them into the pod again, knowing now that it meant doing a shared split-energy. Nox only responded with the huff of air he grunted in defeat. He turned with great effort and started walking back towards his pod. Nova jumped in the air and bounced up and down a few times behind him.

"Thank you!" she mouthed quietly to Kirana as they turned to follow him.

CHAPTER
FORTY THREE

Kirana half covered her mouth with her fingertips, partially con-cealing the smile she couldn't contain. Nova barely touched the ground for how excited she was. She grabbed one of Kirana's hands and ran, pulling her to catch up with Nox where she grabbed his hand as well. Just a moment later, they were standing in front of Nox's pod. Nox opened the door and stepped inside. Kirana saw the same silvery film over the opening that she had seen on Anala's pod. Nova was skipping forward, headed straight for it.

"Nova!" Kirana cried, trying to reach for her but missing. Nova passed through the field unharmed, turning around to see what Kirana had called her name for. Then Nox reappeared.

"Don't worry! I already cleared her," he explained, pointing to the names hovering just inside the doorway that she could see clearly now. The film was gone. "And I just cleared you as well." He smiled and kindly offered his hand. She took it and stepped inside. It wasn't decorated at all like the test pod they had trialed together. The floor was mostly dark, and shadows cast over it in jagged patterns, but the line around where the floor met the domed walls was another story. Purples, reds, oranges, pinks, and every shade in between, danced and moved ever so slowly along the edges, creeping upward. As she followed the colors with her eyes, it became lighter and lighter, touching into blues and whites.

"Wow," Kirana couldn't help but utter as she turned in a slow circle, taking it in.

"I was inspired," Nox said so quietly that she wasn't even sure she heard correctly. She looked over at Nox where he was fiddling with something on the wall, not looking at her. Nova was making herself at home, also avoiding Kirana's eyes while hiding a smirk. She was over by a large floating bench of sorts. It looked like it was strung by invisible string, and if you looked from the right angle with the right lighting, you could catch a shimmer. Kirana joined Nova on the bench. It was kind of stretchy, kind of springy and very comfortable. Nox went over to the door and closed it, bringing a panel with him to the bench where he joined them. He went over the same instructions and warnings with Nova as he had with Kirana, but Nova looked shiny and ready to go. She was unphased. Kirana listened intently even though it was her second time, making sure she knew everything.

"Are we going to be the same kind of Being as last time?" she asked Nox.

"Is that what you'd like to do?" he answered. She nodded emphatically. He looked at her for a moment, as if he were considering something.

"Okay, I have an idea," he shared. "It will be the same, but different." He had a lopsided grin when he said it. It seemed like it didn't matter to Nova, who was anxiously waiting for them to get started. She started bouncing a little on the bench, which shook Kirana and Nox slightly as well. "Hey now," said Nox laughing. "One more thing. Remember that we will be connected to each other, so if you need anything or you get nervous about anything, I'll be there with you. Reach out with your thoughts, and I'll know." He looked from Kirana to Nova to make sure they both acknowledged this.

"Come onnn!" Nova begged. And with that, Nox hit the button. Kirana felt everything rush to her, into her, through her—just like last time. She hadn't moved. She preferred this to the Sims. She closed her eyes, though somehow in this place, she didn't feel like she had eyes the same way as she was used to. It was more like turning inward so that she could take in the feelings of it. The sensations were all encompassing. Soft and hard, light and heavy, hot and cold; she could find it all. After the initial shock when she passed the threshold into being in this state, again it felt like this was always her. She had been like this forever. In this state of change. It was odd to think about the irony that continuous change was a comforting familiar state. They seemed to be opposites, yet they were in perfect balance. She allowed her knowingness and her awareness to expand now to the tickling movements and the gentle swaying, and she stretched into the deep, deep groundedness. That's where she felt the connection to Nox and Nova. She felt Nox's steadiness and Nova's pure delight. She leaned into it more, letting them know she was there. Instantly, she just knew that they knew.

She could turn her attention to different things, while still knowing the rest in the background. She felt like the ultimate multi-tasker, with millions of billions of parts of her all doing different jobs. But like before, she just knew what to do and everything worked together. She could feel the synchronized harmony with those outside of her as well. When she felt deeper into her connection with Nova, she was happy to find that they were more connected than ever. She didn't have to speak or ask anything. She just knew. And in that moment, she knew what Nova knew. Nova was going to be on her team as a Jr. Guide this iteration. And Nova knew that Kirana knew. And Nox knew that they both knew. What Kirana didn't know was where all this knowing came from. And then she knew, instantly. It came from her, and him, and her, who were sitting together in the pod. But it also came from here. It was part of the nature of this life force here where she also was. She admired, she felt, she was in awe, and she also discovered odd sensations. Some that weren't pleasant. They weren't bad, she just didn't prefer them. And then she was excited to have discovered that. It continued.

Finally, at some point, milliseconds or centuries later, the colors from Nox's pod were moving and changing and swirling, bringing her fully back. She realized where she was and what she had just done. She turned and saw Nova, whose face full of emotion mirrored her own. Nox was glowing a deep evergreen. This time it was Kirana who reached for one of Nova's hands and one of Nox's. They stayed like that momentarily, basking in the afterglow, and then Nova turned to Nox.

"What is that called?" asked Nova.

"It's called Tree," said Nox with a soft smile.

When Nova and Kirana got back to their residence, the beautiful display that had covered it was fading, and it was resuming its usual changing patterns. It looked to be a sort of swirling midnight blue underneath the colors. She had filled Nova in on the video apologies from Alev and Ravi and how Anala was glowing orange again, now that she was back in contact with him. They hadn't said anything about the pod experience yet in public. They had somehow decided they would talk about it when they got back. Kirana wasn't sure how, but she knew that they had an understand. She went up to her nest, and Nova went into hers. A little while later, Nova took the light string into Kirana's nest, which was no surprise to Kirana. They hopped on her chestnut light string and went into the nook.

"So," Kirana said softly, "you're going to be on my team?" Nova reached over and squeezed her hand, not saying a word. "How did I get so lucky," Kirana gushed. "I could burst!"

"Oh, but don't do that," laughed Nova. "If you burst, then I have no more excuses to be a Jr. Guide. I'd have to leave campus, and it would be a whole thing," she carried on, mimicking annoyance as she teased Kirana. "It's because of Nox and Kylo. They both have been behind me this whole time, insisting to the Guardians that you and I need each other."

"Well, I do," smiled Kirana. "I couldn't bear to go into this iteration knowing that you weren't even on campus anymore." Nova gave her a big cheesy grin.

"I have an idea," she declared suddenly. Kirana was instantly suspicious.

"I can't sneak you in," she laughed.

"No, that's not it!" Nova chuckled, trying to be serious now. "Kylo is your family, but he's a Guide this iteration, not a Seed with you—"

"But he'll still be with me," Kirana interjected. "He chose the same location." She was clinging on to this fact as hard as she could, still not knowing what exactly the difference was in being a Guide. Nova hesitated, then continued, taking a slightly different approach.

"Right, well, Kylo is in your family, and Nox is in mine. Nox will also be a Seed this iteration. What if—" she began, treading carefully. "What if you find Nox in this iteration?" Kirana tried to block out what she thought Nova might be insinuating. She flustered slightly, but Nova decided to go all the way. "Kirana, we could join our families! We're mates, but they're not wrong. I need you too."

"Nox chose probably the furthest location possible from Kylo and me," she said helplessly, though she couldn't help but think about trying to find him once they got there.

"I don't think it's that big. At least, I don't think it's so big that you couldn't find each other," Nova maintained. Kirana looked at her thoughtfully, letting herself take Nova seriously now. She imagined what it could be like. Then, a hint of Ravi fluttered into her mind. He would be nearby already, and they sort of had a thing going on, though she didn't even know where they stood right now.

"I'll think about it," Kirana promised, partly to appease Nova and partly because she really did need to process the idea. She wondered if it might be possible or what it could mean. That was enough for Nova for now.

"Are you getting excited to rejoin more of your family there?" Nova asked her. Kirana, and many of them really, had family members on different schedules already in iterations now.

"Yes!" Kirana said evenly. "It's weird though, I haven't thought about it much because I've been so focused on figuring out my own plan and what I needed to accomplish. Now that it's mostly preparation work, I feel like I can let myself get excited to see everyone there!"

"They'll be so happy to get both you and Kylo!" Nova cheered.

"I missed him so much last iteration," Kirana said, somewhat off topic. Her mind had circled back to worrying about what he was doing as a Guide. Would it be the same? Would she still be in this iteration with him after all? They were getting close to midterms and turning in their contracts, and she hadn't even been able to set anything up with him yet. Nova must have seen the worry on her face, but only had her last sentence as context.

"He's with you this iteration, so it's okay," she declared. "And," she said, throwing it in one more time for good measure, "there's always Nox."

CHAPTER FORTY FOUR

As Kirana prepared for her next class, she was thinking about the list of experiences she needed to have in order to reach the goals that she had committed to for this iteration. She didn't want to have to organize that many appointments, so she was trying to narrow it down to just the most important things. She could leave some of the other opportunities open for when she arrived. Sometimes lessons and experiences are common, especially in certain areas, so based on the location she had chosen, she was able to make an educated guess as to what things she probably wouldn't need to set up contracts for ahead of time, while still being able to achieve them. Last iteration, she had taken way too many appointments, and it had gotten hectic.

She left her nest and went down to meet Anala out front, per usual. When she opened the door, Anala was there, waiting and chatting pleasantly with Ravi.

"Oh! Hi, Ravi," said Kirana, trying—but not succeeding—to hide the surprise in her voice. He'd been in class lately, but usually arriving late. They had mostly only communicated by waves and smiles and an occasional mist. He beamed at her.

"I thought I'd walk to class with you if that's alright," he commented casually. Kirana glanced at Anala, who looked as if everything was normal.

"Of—of course! Great, let's go then," Kirana stuttered. She was starting to assume that *he* assumed that she had accepted his last apology from that video, which she had, but she hadn't said so explicitly. The tone was light and easy as they started walking together, so it didn't seem right to bring it up. But she did want to know if there was a consensus about Alev.

"How's Alev doing?" she asked either or both of them.

"He's hanging in there," Ravi replied first. Anala had a bit of a dreamy look in her eye.

"He gets to stay on campus! He messaged me more details earlier," Anala reported. "He doesn't get to go to classes anymore or work with Guardian Cosmo or anything, but he can work on redoing his plan while he recovers, and he may just end up on a different iteration schedule."

"Oh, that's great!" Kirana cheered for her mate. "I'm so glad to hear it." Anala nodded. She seemed happy with the decision, and now that everything was out in the open, things had seemed to fall back into place with the two of them. As they approached the Green building, they saw the pods with new eyes.

"Ravi, how do you like your pod?" Kirana asked him. "Did you set up the bright light too?"

"Yeah, of course!" he said. Kirana waited for more, but he didn't add anything. She finally was starting to realize that he wasn't a big talker in general. She laughed to herself. It might not have been entirely in her head after all. Ravi looked in her direction, and Anala jabbed him with her elbow.

"Agh—Right, I like my pod. It's way over there," he said, gesturing in the direction off to the far right, "so I'm kind of in my own space. Where's yours?" Now that they had reached the twin buildings, they could see Kirana's pod. Anala pointed it out to him. "No way! You're right there?" He almost seemed envious in a way, but Kirana didn't understand why. She felt like it was almost too visible of a spot. She blushed a little. "That's cool," Ravi said to her, intentionally catching her eye. He gave her a sparkling smile and then turned to enter the building. Anala followed with Kirana trailing behind. She took a quick glance towards the White building, hoping to spot Kylo and definitely thought it was a long shot. Except he was there! He was talking to someone just out front.

"Kylo!" Kirana shouted. He didn't hear her. "KYLO!" she tried again, but they were deep in conversation. She watched them turn to head into the building. *So close*, she thought to herself as she turned to go into her own building. Ravi and Anala waved her over, and she sat down just as Guardian Beck began to address the group.

"It's just about time for what you've all been working towards! Midterms are almost here, so at this point you should be scheduling appointments for as soon as possible. We will expect signed contracts, and you need time for negotiation and reciprocation as necessary, so please start making arrangements now." She sent her gaze around the room to make sure everyone had heard the direction. Seemingly satisfied, she continued. "In other news, I have heard from Guardian Alder that teams are almost ready to be announced! There are some finishing touches to complete, and they will be assigning pods to the Guides shortly."

Kirana suddenly felt like there were eyes on her, but she didn't want to look. She suspected it was Ravi who was looking at her intently enough for her to feel it. Luckily, Guardian Beck didn't speak that much longer and released them to start setting up appointments. As soon as they got up, Ravi approached her.

"I'd love to set up an appointment with you," he said somewhat hopefully, but with an edge. He already knew she'd say yes, because she told him as much when they were on his roof. She had mixed feelings, remembering that interaction.

"Okay, let's do it," she agreed. Once two of them agreed to set up a contract, they would meet and negotiate based on the things that they needed to encounter during their self-assignments. Since everybody's missions and assignments were different, sometimes it worked, sometimes it didn't. But it made sense to Kirana because Ravi was going to be somewhat close, and she already had an idea for a pretty good fit—on her end at least.

"I'd like to have an appointment with you as well," Anala said to her with a hopeful smile.

"I'd love that," Kirana nodded, smiling back. "Maybe we should just turn our community space into an open office at our residence and get all of our appointments done at once," she joked. She didn't mean it seriously, but Anala seemed to love the idea. She gasped and clasped her hands together, flickering just a little bit stronger.

"Oh, can we?! What a great idea!" she exclaimed. Ravi, who was still standing with them, seemed to agree.

"I'll let Kylo know. We'll be there!" He gave them a sprinkle of gold sparkles. "Well, I'm off then, see you soon!"

"See you soon!" Anala called after him.

"Thank you!" Kirana said at the same time. She was looking forward to connecting with Kylo and glad Ravi would make sure he joined them. Kirana turned to Anala then.

"I'm keeping my contracts to a minimum this iteration, but make sure you invite anyone else you want to," she told her. "Sora's going to love this," she chuckled.

"Oh," Anala said, suddenly turning serious. "Maybe we should keep it to just the graduating class, don't you think? Strictly for contracts? I'm just afraid that it would turn into a party or something, and I would for sure get distracted if Alev showed up."

"Fair enough," Kirana responded. "We'll tell Sora the party can start when the office closes." She grinned, and this relaxed Anala. Kirana looked at her for a moment, trying to figure out if this was really about Alev, or if there was something more. Anala didn't reveal anything one way or the other.

"I'm going to find a few others right now actually," Anala mentioned, looking around at the room that was starting to empty. "See you back there?"

"Okay, see you there!" Kirana responded, waving a mist of gold. She began walking back to their residence on her own. She let her mind wander until she heard someone calling out to her.

"Hey, Kir! Kirana! Light of my existance! Wait up!"

Kirana turned around laughing to see Kylo leaping after her. She waited and watched him run up to her without slowing down. He practically tackled her, but kept them both from ending up on the ground at the last second. He had a hand on each of her arms.

"Hey, Sunshine!" he said breathlessly with a huge grin.

"Kylo, you're wild," Kirana tried to say through her laughter. He let go of her arms when they were steady, and they resumed walking.

"Ravi told me we're making an impromptu office and setting up contracts?" Kylo remarked, almost making it a question. He didn't wait for her response before saying, "I notified Nox." Kirana realized she hadn't even thought of setting up a contract with him. Her mind started racing through the spaces she was hoping to fill. Kylo sensed the hesitation in her non-answer and added, "You know, so all of us can get as much done as we can. You don't have to set anything up with him." He looked at her sideways.

"Of course!" Kirana answered. "I don't know, maybe I'll think of something with him. Although, his location is all the way on the other side. I'm not sure it would make sense." Kylo tilted his head slightly.

"It's not super big," he said. "I don't think it would be a problem." Kirana looked at him, surprised.

"Huh, Nova just mentioned something similar," she said. Kylo didn't say anything to that. As they approached Kirana's residence, the building was mostly fuzzy white streaks, lazily drifting across horizontally. It appeared that nobody was there. Kirana breathed a sigh of relief because she didn't want to have to ask Sora and Nova to leave. They went inside and into the community area.

"Can you help me set things up?" Kirana asked.

"'Course!" Kylo agreed. He walked over to where the congratulatory notes from her green screen were still stacked. "Maybe take these to your nest?"

"Yeah, good point. I'll be right back," she said as she took them and hopped on her light string that was just along the side of the bookcase.

She noticed Kylo watching. When she got back moments later, Kylo was still there next to the light string, waiting for her.

"This is what Alev used to sneak in?" he asked her, his eyes darkening.

"Yes," Kirana responded quietly, "but it's all handled now. No need to bring it up again." He grunted his disapproval but dropped the subject.

"And how about Ravi? Are you two..." he dropped off. When he turned around to look at Kirana, he modified his attitude to be more nonchalant. "Are you two hanging out still?" he asked breezily.

"Not really," she responded. "He's actually been around more, but we haven't really talked about anything more than surface stuff lately. He wants to set up a contract with me though." Then, realizing she made it one-sided, she continued. "I mean, we both want to set up a contract together," she amended. "I'm curious to see how that appointment will go. I have no idea what he'll want me to do." Kylo appeared to be curious as well.

"Well, I certainly want to set up a contract with you, as always," he grinned. "I'll have some limits this time, but I think I can still fill in wherever you need me." Kirana smiled. Kylo was never afraid to take the tough or dirty contracts for her.

"You. Are. The. Best." Kirana said each word as its own sentence and sprinkled him with a different color of sparkles for each one. *Best* was in gold.

CHAPTER FORTY FIVE

Kylo and Kirana had rearranged the room into little meeting areas for two by the time everyone started to trickle in. Kirana pulled out some extra journals and writing pieces in case anyone needed them and set some refreshments in a corner. Kylo put on some ambient sounds and set up air bumpers around some of the areas for noise privacy, as contracts could potentially be very personal. There were some areas that were more open as well. There was not really a formality to this event, so no announcements were made. It stayed somewhat quiet as everyone arrived and moved around the room, preparing to exchange discussions and signatures.

After Kirana felt like everyone was getting settled, she looked around for the few of them that she needed to make arrangements with. She locked eyes with Anala from across the room. It looked like she had been helping others get settled too. One of the sound protected areas was available, and Anala raised her eyebrows at it. Kirana met her at that space.

"Perfect. My first appointment," she said with a smile.

"Mine too!" chimed Anala. "You know, when we first met as mates, I knew immediately that I'd want to do this." Kirana hugged her.

"Me too. I think we can really support each other. You're going to be a little bit far away, but I think it's manageable for sure!" Kirana was reassuring herself, although nobody else seemed concerned about distance. Maybe it was something about the graduating class that she didn't understand yet. She shrugged it off. "Where do you want to start? Why don't you go first," she decided.

"Okay," said Anala, opening her journal. "I actually have two options that I think could be a good fit." She looked up. "It might depend on what you'd like from me, so I'll share them both, and we can decide what works better." Kirana nodded, opening her journal as well, ready to take notes.

"I actually remember my first request of you," Anala said, looking at Kirana somewhat shyly. "To teach me to 'glow steady without flickering so much,'" she quoted herself. "It comes from perfection—or imperfection actually. It makes me flicker! Having to be perfect, to do everything perfectly, it can hold me back. I think you could really help me to push past the anxiety of not being perfect so that I can enjoy more, instead of instantly moving on to the next thing. It takes a lot of energy to make things perfect, and when I don't give myself the chance to enjoy the work I've done, it's possible I could flicker out entirely! I've seen how you can relax into a moment and enjoy it without constantly having your mind on the next thing to do. Perfectly," she added with a grimace. "It could be a Teach by Example contract," she suggested. Kirana was taking notes and writing down ideas as Anala spoke, nodding along. She liked this option.

"What's the second one you're thinking about?" Kirana prodded.

"The second is the one you helped me define a bit better before, under my theme of Being Empathetic. Although, it might be just as frustrating for you as it would be for me for a while, so that's why I think it might depend on what you need on your end. Why don't you share yours before we decide which one matches. Does that work for you?" Anala asked.

"For sure," said Kirana. "You know, I also remember what I said to *you* when we became mates," she grinned. "I wanted you to help me stay strong when things get in my way. I was thinking about that, and it actually fits into my Creating Balance theme. Sometimes when the answer is not black and white, I need a container to give me the space to create gray out of it. Or orange maybe," she laughed. "That analogy works much better for us actually," she acknowledged. "When everything looks red and yellow, I need perspective so I can figure out how to create orange. I need someone to prop me up and help me stay strong until I figure it out." Anala was glowing orange herself by the time Kirana was done talking.

"I would be honored," she whispered, "to be that for you. And I think that my first option is a better match for this. I kind of love that we are going to hold true to our very first instincts of how we could help each other!" Kirana reached her hand over the table and touched Anala's arm.

"Me too. It's perfect," she declared. They worked out the details together and signed each other's contracts in preparation to turn them in.

"First contract, done!" Anala stated loudly. They left the little area for someone else to use. They moved back into the open area where there were many comings and goings as everyone took appointments. Kirana spotted Ravi speaking with someone else and then did a sweep around the area looking for Kylo. She didn't immediately see him, so she decided to get a refreshment while she waited for one of them to become available.

As she waited, someone she wasn't very familiar with saw her and asked to take an appointment. Kirana hesitated, but then decided to take it and see what it was that she needed. They sat in the open area even though one of the more private areas was available. She didn't seem to mind at all. Maybe it was because she had a tough request and thought it would make it harder for Kirana to turn her down if there were others around. Kirana had been on both the giving and receiving side of requests like this before, and was no stranger to them. Everyone needed them at various times to learn various lessons. This classmate basically needed a villain. She needed someone to leave her high and dry, an act of betrayal. A friend-to-enemy of sorts. She was so convincing, but she told Kirana that she couldn't get anyone to do it. It made sense, they weren't especially fun contracts, but they were necessary and had to be arranged sometimes. Adversity could be a quick track to learning lessons. As she looked around the room, she remembered that a lot of the Seeds group were in their first iteration in the graduating class. Maybe everyone was just trying to play it safe, which also made sense.

"Okay, I'll do it," Kirana agreed. She felt better about it when she was showered with loads of dark magenta gratitude until she laughed. It seemed like an important piece of this classmate's iteration. "I don't need anything back, okay? We can do a one-sided contract." They finished the contract and before Kirana could walk away, she felt her grab her arm.

"I would like to return the favor during the iteration," she pleaded. "I'll think of something once we get there. It doesn't have to be official." Kirana gave one nod and a small smile, and she turned away. She did not expect anything from her and would not hold her to it, but it was kind to offer.

By now, Kylo was free. He saw Kirana approaching and waited for her near a private area.

"After you," he said, sweeping his arm open to usher her into the seats. She grinned and sat down, and he sat across from her.

"Tough negotiation?" he asked, looking at her closely.

"More of a tough agreement," she sighed. Kylo nodded in understanding.

"I know all about those," he sympathized, "and I suspect I'm about to set one up right now." His eyes twinkled at her. "But I've got you, don't worry," he grinned. "Want to go first?" Kirana put her head in her hands.

"Not really," she said, her voice muffled.

"C'mon, you've got this. Tell me what you need," he encouraged. He gently pulled her arms out from under her, creating the necessity for her to hold her head up again and look at him.

"I rely on you too much, and we both know it," she began. "I hate this so much, but I need to break it this iteration. I'm in the graduating class now. I have to have the courage to do this, with or without you." Kirana could've sworn she saw a passing look of relief across Kylo's face. She tried not to take it any sort of way. "I'm not saying I don't want to do iterations with you any more after this, I just need to know that I'm brave enough, strong enough, to carry on." She hesitated now, looking down at the table and letting that look she saw on his face go to her head. He must be so looking forward to not having her need him all the time. Kylo was silent for a moment, and when she looked back up at him, he had a look—a different look—deep in his eyes.

"You know I'll always be here for you. Always." He took each of her hands in his own. "I don't think you'll need me as much after this iteration either, but... probably for different reasons than you're thinking."

Kirana looked at him, confused. "Anyways," he continued, "your request fits exactly with what I need from you as well." This made Kirana more confused. He needed her to not need him in this iteration?

"I need you to be able to continue on without me in this iteration. You have huge tasks ahead of you, and I—," he stopped. He basically just confirmed what she thought. Kirana shook her head a little. This wasn't making sense. Kylo let out a big sigh.

"I can't say much, but you know that being a Guide is different. I'm not supposed to share this yet, but you're my Seed," he said, his voice falling to a whisper. Kirana's eyes got wide. "I'm part of your team," he confirmed. At this point, he couldn't hide his smile. "Because I'm a Guide, I don't really have my own mission. My mission is you. My mission is to help you complete your self-assignment." Kirana still didn't say anything. She wasn't understanding. Then Kylo said the thing that cleared it up, both in the best and worst way possible. "In order to be with you on location, I had to choose an option available to Guides, and—" He paused again. "Kirana, Guides are there on location way shorter than most Seeds. My assignment isn't long enough. I have to leave here earlier than you, and I'll be leaving way earlier from there as well. You'll still be on location long after I come back. I need you to be okay. I'm so sorry," he said finally.

Kirana blinked, watching his face. The relief she had seen on his face earlier was not that he was happy to be rid of her, it was that he was afraid she'd be upset with him that he'd chosen to be a Guide after all. "I didn't actually know that detail when I made the choice." He looked down at the table. "I'll still be on your team, but I won't be able to be on location with you after a certain period." They sat in silence for a moment. Then Kirana put her hand on his arm.

"Okay," she whispered. Kylo looked up at her. "We'll figure it out. I'll be okay. I'm sure I'll miss you, but I'll learn to carry on, just like I said I needed to do." She smiled weakly, half regretting her request now that it was going to be granted.

"I know you will be," Kylo responded. "Okay then, let's write up the contract?" Kirana tried to practice being brave as they finished it up together, but she didn't feel brave.

After they got up, he hugged her for a long time. Then he spun her around with his big Kylo smile back in place.

"Kir, there better be a party after all this hard work," he teased her. She giggled.

"I'm expecting it too!" she squealed as he spun her again. Feeling better, they left the area to see that several others looked like they had also accomplished a lot in these appointments.

"Any other contracts you were hoping to get settled now?" Kylo asked her. Kirana looked around the room for Ravi.

"One more in particular actually," she said, spotting him near the entry. Kylo turned to where she was looking.

"Ah, I see," he said. "Well, I'll be around. Come find me when you're done!"

"Sounds good!" Kirana said as she moved towards Ravi. Whoever Ravi was talking to was headed out the door as she was walking up.

"Hi, Kirana," Ravi greeted her. He tossed her a glow, still holding the door open.

"Hey!" she greeted him back. "Want to talk about a contract?" she asked him, glancing at the door and wondering if he had been planning to leave without having an appointment with her.

"What do you have in mind?" he asked her. She explained what she needed, right there in the doorway entrance. Ravi looked hesitant.

"That's not exactly the contract I had in mind," he said, putting a hand on the back of his neck. Someone had walked up and it seemed they had overheard the conversation through the open door.

"I'll do it," said a voice from the doorway, and Nox stepped inside.

CHAPTER FORTY SIX

K irana's heart dropped. That surprised her though. She didn't know why it reacted so dramatically to Nox offering to take the contract she offered to Ravi. She looked between the two of them.

"Hey," Ravi said to Nox in greeting. "That's cool, thanks." Ravi didn't seem to have a problem with it at all. Then he turned to Kirana.

"I'll be right back, okay?" He smiled at her. "I'm going to go get Alev and some of the other FI group that are at my residence. I think Sora might be there too. I'll be back though. Let's talk about our contract then?" Kirana didn't know what to say, but he was walking out the door so she had to respond somehow.

"Oh—okay," she stammered, and he was gone. She was left standing there with Nox. As she turned to him, she felt comforted, although she wanted to rethink her contract request.

"Hi," she greeted him with bright eyes. He smiled.

"Hi," he said. "You know I'm serious, right? If that's what you need, I'll do it." Kirana was lost for a moment. Once she realized she was staring, she scrambled to figure out what to say. Nox didn't seem to mind; he just waited patiently for her response.

"I think I might restructure my request now that I think about it," she finally said. He considered this.

"Want someone to talk it through with?" Nox offered. She realized they were still standing in the doorway.

"Sure," she accepted with a smile. "That might actually help a lot." They walked over to where there were two little meeting areas still set up. Kylo and some of the others were rearranging things again as everyone prepared to relax and have some fun. They sat down, and Kirana looked at Nox curiously.

"Aren't you going to be on the other side of the globe entirely?" she inquired. Nox shrugged.

"Yes, but that's just a starting point. We can always move around," he explained. Kirana hadn't really considered this. It opened up a lot more opportunities when she thought of it that way. "So tell me more about your contract. What's the theme?" he asked.

"It's about trusting myself," she swallowed. Somehow she felt silly all of a sudden. She should've mastered this a long time ago and here she was taking it into her graduating class now. When he didn't react, she continued. "It's important for me to learn to follow my intuition, *especially*," she emphasized, "when everyone else is doing something different or telling me to follow a certain path. Sometimes I'm too easily influenced to follow along with what everyone else wants me to do, and I need to be able to trust myself that I already know what to do. Even if it doesn't make sense to everybody else." She took the chance and looked in his eyes, hoping she wouldn't fall too deep. "I think it's the only way I'll be able to complete my self-assignment," she whispered. "I have to be in situations where others want me to do something, and I have to go against the grain, because eventually, I have to be able to expand when it's uncomfortable or makes others react." Nox sat quietly, looking into her eyes. He didn't try to offer a suggestion, he just offered his presence. Kirana realized this was the first time she had connected with him without getting lost. In fact, she felt entirely found. "That's why I suggested what I did to Ravi. Now I'm thinking that's not such a good way to go about it." *Especially if it's you who's going to take the contract*, she thought to herself.

"Can I offer another idea?" he asked her.

"Yes, please, of course!" she said, a little too emphatically. She realized she was used to others offering advice, even when she hadn't asked for it. It was pleasant to have the choice to hear advice and ideas, or not. There were definitely times when she would choose to not have to hear what someone else thought of her situation or what they thought she should do.

Nox went on to explain a simple adjustment to her original idea. As he explained it, Kirana realized she could get two contracts out of this. One with Nox and one with Ravi, and they'd both be helping her in different ways.

"It looks like you thought of something?" Nox said as a question as he watched Kirana start to grin.

"Thanks to you!" Kirana said, sending him warm flecks of gold with her eyes. This seemed to take him off guard for a moment, and she saw a look she didn't recognize flicker across his face, but then it was gone. Just as they were finishing up a contract together, Ravi appeared in the corner of Kirana's eye. He appeared to be waiting for her. Nox noticed as well.

"One more contract to go?" Nox asked her. She nodded, turning her attention back to him.

"Thank you so much for your time," she said earnestly. She meant it so much that gratitude unintentionally leaked from her. The depth in Nox's eyes intensified.

"I've got you," he said, his voice deep. He was gone before Kirana could register it. She was still trying to process the whole interaction with him when Ravi appeared at the door, grinning and bright.

"I'm ready now!" Ravi sprung on her, shaking her out of her daze. She blinked up at his glow and smiled.

"Okay," she chuckled. "I have a new plan now anyways. Maybe you'll like this better." Ravi sat down, and she told him what she needed now. He was much more amenable to her revised contract idea, and it balanced out what he had in mind as well, although he did have to make a concession on his end too. He was very light about it though, and by the end of their appointment, they were both laughing and playfully teasing each other.

"We've got this, Kirana!" he cheered as they completed the job. "Ready to party?!" He jumped up and looked around. They were the last two working. Everyone else was relaxing, chatting and dancing. "Can I get you a refreshment?" he asked her.

"Sure," Kirana agreed brightly. As Ravi went to get them something, she started to reorganize that last little space they had been using and get rid of the last air bumpers. Kylo saw her pulling furniture and hopped over to help her.

"You're all done?" he asked her, his eyes giving her face a once-over.

"Yep!" she said. "Done!" Kylo seemed satisfied with her response and whatever he found in her eyes.

"Well, that was an effective way to go about contracts," he laughed. "We should probably make that the standard!" He lingered there a moment, and Kirana knew Kylo well enough to feel his questions before he even asked. She grinned at what he was holding back saying and just told him anyway.

"I have contracts with both Nox and Ravi," she said. "They'll both be helping me on the same theme." Kylo accepted this.

"That's great," he said. "I'm glad you got it all worked out." She wasn't entirely sure what he meant by that last part, but let it go as Ravi returned with refreshments.

"Dance later?" she asked Kylo. His grin widened.

"You got it, Kir. Dance battle! Get ready," he emphasized with his eyebrows. Kirana laughed, and he floated away.

As Anala and Kirana headed to class, ready to turn in their midterms, there was an energy of excitement buzzing back and forth between them.

"We should be getting our team assignments, right?" Anala asked, though she knew Kirana only knew as much as she did.

"I'm sure we will! They keep talking about how the Guides need to leave as soon as possible, so they must have it figured out!" As Kirana responded, she felt the pang of missing Kylo ready to set in. She knew that eventually she wasn't going to be able to brush it away. She'd have to go deep into the feeling. But it wasn't time for that yet, so she allowed herself to drop it and remain looking forward to what was ahead.

They entered the Green building and looked around for Ravi but didn't see him. They sat where they had a good view of the screen and saved him a spot.

"My dear graduating class," Guardian Beck greeted them with a wistful, wobbly smile. "You've made it so far! Now is the time to turn in all your contracts, and we will be revealing all the teams. Just so you're aware, your Guides have already known who they're with so if you've seen anyone in pods near yours lately, the secret may already be out." She grinned. "But everyone will get clarity as the teams get posted to the screen after everything is turned in. Just like midterms last semester, we will have everyone go up one at a time, insert your contracts, and your name will appear with your team listed below it." Anala grabbed Kirana's hand in anticipation. "Let's get started," Guardian Beck declared.

When Anala went up, she turned in her contracts, and her team appeared. She would have two Guides on her team. She was glowing a deep orange as she sat back down next to Kirana.

"I'm so happy," she whisper-squeaked. Kirana gave her a big smile and squeezed her hand. She knew she would be going up in a moment. Except names kept getting called and pretty soon all the names from the first iteration of the graduating class were done, and they were moving on to everyone else. Kirana was so distracted after she was skipped that she hadn't even noticed Ravi's team list as it came and went. Anala could feel her fear.

"Do you think it was an accident that they didn't call you?" she asked Kirana.

"It must be," Kirana said half-heartedly. At the end of class, everybody was happy and chattering as Guardian Beck came back to the front.

"Thank you so much everyone," she boomed. "Congratulations on your team assignments! It may do you good to meet with them while most are still here, but be quick! They'll be leaving soon. That's all for now!" Everyone started to get up. "Kirana, please stay after," Guardian

Beck said, while most were distracted and getting their things to leave the building. Kirana stayed frozen in place.

"Do you want me to wait with you?" Anala asked her, concerned. Kirana shook her head.

"No, no, it's alright. You should go meet with your team," she insisted.

"Are you sure?" Anala asked again.

"I'm sure. I'll meet you back at the residence," said Kirana. Anala gave her a nod and a shoulder squeeze, and she left with the rest of the group. Kirana walked up to the front where Guardian Beck was organizing her class things.

"Hi, Kirana. Can you please turn in your contracts?" Guardian Beck asked, smiling at her like everything was normal. She didn't say anything in response but inserted her contracts like everyone else had done. She followed Guardian Beck's eyes to the screen where she saw her name pop up. Her eyes widened as she saw the list of names that followed. Kylo, Makani, Nova, Nox. She blinked a few times, thinking maybe her vision was blurry, but she kept seeing Nox's name on this list. Kylo and Nova had both already slipped and told her she was their Seed, and she was delighted to see Makani's name as well. But Nox was a Seed. She even had a contract with him. How was he showing up as part of her team?!

CHAPTER
FORTY SEVEN

"We know this is a little unconventional," Guardian Beck said gently. She smiled at her. "And maybe a bit surprising," she added as she noticed Kirana's face. "To be clear, which part of this list is the most surprising for you?" With Guardian Beck being new this iteration, she wasn't as familiar with Kirana, her mates or her family. Kirana wondered why she wasn't having this conversation with Guardian Era or Guardian Gaia instead. Guardian Beck seemed to take note of this too. "Guardian Era is otherwise occupied, but I'm sure he would be open to a conversation if you feel this support will not be sufficient," Guardian Beck explained. "They just asked that yours be disclosed in private."

"Oh, no, it's very much okay!" Kirana reassured her. "I'm just surprised about Nox. Isn't he also a Seed? Won't he have his own self-assignment to focus on?"

"As far as I understand, Nox may be moving into a Guardian role soon. He has a small self-assignment to complete in this iteration so he wants to go back and do it, and he offered his support as a Guide as well. Being that you have two Jr. Guides, one of them working with Nox already, it made sense to add him to your team," Guardian Beck explained. "We're all quite pleased with how it worked out." Kirana felt pleased as well—and fortunate. In fact, she couldn't believe how deliciously lucky she was with her team. And two of them would even be on location with her! "Do you need anything else, Kirana?" Guardian Beck asked her. "Feel free to stop by my office if anything comes up, otherwise you are free to meet with your team now." She was looking at Kirana expectantly. She was not one to stand still for too long; she liked to flow. Kirana shook off the surprise and put her palms together in front of her heart.

"Thank you, Guardian Beck," she said. As she turned to walk out of the room, she took one last glance at the floating screen. Her name was shining there with the four others who would be supporting her, rooting for her and there for her through everything she was about to encounter. A warmth radiated in her as she left, and it only grew because from the building exit, seeing her team at her pod was unavoidable. No words were necessary for a moment. She ran over to them, and they had their first team hug of many to come.

Nova's chatter to Makani and Kirana did not stop as they walked back towards their residences. Kylo and Nox had to get back to work. Kirana discovered they would both be leaving early. And that meant very, very soon, almost immediately. There was a short period as they got settled where she would still have access points with them, but after that, she'd have to wait until she got there to connect with them again. She felt utterly surrounded and protected though. As they reached Makani's residence, Kirana gave her a hug. Before she could speak, Makani whispered in her ear.

"I am beyond lucky to have this opportunity to support such an important mission," she said, and then stepping back from the hug, she looked Kirana in the eyes. "I know I'm just a Jr. Guide, but I promise I will put everything I am into helping this be a success." Kirana was touched.

"I'm the lucky one," Kirana contested. Then she pulled Nova in closer and said to them both, "I really couldn't have asked for a better team." They all glowed and sparkled. Nova and Kirana continued on to their own residence, and both of them went to their nests with plans to reconnect later. Kirana was full of energy and her head was spinning so she paced around her nest, letting the energy regulate. She felt like there was a lull now that midterms were over. She had her team assignment, she had her self-assignment defined and her contracts were completed. Typically, those had been the last steps before the iteration began, but because of all the changes, there was still some time before she left. The remainder of her classes would be Sims, and with the benefit of having Jr. Guides who would be staying here, she suspected she had time to work with them on communication codes.

Kirana's level of energy wasn't dissipating, so she hopped on her light string to the community area just to move around some more. The movement seemed to help a bit. She went back and forth from her nest to the community area a few times. Just as she hopped on going back to her nest, she heard someone in the residence entry. She decided to go down (not by light string) to see who it was.

Anala and Alev had come in, and she could hear Anala's animated talking before she rounded the corner into the community area. Anala spotted her, and her sentence turned mid-speech to greet her.

"—Kirana, you're here!" she rushed over. "Everything okay?" she said in a hushed voice, as if to give her a little privacy from Alev. Kirana gave her a big smile.

"Yes! I found out my team assignment, and everything is great!" she assured her, hoping she wouldn't ask more questions right now with Alev present. Anala seemed to be enduring the same energy extension that she was, and she just kept right on talking without asking any more questions.

"Oh, good! I'm so relieved! I was nervous something happened with your self-assignment or your team or something! This is great, isn't it? We're so close to starting the iteration! Honestly, I'm so wired right now. It feels like we should be leaving, but we're not." She finally took a breath. Kirana was eyeing Alev with uncertainty while Alev listened to Anala with interest. Anala looked back and forth between them. "Ah," she noted. "Have you two..." she paused, "talked since..." She didn't need to finish the sentence. Kirana shook her head no. Alev was looking pale. He certainly was not back up to what his energy levels should be either. Kirana wondered why they let him stay on campus. "You know what," Anala spoke again. "I'm going to put my things away in my nest, and I will be right back!" she declared as she disappeared. Kirana smiled internally at Anala's departure. It was kind of her to give them a moment to talk out what had happened. She sat down near, but not next to Alev in the community area and waited, giving him the opportunity to start talking and explain himself. She started to think he might not actually say anything at all and wondered if maybe he was waiting for *her* to say something. It was getting ridiculous.

"I saw your apology video," she said to him. He looked sick. "I've already forgiven you," she added quickly.

"Thank you, Kirana," Alev choked out. "Really, I'm sorry, again. I just let things get out of control. I—" he turned towards where Anala had walked away. When he turned back, he spoke even quieter. "I don't want to lose Anala, and I care about you as her mate too. I almost ruined everything." He put his head in his hands. Kirana felt the urge to comfort him, but at the same time, she felt unsurprised that he was experiencing the consequences of his actions. In the end, she reached over and put her hand on his shoulder. He looked up again, accepting her hand as a peace offering.

"Can we start over?" he implored. She looked hard into his eyes.

"Are you still trying to help Guardian Cosmo take my self-assignment?" she asked him. It was more direct than she usually ever was, but she had to know once and for all. Alev shook his head fiercely.

"NO," he said definitively. "I'm not working with him anymore, and I refuse to be in his class. I don't like the influence he has on my energy. Next iteration, I will likely be going straight to Guardian Nika's group. I've learned my lesson." Kirana chose to believe him.

"Let's start over," she concurred, softening her eyes and posture. Alev gave one strong flicker of orange, smiling with relief. Anala appeared then, eyeing the conversation from a distance before confirming it was an appropriate time to come back.

"So, where were we," she said with a smile.

"I think Kirana was just about to tell us who's on her team," said Alev. Kirana was a bit taken aback with his response. It didn't feel right to her.

"Ooh! Yes!" Anala turned to her with bright eyes.

"Sorry, I actually have to head out, but we can talk more about it later!" Kirana got up and made a move to leave the room. She made the excuse because she wanted to keep her team quiet for now, particularly from Alev, and particularly since Guardian Beck kept it from the entire graduating class so far.

"Okay, see you later!" Anala sang, unphased. Alev didn't say anything, but he did flicker some faint sparks in her direction. As Kirana left the room, she heard Anala scolding him for using energy when he should be saving that up to get better right now. It wouldn't make sense for her to just go up into her nest when she said she had to leave, so she headed through the entry and left the residence. Maybe a walk would do her good anyway.

Kirana wandered around, staying somewhat nearby. She found the gardens and art displays that Anala had talked about after a date with Alev a while back and walked the labyrinth path there. That was immensely helpful to refocusing her energy. As she walked back towards her residence, she ran into Sora, who was also returning.

"Hi, Sora," Kirana greeted her. "How did your midterms go?" The FI class was the only group that didn't swap their Communications with their Sims term, so Sora had been spending a lot of time in the Sim Buildings. Her midterms would have been a variety of Sim tests based on the location she had chosen.

"So good!" she twinkled. "I love my location choice, so it was easy! How about you?"

"Mine went well too," Kirana echoed. "Do you have a favorite Sim building?" Sora thought about this for a moment, likely because she was fond of several.

"Maybe the Comms Building," she concluded. "Although, it could be because I know I'm about to spend a lot more time on communications specifically." Kirana smiled at this because Sora was always the first one ready to host a party at any time, and she was always wanting to be around others.

"Maybe, but I also think that's just a strong trait of yours," she suggested.

The FI class was different from the rest of the groups in more ways than one. Their Communications studies were more focused on practicing how they would communicate once they arrived at their location versus setting contracts and getting teams. They did not have teams exactly, though the Guardians were always there to offer support throughout the iteration. It was more of a collective support than a dedicated team. And contracts were used, but less so in the very first iteration, so they were optional.

As they approached the residence, Kirana asked Sora about the conversation they hadn't finished.

"Did you want to talk more about our conversation from earlier? About doing split-energies?" she asked. A mix of fear and excitement crossed through Sora's eyes, so briefly that Kirana barely caught it. Sora stopped her in front of their residence. She faced Kirana towards herself and took a step back.

"Don't be scared," she told Kirana. "I'm going to tap you on the shoulder. Okay?" Kirana was a little confused, but agreed. Sora took a deep breath and closed her eyes, slowly turning opaque. Once opaque, she turned clear again in an instant. Then, without moving from her position or raising her arm to tap Kirana's shoulder, Kirana felt it on her shoulder anyway. *Tap tap tap.*

CHAPTER
FORTY EIGHT

Sora had already told Kirana she could do split-energies and that her split became invisible when she did. That didn't stop Kirana from being startled to see it happen. Or not see it, but feel it, rather. Sora quickly stopped doing the split-energy and returned to normal, opening her eyes.

"So, that's what happens," she said with a little smile and a little shrug. They were standing outside their residence now, and for some reason, Kirana wanted to stay out there while they had this discussion. That reason, Kirana let herself admit, was Alev. If Alev knew Sora could do this, maybe he would tell Guardian Cosmo, and then maybe Guardian Cosmo would push her into doing it more. She wasn't sure how valid her concern was, but nevertheless, Sora didn't seem to mind talking where they were.

"It seems easy for you," Kirana said. "So it's commonplace now? Do you think all of you in the FI class can do it?" Sora appeared to not want to answer.

"Have you ever done it?" she asked, instead of answering. Kirana shook her head.

"Actually, no, I don't think I have," she said. "Nobody ever taught me, and there didn't seem to be a purpose, so I just... didn't." She didn't really know how else to answer that. It wasn't ever a focus or part of their lessons. She knew about it, but she just assumed it was a more advanced practice, or maybe it was looked down upon for doing it without instruction. Turns out things had changed. She didn't necessarily think it was a bad thing, it just made her feel behind.

"I could show you if you want," Sora offered. Kirana was a little surprised. The last time they had talked about this, it seemed like Sora was scared for anyone to know what she could do, but now it seemed easy for her, and she was offering to teach Kirana.

"Okay," Kirana said hesitantly. "I think I should probably learn if that's going to become the standard for everyone." Sora sensed her hesitation.

"No rush!" she said lightly. "Just let me know when you're ready or if you want to try it!" She smiled at Kirana and flitted away inside their residence. Things seemed very different since the last time they had talked. Something steeled in Kirana. She turned on her heels and walked towards the Impressions Office. She needed to talk to the source.

As she entered the building, she walked around looking for Guardian Cosmo's office. She found it in the middle of a hallway. She knocked on the door, and it opened before she could knock a third time, leaving her hand swinging forward in the air. Guardian Cosmo was sitting in a darkened room near a fireplace and a glowing screen, looking at her standing in the doorway. Kirana assumed he had done a split-energy to open the door, but she didn't see it happen. She realized she wasn't very familiar with Guardian Cosmo, other than their limited interactions and what Nova thought of him.

"Yes?" Guardian Cosmo inquired stiffly. "Can I help you?" Kirana stepped into the room so she wasn't just yelling from the doorway.

"I—I'd like to talk to you," she stammered. She hadn't really considered what she wanted to say. She just knew that she needed to talk to him.

"If you must," Guardian Cosmo began, "then please come in and have a seat. What is it you'd like to discuss?" Kirana built up her courage as she walked past him to sit down where she could face the room.

"Thanks for your time," Kirana began, slower than she wanted to. She wanted to dive right in and drill him on so many things, but that didn't seem right. "I just wanted to address a few things with you." Guardian Cosmo blinked at her with a slight bit of impatience near his edges. "Okay, just two things. Why did you teach the FI class to do split-energies?" Guardian Cosmo looked caught off guard for a moment and quickly recovered.

"While the syllabus is generally standard, everyone has their own style, do they not?" He asked her. "Did Guardian Beck do everything the same as Guardian Nika did?" His eyes bore into hers, but she held his gaze.

"Well, those are different groups entirely," she tried to explain. "The graduating class is different."

"So is the First Iteration class," he retorted. She couldn't argue with that. "Did you also meet with them and ask why they taught what they taught?" Kirana thought that was a rhetorical question, but he stared at her as if asking for real.

"No," she said simply, still holding his gaze. "I did not. They haven't endangered any students." That last part was a risk, but it didn't seem like this meeting was going anywhere fast. Guardian Cosmo's eyes sparked.

"Students succeed, and students fail. It's been quite some time since you've been in the first iteration. Things have changed, and we have to change with them. Now if you'll excuse me, I was in the middle of something." He broke their eye contact and looked at the glowing screen. He seemed to be watching a meeting of some kind.

"I have one more question," Kirana said, not stopping for his response. "I was told that you want my self-assignment. That you think you should be taking it." That worked to get his attention back on her.

"That's not a question," he said, not denying its truth. Kirana didn't really know what to say for a moment.

"Well," she began, trying to think quickly so she didn't stumble over her words. "I've accepted it. I'm going to complete it."

"We'll see," Guardian Cosmo responded, looking away again as if disinterested. Kirana didn't think this conversation was really all that useful so she stood up to leave.

"Thank you, Guardian Cosmo, I suppose I'll see you later," she said, and she walked towards the door. Something in him snapped.

"You will. You'll see me later," he said. Kirana stopped and turned back towards him. She was surprised but didn't show it as he continued. "That assignment should be mine. It was supposed to be mine. Everything was taking so long, so I took a couple iterations to be a Guardian, and it still wasn't time. But now, I can do split-energy so expertly that I could've continued my commitment here as well as taken on a self-assignment in the graduation iterations. This is only your first iteration in this class. Obviously I can do it better." Kirana just stared at him, shocked.

"I'm sure other tasks will come up that you can assign yourself to after this iteration," Kirana maintained. Then she turned and left the room. As she was closing the door, she heard him say one more thing.

"The assignment is mine."

Sims classes had begun, and Anala was breezing through as usual, making things look easy to Kirana. But the two of them shared a restless energy. It's not that the Sims were all that difficult, Kirana just knew that their experience would be tremendously deeper and bigger and terribly more intense than just one focused Sim. She felt like she was going through the motions now and was anxious for the iteration to get started. She knew she'd learn the best once she was there, immersed in it.

Nox and Kylo had already left. Kylo had one more point in time where he could meet with her before she wouldn't see him until she joined him on location. He didn't have his own self-assignment as a Guide, other than to support Kirana's work, so he was just getting a lay of the land, so to speak, and trying to acclimate in order to support her once she arrived.

The energy around the campus was different now. It was quieter, more focused. Everyone was finishing up their final studies and practices. This semester didn't have finals because everyone left to go take on their self-assignments instead.

The pods were such a great addition to the campus—allowing them to both have somewhere to stay as well as provide an easier support system. Before this iteration, Kirana wasn't totally sure about how they managed. She'd have to remember to ask Kylo or Nox. Kylo had struggled, she knew, but that was only his first time. Maybe after this iteration as a Guide, he'd be more apt to try again. Nox had been in the graduating class for a long time. Probably as long as Guardian Cosmo. She was curious to hear from him, once they got back, what he thought of this iteration's changes in comparison to previous iterations.

Kirana was thinking about all this while she went from her latest Sim class back to her residence, where she was going to get together with Nova and Makani to make a plan for communication and set up some codes. She was excited to discuss ideas about how they could stay connected—her own signs and signals.

As she walked up to the residence, the building was quiet on the surface. A drifting midnight blue. But she could see it was covering blasts of orange and green and yellow underneath, just showing how ready they all were to get started.

Nova and Makani had spent all this time in classes together because Makani was Tali's mate, so it was a perfect match for them to be teaming up to support Kirana. They had been inseparable since the announcement and constantly asking Kirana questions about her self-assignment, about her preferences and even about some special surprises she might like to encounter when she got there. She knew they were scheming all kinds of ways to support her, and it made her feel warm and fuzzy.

Kirana went inside the residence, then popped her head through the open door into Nova's nest where they were waiting for her. Nova and Makani squealed when they saw her.

"Come in! We have so many ideas!" called Nova. Kirana couldn't help but smile. She stepped inside and again soaked in the energy from Nova's nest of emerald and moonstone. She eyed the cottony cloud cushions, and Nova caught her looking.

"Race you!" she called, launching herself towards them to try to beat Kirana. They both scrambled for the clouds with Makani not far behind.

Nova reached them before Kirana by the slightest of moments. Once the three of them were situated, they began to discuss ideas.

"Can I go first?" asked Kirana. "I've been thinking about how to equip myself." Nova and Makani nodded enthusiastically, encouraging her to continue.

"It will give us a good understanding of how you're likely to connect," Makani confirmed.

"Okay, well, Intuition and Trusting Myself is already a strong theme for me, so I'm going to use that as much as I can to give myself positive reinforcement to keep doing it. Those will likely be times I'll need encouragement that I'm doing it right or that I'm not alone." Kirana paused as she waited for the furious note taking by the other two to subside. "And the other main idea I had was to travel and get messages while resting. I want to open that channel of dreams." Nova's eyes sparkled.

"Love it! I'll take that. We can check in there, and I'll be able to tell you if you're on the right track," Nova approved.

"And I'll take the signs and signals that we're with you!" Makani jumped in. "I've been thinking about synchronicities and symbols, anything that I can use with you on the move."

They talked through a few more ideas and nailed down some specifics for each of them. Kirana was certain that with the level of support she had, she'd be able to accomplish everything she set out to.

CHAPTER FORTY NINE

Kirana waited anxiously in her pod for Kylo to meet her. With her door open, she could poke her head out and see his pod. The door was still closed. She paced around and checked again. Still closed. She tried to relax, but she couldn't sit still. Finally, she heard something outside of her pod. This time when she poked her head out, still nothing! It was just another Guide heading towards their own pod.

"Ugh," she groaned. She closed her pod and made her way to the Green building. She went inside and sat near some huge, fragrant blooms. As she admired them, they seemed to be admiring her too. She got up and went into the middle of a group of them and sat down. They almost leaned into her, and she actually felt herself able to relax. Moments later, Kylo walked in through the front door, eyes bright and voice booming.

"Hey, Sunshine!" he said with his arms open wide when he spotted her in the midst of the colors. She hopped up and ran straight into them.

"Kylo! How's it going so far?" She stood back and looked at him. He was glowing a pale blue and seemed to be utterly comfortable and happy.

"Here," he said, grabbing her hand and pulling her behind him. "Let's find someplace nice and snug. I don't have long." They stopped in a small grove surrounded by tall lines, creating a little haven for them to have privacy in the building. They sat down in the soft green, and Kylo told her what he could.

"Everything is great," he said. "You're going to love it. You really know how to pick your location! I can keep an eye on everything just as well as I hoped I would be able to. Don't think about this too much, but it might take you a while to recognize me. Focus on my eyes, okay?" This wasn't really making sense to Kirana, but she nodded along. He could tell she wasn't following. "It doesn't matter. I'm there, and you won't be alone, okay? I probably should be getting back about now." He stood up, smiling at her. "We're going to have fun."

"I have a lot to accomplish in my self-assignment!" Kirana protested.

"Time works differently there. You know that—haven't you been practicing in the Time Sim building?" Kylo raised his eyebrows at her. Kirana silently chided herself for not paying as much attention lately as she should be. "Anyways, you'll see when you get there." They started walking back to the front of the building together, and Kylo slung an arm around her shoulder. Kirana noted his relaxed demeanor, and the happiness was sliding off him in waves. She smiled to herself. This was a very good sign. Except, why wouldn't she recognize him?

"You said I wouldn't recognize you?" she tried to mention casually. He hesitated, not able to share exactly what he meant.

"It's uh, well, we're not the same type of..." he tried. Kirana wasn't sure if he didn't know how to describe it or if he really wasn't supposed to. "Just focus on my eyes. You can always recognize me that way." Kirana shrugged. It should be fine. She'd never had a problem finding him before. Sometimes it took longer than others, but they should be together from the beginning this time. She walked him out the exit and towards his pod next to hers. She grinned at that detail. As he gave her one more hug, spin included, he was still beaming.

"See you soon, okay? Oh! I almost forgot," he laughed. "I've been working on your name!"

"What?" Kirana asked curiously.

"Yeah," Kylo glowed proudly. "I've been working on them, and they're getting so close."

"Wait, what's your name?" Kirana asked him.

"Can't say," he responded, wrinkling his nose. "They were nowhere near with mine, but I'm going to keep trying with yours."

"Okay, let's see how you do then," Kirana responded, smiling at their little game.

"Gotta run! See you there, Kir!" Kylo disappeared into his pod and as the door was closing, he blew her some deep blue bubbles that lingered on her fingers. Kirana walked away feeling confident that everything was going to be alright this iteration. Better than alright.

Ravi came by to walk with Anala and Kirana to the Green building for their last instructions. There was a soothing calmness blanketing their energy peaks of anxiousness or impatience as the time had finally arrived. Guardian Beck stood at the front appearing larger than normal, but speaking quieter.

"One more time, I'd like to thank you for your contributions to this iteration. Every single one of you has an impact bigger than you know. Thank you for volunteering to be a part of this incredible opportunity," she said in a fluid way, pouring the words over them. "As you get yourself set up in your pods, you'll have a short time where you can return with questions or to touch base with your team before you need to stay." Kirana was glad she had just seen Kylo do this, so she knew it was easy, and she could do it if she needed. Guardian Beck finished with one final note. "Support each other," she said, looking each of them in the eyes. "You'll recognize each other in some way at some point. Support each other. You're all on the same mission in the end, each of you holding up a different part, but the goal is the same."

Then, Kirana felt Anala's hand on hers. She took it and felt for Ravi's hand on her other side. Across the room, all of them were connecting. They all held hands, including Guardian Beck. She nodded in approval, her eyes glistening.

"Proud of you all!" she said, her voice not as smooth as it was before. "Now off you go."

Somehow, maybe it was the turning of the energy in the room, or maybe it was because it was finally time for the iteration to start, but either way, the anticipation and the anxiety were gone. Kirana was calm, and she was filled with a feeling that she had everything she needed.

They all wished each other well and gave each other hugs, then everyone started breaking off to head out to their pods. Ravi walked with Kirana and Anala to where their pods were nearby.

"See you both there," Ravi said quietly. It looked like everyone had gotten a dose of calm.

"See you, Ravi!" Anala said, giving him a hug. Then Ravi turned to Kirana.

"Can't wait to work on our agreement," he smiled. "One more glow to hold us over until we get back?" He held his hand out to her. She smiled and took his hand happily. Anala covered her eyes, knowing the bright light was coming. They all laughed.

"See you, Ravi," said Kirana. As he turned to walk towards his own pod, Anala poked Kirana in the side with her elbow.

"I want to hear all about your contract when you get back," she teased her. "And I can't wait to meet up for our own. I was thinking about it," she began. Kirana waited for her to say more. "I know I'm not a Guide, and I have my own work to do, but... I support you, Kirana."

"I know that!" Kirana responded. "I support you too!" Anala shook her head slightly, like there was more to it.

"I'll be there, in my own way. I'm going to keep an eye on you as much as I can. I spoke with Nova, and we came up with a signal," Anala continued. Kirana blinked, surprise on her face. This made Anala give her a little smile.

"I know I can't do much, but when you see a flickering light, I'm with you. You're not alone. Okay?" Anala looked at her with eyes that asked for approval. Kirana couldn't believe the mates she'd been blessed with.

"You're the best, Anala. Thank you. I feel so honored," Kirana said, feeling like that wasn't enough. But Anala seemed to take it as if it was more than enough. They hugged one more time, and Anala left for her pod. Kirana sent her some orange and gold sparkles and turned to step into her own. As she settled in, following the outlined procedure along with the memory of what she had seen Nox do previously, she took one last deep breath. This moment in her past iterations had always been a delicious feeling of endings and beginnings. She savored it as long as she dared, and she pressed the button.

CHAPTER FIFTY

There was typically an incubation period of sorts. It was a time to calibrate her energy and prepare herself to fit into the environment of the location she had chosen. This time it was comfortable and warm, and she actually felt a lot. Movement, texture and all kinds of vibrations. She was able to pick up on more and more over time. She never felt the need to go back to campus, and didn't think it would send the right message to Guardian Cosmo anyway, so she stayed. She began to fall in love with her environment and the generally peaceful bubble she was in. There were sounds sometimes that she just adored. Sometimes they were tinkling on high notes, sometimes rumbling on low ones. But they flowed, went up and down and all swirled together. It felt magical.

After some time had passed, which Kylo was so right about how different it was, she began to get that familiar feeling. The knowingness that it was time. She was calibrated and fully ready now to enter. This part could be uncomfortable, but she was getting uncomfortable as it was, so it seemed like the better option to dive right in. She went over her mission one last time and started the process.

Kirana thought she may have disappeared a time or two. Feeling uncomfortable was an understatement. This process was more intense than she remembered, or maybe it just hadn't been quite like this. She felt like she couldn't do anything. She just had to ride it out. The thought crossed her mind that maybe these graduation iterations really would be as tough as Kylo had made it out to be. Although, he seemed happy and everything seemed alright, so she decided she just needed to concentrate on getting through this. She tried to make it as easy as she could on her end, hoping it made a difference for any others involved.

Finally, all the intense action stopped, and Kirana was bombarded with sensation. She vaguely thought to herself that they really needed to update the Sim building because this was entirely shocking. Rather quickly after the process was complete, she settled, warm again in a different way, and went into her dream channel. She was so glad she had set it up. Nova was waiting for her there.

"Kirana!" Nova exclaimed. "How are you? Is everything alright?" Nova's eyes were big. She had only experienced one iteration and had certainly never helped anyone else through one. Kirana smiled at her, ironically calming her own Jr. Guide.

"I made it!" Kirana said. "All good! The calibration is done, and I'm on location. Things are... weird," she said, making a face. "I'm not so sure the Sims are up to date, but I'll figure it out!" She still felt confident.

"Okay," breathed Nova. "Well, I'm here. Let's just keep in touch as often as you can for a while." Kirana nodded. She tilted her head, all of a sudden hearing those sounds from earlier. Those pleasant, clear notes that danced and fluttered around.

"I want to check something out. I'll be back later, okay?" Kirana told her.

"Sounds good!" Nova said, appearing relieved. Kirana brought her consciousness back to her location to hear the sounds better. Then she heard voices on top of it.

"Turn that off! I think it's waking her up!"

"No, I think she likes it!"

Kirana blinked, but couldn't really see anything like she was used to. There was a haziness and some blended color, but that was mostly it. She felt like she couldn't move. She wasn't even sure how to move anyway. Was that another bad Sim that needed updating? Something blinked in her mind, and she couldn't remember if she had just not prepared herself properly or if she was forgetting what the Sim buildings were like. *Weird*, she thought to herself. She refocused on the sounds and trying to see something. Anything. Maybe she needed to go back to talk to Nova after all. Nothing seemed to be working. As she was about to enter the dream portal again, she heard the voices above her. The vibrations carried, making her feel cozy and protected.

"Hi, Baby Girl," a voice cooed at her. She relaxed even further. "Welcome to Earth, Kira. We've been waiting for you." As she drifted off, she smiled to herself because Kylo really had gotten them so close to her name.

ACKNOWLEDGEMENTS

The fortune that I have to be surrounded by people who always support me in the end, even when they don't understand why I do what I do, is very nearly unmatched. Thank you to my parents, Greg and Kathy, for endlessly rooting for me. Special shout-out to my mom for the enormous task of being the first set of eyes on this book. Your insights were nothing short of invaluable. Another huge thank you to my sister, Danielle and my brother-in-law, Karl who have dropped everything, time and time again, to help me when I needed something. The energy of this book came to be while I was in your midst, and it seems it couldn't have happened without you. And to the rest of my family, I'm honored we've chosen this time and space to be together, and I truly believe it's for a reason.

Kirana's mates echo many of my own special bonds, and I have to express enormous gratitude to some dear mates of mine. Some who have impacted me for 20 years, and some who have only entered my life more recently. Monica, who unknowingly gave me the first line of this book on a phone call, Heather, who I continuously thought of in one of the characters, and Ana, my fellow Seed, one of the first ones to know about this story and who always encourages me to be seen. Your impacts on my life are great, and I hope you know it.

And to all the people along the way who enthusiastically supported and encouraged the idea of me writing a book without knowing a thing about me or it, your contracts are complete. I send you immense gratitude in the form of mauve sparkles. Thank you.

Author's Note:

This book existed as an entity itself, and I merely recorded the words. I believe this is what they call being in flow. Often the writer knows a lot more about what's going on or what's going to happen than the characters or readers do. But in this case, not even the writer knew how things would unfold until they did. It's quite an experience to be a writer and a reader at the same time.

Readers may or may not pick up on the subtleties laced throughout the book. I'm quite satisfied with that, because it allows the story to land on whatever level a reader is at in their journey. I hope it is enjoyable to many.

What if those little synchronicities, the encounters that leave you speechless and even the tiny feelings that call to your intuition are simply windows—quick glimpses into something greater—to *you* beyond your flesh and bone? May this book carry something to help remind you of who you are.

ABOUT THE AUTHOR

Heart in the mountains and creating her own wonderland. Where she lives now won't be where she lives by the time you read this so no sense in sharing anything more specific than Earth.

Forever inspired by the likes of Dr. Seuss and Shel Silverstein, she is the author of the best selling children's book, The Search for Color.

This is her debut novel.